SCHOOL'S OUT!

www.transworldbooks.co.uk

Also by Jack Sheffield

Teacher, Teacher!
Mister Teacher
Dear Teacher
Village Teacher
Please Sir!
Educating Jack

For more information on Jack Sheffield and his books,
see his website at www.jacksheffield.com

SCHOOL'S OUT!

The Alternative School Logbook 1983–1984

Jack Sheffield

BANTAM PRESS

LONDON · TORONTO · SYDNEY · AUCKLAND · JOHANNESBURG

TRANSWORLD PUBLISHERS
61–63 Uxbridge Road, London W5 5SA
A Random House Group Company
www.transworldbooks.co.uk

First published in Great Britain
in 2013 by Bantam Press
an imprint of Transworld Publishers

A CIP catalogue record for this book
is available from the British Library.

ISBN 9780593069707

Addresses for Random House Group Ltd companies outside the UK
can be found at www.randomhouse.co.uk
The Random House Group Ltd Reg. No. 954009

The Random House Group Limited supports The Forest Stewardship
Council® (FSC®), the leading international forest-certification organisation.
Our books carrying the FSC label are printed on FSC®-certified paper.
FSC is the only forest-certification scheme supported by the leading
environmental organisations, including Greenpeace. Our
paper procurement policy can be found at
www.randomhouse.co.uk/environment

Typeset in 11/15pt Palatino by
Kestrel Data, Exeter, Devon.
Printed and bound in Great Britain by
Clays Ltd, Bungay, Suffolk.

4 6 8 10 9 7 5 3

MIX
Paper from
responsible sources
FSC® C016897

For Phil, Molly, Oscar,
Sam and Clara Patterson

Contents

Acknowledgements	9
Map	11
Prologue	13

1	The Sensitive Child	17
2	The Wisdom of Vera	35
3	Ruby and the Coffin Polisher	55
4	Important Decisions	74
5	A Friend in Need	92
6	Sewing for Boys	109
7	Broken Blossoms	124
8	A Surprise for Santa	141
9	The Length of Our Days	158
10	Bobble Hats and Breadcrumbs	171
11	George Orwell's New World	182
12	Raining in My Heart	200
13	Dorothy's Dirty Weekend	218

14	The Miner's Daughter	235
15	A Cow Called Clarissa	254
16	Terry Earnshaw's Bob-a-Job	272
17	Extra-Curricular Activities	290
18	A Bolt from the Blue	304
19	School's Out!	319

Acknowledgements

I am indeed fortunate to have the support of a wonderful editor, the superb Linda Evans, and the outstanding team at Transworld including Larry Finlay, Bill Scott-Kerr, Elizabeth Swain, Vivien Garrett, Bella Whittington, Brenda Updegraff, and the excellent Publicity Manager, Lynsey Dalladay, plus the 'footsoldiers' – fellow 'Old Roundhegian' Martin Myers and the quiet, unassuming Mike 'Rock 'n' Roll' Edgerton.

Special thanks, as always, go to my hardworking literary agent, Philip Patterson of Marjacq Scripts, for his encouragement and good humour.

I am also grateful to all of those who assisted in the research for this novel, in particular: Patrick Busby, Pricing Director, church organist and Harrogate Rugby Club supporter, Hampshire; Janina Bywater, neonatal nurse and lecturer in psychology, Cornwall; the Revd Ben Flenley, Rector of Bentworth, Lasham, Medstead and Shalden, Hampshire; Tony Greenan, Yorkshire's finest headteacher (now retired), Huddersfield, Yorkshire; Ian Haffenden, ex-Royal Pioneer Corps and custodian of Sainsbury's, Alton;

David Hayward, retired environmental scientist and radio-controlled model-aircraft enthusiast, Hampshire; Ginny Hayward, Family Record Keeper, Hampshire; John Kirby, ex-policeman, expert calligrapher and Sunderland supporter, County Durham; Roy Linley, Enterprise Architect, Unilever Global Expertise Team, and Leeds United supporter, Port Sunlight, Wirral; Sue Maddison, primary school teacher and expert cook, Harrogate, Yorkshire; Sue Matthews, retired primary school teacher and John Denver enthusiast, Wigginton, Yorkshire; Dr Alison Rickard, General Practitioner, Alton, Hampshire; Elaine Roberts, ex-teacher and gardening expert, Haxby, Yorkshire; Irene Ross, dressmaker, Alton, Hampshire; and all the terrific staff at Waterstones, Alton, including Rob, Simon, Sam, Kirsty, Louise, Fiona and Mandie.

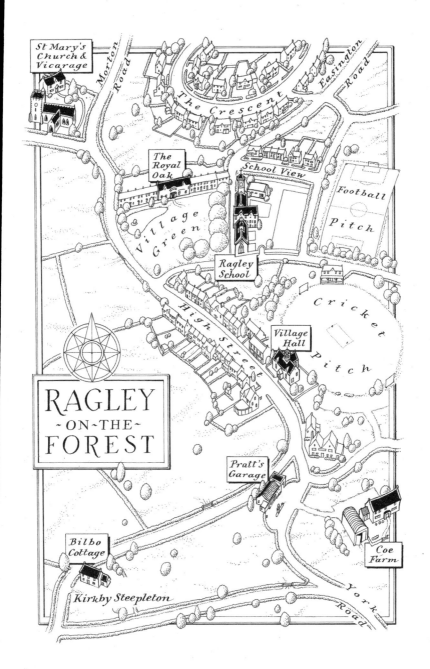

Prologue

Change touches us all with cool fingertips . . . it is a pathway of unknown consequences.

Meanwhile, time is a great healer – or so they say. However, when I reflect on the academic year 1983/84, the memories remain sharp as sunlight yet cool as moonbeams. It was a year of triumph and tragedy.

Life is a collection of moments. Some sear the soul while others are like balm on a wounded heart. Looking back on that time I recall a day that gave hope to a lonely child and another that was filled with sadness. There was also a time when the unexpected reared up and stunned our senses. I can recall it now with the clarity of a living dream . . . a day etched in the memory of youth and living on in an old man's reminiscences.

Destiny can be a cruel companion. However, all was still and quiet on that long-ago autumn morning when another school year was about to begin. It was as if the world were holding its breath and only the light breeze that stirred the branches of the horse chestnut trees at the front of our village school disturbed a scene of perfect tranquillity.

It was a year that began in hope and expectation and, as always, the familiar pattern of the school terms stretched out before us – autumn, spring and summer, the very fabric of our working lives. It was a journey that would end in a maze of confusion, but it had begun simply with the birth of a child . . . a teacher's child.

My wife Beth had given birth to our firstborn, a son, during the early hours of Sunday morning, 24 July 1983, and we had named him John William after our respective fathers. That was six weeks ago and life had moved on.

It was Thursday, 1 September, and I was sitting alone in the school office. On that distant autumn day my seventh year as headmaster of Ragley-on-the-Forest Church of England Primary School in North Yorkshire was about to begin. The dawn of a new school year was always an exciting time, but little did I know what lay ahead. A new destiny was in store.

The clock ticked on. I took a deep breath and sighed as I unlocked the bottom drawer of my desk, removed the large, leather-bound school logbook and opened it to the next clean page. Then I filled my fountain pen with black Quink ink, wrote the date and stared at the empty page.

The record of another school year was about to begin. Six years ago, the retiring headmaster, John Pruett, had told me how to fill in the official school logbook. 'Just keep it simple,' he said. 'Whatever you do, don't say what really happens, because no one will believe you!'

So the real stories were written in my 'Alternative School Logbook'. And this is it!

Chapter One

The Sensitive Child

91 children were registered on roll on the first day of the school year following a large intake from the extension to the council estate on Easington Road. An advertisement was put in the Times Educational Supplement *following Mrs Hunter's appointment to take up a new post at Priory Gate Junior School in York in January 1984.*

Extract from the Ragley School Logbook:
Monday, 5 September 1983

'Our Madonna's very sensitive, Mr Sheffield,' said Mrs Freda Fazackerly.

I was heading for the school office but this formidable Yorkshire lady was waiting for me in the entrance hall.

'Is she?' I asked.

'She is that . . . an' we're proper flummoxed.'

'Oh, I see,' I said, glancing down at her tiny four-year-old daughter. Madonna was wearing a Wham! T-shirt, a grubby green cardigan, black stone-washed jeans and red pixie boots. Her fair hair sported two pigtails tied with large pink bows and she grinned up at me, apparently unaware of the two green candles of snot that dangled unattractively from her nose. 'And why are you, er, *flummoxed*, Mrs Fazackerly?' I asked.

'Well, me an' Ernie, that's 'er dad, we was wond'ring 'ow she'd *mek 'er mark*, so to speak, jus' like we did.'

I removed my black-framed Buddy Holly spectacles and began to polish them with my new eighties slim knitted tie.

'Make her mark?'

'Yes, Mr Sheffield, 'cause long afore your time ah were captain o' netball 'ere at Ragley, an' my Ernie were captain o' football, an' 'is dad were t'best runner in t'school. So our Madonna's t'third gen'ration o' F'zackerlys an' we want 'er t'*mek 'er mark* as well . . . 'xcept she's a bit on t'*sensitive* side, if y'tek m'meaning.'

'Sensitive?'

'Yes. Like this morning, f'instance . . . wi' *dead things*,' said Mrs Fazackerly, leaning towards me as if sharing the secret of the universe.

I shifted my gangling six-foot-one-inch frame and took a step back towards the office door. 'Dead things?'

'Yes, Mr Sheffield,' said Mrs Fazackerly. 'That's why she's not quite 'erself this morning. It's put 'er in a reight pickle, ah can tell you.' She pulled Madonna's arm and the little girl looked up expectantly. 'Go on, luv, tell Mr Sheffield what 'appened to our 'Enry this morning.'

Madonna shook her head, wiped the snot from her nose with the sleeve of her cardigan and said nonchalantly, 'Ah pissed in 'is ear.'

'Pardon?'

The little girl clearly assumed I was deaf. 'AH PISSED IN 'IS EAR,' she shouted.

Mrs Fazackerly nodded vigorously. 'That's reight, Mr Sheffield.'

'I'm not quite following,' I said.

'Well, our 'Enry 'ad jus' 'ad a bowl o' 'is fav'rite liver-flavoured Kit-e-Kat Supreme an' then all of a sudden 'e were jus' lying there on t'doormat like a lost soul,' said Mrs Fazackerly.

'Ah, Henry's a *cat*,' I said.

Mrs Fazackerly gave me a puzzled look. 'Yes, o' course . . . an' our Madonna tried t'wake 'im up.'

'Wake him up . . . by, er, doing what you said?'

'That's reight, Mr Sheffield – our Madonna knelt down proper quiet like, 'cause she's real *sensitive* wi' animals, an' whispered *psssst* in 'is ear but 'e couldn't 'ear 'er . . . 'cause t'poor little sod were dead.'

'Ah.' The penny had dropped.

'So t'day, on 'er first day, she might be a bit, y'know . . . backwards in comin' forwards so t'speak.'

'I'm sure Mrs Grainger will look after her, Mrs Fazackerly, and we'll all try to give Madonna plenty of encouragement,' I said reassuringly.

Mrs Fazackerly appeared satisfied. 'Well, y'can't say fairer than that, Mr Sheffield,' and she hurried out of the entrance hall, dragging a bemused Madonna after her.

I glanced up at the clock on the office wall with its faded Roman numerals. It was 8.30 a.m. on Monday, 5 September 1983, the first day of the autumn term. My seventh year as headteacher of Ragley-on-the-Forest Church of England Primary School in North Yorkshire had begun.

*

'Another Fazackerly,' said a voice from the other end of the entrance hall. It was Anne Grainger, the deputy headteacher, who had emerged from the stock cupboard clutching two huge tins of powder paint.

Anne, a slim brunette who looked nothing like her fifty-one years, was the reception class teacher and had taught at Ragley School for as long as she could remember. 'Freda was in my class twenty years ago, Jack,' she went on, with a wry grin. 'If the little girl is anything like her mother, we're in for interesting times,' and she hurried off to her classroom.

When I walked into the school office Vera the secretary was on the telephone and she didn't sound pleased.

'But surely this should have been done during the summer holiday.' She shook her head in disbelief and wrote a note in neat shorthand on her spiral-bound pad.

Vera Forbes-Kitchener, a tall, slim, elegant sixty-one-year-old, was clearly irritated. 'Yes, I do understand what you are saying about your programme for school maintenance, but today is the first day of term and the playground will be in use.' She replaced the receiver and stood up. 'Good morning, Mr Sheffield. Not such a good start, I'm afraid.'

I smiled. Even after working together for six years, Vera still chose to retain the formality of calling me *Mr* Sheffield. For our superb school secretary it was the proper thing to do. She smoothed the creases from the skirt of her crisp new Marks & Spencer pin-striped suit and picked up the pile of school registers.

'So, what is it, Vera?' I asked, picking absent-mindedly at the frayed leather patches on my herringbone sports coat.

'The office has informed us that a workman is coming today to repaint the lines on the netball court on the playground . . .' she glanced at her notepad, '. . . arriving at lunchtime.'

'Well I'm sure we'll manage,' I said.

'We always do, Mr Sheffield.' She gave me her usual enigmatic *we've seen it all before* smile, picked up the pile of new attendance and dinner registers and hurried off to deliver them.

In the school hall the other two teachers were deep in conversation. Sally Pringle had her arm round Jo Hunter's shoulders. 'It will be fine, Jo,' she said. 'A new teaching post . . . a fresh opportunity.' Sally, a tall, ginger-haired and freckle-faced forty-two-year-old, taught the eight-year-olds and the nine-year-olds with summer term birthdays in Class 3. As usual, Sally remained faithful to her flower-power days in her mint-green cords, a baggy purple blouse and a vivid, pillar-box-red waistcoat. 'It's the next stage of your life,' she added with an encouraging smile.

Jo Hunter, a diminutive, athletic twenty-eight-year-old, dressed in a figure-hugging tracksuit and Chris Evert trainers, taught the six- and seven-year-olds in Class 2. Her long black hair was tied back in a familiar pony-tail. It was a time of all change for Jo and she was facing the new school year with mixed feelings. Her husband, Dan, the village bobby, had recently been promoted to sergeant at the main station in York and they had been offered a police house in the city centre.

'My last term at Ragley School,' she said sadly. 'I can't believe it.' Last week she had enjoyed a successful interview for a Scale Two responsibility post for science and girls' games at Priory Gate Junior School in York, to commence in January 1984. It was a well-earned promotion for Jo, but it was clear she would be sad to leave our little village school and her first teaching post since graduating from college six years ago.

Vera handed out the new registers and Jo looked at her name written in our secretary's beautiful copper-plate handwriting. 'I wonder whose name will be on it next term?' she mused.

'We'll know by half-term,' I said.

'Let's hope they enjoy netball,' commented Jo, who was proud of her school team.

'And, hopefully, computers,' added Sally with a wry grin. Jo had led the way at staff meetings with the new technology and we were all still struggling to catch up.

I looked up at the hall clock. 'I'll go down to the school gate and welcome the new starters.' Sally and Jo hurried back to their classrooms to make final preparations and I returned to the entrance hall.

The ancient oak door swung open on its giant hinges and I walked down the stone steps to the tarmac playground, surrounded by a waist-high wall of Yorkshire stone topped with metal railings. Groups of children with rosy, sunburned faces were running, skipping and playing games, and they waved in acknowledgement.

We had a mixed intake from all walks of life. They included the sturdy sons and daughters of local farming families and others whose parents were executives at the prestigious chocolate factory in York. Also, during the past year, new building on the council estate had gradually increased our number on roll, so more rising-fives than usual were due to be admitted to Anne's reception class.

One of the new starters was holding on to the hand of her elder sister.

'Hello, Mr Sheffield,' shouted eight-year-old Sonia Tricklebank. 'Our Julie starts today. Ah've told 'er where 'er coat peg is, so she'll be all right.' Her four-year-old sister, immaculate in a starched blue-checked gingham dress, brown leather sandals and white ankle socks, grinned up at me. Meanwhile her mother was chatting with Brenda Ricketts, mother of four-year-old Billy, who had run on to the playground to balance on the faded white lines of the netball court as if he were a tightrope-walker. It was clear that young Billy was not lacking in confidence.

I smiled. There was something special about the first day of a school year and I felt that familiar excitement mixed with trepidation. Our school was an integral part of village life and the centre of the community. I had found peace, contentment and a way of life in this quiet corner of God's Own Country and I breathed in the clean air as I walked down the cobbled drive to the school gate.

In the cycle shed ten-year-old Molly Paxton was holding a loop of taut string between outstretched fingers and thumbs and teaching six-year-old Katie Icklethwaite how to do a cat's cradle. Ten-year-old Sam Borthwick was playing conkers with nine-year-old Harold Bustard, oblivious to the chanting girls behind them as they jumped in and out of a skipping rope. One of the girls ran up to me.

"Ello, Mr Sheffield,' said ten-year-old Hazel Smith, the cheerful daughter of our school caretaker. 'Don't f'get that y'said me an' Molly could be in charge o' t'tuck shop,' she added with a touch of anxiety. After all, this was a monitor job that held high status.

'Don't worry, Hazel,' I replied with a grin, 'I haven't forgotten,' and she ran back to her friends.

I leaned on the wrought-iron gate and looked around me. Above my head a gilded light shone through the translucent leaves of the horse chestnut trees and lit up the school wall like amber honey. Ragley School was a severe, traditional Victorian building of reddish-brown bricks with a steep grey-slate roof, high arched windows with pointed tops and an incongruous Gothic bell tower. Opposite our school was the village green, with a duck pond that nestled under the welcome shade of a weeping willow tree. Alongside ran a row of cottages with pantile roofs and tall brick chimneys and the green was domi-nated by the white-fronted public house, The Royal Oak. Off to my left, down the High Street, Ragley village was coming alive.

Miss Prudence Golightly was standing outside her General Stores & Newsagent and chatting with Old Tommy Piercy, who was about to open his butcher's shop. Eugene Scrimshaw was in the village pharmacy accepting a delivery of Pond's Cream, while next door the meticulous Timothy Pratt was arranging a neat row of enamel watering cans on a trestle table outside his Hardware Emporium. In the open doorway of Nora's Coffee Shop stood the assistant, Dorothy Humpleby. She was listening to the number-one record, 'Red Red Wine' by UB40, and looking at a poster of *Fame*'s Irene Cara sellotaped on the window of Diane Wigglesworth's Hair Salon. Finally, at the end of the row of shops, Miss

Amelia Duff was at the counter of her village Post Office, counting out her second-class twelve and a half pence stamps and hoping she had sufficient to last the day. Amelia knew her customers well and it was unlikely that first-class stamps would be in demand at the exorbitant new price of sixteen pence.

For this was 1983. Average house prices had shot up to almost £30,000, Margaret Thatcher had been re-elected with a landslide majority and the film *Gandhi* had won eight Oscars. London police had started using wheel clamps, seatbelts had become compulsory for drivers and front-seat passengers, while Björn Borg had retired from tennis. In popular music, Culture Club's 'Karma Chameleon' was destined to become the United Kingdom's best-selling single of the year and we said a sad and final farewell to Karen Carpenter and Billy Fury. Microsoft advertised something called Word software, McDonald's introduced the McNugget and a range of strange dolls by the name of Cabbage Patch went on sale. Meanwhile, in the Bahamas there had been an explosion in the use of a little-known drug called crack cocaine. The world was changing fast, but in the tiny village of Ragley-on-the-Forest life moved at a slower pace and on this perfect September morning the residents of the High Street were going about their business in their own quiet way.

'Mr Sheffield, Mr Sheffield!' cried an eager voice. Off to my right, ten-year-old Louise Hartley was turning the corner of School View from the council estate with her sister, nine-year-old Maureen, known affectionately as Little Mo. 'Please can ah ring t'bell, Mr Sheffield, like y'said?'

'I promised you could be bell monitor, Louise, so yes

you can,' I looked at my watch, 'but remember to wait until *exactly* nine o' clock. Go and see Mrs Grainger and she will tell you when to ring it.'

'Thanks, Mr Sheffield,' she shouted and they ran off to play hopscotch with the Buttle twins.

''Ere we go again, Mr Sheffield,' shouted a familiar voice. Ruby the caretaker in her bright orange XX overall appeared from the cycle shed carrying a yard broom and a black bag. Her cheeks were flushed and she leaned on her broom and waved.

'Morning, Ruby,' I said. 'Thanks for all the hard work.'

She looked, misty-eyed, at the children playing in the playground and on the school field. 'Our 'Azel's las' year,' she said sadly. 'M'las' one at Ragley.' All of Ruby's six children had attended our village school and it was the end of an era for our hardworking caretaker.

'Let's make it a good one, Ruby,' I said and hurried back up the drive.

Ten-year-old Terry Earnshaw sped past me. 'Ah'm Steve Ovett, Mr Sheffield!' he shouted triumphantly as he ran on to the playground. The British runner had just regained his fifteen hundred metres world record in three minutes 30.7 seconds. Along with Kevin Keegan and his big brother, Heathcliffe, the Olympic athlete was one of Terry's heroes, and I smiled at his eagerness not to be late.

At nine o' clock Louise Hartley untied the bell rope from its metal cleat and, as it had done for over one hundred years, the school bell rang out to welcome the children of Ragley village for the start of another school year.

*

The top juniors in my class soon settled in and, apart from having to send Terry Earnshaw out to wash his hands before we started work, all was well. Once again, as in all the classes, it was a group of mixed ages. The children who had been in my class last year would all pass their eleventh birthday during the academic year, while the younger ones, the nine-year-olds, would have two years in Class 4. Soon they were busy decorating a personalized sticky label on the lid of their tin of Lakeland crayons, putting their names in their *New Oxford Dictionary*, filling in their reading record cards and labelling their manila-covered exercise books for a variety of subjects. Predictably, many of them had forgotten how to write during the six-week holiday. However, old habits were soon recalled as they wrote their first paragraphs of news . . . even if the occasional spelling didn't quite meet expectations.

Nine-year-old Charlotte Ackroyd wrote, 'We went to France for our holidays. We all got on a fairy and I was sick.' Tongue in cheek, I wrote the word 'ferry' in the margin. Meanwhile, new pupil ten-year-old Lee Dodsworth had visited the local RAF station where his father was an engineer. He wrote, 'My Uncle Jim showed us his helicopter. My mam says he's really clever because he can go straight up and hoover.'

Morning assembly was always a special occasion at the beginning of a school year, with the new starters, sitting cross-legged in the front row, waving to their older brothers and sisters. Anne played the piano while we sang 'Morning Has Broken' and I welcomed everyone and promised exciting times ahead. Sally accompanied 'Kumbaya' on her guitar and finally ten-year-old Betsy

Icklethwaite, the tallest girl in the school, who, predictably, had volunteered to be Class 4 blackboard monitor, led us in our school prayer.

Dear Lord,
This is our school, let peace dwell here,
Let the room be full of contentment, let love abide here,
Love of one another, love of life itself,
And love of God.
Amen.

At half past ten Louise Hartley rang the bell for morning playtime and I followed a stream of excited children out of the classroom for our first morning break of the school year. I had volunteered to do playground duty and my opening task was to remove a stick of chalk from Madonna Fazackerly's tight little fist after she had drawn a pig on the door of Ruby's store cupboard.

Meanwhile, in the staff-room Vera had prepared mugs of hot milky coffee and was reading her *Daily Telegraph*, shaking her head in dismay. An opportunist thief had stolen Daley Thompson's decathlon gold medal from his parked car. Happily, her favourite newsreader, Angela Rippon, was recovering nicely from a riding accident in which she had broken both her wrists and was about to return to broadcasting. 'I'm so glad she's getting better.'

'Anything interesting in the paper, Vera?' asked Jo.

Vera shook her head and pointed to the front page. 'Well, I'm afraid that ginger-haired Welshman has emerged as the principal candidate for the leadership of the Labour Party,' she remarked with more than a hint of disapproval.

'I like Neil Kinnock,' said Sally, who didn't share Vera's political views. 'He talks sense and of course red hair is distinctive.' She shook her Pre-Raphaelite curls in defiance.

'Margaret will soon show him the door,' said Vera. She looked across the staff-room at Sally. 'But of course I do agree that red hair *can* be very striking . . . regardless of colour-coordination difficulties.'

Sally simply smiled reflectively and returned to her list of possibles for the school orchestra.

At twelve o' clock the bell rang for lunchtime and I called in to the office to see if there were any messages. As I walked in the telephone rang.

'For you, Mr Sheffield,' said Vera, holding out the receiver. 'It's *Mrs* Sheffield.'

'Thanks, Vera,' I said.

She walked to the window and I sat in her chair. 'How's John?' I asked.

'Fine,' said Beth, 'I've just fed him.'

Our baby son, John William, was now six weeks old and growing fast.

'I think he's just discovered his hands, Jack,' added Beth. 'He's staring at them now.'

'I wish I was there,' I said. 'You sound tired.'

'Hmmn . . . your son could drink milk for England,' she replied a little wearily.

Beth was breastfeeding the baby every four hours and our lives had changed. Broken sleep made us constantly tired, but it was remarkable watching him grow. He had begun to 'coo' and gurgle and make happy noises when he was feeding, and had recently survived his first cold.

At four weeks he had smiled properly and now he had a kick like a mule. It appeared he was destined to be a very active little boy.

'I shouldn't be too late tonight,' I said. 'There's plenty of paperwork but I can do most of it at home.'

'Fine,' said Beth, 'see you later, and when he goes to sleep I'll get on with my next assignment.' Beth was taking maternity leave from the headship of her village school but was still finding time to complete a part-time Masters Degree in Education at Leeds University.

'Bye,' I said. 'Don't overdo it.'

There was a chuckle down the line as she rang off.

After checking the latest circular about a proposed common curriculum for all schools in England I decided to catch up with Jo Hunter in the staff-room. We discussed the possibility of arranging a half-day for her to visit Priory Gate Junior School to familiarize herself with her new teaching post.

'Thanks, Jack,' she said and we went to the office to check our list of proposed dates in the school diary. Vera was looking out of the window and shaking her head in dismay. A little white van had driven on to the car park and a short man in a flat cap and grubby white overalls climbed out, opened the rear doors and surveyed his collection of paint buckets and balls of string.

I walked out to meet him. 'Good afternoon,' I said. 'I'm Jack Sheffield, the headteacher.'

He shook my hand. 'Name's 'Umble, Mr Sheffield, Percy 'Umble . . . line-marker *extra-ordinaire*. Straight lines guar'nteed.'

'Pleased to meet you, Mr Umble,' I replied.

He removed his flat cap and looked at me quizzically.

'It's 'Umble, Mr Sheffield, beggin' y'pardon – with an aitch . . . 'Umble by name an' 'umble by nature.'

'Ah, Mr *Humble*,' I said, emphasizing the aitch. 'Thank you for coming. We'll send the children on to the school field for afternoon playtime so they will be out of your way.'

'Thank you kindly, sir,' he said and then he sniffed the air like a French wine-taster. 'Perfec',' he whispered, almost to himself. 'No wind.'

'No wind?' I asked.

'Yes, ah allus sweep t'playground where m'lines are goin' so there's no dust when ah'm painting. Y'see, Mr Sheffield, ah'm what y'call a perfectionist . . . there's straight an' there's *straight* – an' my lines are *straight*.'

'That's good to hear,' I said. 'I'll leave you to it then.'

'That's reight, Mr Sheffield, 'umble is as 'umble does.' And with the accuracy of an Egyptian pyramid-builder he began to mark out the playground.

When I walked back into school I noticed to my surprise that in Class 1 Anne was on her hands and knees in the Home Corner. She was washing the classroom walls.

'Don't ask,' she said with a tired smile. 'You'd think I was experienced enough not to take my eyes off a group of children mixing powder paints.' A line of bright-red handprints stretched round the walls and across the door.

'Who was it?' I asked.

'Madonna,' said Anne tersely as she dipped a sponge in her bowl of soapy water. I decided to leave her to it. It wasn't the moment to discuss arrangements for the afternoon, when the school playground would be out of bounds.

*

Back in the staff-room Sally was marking a pile of exercise books and sharing with Jo a passage of writing by eight-year-old Mary Scrimshaw. The local pharmacist's little daughter had written, 'My Uncle Terry's an accountant so 'e knows a lot about moths.'

When I walked in Sally looked up. 'Jack, sorry to spoil your day, but that new girl, Madonna, has been in my classroom and almost exterminated Tarzan and Jane.' Sally's goldfish were a popular addition to her nature table. 'She dropped that ammonite from Robin Hood's Bay into the aquarium . . . but don't worry, it's all sorted and I told Mrs Critchley to keep an eye on her.' Doreen Critchley was our dinner lady and, as *Mr* Critchley could confirm, she didn't take prisoners.

'Oh dear,' I said. Someone needed to break the news to Anne.

At a quarter past three the parents of the new starters came into Anne's class to collect their children. Anne explained that everyone should leave by the side entrance of the school to avoid the playground.

Meanwhile, Ruby the caretaker had arrived at the top of the cobbled school drive ready for her evening work. She paused to chat with Yvonne Higginbottom, who had just collected her five-year-old son, Scott. Yvonne had spent eighteen pence that morning on a *Daily Mail* and she took it out of her shopping bag and pointed to the headline: 'Diana in New Baby Mystery'. Princess Diana had left Balmoral suddenly without either Prince Charles or fourteen-month-old Prince William for a private visit to a London clinic.

'She might be 'aving another baby,' said Yvonne.

'Ah wunt be s'prised,' said Ruby. 'She wants another as sure as eggs is eggs.'

Yvonne nodded in agreement, as Ruby had a significant source of information. It was well known in the village that Ruby was a dear friend of Vera the secretary, who seemed to know *everything* about the royal family. They both looked at the stooping figure of Percy Humble on the playground as he completed yet another perfectly straight line. 'What's Van Gogh up to?' enquired Yvonne.

'Ah'll be glad when 'e's gone,' said Ruby. 'Ah don't like people messin' wi' m'playground.'

'Men,' said Yvonne dismissively, 'who needs 'em?'

It was then that Freda Fazackerly rushed up the drive, dashed into Anne's classroom, grabbed Madonna and left by the usual route through the main door. Predictably, Madonna ran off, stepped on to the wet paint and balanced precariously on the newly painted lines before wandering off towards the school drive.

'Oy!' shouted Percy Humble. 'Gerrof m'lines.'

'Who rattled your cage?' shouted Freda Fazackerly in response. Little Madonna stuck out her tongue and they both walked down the drive, oblivious of the trail of small white footprints behind them.

'Ah'll swing f'that one,' said Ruby as she rushed into school for her mop and bucket.

Anne and I stood by the staff-room window and stared out as Freda Fazackerly took Madonna's hand and strode out towards the council estate. Meanwhile, Ruby set about cleaning up the mess.

'Don't worry, Mr Sheffield,' said Vera with a reassuring smile, 'we've survived the first day.'

*

It was six o'clock when I had finished enough of the day's paperwork to leave for home, three miles away in Kirkby Steepleton. As I drove out of the school gate Freda Fazackerly was walking across the village green from the shops. She was gesticulating, so I slowed and wound down my window.

'Well, Mr Sheffield,' she shouted, 'did she mek 'er mark?'

I recalled the graffiti, the handprinted wall, the near-death experience for two goldfish and the white footprints that now decorated the playground.

'Yes, Mrs Fazackerly . . . she did,' I yelled back.

As I drove away the thought occurred to me that some days were better than others. At least I hoped so.

Chapter Two

The Wisdom of Vera

The Revd Joseph Evans recommenced his weekly RE lesson. Major Forbes-Kitchener, school governor, visited school to discuss the applications for a new teacher at Ragley School and tomorrow's Harvest Supper. The newly appointed Easington Area Health & Hygiene Inspector visited the school kitchen. County Hall requested responses to their discussion document 'A Common Curriculum for North Yorkshire Schools'.

Extract from the Ragley School Logbook:
Friday, 23 September 1983

Vera had a problem . . . and she couldn't solve it.

She paused for thought, staring at her reflection in the leaded windows of Morton Manor. Pale shafts of morning sunlight danced across the spacious grounds while, through the branches of the high elms, a parliament of rooks stared down unforgivingly with beady eyes.

It was Friday, 23 September, the day before the annual

Harvest Supper in the village hall, and Vera was finding it difficult to concentrate on the list of ingredients for her Harvest Festival Cake. With a sigh she placed the shopping list in her leather handbag, put on her coat and silk scarf and set off in her new Austin Metro for what was destined to be a most eventful day at Ragley School. Vera prided herself on being the supreme problem-solver, but just occasionally one came along that surpassed even her great wisdom.

Nine months ago Vera had lived with her younger brother, the Revd Joseph Evans, in the beautifully furnished vicarage in the grounds of St Mary's Church on the Morton Road. Her life had been one of careful routine and order. However, last December she had married Major Rupert Forbes-Kitchener, a rich widower and owner of the magnificent Morton Manor. It had proved to be a dramatic change for Vera, even though she had brought with her the comforting companionship of her three cats, Treacle, Jess and Maggie. Her favourite, Maggie, a black cat with white paws, was named after her political heroine Margaret Thatcher. However, while her busy life continued to be filled with the twice-weekly Cross-Stitch Club, church flowers and Women's Institute meetings, her world had changed. Vera had a problem and it wouldn't go away – and it wasn't simply the fact that Maggie had fleas.

A few miles away, in the second bedroom of Bilbo Cottage in Kirkby Steepleton, I was becoming a moderately proficient changer of nappies. Our second bedroom had been decorated by Beth during the latter part of her pregnancy and it was now baby John's nursery. The cot was in the corner and a plastic changing mat adorned the floral-patterned sofa.

'The health visitor is coming this morning, Jack,' said Beth. Even at this early hour she looked stunning in a cream sweater and tight, stone-washed jeans that emphasized her natural beauty. Her honey-blonde hair caressed her high cheekbones.

'Just routine, I expect,' I replied.

'And don't forget I'm bringing John into school later this morning to help with Anne's Growing Up project.'

I smiled. 'Everyone will love him,' I said and we walked downstairs.

While I ate my cereal at the kitchen table Beth was holding John and flicking hastily through the pages of the *Times Educational Supplement*. Suddenly she said, 'This is the one, Jack,' and picked up a pencil and circled an advertisement on the Primary Headships page. 'What do you think?'

It read: 'Badger Hills County First School, Hampshire, Group 4. NOR 165. Required for 1st January 84. Salary Scale £10,572–£11,784. Full details from the Area Education Office in Lymington.'

'Just think of it, Jack,' said Beth, 'a five-figure salary!'

I was unsure how to respond. 'Well . . . it's certainly a lot of money.'

'And it's in a beautiful part of my home county,' she added with a smile. Beth's parents lived in a lovely cottage in Little Chawton in Hampshire.

I was quiet while I packed my old leather satchel. I loved being a village school headteacher here in North Yorkshire and was happy with my life. Occasionally I found it hard to keep up with Beth. Somehow, as well as being a great mother, she had continued with her degree course and had made it clear that she intended to return to work as soon as she could. Ambition takes many forms and, on occasions, I was left breathless in its wake.

As I was about to leave she kissed me on the cheek and asked suddenly, 'Jack – what do you think about a nanny?'

'A nanny?' I said. 'Well . . . it's a big decision.'

Beth smiled knowingly and, as always, I felt she could read my thoughts.

My journey on the back road to Ragley village lifted my spirits as the early-morning sun broke through and lit up the fields around me. It was a joy to live in this beautiful part of Yorkshire and I wound down my window and drank in the clean air. However, the natural wonders of our world were soon forgotten when I pulled into the school car park. A smart three-door Ford Sierra was in Vera's parking space.

Vera was sitting at her desk when I walked into the school office, typing an alphabetical list of applicants for the new teaching post on our state-of-the-art typewriter with its golf-ball head.

'I've put the folder of applications on your desk, Mr Sheffield,' she said. 'We've had a good response.'

The advertisement in the *Times Educational Supplement* had stated that the closing date for applications for the full-time teaching post at Ragley Church of England Primary School was Friday, 23 September. So today was the final day and the village postman, Ted Postlethwaite, had already delivered the morning mail.

'And there's a lady waiting to see you. I put her in the staff-room.'

'A lady?'

Vera glanced down at her spiral notepad. 'Yes – a Ms Piddle,' she said, with an emphasis on the Ms so that it sounded like the buzzing of a bee. Vera had always preferred Miss or Mrs.

'Piddle?'

'Yes, Mr Sheffield,' said Vera with a hint of a smile. 'Piddle – as in the Dorset river . . . apparently.'

I glanced up at the clock. It was 8.20 a.m. 'I had better see her now,' I said and hurried up the narrow corridor that linked the office to the staff-room.

A short, plump, grey-haired lady dressed in a loud, checked two-piece suit, cream blouse buttoned to the neck, thick unseasonal stockings and low-heeled Blaze Taupe Hush Puppies was waiting for me. She was in the process of stroking a stubby finger over the top of the window frame and appeared to be checking for dust.

'Hello,' I said, 'I'm Jack Sheffield, headteacher. Welcome to Ragley School.'

'Good morning,' she replied in a voice that sounded as if she had spent the previous twenty years in elocution lessons. 'I am Ms Piddle – as in the Dorset river.'

'Ah, yes, I see,' I said. 'Well, I'm pleased to meet you, Ms Piddle.'

She inspected the tip of her finger, looked up at me as if I had just failed my driving test and shook her head dismissively. 'Mr Sheffield, I'll get right to the point,' she said with a flourish of her official-looking clipboard. 'I'm here to check on kitchen hygiene and procedure . . . and perhaps, if time permits, I shall give you some advice on other related matters in accordance with the Health and Safety at Work Act 1974.'

I was beginning to dislike this lady's abrupt manner. 'Yes, well, we do have a policy, of course,' I said, 'and County Hall has always been pleased with our efforts.'

She selected a green biro from her black leather handbag. 'I shall examine that as well,' she said and added a note to her neat chart.

'Would you like some refreshment – tea or coffee?' I asked.

Ms Piddle wrinkled her nose. 'Artificial stimulants? No, I think not. My body is my temple.'

More a bungalow I thought, but said nothing.

With a sinking heart I took this irritating little lady into the kitchen. 'Good morning, Mr Sheffield,' said Shirley in her usual cheerful voice. Shirley Mapplebeck was an excellent cook, worked wonders with limited ingredients and loved her job.

'Hello, Shirley,' I replied. 'This is Ms Piddle from County Hall, here to check on health and hygiene, so perhaps you and Doreen could show her round your kitchen.'

Shirley looked warily at the newcomer while her assistant, the formidable Doreen Critchley, merely flexed her biceps and guarded her territory like an Easter Island statue. 'We're spotless in 'ere,' she said bluntly. Doreen didn't waste words.

'We shall see, won't we, ladies?' said Ms Piddle. 'After all, a clean bill of health is all in the *detail*.'

I prayed that all would go well and hurried back to the office.

*

The most recent applications for our new teaching post to begin next January were piled neatly on my desk. Vera had created a special file for them and, each time the Revd Joseph Evans, her younger brother and chairman of the school governors, visited school we both scanned the information about each applicant.

'Thanks for this, Vera,' I said and began to work my way through the letters and completed North Yorkshire forms.

After registration we all walked quietly into the hall for morning assembly. Anne had put her LP record of the *Peer Gynt Suite* on the turntable and strains of Edvard Grieg's 'Anitra's Dance' echoed in the Victorian rafters as the children sat cross-legged on the floor. Joseph Evans, a tall, slim, angular figure with a prominent Roman nose, took the lead and we all finished by reciting the Lord's Prayer.

As the children trooped out, eight-year-old Barry Ollerenshaw tugged his sleeve.

''Scuse me, Mr Evans,' said Barry politely.

Joseph loved good manners and crouched down beside the eager little boy. 'What is it, Barry?' he asked.

'Well, Mr Evans,' said Barry, 'ah was wond'ring why we say "old men" at t'end of prayers?'

Joseph was puzzled. 'Old men?'

'Yes, Mr Evans. We allus say it – y'know, t'power and t'glory, for ever an' ever, old men.'

'Ah,' said Joseph as the penny dropped.

'It's jus' that ah don't know any old men,' said a confused Barry, ''xcept mebbe f'you.'

Joseph smiled. 'Well, it's like this . . .'

*

Back at Bilbo Cottage Beth was in earnest discussion with the health visitor, a cheerful young woman who was new in the job.

'He looks fine, Mrs Sheffield,' she said. John was now eight and a half weeks old. 'And regarding a nanny – you need to advertise in the local paper and interview a few people. It's obviously an important decision.'

Beth looked at the cheerful, innocent little boy on her lap and kissed his rosy cheeks. 'I know . . .' she said quietly, '. . . and I'd miss him.'

After changing his nappy Beth strapped John into the baby seat in the back of her light blue Volkswagen Beetle and set off for Ragley and Anne's classroom. John was about to be weighed, measured and fed as part of Class 1's health education programme.

At morning break Sally appeared to be dropping a tiny tablet into her coffee when I walked into the staff-room. 'What's that?' I asked.

'It's Sucron, Jack,' she explained, 'an alternative to sugar, four times as sweet, so you use less.' Then she selected a Garibaldi from the biscuit tin and munched contentedly.

Vera glanced knowingly over her pince-nez but said nothing. She was studying her *Daily Telegraph* and was equally unimpressed by the photograph of a bespectacled John Selwyn Gummer, who had been appointed that summer by Mrs Thatcher to be Chairman of the Conservative Party. While she would never criticize the venerable Margaret, Vera remained unconvinced that this bookish little man was the ideal choice.

I picked up the *Times Educational Supplement* and flicked through the pages while I drank my coffee. As usual the weekly journal was full of varied articles, including one entitled 'Crisis in the Teaching of Handwriting'. It was reported that the majority of sixteen-year-olds were unable to write a decent letter of application for a job. Of more concern was the new training film for teachers advertised under the banner headline 'What Line to Take on Glue-sniffing?', and I recalled the rubber glue with its distinct and very appealing pear-drop smell that we used each day in our classrooms.

Sally put down her *Art & Craft* magazine. 'Let me show you the back-page article, Jack – it's hilarious.'

The witty educationalist Ted Wragg had written a satirical response to the proposal that 'Teachers should be awarded points and the best teachers should be paid more!' However, in amongst the shared laughter when Sally read it out there was the nagging doubt that our educational world was changing and that even the daftest ideas might one day come to pass.

In the middle of all this there was a tap on the door and Doreen Critchley came in. ''Scuse me, Mr Sheffield.' She had a face like thunder.

'Yes, Doreen?' I asked somewhat apprehensively.

Doreen had the build of a professional weightlifter and the only thing she hated more than men was a bossy woman. 'Someone 'ad better come into t'kitchen afore ah throttle that woman,' she said. 'She's upsettin' Shirley summat rotten.'

Vera was the first to respond. 'I'll go,' she said.

'And I'll join you,' I added. We followed Doreen into the kitchen.

Ms Piddle, looking animated, was waving her finger at Shirley as if reprimanding a child. Our school cook seemed dejected but Ms Piddle was in full flow.

'Now, Mrs Mapplebeck,' she said, opening and shutting cupboard doors, 'we must also ensure that your protective clothing is properly looked after and that adequate first aid facilities are available.'

'We need t'get on wi' t'Spam fritters and t'treacle sponge,' said Doreen gruffly.

'Plenty of time for that,' replied Ms Piddle. 'Now,' she continued, ticking her list, 'I have to check toilets, washing facilities and drinking water.' She gave a sinister Cruella de Vil smile. 'It is all in the *detail*, dear,' she repeated, adding a note to her list, this time using a red biro.

'Is there a problem?' I asked.

Ms Piddle looked me up and down. 'It is important to *always* comply with the rules, Mr Sheffield,' she said.

Before I could reply Vera stepped forward. 'We've always found that it is important to note that legal information must be used with a degree of caution,' she said.

'Perhaps so, Mrs Forbes-Kitchener, but may I remind you that in the Bible it says "*Wisdom* is the principal thing",' retorted the officious Ms Piddle.

Words such as 'red rag' and 'bull' came to mind. Vera clearly bristled with indignation. 'Yes, Ms Piddle, I *am* familiar with Proverbs, chapter four, verse seven.'

'Oh, are you?' said a surprised Ms Piddle and retreated towards the fridge door.

'Yes,' said Vera firmly. She took another step towards the now-hesitant inspector and fixed her with a steely stare, 'but it goes on to say "therefore get wisdom: and with all thy getting . . . get *understanding*".'

Ms Piddle was not to be outdone. 'Yes, but we need *knowledge*, Mrs Forbes-Kitchener – *knowledge*,' she said with emphasis.

Shirley looked crushed. Doreen, a glowering presence, leaned forward but Vera stepped between them. 'What exactly do you mean, Ms Piddle?' she demanded. Ms Piddle gave her a hard stare but Vera's eyes never flickered.

The inspector picked up a ripe tomato from the chopping board and held it aloft as if she had just declared peace in our time. 'For example, *knowledge* is knowing a tomato is a fruit,' she said with a confident grin.

Vera took the tomato from her, rinsed it under the tap and placed it back on the chopping board. 'Yes, Ms Piddle,' she said quietly, 'but *wisdom* is knowing not to put it in a fruit salad,' and she turned on her heel and walked out.

'Perhaps we could have a word before you go, Ms Piddle?' I asked.

'It will be after school lunch,' she replied haughtily, 'and then I shall go home to write my report.'

In the school entrance the mood was different. Beth had arrived and John was gurgling and bubble-blowing in his pushchair.

Sally and Anne were leaning over and tickling John's chin when Vera and I joined them. 'I think he looks like you, Beth,' said Sally.

'Definitely your eyes,' added Anne.

'And maybe Jack's square chin,' suggested Vera.

I rubbed my chin ruefully, hoping this was a compliment.

'He's certainly got your smile, Jack,' said Anne.

'And John William is a perfect name,' confirmed Vera.

'It said in the paper,' said Sally, our fount of miscellaneous facts, 'that the most popular names in 1982 for boys were James, Edward and William.'

'And what about girls?' asked Beth.

'Elizabeth, Louise and Jane,' supplied Sally with perfect recall.

'I like all of those,' said Beth with a mischievous grin in my direction and they all set off to Anne's classroom.

At twelve o' clock Louise Hartley rang the bell to announce lunchtime and I walked into the entrance hall, where Beth was preparing to leave with Vera.

'I'm just going to the General Stores, Mr Sheffield. I won't be long.'

'And I'll see you tonight, Jack,' said Beth.

John, after an hour of celebrity status, had fallen asleep in his pushchair and I stooped to kiss him goodbye.

'Thanks for coming in, Beth,' I said, 'and see you later, Vera.'

As they walked out to the car park the perceptive Vera looked inquisitively at Beth. 'You seem preoccupied, Beth – is all well?'

'I'm wrestling with the problem of going back to work next term,' explained Beth. 'The health visitor recommended a childminder or that I should advertise for a nanny to look after a six-month-old baby at the cottage.'

'You would need good references, Beth,' said Vera cautiously.

Beth looked longingly at the sleeping baby. 'It's just that . . .'

Vera put her arm round Beth's shoulders. 'You would miss him if you went back to work.'

Beth nodded and sighed. 'Yes, I would.'

There was a heavy silence. 'I understand,' said Vera quietly.

'I'm not sure we'd manage on just Jack's salary,' added Beth suddenly.

'Many do,' replied Vera.

'I suggested a bigger headship this morning,' Beth told her.

'And what did he say?' asked Vera.

'You know Jack,' said Beth simply.

'I do, my dear – I do.'

Just then Ms Piddle came out to her car, opened the boot and searched in an executive black briefcase for a document.

'I know that lady,' said Beth mysteriously.

'Oh yes?' asked Vera.

'She's a member of the Hartingdale WI and there was a lot of fuss last year about her competition entry in the annual fête.'

'Really?' exclaimed Vera, suddenly very interested. 'Tell me more.'

In the staff-room Sally was taking a slightly malicious delight in seeing a photograph of Kenneth Baker, the Minister for Information Technology, who was looking clearly perplexed as he tried to get to grips with one of the new computers. She smiled up at Jo and passed her the newspaper. 'Good to see I'm not the only one struggling with the new technology,' she said.

Jo looked up from her Heinemann catalogue advertising

computer software and nodded. 'Even Ladybird books are going micro,' she said.

'Micro?' murmured Anne from the other side of the staff-room. A whole new world with strange vocabulary had arrived.

Vera crossed the High Street and walked into Pratt's Hardware Emporium. Fortunately there were no customers around. 'Timothy, I need a quiet word,' she said.

Tidy Tim took the hint and ushered Vera to the private space behind the tall shelf of Black & Decker orbital sanders and heavy-duty grinders. He touched the side of his nose with a beautifully manicured finger. 'Y'word is my command, Mrs Forbes-Kitchener,' he said.

'I'm afraid it's *fleas* again, Timothy – and this time it's Maggie.'

The gravitas of Vera's words struck home. Maggie was her favourite cat. 'I've got just the thing,' Timothy re-assured her. 'Ah took delivery today of the new range of improved Sherley's Super Flea Band – 'specially f'*superior* cats.'

Vera nodded in appreciation of the recognition that Maggie was undoubtedly no ordinary cat. 'But will it work, Timothy?' she asked anxiously. 'I can't have fleas at Morton Manor. The major would never forgive me.'

Timothy unwrapped one of the boxes. 'Here y'are,' he said. 'Guards against fleas for up t'five months.'

'Thank you, Timothy,' said Vera gratefully, 'I do appre-ciate your support . . . and, of course, your *discretion*.'

The next stop was Prudence Golightly's General Stores, but opportunity beckoned when Vera saw Diane

Wigglesworth outside her Hair Salon, enjoying the afternoon sunshine. Diane was sitting on a folding chair and skimming through the pages of an old sixty-pence copy of *Hair Flair* magazine. She had half an hour before Petula Dudley-Palmer was due to have an Irene Cara.

'Diane,' said Vera quietly, 'I have a problem and I wondered if you could help.'

'Of course, Vera,' replied Diane.

A few minutes later, Diane smiled. 'Don't worry, Vera,' she said, 'we'll sort it.'

Meanwhile, in the staff-room, Sally was spreading some Outline Low Fat Spread on a cracker and was conscious of Jo looking thoughtfully at the process.

'Only nine hundred and thirty calories per pack,' said Sally with little enthusiasm.

Jo offered what she hoped was a supportive smile and returned with relish to her after-lunch Bakewell tart.

Ms Piddle had clearly seen enough and announced her departure. 'I am going now, Mr Sheffield, and you'll have my report next week.' It didn't sound promising and there was no time for further discussion.

When she reached the car park Vera was putting her shopping into the boot of her car. 'A word, please, Ms Piddle, before you go,' she said.

Soon they were deep in conversation.

After school, Major Rupert Forbes-Kitchener met Joseph Evans at the school gate. Eleven-year-old Jimmy Poole, who had been in my class last year, walked by with his Yorkshire terrier, Scargill. The frisky little dog immediately took a fancy to the major's cavalry twills.

'Thtop it, Thcargill,' lisped Jimmy, 'that'th naughty.' He tugged the lead and they hurried away up the High Street.

The major was soon placated when Vera served them tea in the staff-room. We were due to select the candidates for interview for the new teaching post and the major and Joseph had come to represent the school governors. Rupert, immaculate as ever in a lightweight shooting jacket, crisp white shirt and East Yorkshire regimental tie, was in good spirits. 'A fine day, Joseph, what?' he said cheerily.

'Yes, Rupert,' replied Joseph quietly. Life had never been the same for him since his sister had left the vicarage to marry this larger-than-life ex-soldier.

I collected the folder of applications while Vera tidied her desk. Joseph took me to one side in the entrance hall as the major went into the staff-room. 'Just a thought, Jack,' he said. 'I know you will think of the *school* and won't be swayed by the applicants you *know*. Obviously, first and foremost we need a first-rate teacher with excellent references, but we also need to look at the *skills* they can offer. I'm sure we can cover girls' games but, whether we like it or not, computers are here to stay.' He made a steeple of his fingers and rested them against his chin. 'Jack – we really need someone to lead us in the new technology,' and with a gentle smile he followed me into the staff-room.

It was seven o' clock when we finally agreed on the four we wanted to interview. They were Mrs Mary Blaythewaite, age thirty-seven, currently teaching reception in York; Ms Pat Brookside, age twenty-six, infant teacher from Thirkby, and looking for a change; Mr Tom Dalton, age twenty-four, a teacher at a North Yorkshire village school that was due for closure; and Miss Valerie Flint, age sixty, our regular supply teacher. As I drove home I prayed we had made the right choices. Meanwhile, Beth and I had our own choices to make and they were more complex.

By Friday evening, in the kitchen at Morton Manor, Vera had completed her preparations for her Harvest Festival Cake. She had put cider, apricots and prunes in a bowl and covered it to soak overnight. In another bowl she had mixed apricots, cherries and sultanas in cider for the topping. She put away her ancient weighing scales and brass imperial weights, tidied the surfaces and then made an important telephone call to a certain inspector. It wasn't long before the matter of an infamous Dundee fruit cake, circa 1982, cropped up in the conversation.

On Saturday morning I looked out of the bedroom window of Bilbo Cottage. A gentle breeze stirred the distant cornfield and the cut stalks swirled in a living pattern as if touched by the breath of God. The countryside had come alive on this sunlit autumn morning.

Beth came in carrying baby John. She took a deep breath. 'Jack,' she said, 'I've been thinking.'

'About what?'

'Something Vera said – about the nanny idea.' I wondered what was coming next. 'It would have to be the very best for John.'

The significance dawned. 'Of course,' I agreed.

'I was thinking of the expense,' continued Beth.

'Don't worry,' I replied, 'we'll manage.'

No more words were needed. Beth smiled and we kissed. Then she wrinkled her nose. 'And, by the way, your son needs changing.'

A mile away on the Crescent, Anne was listening to Radio 2 while chopping a banana to add to her Weetabix. Terry Wogan had just told the nation that Cyril Smith, the heavyweight Liberal MP, had stormed out of a meeting with party leader David Steel. However, Anne was much more impressed with the news that actress Joan Collins, at the age of fifty, had been voted one of the ten most desirable women in America. The Irish raconteur also mentioned that the Everly Brothers had performed the night before in a reunion concert at the Albert Hall and he introduced an old favourite, 'Cathy's Clown'; Anne, word perfect, sang along and swayed her hips.

Meanwhile, her husband John was engrossed in his *Woodworker* magazine and the new range of Nobex mitre saws. As she sat down at the kitchen table, Anne smoothed the seat of her figure-hugging tracksuit bottoms and wondered about her life.

Back at Morton Manor a contented Vera was listening to the news bulletin on Radio 4. She was concerned to hear that a man with a knife had been overpowered outside Buckingham Palace by a heroic policeman wielding nothing more than a rolled-up umbrella. Equally worrying for Vera was the report on Captain Mark Phillips and Princess Anne. They had flown to Australia, where he was due to ride in the Melbourne Cup three-day event. However, it appeared the couple would be apart for their tenth wedding anniversary and Vera reflected on the problems of other people.

However, the main problem that had caused this proud lady such concern was about to be solved. The doorbell rang – Diane the hairdresser had arrived. She unpacked her bag in the room Vera used for her sewing. 'Now, Vera,' she said, 'just relax and we'll sort you out.'

Vera, fingertip softly, touched the distinct grey-white roots at her temples. She had been embarrassed for some time as her beautiful wavy hair had finally succumbed to the remorseless wheel of time. The thought of treating it in public view was unthinkable to Vera and, as she relaxed under Diane's expert care, she wondered if *vanity* really was a sin.

Meanwhile, in the kitchen the major was eating his cornflakes and scratching his shin. 'Feels like a jolly old flea bite,' he said to himself. 'Probably that dratted little Yorkshire terrier in the village, what?'

It was an eventful weekend. Following some careful financial accounting Beth advertised for a nanny and Jo Hunter volunteered to be our babysitter so that Beth and I could go to the Harvest Supper.

The evening was a success and Vera's cake was judged to be the best she had ever made. The major forgot to blame the unfortunate Scargill as the threat of flea bites was overlooked and remembered to praise Vera on the beauty of her perfectly coiffured hair.

On Monday morning when I walked into the school office, Vera was on the telephone. 'Thank you, Miss Barrington-Huntley,' she said, 'I'll inform Mr Sheffield.' I stopped in my tracks. The chair of the Education Committee at County Hall rarely got in touch to pass the time of day.

Vera replaced the receiver and gave a calm smile. 'Good news, Mr Sheffield,' she said. 'Miss Barrington-Huntley called to say well done.'

'Really? Whatever for?'

'Our Health and Hygiene report was . . .' she glanced down at the shorthand on her pad, '. . . *outstanding* in all areas'.

'That's wonderful, Vera! What did you say?'

Vera smiled with the contentment of the ultimate problem-solver, touched her hair lightly and said, 'Simply that – *it's all in the detail*, Mr Sheffield.'

Chapter Three

Ruby and the Coffin Polisher

Mrs Hunter invited the grandparents of children in Class 2 to visit school this morning as part of her portrait-painting activity. Preparations were made for the annual Parent Teacher Association Jumble Sale on Saturday, 8 October. Parents sorted jumble after school in preparation for an 11.00 a.m. start on Saturday. County Hall requested copies of our history syllabus in preparation for their working paper towards a common curriculum.

Extract from the Ragley School Logbook:
Friday, 7 October 1983

'Mrs F – ah'm worried about my Ronnie,' said Ruby the caretaker. She stood by the office door absent-mindedly polishing the brass handle, a familiar pose when Ruby wished to discuss her dysfunctional life.

Vera looked up from searching in our huge four-drawer filing cabinet for a spare copy of our history syllabus following a request from County Hall. 'And what is the problem, Ruby?' she asked.

'Well, 'e's jus' bone idle, Mrs F, allus was, allus will be,' said Ruby sadly. Ronnie Smith was Ruby's fifty-two-year-old husband and his life revolved around his racing pigeons, managing the Ragley Rovers football team and propping up the bar in The Royal Oak.

'How is the job going at the funeral parlour with Mr Flagstaff?' asked Vera.

''E's goin' in late t'day,' said Ruby. 'Sez 'e's poorly.'

After a lifetime of unemployment for Ronnie, last year Vera had managed to get him a job by using her influence with an old friend, Septimus Bernard Flagstaff, the local funeral director. So it was that Ronnie had finally joined the ranks of the employed as a part-time coffin polisher. 'Mr Flagstaff won't be happy if he's absent,' commented Vera.

'That's what ah told 'im, Mrs F,' said Ruby and she dabbed away a tear with the corner of her fluffy duster. 'But does 'e listen? Does 'e 'eck.'

Vera took pity on her dear friend, closed the drawer of the filing cabinet and sat down. 'Come in and tell me about it.'

Ruby walked in, shut the door and began to cry. Vera offered her a lace-edged monogrammed handkerchief and Ruby accepted it gratefully. She blew her nose like a snorting buffalo and sat down in the visitor's chair. When she offered to return the handkerchief Vera politely refused. It was shortly after nine o' clock on Friday, 7 October and life was proving difficult for our school caretaker.

Ruby was a popular member of the Ragley community and a cheerful sight skipping round the school with her mop and galvanized bucket, singing songs from her favourite film, *The Sound of Music*. Ruby and Ronnie had six children. Thirty-two-year-old Andy was a sergeant in the army and thirty-year-old Racquel was the proud mother of Krystal Carrington Ruby Entwhistle, who, at just over fourteen months, was Ruby's pride and joy. Ruby's other four children shared their cramped council house. Twenty-eight-year-old Duggie, nicknamed 'Deadly' as he also worked for the local undertaker, was content to sleep in the attic; twenty-three-year-old Sharon was engaged to Rodney Morgetroyd, the Morton village milkman with the Duran Duran looks; and twenty-one-year-old Natasha worked part-time in Diane's Hair Salon. Finally, the youngest in the family, ten-year-old Hazel, was in her final year at Ragley School. Feeding her large family was always a struggle for Ruby.

Meanwhile, on the other side of the High Street, Ronnie was rubbing his stomach and leaning on the counter of the village pharmacy. Eugene, the eccentric pharmacist who wore a *Star Trek* outfit under his white coat, looked concerned.

'Ah gorra upset stomach, Eugene,' said Ronnie.

'Mebbe y'should go to t'see Doctor Davenport,' said Eugene.

'No thanks. Ah jus' think one o' them pints ah 'ad last night were a bit off,' said Ronnie. 'It were either t'seventh or mebbe t'eighth, so ah jus' need summat t'get me back on t'straight an' narrow, so t'speak.'

Eugene looked on the shelf behind him and selected some Bisodol tablets. 'These are f'indigestion, Ronnie. So see 'ow y'get on an' come back if y'not better.'

'Thanks, Eugene,' said Ronnie with a pained expression.

'It's tough being a man – y'know, never complaining.'

Eugene glanced nervously to make sure his wife Peggy was not within earshot. 'Y'reight there, Ronnie. We're *martyrs*, you an' me.'

It had been a busy morning in my class. I had spent time hearing every child read, updating record cards and helping Terry Earnshaw understand the mysterious world of fractions. Finally, at a quarter past ten, Louise Hartley rang the bell for morning assembly and the children put away their School Mathematics Project workcards and exercise books and we filed into the hall.

Around twenty extra chairs had been put out as Jo Hunter had organized a portrait-painting activity with her class and had invited the children's grandparents to come in. They strolled up the drive, chatting in happy groups and recalling the days when they used to attend the village school before the Second World War. Also many of them dropped off bags of jumble in the entrance hall in preparation for tomorrow's annual PTA Jumble Sale. The last to arrive was a stick-thin peroxide blonde with hard features, a pink polo-neck sweater, tight black miniskirt and high heels. She took a last puff of her cigarette, tossed it on the entrance steps, crushed it with the pointed sole of a black stiletto and tottered in.

I leaned over to Jo. 'Who's that?' I asked.

'Thelma Badstock,' said Jo, 'Charlie Cartwright's grandma.' She glanced left and right, then leaned over to whisper, 'Vera told me she has just divorced her third husband.'

It was Anne's turn to take assembly and she had brought one of her classical LPs into school. With the utmost care she wiped the surface of the vinyl record with a soft cloth and placed it on the rubber turntable of our music centre, a Contiboard contraption on castors with two huge speakers on the lower shelf. She selected 33 revolutions per minute, raised the plastic arm and lowered the sharp stylus on to the surface of the spinning record in exactly the correct groove. Moments later Johann Pachelbel's *Canon in D Major* echoed in the lofty roof space. As always, it proved a calming influence on the children as they walked in and sat down cross-legged on the polished wood-block floor.

It was a happy occasion during which four-year-old Julie Tricklebank and five-year-old Rosie Spittlehouse held up their paintings upside down and no one noticed the difference. After the bell for morning playtime our visitors cheered when Shirley wheeled out a trolley with a steaming Baby Burco boiler, a battered aluminium milk jug, a bowl of sugar, a variety of crockery and a tin of digestive biscuits.

On the council estate at 7 School View, Ronnie was looking preoccupied while Ruby, tired after her morning shift, was drinking a mug of tea as she sat on their battered sofa.

'Y'should be gettin' off t'work,' she said.

'Where's t'plate wi' t'breadcrumbs?' he asked.

Each day Ruby collected every breadcrumb and spare scrap of food and piled it on an old chipped 1953 Coronation plate, then Ronnie took it out to feed his racing pigeons. 'In t'kitchen where it usually is,' she replied.

Ronnie reappeared with the plate and headed for the back yard.

"Ang on a minute, Ronnie,' said Ruby, 'ah need a word.'

'What's that, luv?' enquired Ronnie guardedly.

'Our 'Azel needs new shoes.'

Ronnie shook his head forlornly. 'Sorry, luv, ah've nowt t'spare. There's not much goin' on at t'fun'ral parlour. Things'll pick up in winter.'

'She needs 'em *now*, Ronnie,' said Ruby.

'It's t'school jumble sale t'morrow,' said Ronnie, opening the back door. 'We've allus done well out o' that.'

Ruby shook her head in dismay. 'Ronnie – dresses and jumpers is fine but ah don't want our 'Azel 'aving t'wear other people's shoes,' she said. 'It's not good for 'er feet.'

'Beggars can't be choosers, luv,' said Ronnie and slipped out, shutting the door behind him.

So that's what it's come to thought Ruby. She put down her mug on the arm of the sofa and stared at her work-red hands.

Back in school, the children in Class 2 were wearing outsize, paint-splattered shirts back-to-front and were hard at work painting portraits of their bemused grandparents. As usual, some showed great skill and attention to detail, whereas others applied more paint to their faces and hands than to the large A2 sheets of thick white sugar paper. A few unwitting advocates of the French Post-Impressionist school were emerging, not least six-year-old Charlie Cartwright, who was about to discover the art of pointillism. Although he had never heard of Georges Pierre Seurat and his famous large-scale painting *Un dimanche après-midi à l'Île de la Grande Jatte*, the little boy sat there with bristle brush poised, studying his Grandma Thelma intently.

'An' what y'painting now, Charlie?' asked Thelma, who, at the age of fifty, couldn't recall having her portrait painted before. She had once enjoyed a brief passionate affair with an interior decorator from Grimsby but the only thing he had painted was her bedroom ceiling.

'Ah'm paintin' y'face, Grandma,' said Charlie. He pursed his lips in concentration and stared even more closely than before.

'Can ah 'ave a look?' asked Thelma.

'Yes, Grandma,' said Charlie.

Thelma was impressed. Charlie had mixed a splash of red into a small saucer of white poster paint and stirred it vigorously to create a delicate fuchsia pink. The representation of Thelma's artistically enhanced face made her look thirty years younger. 'Oooh, that's lovely, Charlie – what a clever lad you are,' she said with enthusiasm. 'An' you've got me earrings jus' right.' Thelma was proud of the pair of large plastic strawberries that hung from her pierced ears on long, thin pendulous chains.

The painting looked finished so she stood up. She was dying for a cigarette and she looked at the other grandmothers with a self-satisfied smile on her face. In *her* eyes her portrait made her look much younger than this motley crew. 'Ah'm off now, luv,' she said and, after smoothing the miniskirt over her skinny hips, she picked up her imitation leopard-skin handbag and walked out of school.

However, unknown to Thelma, Charlie *hadn't* finished. He selected a small brush and began adding dirty brown dots of paint with gay abandon. Jo was going round the class, encouraging each child. Slightly puzzled, she leaned over.

'Finishing touches, Charlie?'

'Yes, Mrs 'Unter,' replied Charlie, continuing with impunity.

'So what are you doing?' asked Jo.

Charlie's brush tapped up and down with the demeanour of a demented woodpecker. Georges Seurat had required three and half million dots to complete his masterpiece. Charlie needed a mere fifty-seven.

'Ah'm paintin' all t'wrinkles, Mrs 'Unter,' he explained enthusiastically.

Jo smiled and reflected that children never ceased to surprise you.

In the funeral parlour in Easington an unexpected opportunity had arrived for Ronnie Smith.

'It's a rush job, Ronnie – cash in hand,' said Septimus. He took a large brass watch from the pocket of his black waistcoat and looked anxious. 'Time's short,' he added.

''Ow much, Mr Flagstaff?' asked Ronnie.

'Finish it by six o' clock tonight and there's a tenner for you.'

'A tenner?'

He tapped the side of a prestigious top-of-the-range mahogany coffin. 'I need it polished, Ronnie, and I'm in a rush . . . so is it a deal?'

'Good as done, Mr Flagstaff,' said Ronnie.

After school lunch, in the staff-room Anne and I were making a chart of the children's reading ages and Vera was sipping Earl Grey tea and reading her *Daily Telegraph*. Jo and Sally were in Jo's classroom pegging up the wet paintings on a temporary washing line made of thick string.

Vera looked content. She was studying an article about the wreck of the *Mary Rose*, the Tudor warship that sank off Southsea in 1545. It had gone on show for the first time, with the ship's hull being sprayed with icy water for eighteen hours each day. Then she frowned when she turned the page. 'Oh no,' she said and looked up to ensure Sally was not in the room. 'Here's that ginger-haired Welshman again. I'm so sorry he's been elected leader of the Labour Party.'

During afternoon school I walked into Jo's class, where the children were busy doing the mathematics lesson that would have taken place in the morning but for the portrait-painting session. Jo was sitting at a trapezoidal table with her youngest group of budding mathematicians as they worked their way through a long multiplication workcard from the green box of the School Mathematics Project.

She scribbled a figure on a piece of card. 'And this is the *remainder*,' she said with a confident smile. The usual follow-up rhetorical question was not far behind. 'So the *remainder* is?' she asked.

There was a hesitant silence, finally broken by, 'Ah know what a remainder is, Miss,' from the enthusiastic six-year-old Ted Coggins. 'It's what pulls Santa's sleigh.'

Jo gave me a sheepish *well I'm trying my best* glance.

I smiled and passed on the message: 'Vera says she has time to mount the portraits on the big display board in the entrance hall if you want to send them along.'

Jo looked relieved. 'Thanks,' she said, 'that's terrific. I'll do it now.'

'She also said if you could make sure they're all labelled with the subject and artist's name it will help.'

'Fine,' said Jo and returned to the difference between *reindeer* and *remainder*.

Shortly before the end of school a posse of willing mothers arrived in the entrance hall and began to sort the jumble for tomorrow's sale.

Meanwhile, in my classroom, the Buttle twins appeared to be in a hurry.

'It's a long walk back to t'farm, Mr Sheffield,' said Katrina.

'An' we want t'be 'ome by twenty past four,' added Rowena, hastily packing her bag.

'And why is that?' I asked.

They both looked at me as if I lived on another planet. ''Cause it's *SuperTed and the Inca Treasure*,' they said in perfect unison and ran off down the school drive.

Ruby arrived to empty the bin. She looked preoccupied and Hazel gave her a hug.

'An' what y'doin' now, luv?' asked Ruby.

'Ah'm off t'Molly Paxton's 'ouse, Mam, t'watch *Blue Peter*. Ah think Peter Duncan's mekkin' a model out o' matchsticks.'

Ruby smiled. 'OK, luv, you get off an' don't be late 'ome f'tea.'

Two hours later, Ruby rushed home and cooked egg and chips for Ronnie and Hazel.

Ronnie looked unimpressed. 'This dunt look much for m'tea, Ruby,' he said disconsolately. 'Ah'm gettin' like a bag o' bones.'

'Well mebbe y'should work a bit o' overtime f'Mr Flagstaff an' then we'd 'ave some brass t'buy some chops for a change.'

Ronnie fingered the ten pound note in his pocket. 'Ah work m'fingers to t'bone as it is, Ruby.'

'Y'could spend less on them cigarettes,' said Ruby.

Ronnie looked aghast, removed the cigarette from his lips, coughed twice and said, 'It's me only pleasure, Ruby, my love. Y'wouldn't deprive me o' that.'

Ronnie had begun smoking Woodbine cigarettes at the age of twelve and had progressed to roll-ups during his teens. Once the children had come along he had smoked his way through countless packets of Kensitas cigarettes in order to collect sufficient coupons for a child's swing, a slide and a dartboard.

'An' beer,' added Ruby sharply. 'You'll drink that pub dry one day.'

'That's jus' me bein' sociable, Ruby,' protested Ronnie. 'Ah 'ave me position t'up'old as manager o' football team. Ah 'ave *responsibilities*. Anyway, ah'm off now.'

'Well wear a clean vest in case y'get knocked down an' go to t'ospital,' shouted Ruby.

'Ah'll 'elp y'wash up, Mam,' said Hazel.

After updating our history syllabus for County Hall I tidied my desk and locked the school. Beth had taken John down to Hampshire to visit her parents so I decided to have a meal at The Royal Oak on the way home.

It was full of regulars, including Ronnie and the Ragley Rovers football team. Sheila Bradshaw, the landlady and barmaid, was pulling pints with her usual dexterity and chatting with the customers. She was wearing tight black leather hotpants, a royal-blue boob tube and a gravity-defying bra that supported the best cleavage in the village. Her mascara had been applied liberally to create her favourite Dusty Springfield look and she smiled as I approached the bar.

'What's it t'be, Mr Sheffield?' she asked.

'A pint of Chestnut please, Sheila,' I said, placing thirty pence on the counter.

'An' is there owt else y'fancy?' she asked with a secret smile.

When I looked up at the chalkboard menu it was clear that Pete the poacher had paid a recent visit. As well as the regular dishes, today's list included smoked squirrel and smoked partridge. 'I'll have chicken and chips in a basket please,' I said quickly. Sheila pulled on the pump and fluttered her false eyelashes. 'Ah like a man who knows what 'e wants. She's a lucky woman, that wife o' yours.'

'Don looks busy,' I said, keen to change the subject, as her red-faced husband appeared once again from the direction of the cellar.

''E's jus' put another barrel on,' said Sheila and then leaned provocatively over the bar. As usual, I averted my eyes from her astonishing cleavage and stared at the bottled shandy on the shelf behind her. 'It's a 'ectic night, Mr Sheffield,' she added. ''E's been up an' down more than a bride's nightdress,' and she gave me a wink.

In an earlier life Don had wrestled under the slightly disconcerting title of The Silent Strangler, so it was wise never to upset him. 'Thanks, Sheila,' I said as the massive frame of her husband appeared at her elbow and collected some empty glasses from the bar.

'Evening, Mr Sheffield,' said Don. ''Ow's little un shaping up?'

'Fine thanks, Don,' I replied. 'He's more than ten weeks old now.'

'Ah remember our Claire when she were that age, Mr Sheffield,' said Sheila wistfully. 'Er skin were soft as silk.'

'John can hold a rattle now,' I added proudly, 'and he loves sitting in his bouncer chair.'

'Well, mek t'most of it 'cause they soon grow up,' said Don, 'an' then y'trouble starts.'

'Shurrup, y'big soft ha'penny,' said Sheila. 'Y'know nowt.'

I glanced up at the television perched on a shelf above the tap-room bar. Assorted members of the football team were watching Culture Club perform their number-one record 'Karma Chameleon'.

Ronnie walked in and glanced up at the television. 'Ah reckon 'e's a poofter,' he said bluntly and ordered a pint of Tetley's bitter. It was then that something caught his eye. Thelma Badstock was sitting at a corner table, rummaging in her handbag. She looked up and smiled. Ronnie removed his Leeds United bobble hat, nervously flattened a few wisps of greying hair and walked over. ''Ello, Thelma. Y'back then,' he said.

'Been a long time, Ronnie,' she said. 'Ten years.'

Thelma opened a pack of Regal King Size, selected a cigarette and beckoned to Ronnie for a light. She cupped her long fingers round his shaking hand, then leaned back and crossed her legs. 'Ah prefer them *mental* cigarettes now, Ronnie, but these allus settle me nerves,' she said huskily.

'So what y'doin' back 'ere?' asked Ronnie.

'Movin' on wi' me life,' said Thelma. 'That Norman Badstock were as twisted as a corkscrew . . . ran off wi' 'is secret'ry.'

'Ah'm sorry, Thelma,' said Ronnie. 'Do y'want a drink?'

Thelma laughed. 'That teks m'back, Ronnie. Remember back in t'fifties when y'used t'buy me them erotic drinks like Cinzano Bianco?'

'Ah remember,' said Ronnie.

'Ah'll 'ave a double G an' T,' said Thelma. ''Ave you 'ad y'tea yet, Ronnie, 'cause ah fancy summat t'eat.' She opened her purse.

'No – ah've got brass,' said Ronnie, pulling out his ten pound note.

'In that case ah'll 'ave steak an' chips an' peas,' said Thelma quickly.

'That's what ah fancy,' said the affluent Ronnie and he hurried back to the bar.

Twenty minutes later they were tucking into two well-done steaks and swapping stories. 'So y'still wi' Ruby then?'

Ronnie nodded but didn't look up from making a chip butty.

'What's y'job, then, Ronnie?' asked Thelma.

'Ah'm in t'furniture . . . 'igh quality.'

'That's wonderful,' said Thelma. 'Like they say – don't 'ide y'light under a bucket.'

She delved into her battered handbag and in among the clutter found a dog-eared photograph with the year 1951 scrawled on the back. The subject was a smiling eighteen-year-old Thelma leaning against the seafront railings at Morecambe and smoking a cigarette.

'Ah 'ad a lovely Terylene pleated skirt,' she said, 'an' them Twinco sunglasses cost me one an' ninepence.'

'Y'look a stunner, Thelma,' said Ronnie in appreciation.

Thelma studied the detail of her younger self. 'Ah
used t'smoke Capstan in them days an' ah moved on
t'Rothman's King Size when ah got a proper job,' she said
proudly. 'It's a shame ah didn't meet you then, Ronnie.'

Ronnie fingered the change in his pocket. ''Ow about
another drink, Thelma?'

'Oooh, ah do like a gen'rous man,' said Thelma, re-
crossing her legs.

By ten o' clock Ronnie was half drunk and completely
broke. He made his excuses and wandered home under
an ethereal night sky. When he fell asleep on the bed and
began to snore Ruby removed his shoes but left on his
bobble hat. After all . . . the nights were getting chilly.

On Saturday morning it was a slow dawn and a grudging
grey light spread over the sleeping land.

In Ruby's household, on Mike Read's Radio 1 show,
'I'm Still Standing' by Elton John was blasting out
while Ruby and Hazel made a breakfast fry-up. On the
Crescent, in Anne's kitchen, Terry Wogan on Radio 2 had
just introduced Peabo Bryson and Roberta Flack singing
'Tonight I Celebrate My Love' and Anne sang along
while imagining David Soul tapping on her bedroom
door. Meanwhile, at Morton Manor, Vera was listening
to Édouard Lalo's *Concerto for Cello and Orchestra* on Radio
3's *Morning Concert* while enjoying a slice of toast with
home-made marmalade.

The Earnshaw household was also waking up.

'Terry,' shouted Mrs Earnshaw, ''ave y'washed be'ind
yer 'ears?'

'Yes, Mam,' said Terry quickly. It was a regular question posed by his mother and he had never quite understood its significance. He was happy that he had given an honest answer and felt no regret whatsoever that he hadn't bothered to wash the *front* of his ears, not to mention his face. In the meantime, he was looking forward to the jumble sale. Before he left school yesterday he had noticed a model Darth Vader with a broken light sabre in a cardboard box of toys and he was hoping to add it to his collection.

By the time I left Kirkby Steepleton the sun had come out and lit up Twenty-acre Field on my way into Ragley. Joyce Davenport, the doctor's wife, and a friend were stooping under the shade of a huge oak tree and they waved as I drove past. They were gleaning stalks of corn missed by the combine harvester. Their intention, I discovered later, was to make decorative stars for the Christmas WI stall. However, my thoughts were elsewhere. The School PTA annual Jumble Sale was always a popular village event and a busy morning was in store.

A few minutes before eleven o' clock the school hall was a hive of activity. As usual, Vera was helping Ruby scavenge jumpers, skirts, boilersuits and footwear before the doors opened.

'These'll do nicely f'our 'Azel, Mrs F,' said Ruby, holding up an almost-new pair of stout winter shoes.

'We'll put them safe in a bag under my desk,' said Vera and they both hurried into the school office.

'My Ronnie's comin' round t'collect what ah bought,' said Ruby.

Vera looked at her dear friend and closed the office

door. 'Let's sit down for a minute,' she suggested.

Ruby sat down, took out yesterday's monogrammed handkerchief, dabbed her eyes and stared out of the window. 'He once bought a record f'me, Mrs F – that Max Bygraves singing summat abart a pink toothbrush.'

'I remember it,' said Vera.

'An' 'e sed 'e'll tek me t'London one day,' added Ruby wistfully.

'That would be lovely, Ruby,' said Vera quietly.

'Ah've never been t'London,' Ruby went on with a sigh.

'It's a wonderful place,' said Vera.

'Ah'd love t'see all them sights – y'know, Nelson's Colon, Piccalilly Circus, that Convict's Garden . . . all them famous places.'

Vera smiled and nodded. 'Yes, Ruby.'

'Ah think 'e means well, Mrs F – but 'e does nowt. Goin' t'work never suited 'im. It's like transplantin' a flower that doesn't tek.'

Vera said nothing but thought volumes.

In the entrance hall a group of women were looking at the display of Class 2's art work. 'Y'can tell who they are, can't you?' said Connie Crapper, mother of five-year-old Patience, appreciatively.

Mary Cartwright, mother of six-year-old Charlie, wasn't so sure. 'M'mother won't be pleased,' she said, looking dubiously at little Charlie's portrait of his grandma Thelma. With the addition of the wrinkles it resembled a pineapple with earrings. 'Anyway, c'mon,' continued Mary, 'ah've jus' seen an Orville the Duck on t'toy table.'

Ronnie followed Betty Buttle and Margery Ackroyd into the entrance hall and they stopped and laughed when they saw Thelma's portrait. 'Flippin' 'eck – what a picture!' exclaimed Betty.

'That's jus' perfect,' said Margery. She looked into the school hall, where Thelma had sidled up to the bemused bachelor Maurice Tupham.

'An' she's lookin' for 'usband number *four* by all accounts,' added Betty.

'Well, y'know what they say about Thelma,' said Margery.

'What's that?' asked Betty.

'Badstock by name an' *bad stock* by nature,' said Margery and they set off arm in arm.

Ronnie watched them walk away to the stall displaying leather boots, pink stilettos and Doc Marten boots. He sighed and put his hands in his pockets. He had no money, only a single cigarette in a crumpled packet, and he walked out and leaned against the school wall. From the office window Vera and Ruby saw him light up, hunch his shoulders and stare at his shoes.

'Shall we go back out?' asked Vera.

'It's too much argy-bargy f'me, Mrs F,' said Ruby. She looked tired.

Suddenly there was a knock on the door.

'Come in,' said Vera.

It was little Hazel Smith. ''Scuse me,' she said politely to Vera and then turned to her mother. 'Mam, ah cut m'finger 'elpin' Terry mend 'is light sabre.'

'I'll get a plaster,' said Vera and hurried off to the staff-room.

Ruby held up Hazel's finger and kissed it. 'Love 'eals wounds better than Elastoplast,' she said.

There was silence between them until Hazel looked up

at her mother. 'Mam – ah know what love is,' she said thoughtfully.

'An' what's that, luv?'

'It's what meks y'smile when y'tired,' said Hazel.

Ruby looked at her youngest daughter and realized she was growing up. 'Mebbe y'reight – in fac', y'spot on.' And she leaned over and gave her a hug.

Chapter Four

Important Decisions

Interviews were held today for the post of the new teacher for Class 2 commencing January 1984. The interviewing panel comprised the Revd Joseph Evans, Major Rupert Forbes-Kitchener, the deputy headteacher Mrs Anne Grainger and the headteacher. School closed for a one-week half-term holiday and will reopen on Monday, 7 November.
Extract from the Ragley School Logbook:
Friday, 28 October 1983

'I think it's the right decision, Jack,' said Anne. I looked round the school office. The interviews were over and it was time to make a choice.

The major spoke confidently. 'All jolly good teachers, what?' He fixed us all with a look of absolute authority. 'I'm sure the governors and the education office will back the decision of the head and chair of governors.'

Joseph responded with a gentle smile and then looked at me, presumably for reassurance. 'Well I'm happy, Jack – clearly the best candidate as far as I'm concerned.'

'Anne?' I asked quietly.

Anne looked up from stacking the letters of application into a neat pile. 'I agree,' she said. 'Replacing Jo was always going to be difficult, Jack, but I'm sure this will be good for the school. It will complement the team.'

I took a deep breath and underlined one of the four names on the sheet of paper in front of me. 'So, if we're agreed,' I said, 'it looks like we have a new teacher.'

Anne stood up and looked at each of us in turn. 'I'll go, shall I?' I could see the relief on her face.

'Yes please, Anne, it's time to ask *the question* . . . and then I'll have a word with the others.'

As Anne left the office to walk through the narrow connecting corridor to the staff-room I glanced up at the clock. It was exactly six o' clock, the interviews were completed and a new teacher to take over from Jo Hunter had been selected. As chair of the school governors, Joseph was about to offer a permanent teaching post to the successful candidate and we presumed the answer would be 'Yes'.

I sighed and reflected on the past twelve hours. It had been an eventful day . . . a day of important decisions.

It had begun in the early hours when a reluctant dawn light crept into the second bedroom of Bilbo Cottage. Baby John was three months old now and clearly enjoyed chewing his fists and fingers. He had begun to laugh and I marvelled at his development. He needed feeding and changing and Beth and I moved like slow-motion dance partners. Lack of sleep had become a way of life for us. We had a routine and few words were spoken, simply two tired people, each with their own thoughts, doing what needed to be done.

A journey begins with one small step – and big decisions sometimes begin with small sentences. So it was that later, over a hurried breakfast of cereal and toast, John was gurgling happily and Beth was sipping at her mug of tea. She looked distracted. Faintly, in the background on Radio 2, Barbara Dixon was singing 'The Long and Winding Road'. It somehow seemed appropriate.

'Jack, do you think we can manage on one salary?'

It took me by surprise. 'Why – what are you thinking?'

Beth didn't turn to look at me. 'It's just that I have to make a decision about going back to my headship.'

'I thought you had decided to go back in January.'

She replaced the spoon on John's plastic tray and wiped his face. 'I feel different . . . it's hard to explain.'

I put down my mug of black tea. 'Tell me,' I urged.

'Well, we may not find a suitable nanny,' she said, 'and I enjoy being at home with John.'

'I can understand that.'

'So I've been thinking . . . perhaps we should consider me taking the full academic year off and staying here to look after John. The school can survive without me, my deputy's doing a good job, I can still do my Masters degree – and we would save money on a nanny.' She broke off to adjust John's 'I Love My Daddy' bib, a present from Ruby. Then she nodded towards our 'Views of York' kitchen calendar. 'But I'll need to tell the school governors tomorrow so they have a couple of months' notice to sort out staffing and then let County Hall know.'

It was an important decision. Once again we were at a crossroads. I leaned over and held her hand. 'I think that's a wonderful idea and, yes, I'm sure we can manage. Plenty of others do it.'

Beth looked relieved. 'Thanks,' she said. 'I'll give it some thought today and maybe we can talk about it again tonight.'

I looked at the kitchen clock. 'I have to go,' I said and kissed her on the cheek. Then I bent to kiss John good-bye.

'And good luck with the interviews,' she called out as I shut the front door behind me.

During the drive on the back road to Ragley village my mind was filled with thoughts of what lay ahead. The school that was a cornerstone of my life was about to change, and with it the job I loved.

Meanwhile, the season was changing and as I drove up the High Street the residents of Ragley were hunched in their winter coats. The temperature was dropping and dark nights and cold winds were upon us. Early frosts had blackened the fragile petals of the last floribunda roses and dead leaves gathered in eddying swirls. In the hedgerows the intricate webs of countless spiders looked like fine lace, while small creatures plundered the red hips of dog roses. A robin, perched on the noticeboard outside the village hall, sang a mournful song while tiny wrens were busy claiming territory and goldfinches searched for seeds in among the teasels. Winter was coming.

Vera was busy when I arrived at school. 'Good morning, Mr Sheffield,' she said. 'The list of applicants is on your desk.'

'Good morning, Vera, and thank you. I'm sure every-thing is in place for today.'

Vera was her usual confident, well-organized self and she picked up a copy of the programme for the day. 'All the applicants have been invited to arrive at twelve and sit with the children for lunch. As you suggested, I've arranged for Anne, Sally, Jo and myself to meet them and then, as you requested, no doubt you can have a word with them all before afternoon school when they are free to walk around and visit the classrooms. Then Rupert and Joseph will be here at afternoon break to meet them in the staff-room and answer their questions before the interviews commence at the end of school. We've timetabled up to thirty minutes each for that.'

'Excellent, Vera,' I said. 'I'd be lost without you.'

Vera gave a modest, unassuming smile, took out her late dinner money tin and register and prepared for an otherwise usual Friday morning.

It was my turn to supervise morning playtime and once again I was amazed by the children, who seemed impervious to the sharp north wind and the dark clouds rolling in from the Hambleton hills.

I leaned against the stone wall with a welcome mug of hot coffee and reflected on my life in this community. My time at Ragley School had proved to be a long and busy road shared with countless children and the riches of childhood. I was a teacher of the young and we needed to prepare the children in our care for an uncertain future.

Suddenly a loud shout shattered my reverie.

Little Ted Coggins was playing lions-and-tamers with Charlie Cartwright while Jemima Poole watched open-mouthed.

'Ah'm gonna do one o' m'blood-curdlin' roars,' said Ted Coggins proudly.

'Blood-curdling?' queried Jemima, discovering yet another new word.

'Yeah,' said Ted with bravado, 'y'can't beat a bit o' curdlin'.'

I walked out to the area of the playground that was sheltered from the bitter wind by the school cycle shed. The Buttle twins, Rowena and Katrina, were winding a skipping rope while two eight-year-olds, Mary Scrimshaw and Sonia Tricklebank, stood alongside chanting:

> *Pease pudding hot,*
> *Pease pudding cold,*
> *Pease pudding in the pot,*
> *Nine days old.*
> *O-U-T spells OUT!*

Meanwhile three ten-year-olds, Betsy Icklethwaite, Hazel Smith and Molly Paxton, jumped in and out with skilful steps. I smiled at their zest for life. It was a song of childhood. Adolescence was still a distant world and a journey yet to be made.

At lunchtime Vera and I were in the school office when she looked out of the window. 'Here they come,' she said.

First to arrive was Mrs Mary Blaythewaite, an experienced thirty-seven-year-old and a strong candidate, as she was currently teaching a reception class at Kingsdale Infant School in York. She was dropped off at the school gate and waved a fond farewell as the driver sped away. A short, stocky lady, she walked purposefully towards the entrance door, where she was met by Anne, who took her on a brief guided tour of the school.

Next to arrive was Valerie Flint, our regular supply teacher and, at the age of sixty, she was by some distance the most experienced teacher. Valerie was generally regarded as 'a safe pair of hands' and, having taught every class in the school over the years, she knew Ragley and its children very well. She was met by Vera, both long-standing friends at the Women's Institute, and they shared the formality of a familiar walk round the classrooms.

Back in the staff-room Sally and Jo were waiting for the other two candidates. 'I imagine this must be Mr Dalton,' said Sally.

'And the netball player,' added Jo with a grin.

Two cars had arrived at the same time and eased their way into the last parking spaces in the car park. Ms Pat Brookside parked her 1970s Mini Clubman Estate, picked up a manila folder from the passenger seat and jumped out. She was a tall, slim, leggy, twenty-six-year-old blonde and, on paper, was another particularly strong candidate, having taught infants for the past four years at Thirkby Primary School, where she also ran the school netball team. She paused on the grassy bank that separated the car park from the playground and waited for a battered, rusty and once-royal-blue Renault 4 to squeeze into the space next to her.

A young man, probably three inches shorter than me at around five foot ten, with broad shoulders and an open, friendly face climbed out.

Ms Brookside gazed at the handsome newcomer and smiled. 'I'm here for interview,' she said.

'So am I,' replied the young man with a sheepish grin.

Tom Dalton was twenty-four years old and the youngest candidate. He wore a smart if slightly crumpled dark grey suit, blue denim shirt, a cheerful red tie and recently polished black shoes. His dark, shaggy hair flopped over his beetle brows and hung over his collar.

Both of them paused to look up at the bell tower and then smiled at the children playing on the playground. Sally and Jo went out to meet them and took them in to school lunch. The children were intrigued by our new visitors and were full of questions as they queued up with their plastic trays. Shirley the cook served them with sausages, mashed potato, carrots and a splash of gravy while Doreen added a hefty slice of sponge cake and lurid purple custard.

'So none o' you are one o' them *vegetarians*, then,' announced Doreen with a voice of doom. Only the bravest vegetarian would have replied 'Yes'. Then they settled down with the groups of children round the Formica-topped trapezoidal tables for their pre-interview meal.

Ms Brookside was soon in conversation with nine-year-old Harold Bustard.

'So what have you been doing this morning?' she asked.

'We've been doin' Moses wi' t'vicar, Miss,' said Harold bluntly.

'And what do you know about him?'

"E comes in ev'ry Friday,' said Harold.

'No,' said Ms Brookside with a smile, 'I meant Moses.'

'Oh well – what m'mam says,' answered Harold.

'Really – and what does she say?'

'She says 'is real name were Charlton 'Eston an' 'e were reight 'unky.'

*

Half an hour later I was in the entrance hall. One of the doors led to the school stock cupboard and I walked in and propped the old wooden ladder against the top shelf. The cupboard was an Aladdin's cave of powder paint, frieze paper, corrugated card, manila exercise books, countless boxes of white chalk, bags of clay, crêpe paper, large sheets of card, tins of Lakeland crayons, rolls of coloured foil and boxes of HB pencils. We needed A4 notepads, Berol pens and manila folders for each member of the interviewing panel and I had told Vera I would collect them.

When I came out I saw Tom Dalton on the other side of the double doors that led from the entrance hall to the school hall. He had been stopped in his tracks by the inquisitive six-year-old Charlie Cartwright. ''Ello, Mister, are y'looking for t'teachers?'

'Yes, I am. I'm Mr Dalton and I'm here to visit your school and talk to Mr Sheffield.'

'Well, Mr Dalton,' said Charlie politely and in the manner of an official tour guide, 'after dinner they all go to t'staff-room for a cup o' tea.'

'Thank you very much . . . and what's your name?' Tom asked.

'Charlie. Ah was named after m'dad – 'e's called Frank,' said Charlie.

'Frank?'

'Yes, but ev'rybody calls 'im Charlie. M'mam says it's 'cause 'e walks funny.'

'Oh I see.'

Charlie was obviously weighing him up and came to a decision. 'Mister,' he said in a conspiratorial whisper, 'would y'like t'see my pet?'

Tom Dalton grinned and crouched down so his head was on the same level as Charlie's. 'Yes, let me see,' he said.

Charlie produced a matchbox from the pocket of his thick corduroy shorts and opened it as if it were a rare casket of precious jewels. Inside was a wriggling and very active spider. 'This is Sammy,' he said with reverence, 'an' ah'm goin' t'make him better.'

'Why, what's wrong with him?' asked Tom, peering closely into the box.

''E's gorra limp,' said Charlie, ''cause of 'im only 'aving seven legs.'

Tom studied the limping spider. 'And how many do you think he is supposed to have?' he asked.

'Eight,' said Charlie in surprise. 'Ev'rybody knows they 'ave eight – four on each side. That 'elps 'em balance.'

'I see,' said Tom. There was a moment of silence as he looked from the spider to the little boy whose lips were pursed in anxiety. 'I can see you're worried about him,' he added.

'I am,' said Charlie, 'an' 'e's not 'ad any dinner. Ah couldn't find any dead flies, only live ones, an' ah can't catch 'em.'

'Perhaps we should let Sammy spin his own web,' suggested Tom quietly. 'I bet he could do it, even with seven legs. He looks a strong spider to me.'

'Mebbe so,' said Charlie.

'There were a lot of spiders' webs in the hedgerow by the school gate when I arrived. If we put Sammy there he would be among his friends.'

'An' ah could look t'see 'ow 'e's gettin' on at t'end o' school,' said Charlie, clearly warming to the idea.

'We could do it now,' said Tom.

There was a pause and a sigh from the little boy. 'OK, Mister – an' thanks.'

As they walked down the drive Vera was in the office locking away Class 2's late dinner money which Sally had just delivered. Sally was staring thoughtfully out of the window.

'Looks like Charlie Cartwright has taken a liking to Mr Dalton,' she said.

Vera smiled. 'Yes, it's good to see,' and she looked approvingly at the young man with the confident manner and engaging smile. 'And he is rather handsome, I suppose.'

'Handsome?' said Sally. She picked up her dinner register and grinned. 'Vera, he's absolutely drop-dead gorgeous.'

The events in school had not gone unnoticed in the village. Friday was always a busy day in Diane's Hair Salon. Diane had just sprayed Yorkshire Pale Ale on Amelia Duff's hair as a setting lotion before adding a colourful collection of giant plastic rollers. Then she glanced up at the clock. 'Margery will be here any minute,' she said and went into the little kitchen to boil some water for a hot drink.

Meanwhile Amelia relaxed in her chair and skimmed through a recent edition of *Woman's Weekly*. After reading an article about television heart-throb Anthony Valentine, she was studying the instructions for a cut-out and ready-to-sew pinafore dress when Margery Ackroyd walked in. Margery was a dedicated gossip: for her it was a way of life and she couldn't wait to share her news.

'We've seen 'em, Amelia – all four of 'em – large as life,' she said excitedly as she sat down on the second of the pair of hairdresser's chairs.

'An' who's that then?' shouted Diane from the kitchen.

'T'new teachers, Diane,' said Margery, 'come for interview t'tek over from Mrs 'Unter.'

'And what are they like?' asked Amelia.

Diane reappeared with two cups of coffee and put each one on the shelf below the large mirror. 'Let's 'ear it then, Margery,' she said and settled down on the bench seat in the corner. She leaned back, lit up a John Player King Size Extra Mild cigarette, took a contented puff and relaxed. Diane knew from past experience that there was no point starting Margery's hair while she had a story to tell.

'Well, there was Miss Flint who we all know,' said Margery, 'in that safari trouser suit that she likes, an' two women who looked all right, 'cept one could 'ave been Miss World,' she took a sip of her coffee, '. . . an' a *man*.'

'A man!' exclaimed Diane, suddenly full of interest.

'An' 'e's a looker,' added Margery in a knowing way. ''E reminds me o' that Richard Chamberlain.'

'I loved *The Thorn Birds*,' said Amelia. 'It was so romantic.'

'Yes, well 'e's not *'xactly* like Richard Chamberlain but 'e 'ad that *walk* . . . y'know, like Richard Gere.'

'Oooh, now y'talkin',' said Diane appreciatively.

Amelia tossed her *Woman's Weekly* on to the coffee table, unable to contain herself. 'Oooh, Richard Gere . . . I saw *An Officer and a Gentleman* twice last year, once with Ted and once with the brass band,' said Amelia, warming to the discussion. 'It's my favourite film.'

'Yes,' said Margery, staring dreamily into the mirror, 'probably more Richard Gere than Richard Chamberlain.'

Diane pinched the end of her cigarette and left it in the ash tray on the window sill. She decided to bring their attention back to hairdressing. 'Well, it looks as though we're all agreed on Richard Gere, then . . . So what's it t'be, Margery?'

'An Olivia Newton-John please, Diane – but like she 'as at t'end o' *Grease*, not t'beginning,' said Margery.

Diane smiled and reached for her extra supply of rollers.

'Wonder if 'e's gorra girlfriend?' added Margery for good measure, and Diane gave Amelia a knowing look.

Further down the High Street in the General Stores & Newsagent, Prudence Golightly was serving Julie Earnshaw.

'A tin o' 'Einz Baked Beans please, Prudence,' said Julie, 'an' a white loaf. That'll 'ave t'do f'tea.'

'That's twenty and a half pence for the beans, Julie,' said Prudence, 'and thirty-two pence for the loaf. Was there anything else?'

Julie rummaged in the bottom of her purse and found a couple of spare coppers. 'An' a Curly Wurly for our Dallas, please.' Three-year-old Dallas Sue-Ellen Earnshaw smiled a toothy smile and with practised ease bit off the paper wrapping.

The bell over the door rang urgently and Betty Buttle and Connie Crapper walked in. 'Guess what?' said Betty and hurried to the counter. 'Ah've seen 'em what's come for t'new teachin' job.'

Prudence hated gossip, except this was definitely

interesting gossip. She looked up at Jeremy Bear, her lifelong friend. Yorkshire's best-dressed teddy bear was sitting on his usual shelf next to a tin of loose-leaf Lyons Tea and an old advertisement for Hudson's Soap and Carter's Little Liver Pills. Prudence took great pride in making sure he was always well turned out. Today he was wearing a white shirt, a tartan bow-tie and a striped apron. Prudence decided this gossip was not for Jeremy's fluffy ears, so she quickly picked him up and put him in the back room. After all, Jeremy was a sensitive soul.

'So, Betty,' she asked, 'what did you see?'

'Well, there were three women – an' a young man,' said Betty.

'A man!' exclaimed Julie. 'What's 'e like?'

'A bit like that feller what dived into t'lake wi' nowt on in *Women in Love*,' she said. 'Y'know –'im who fancied Glenda Jackson.'

'Oliver Reed,' suggested Julie.

'No, t'other one,' said Betty.

'Alan Bates,' said Prudence. 'It's one of my favourite films.'

Betty looked thoughtful. 'Ah'll grant yer 'is 'air is 'xactly like Alan Bates, sort of manly but floppy at t'same time.'

'Well, ah thought 'e were more like Robert Redford – but wi' 'air like Alan Bates,' said Connie.

'Are y'sure?' asked Betty, who was taking some shifting from her dreams. 'Well, ah'll tell y'summat f'nowt,' she continued with absolute conviction, 'ah wish ah were ten years younger.'

There was an awkward silence as the rest of the ladies did the maths and thought *more like twenty*.

'So what's it to be, Betty?' asked Prudence.

'Blessed if ah've f'gotten now,' said Betty and everyone laughed.

At the end of school the children ran down the cobbled driveway into the gathering darkness with happy thoughts of a week's holiday, bonfires and fireworks. Meanwhile, the candidates settled in the staff-room and the interviewing panel – Anne and myself plus Major Forbes-Kitchener and the chair of governors, Joseph Evans – settled ourselves in the office and prepared to interview the first candidate.

Not for the first time, it occurred to me that interviews for a new teacher lacked one thing that was obvious – you didn't actually see the candidates *teach*. You relied on gut feeling based on the personality sitting in front of you, the answers they gave and the report of their previous headteacher.

As the time ticked by on the office clock it was interesting that all the interviews were remarkably different. It felt as though Mrs Mary Blaythewaite interviewed *us* . . . which of course was a good thing. She was confident and clearly very competent, although I felt there were questions about her flexibility and the capacity she may have to adapt to the needs of our village school. To her credit she made it clear that she had never sought promotion and merely wanted a new challenge teaching early years children in a different school.

I liked the dynamic Ms Pat Brookside from Thirkby. She reminded me of Jo Hunter, and was keen to offer to take over the school netball team, particularly as she herself played for York Ladies. However, she appeared to have a phobia about computers and lacked conviction in her responses to questions about the curriculum. I put it down to nerves, and I saw her as a potentially strong candidate who could definitely develop at Ragley School given the chance.

Tom Dalton was remarkably calm and relaxed for such a young man. He had taught a range of age groups in his short career and his village school was about to close, so he was looking for a new post with some urgency. He answered the major's questions about school discipline with confidence and Joseph was clearly impressed with his views on the inevitability of a forthcoming common curriculum for schools and how we would need to adapt. Anne asked him about a quirky addition to his application form. Tom had entered *The Times* Classroom Computer Competition. 'Yes,' he confirmed enthusiastically, 'and the prize is an Atari 600XL computer with a 16Kb RAM memory,' at which Anne glanced across at me and smiled.

Miss Valerie Flint was frank as always. 'I know why I'm here, Joseph,' she said at the end of her interview, 'and you know what you'll get from me – order, loyalty and good teaching.' She was a remarkable lady and I knew the final choice would be a difficult one.

An hour later I felt relieved as I drove back to Kirkby Steepleton. Selecting a new member of staff, particularly in such a small school as ours, was a vitally important decision. However, I knew we had made the right choice. To be effective for the children in our care, it was important we worked as a *team* and made the most of each other's strengths. I relaxed as I pulled into the driveway of Bilbo Cottage and when I opened the door the appetizing smell of delicious cooking floated out to meet me.

Beth was in the kitchen, preparing a shepherd's pie in that particular way I loved so much, simple but effective. She had cooked the onions, removed them from the pan, fried the meat, removed the fat, added a stock cube and tomato purée, then thickened and seasoned to perfection. I dropped my old leather satchel in the hallway, walked into the kitchen and put my arms round her waist. 'Good to be home,' I said, 'and what a wonderful smell.'

'Me or the cooking?' she asked as she spooned the food on to two Denby plates.

'Both,' I said and nuzzled her neck. 'John OK?'

'Yes, he's fast asleep.'

We sat opposite each other at the old pine table. Beth had also found a bottle of Muscadet, a sharp French white wine, in the ancient spare fridge in the garage and she poured a liberal measure for us both.

'What's the occasion?' I asked.

Beth swirled the wine in her glass and stared at it as if for inspiration. 'Jack,' she said at last, 'I've spoken to my chair of governors and to Miss Barrington-Huntley at County Hall and both have agreed.'

I put down my glass. 'Agreed?'

She sipped her wine before delivering the enormity of the next statement. 'I'm staying at home, Jack, to look after John for the rest of this academic year.'

For me it was a relief. 'But that's great news,' I said, 'and I'm sure it's the right decision.'

She gave me a tired smile. 'So, as long as we can manage . . .'

'We'll be fine, Beth,' I assured her with as much conviction as I could muster.

The reality was that, although I was a headteacher,

Ragley was a relatively tiny school so my pay grade was very low. There were young policemen, trainee gas-fitters and pop salesmen earning more than me. While it was the job I loved, it came at a price. However, we touched our glasses across the table with a satisfying clink, drank deeply and began to enjoy the welcome hot food.

Beth looked up. 'Sorry, Jack,' she said, 'but I've not asked yet about the interviews.'

'They went well,' I said, 'and I'm happy with the outcome.'

'So who got the job?'

'The young guy from York – Tom Dalton.'

'What's he like?' asked Beth.

'He'll be fine,' I said.

Little did I know it then, but I couldn't have been more wrong.

Chapter Five

A Friend in Need

County Hall sent the document 'Towards Cooperation – a Vision for the Implementation of a Core Curriculum for Small Schools in North Yorkshire' to all village schools in the Easington area and requested responses from all head-teachers.

Extract from the Ragley School Logbook:
Friday, 11 November 1983

We all need a friend . . . perhaps some more than others.

Timothy Pratt was sorting his socks.

Three colours he thought. *A pair for all seasons and every occasion.*

He stared in admiration and, in that moment of sheer bliss, he knew contentment in every fibre of his organ-ized soul. It was satisfying to create perfection and this was it.

Timothy's bedroom above his Hardware Emporium was functional, some would say minimalist. It comprised a big iron-framed bed with highly polished brass knobs on each corner, an old wooden carver chair, a Contiboard bedside table and a pine chest of drawers painted with anti-dust varnish. Everything was in its place and Timothy was content in his world.

He pulled open the left-hand top drawer, peered in and sighed. *Order from chaos* was Timothy's mantra. So it was that his recently ironed pairs of black socks were placed on the left-hand side, in the middle were perfect piles of blue socks and finally, on the right, equally neat pairs of grey socks. He had *black* socks for funerals and weddings, *blue* socks for summer and *grey* socks for winter. Twice a year the villagers of Ragley changed their clocks: however, the owner of Pratt's Hardware Emporium also changed his socks. There were almost forty-seven million people in the country but few had a sock drawer like Tidy Tim. Timothy's was not only colour-coordinated – it was also in alphabetical order.

However, the life of Timothy Pratt was about to change and his sock drawer was destined never to be the same again.

It was Friday, 11 November and the first frosts had arrived. Outside Bilbo Cottage a coating of frozen mist had settled on the fading leaves of the once-bright dahlias and in the vegetable patch a few neglected onions had gone to seed. Dense morning fog had descended over the Vale of York and the acrid smell of woodsmoke hung heavy in the air.

Beth and John were leaving to spend the weekend with Beth's parents at Austen Cottage in Little Chawton, the pretty little village in Hampshire where they lived. I watched her walk out to her pale blue Volkswagen Beetle. She looked a perfect English beauty in her white polo-neck sweater, a suede fleece, blue skin-tight denim jeans and fur-lined leather boots. A flurry of decaying autumn leaves swirled at her feet as she strapped John into his baby seat.

'Stay safe,' I said.

'We shall,' said Beth. 'Will you survive without me?' she added with a grin.

'Well, I'll get a full night's sleep,' I said and kissed her goodbye.

As she drove away I reflected on the past couple of weeks.

During the half-term holiday family and friends had gathered for John's christening in St Mary's Church. I had collected my Scottish mother Margaret and her sister May from their house in Leeds and that evening they had stayed with Joseph at the vicarage as there was no room in our tiny two-bedroom cottage. Beth's parents, John and Diane Henderson, had accepted Vera and Rupert's kind invitation and they had enjoyed the experience of staying overnight at the elegant Morton Manor. Beth's younger sister, the dynamic and vivacious Laura, had travelled up from her London flat and stayed in the Dean Court Hotel in York. Laura had been asked to move from her post as Assistant Manager of Liberty in London to take over as temporary Manager of the fashion department at their large department store in York for a few months. So she had taken the opportunity to seek out a stylish apartment in the city centre on a short-term let.

The service had gone smoothly and John slept for most of it, only waking when Joseph poured water on him from a baptismal shell. When he made the sign of the cross on his forehead John thought it was feeding time and tried to suck Joseph's finger, much to the amusement of the congregation. It was followed by a low-key but happy and convivial family tea at Bilbo Cottage. Since then Beth had been busy with her latest assignment for Leeds University and I had prepared my scheme of work for the new half term.

When I drove up the High Street Miss Lillian Figgins, known as Lollipop Lil, was on duty as our road-crossing patrol officer and she waved a cheerful greeting. The zebra crossing at the top of the High Street had become part of our village life as the traffic became a little busier each year.

Lillian loved her job and also, thanks to Vera, she was now the regular housekeeper at the vicarage, where she looked after the increasingly lonely Joseph Evans. She often thought of this kindly man as she braved all, and hoped they might be friends one day. Talking to the children each day was the highlight of Lillian's life; she had soon learned all their names by heart and enjoyed the brief conversations she had with them as they marched across the road.

'Ah gorra sticker, Miss,' said Rosie Spittlehouse with enthusiasm, showing her the bright sticky label on the first page of her writing book.

'Well done, Rosie,' said Lillian, waving her across. 'Y'mam'll be proud.'

'An' ah got one as well,' said six-year-old Mandy Kerslake.

'An' Mandy's my best friend,' said Rosie.

'That's lovely,' said Lillian. 'It's good to have a friend.'

95

A mud-covered Land Rover's horn peeped . . . *an' 'e's not one o' 'em*, thought Lillian.

It was Stan Coe, local pig farmer and the bane of Lillian's life. 'Gerra move on,' he shouted. He was always in a hurry and she had to grit her teeth to avoid shouting back at him.

One day she thought, *one day . . .*

Vera was already hard at work dealing with the morning post when I walked in.

'This looks important, Mr Sheffield,' she said, handing me a smart spiral-bound document with a distinctive North Yorkshire County Council crest. It concerned the proposal that small schools should work together towards a new core curriculum. There was an accompanying letter from Miss Barrington-Huntley, chair of the Education Committee.

'According to this, Vera, we have to team up with another school and do some in-service work together,' I said.

'Which school?' she asked.

I scanned Miss High-and-Mighty's letter. 'It simply says we need to work together "as friends in the spirit of cooperation".'

'In that case, Mr Sheffield,' said Vera pointedly, 'we shall need to choose our friend carefully.'

It was a busy morning and, as my class was doing a Second World War project, we joined Sally's class in the school hall for their weekly ITV television programme *How We Used to Live*. It was an excellent twenty-minute broadcast featuring some of the major historical social events between 1936 and 1953. The discussion afterwards was fascinating and, with the Argentine conflict fresh in our minds, Betsy Icklethwaite asked if there was an alternative to war.

Afterwards the children's writing produced some poignant memories. Charlotte Ackroyd's composition was beginning to show great improvement but it was clear she needed to use her dictionary with more care. She had written, 'During the war my Aunty Pauline lived in London so she had to be evaporated and my granddad was captured and was put in a constipation camp.' I corrected the misspellings with a wry smile.

At morning break Jo was full of enthusiasm. She had come across an advertisement in an article in her weekly science magazine and was eager to share her news. 'Jack,' she said, 'there's a Sinclair ZX Spectrum Computer for £129.95 on sale here. It looks to be a bargain and it comes with MEP cassettes in maths, problem-solving and reading.'

'It certainly looks impressive,' I said. 'Let's discuss it at the next staff meeting.'

Sufficiently mollified, she hurried off to prepare her next lesson.

On my way back to class two ten-year-olds, Michelle Cathcart and Louise Hartley, were in the school library and eagerly exchanging stories when I spoke to them.

'Guess what, Mr Sheffield?' said Louise.

I didn't have a chance to reply.

'Me an' Louise are friends now,' said Michelle.

I smiled at their new-found enthusiasm. 'I'm pleased to hear that,' I said.

'Well, we're the same age,' explained Michelle.

'An' our birthdays are in t'same week,' added Louise.

'That's a good reason,' I said.

'An' Louise 'elps with t'library work,' said Michelle.

'An' sometimes ah let Michelle ring t'bell,' said Louise.

'An' we both like Wham!' said Michelle.

'An' David Bowie,' said Louise.

'An' Kajagoogoo,' said Michelle.

'An' 'Eaven 17,' said a bright-eyed Louise.

'Heaven 17?' I repeated, puzzled. 'I've not heard of them.'

'Ah thought teachers knew *everything*,' said a smiling Louise.

'Anyway, Mr Sheffield,' said Michelle, keen to move on, 't'main reason we're friends is 'cause we're t'same . . . but different.'

'Different?'

'Yes, Mr Sheffield,' said Louise, 'Michelle 'asn't got a father and ah've not got a mother.'

'But between us we've got one of each,' said Michelle.

'So that makes us friends,' concluded Louise and they wandered off back to class for a lesson on reflection and refraction followed by a lively half-hour of mental arithmetic without the use of a Casio calculator.

After lunch in the staff-room, Anne and I made a list of children whose reading ages were below their chronological age, with a view to giving them extra help. Conversely, Sally and Jo identified our most able children with a view to ensuring their programmes of work were sufficiently demanding.

Then, while we relaxed over coffee, Vera, Sally and Jo scanned my morning paper, gleaning news according to their interests. Vera was concerned to note that US President Ronald Reagan only worked a three-hour day, whereas Sally read the latest article about the protests on Greenham Common. Not only had the first missile-launchers been unloaded, but the first cruise missiles were expected later in the month. Protesters had been informed that those who got too close would be shot! Meanwhile, Jo was heartbroken. The man who in her opinion was the world's most eligible bachelor, thirty-four-year-old Richard Gere, had got engaged to a Brazilian beauty. 'Oh damn,' she said out loud, much to Vera's surprise.

Across the High Street, in Nora's Coffee Shop, Dorothy Humpleby was in an equally reflective mood. She had put Lionel Richie's 'All Night Long' on the juke-box and was putting extra sugar in Little Malcolm's tea.

Dorothy was beginning to consider that horoscopes weren't all they were cracked up to be. She fingered the chunky signs of the zodiac on her charm bracelet and gazed at Little Malcolm Robinson, the Ragley refuse collector, with new appreciation.

She recalled that Gypsy Fortuna in the *Easington Herald & Pioneer* had reliably stated that her Aquarius sun sign would be in sexual accord with Leo rising because they were opposite signs of the zodiac. She assumed this was because one went up while the other went down. However, unknown to Dorothy was the fact that Gypsy Fortuna was actually Brenda from the bread shop in Thirkby. So it was that, after reading that she would marry a tall, dark and very rich stranger, she had eventually settled on an impecunious and vertically challenged Gemini binman with a heart of gold.

*

Relationships were also the focus of attention for Ruby and Vera at the end of school. Ruby was concerned about her son Duggie.

'Ah'm worried about our Duggie, Mrs F,' she said, as she absent-mindedly polished the brass handle of the office door.

'Oh dear,' said Vera, looking up from her filing.

'Ah 'ave a dickie-fit ev'ry time 'e goes out now,' said Ruby, shaking her chestnut curls. 'Ah don't know if ah'm comin' o' goin' some nights when 'e dunt come 'ome.'

'I see,' said Vera, closing the heavy metal drawer of the filing cabinet.

'It's still that *mature* woman from t'shoe shop in Easington. 'E dunt think o' nowt else these days – she's a reight extraction. 'E's even tekken down 'is poster o' that blonde lass in Abba 'cause 'e sez 'e dunt want t'be unfaithful.'

Vera sat down behind her desk and looked up at her dear and obviously very troubled friend. 'Well, he is twenty-eight years old now, Ruby,' she said quietly.

'Problem is *she's* forty-summat – an' she's 'ad more men than ah've 'ad 'ot dinners.'

'Perhaps he will be able to work this out for himself.'

'Ah won't be 'oldin' m'breath, Mrs F,' said Ruby forlornly.

As she left the office, she paused by the door. 'An' she's allus done up like a dog's dinner,' she added for good measure. As Vera returned to her work she reflected that on occasions friendship is a stony pathway.

After school I worked on a school maintenance document in preparation for the next governors' meeting. The school slowly fell silent and by seven o' clock I was ready for some hot food and a little companionship. The bright orange lights of The Royal Oak were a welcome sight on this cold November night.

Old Tommy Piercy was sitting on his usual stool by the bar when I walked in. He was clearly upset after reading the front page of his *Yorkshire Post*. 'It'll never be t'same again,' he said mournfully. The headline read 'Boycott Out After 21 Years With Yorkshire'. Old Tommy's beloved Yorkshire Cricket Club had finished bottom of the county cricket championship for the first time. The forty-three-year-old Geoffrey Boycott had departed and the youthful thirty-two-year-old David Bairstow had been named to succeed Raymond Illingworth as the club captain.

'Evening, young Mr Sheffield,' said Old Tommy. 'Poor do is this abart *Sir* Geoffrey.' As far as Old Tommy was concerned, Geoffrey Boycott should have received a knighthood long ago.

'I agree, Mr Piercy,' I said.

'What's it t'be, Mr Sheffield?' asked Don the barman.

'A pint of Chestnut and . . .' I glanced at the menu board, 'something hot, please.'

'Sounds like y'wouldn't go far wrong wi' Duggie's girlfriend,' said Don with a deep chuckle.

'Be'ave y'self,' said Sheila, swatting him with a tea towel. 'Tek no notice of 'im, Mr Sheffield.'

I found a table within earshot of the tap-room conversation and settled to enjoy a welcome drink, the warmth of this friendly pub, a plate of lamb casserole and, of course, the lively banter.

''E puts it abart a bit, does our Duggie,' said Ronnie

Smith. "E's still 'avin' it away wi' that *mature* woman from Easington.'

'Mature?' chorused Big Dave and Little Malcolm.

'Well, let's put it this way,' said Ronnie, 'she won't see forty again.'

'Mind you, ah expec' she knows what she's abart in t'bedroom department, if y'get m'meaning,' said Don knowingly.

Ronnie pondered this for a moment. "Spec' so,' he said thoughtfully. 'Women over forty do – well, so ah've 'eard.'

'Ah'm not so sure,' said Little Malcolm. Dorothy was only twenty-six and what she didn't know about the 'bedroom department' wasn't worth knowing.

'Ah, but remember this, young Malcolm,' said Old Tommy. 'T'early bird allus gets t'worm,' he paused and puffed on his briar pipe, '. . . but it's t'second mouse what gets t'cheese.'

Like most things in life, this went above Little Malcolm's head.

Then Old Tommy looked sternly at Duggie Smith. 'Tek my advice, young Douglas,' said Old Tommy, 'y'want t'stay a bachelor.'

"Ow come, Mr Piercy?' asked Duggie.

Old Tommy waited a moment for the hubbub around him to cease. The football team all put down their pint pots to await his words of wisdom. 'Well, if y'think on it,' said Old Tommy, 'a bachelor never makes t'same mistake *once.*'

It was during the raucous laughter that Derek 'Deke' Ramsbottom, local farmhand and occasional snowplough driver, came in with two of his sons, Shane and Clint. As usual, Deke was wearing a cowboy hat, checked shirt, a knotted neckerchief, leather waistcoat complete with sheriff's badge, blue jeans and cowboy boots. Shane was a skinhead psychopath with the letters H-A-R-D tattooed on the knuckles of his right hand and his muscles bulged under his favourite Sex Pistols T-shirt. Meanwhile, his younger brother Clint looked like a cross between Boy George and an extra from *Mutiny on the Bounty*.

"Ow come y'dressed like that?' asked Sheila.

'Well, ah'm a sort o' pirate an' a plunderer,' said Clint, looking down in admiration at his baggy shirt.

'Ah see,' said Sheila, unconvinced. She remembered Clint stealing apples from the major's fruit trees when he was a boy, but there hadn't been much plundering since then. 'So that's why y'dress like Captain 'Ook, is it?'

'Well, we've moved on a bit since Sid Vicious an' Adam Ant,' he replied, pleased that Sheila was showing interest.

"Ow d'you mean, Clint?' asked Sheila.

'It's New Wave, Sheila,' said Clint. 'It's cuttin' edge o'fashion,' and he wandered off to watch the television above the bar.

'Ah don't know where 'e gets it from,' said Deke, supping deeply on his tankard of Tetley's. 'Mus' be on 'is mother's side,' he added as a reassuring afterthought.

'Y'reight there, Deke,' said Big Dave. "S'not nat'ral, a bloke wi' an earring.'

'An' black eyeliner,' added Little Malcolm for good measure.

They looked Clint up and down, staring curiously at his black jeans, which sported a variety of zips for no apparent reason.

"E's a big Mary-Ellen is our Clint,' said Deke sadly. 'Allus 'as been.'

'Mus' be a worry, Deke,' sympathized Don.

Deke settled on a bar stool, polished his sheriff's badge reflectively and leaned over towards Don. 'Between you an' me, Don, ah'm gettin' a bit worried abart 'im,' he confided.

"Ow d'you mean?' asked Don, pausing in wiping a glass tankard with his York City tea towel.

'Well 'e's not 'xactly what y'd call, y'know . . . *normal.*'

'Y'don't mean . . . ?'

'Ah do.'

Don mouthed the words rather than actually saying them: 'Y'mean 'e might be . . . *one o' them*?'

Deke sighed and nodded. "E's allus been a bit light across t'carpet, 'as our Clint.'

'Hmmn, mebbe so, Deke, mebbe so,' mused Don.

Sheila looked up from pulling my pint of Chestnut mild. 'Well, ah won't 'ear nowt against young Clint,' she said with feeling. "E's a lovely lad an' 'e teks a pride in 'is 'ppearance and 'e allus smells nice.'

'A bit *too* nice, Sheila,' replied Deke.

Clint, unaware that he was the centre of attention, had concerns of his own. He was becoming increasingly anxious about the dangers of smoking. In the doctor's surgery he had read that it could cause cancer and he definitely didn't fancy that. To calm his nerves, he lit up a John Player King Size Extra Mild cigarette, took a contented puff and relaxed back in his seat.

'By 'eck,' he said, 'ah needed that.'

Shane flexed his neck muscles at the bar and stared at his younger brother in dismay. "E's a reight nancy boy is our Clint, what wi' 'is poncy shirts an' coloured 'air,' he said.

'An' an earring,' added Don once again.

'An' eyeliner,' repeated Little Malcolm.

''E's as camp as a row o' tents,' said Big Dave with emphasis.

'Y'spot on there,' said Shane, 'but e's m'brother an' ah won't 'ave nowt said against t'little nancy-boy poofter.'

'Well said, Shane,' said Deke.

''Ere, 'ere,' said Don.

'Yer 'ave t'stan' by yer family,' agreed Big Dave.

'Y'reight there, Dave,' said Little Malcolm.

Clint finished his drink and came to join them. 'Ah'm off int'York,' he said cheerfully, 't'meet a mate. ''E said they've got one o' them new video juke-boxes. It's reight modern.'

'Sounds more like bloody *Star Trek*,' shouted Don as Clint hurried out.

'What'll they think of nex'?' grumbled Deke.

'An' ah wonder what 'is mate's like,' said Shane.

'Yes . . . ah wonder,' murmured Deke, and they all nodded knowingly.

On Sunday morning Walter Clarence Crapper, an accountant from Easington, was Turtle Waxing his 1977 Toyota Corolla Estate while glancing anxiously at the scudding clouds. He returned his chamois leather to the exact place in his box of cleaning materials, cleared up and went inside. It was time to set off to Pratt's Hardware Emporium to meet his friend Timothy.

In his mid-forties, Walter was the younger brother of Ernest Crapper, the Ragley encyclopaedia salesman, and his hobby was making model aircraft. Thanks to Timothy, Walter had recently enjoyed a Eureka moment – he had discovered how to make perfect dummy rivets.

He was approaching the end of a two-year project to build a one-sixth scale model of a United States Army Air Force World War II aerobatic training aircraft – a Fairchild PT-19 Cornell. With a wingspan of seventy inches it was Walter's greatest creation so far. The problem was how to apply the finishing touches and attach tiny artificial rivets to the smooth body.

It was then that Timothy came up with the idea of using some of the minute dome-shaped sequins from his late mother's Victorian sewing box. At a fifth of an inch in diameter and with a small central hole, they were perfect.

So it was that on this quiet Sunday morning Walter and Timothy were sitting at Timothy's kitchen table, each holding a delicate artist's brush and painting sequins with bright yellow fuel-proof paint. Each rivet was then left to dry on an upturned jam-jar lid.

'How many more, Walter?' asked Timothy enthusiastically. He was enjoying himself. The work required immense attention to detail, which, of course, was right up Timothy's street.

'One hundred and eight please, Timothy,' answered Walter without raising his head, 'plus twelve dark blue ones for the rear end of the fuselage.'

Timothy smiled at his trusted friend. Walter was always so precise, and precision was one of the cornerstones of Timothy's organized life.

When they had finished they enjoyed a cup of tea together.

'It's been a wonderful day, Walter,' said Timothy.

There was silence between them as Walter came to a decision and looked inside his leather satchel. 'I've bought you a present, Timothy,' he said. He took out a small attractive carrier bag with the words 'Browns Department Store' on the side.

Timothy was almost too excited to speak. 'Th-thank you, Walter,' he said. However, when he looked inside he really was speechless. It was a pair of socks.

'Do you like them, Timothy?' asked Walter eagerly.

Timothy took a deep breath. 'Yes, thank you, Walter. They're, er, perfect.'

Walter gave a sigh of relief. 'I guessed the size,' he said.

'Well, y'know what they say, Walter,' said Timothy.

'What's that?' asked Walter.

'A friend in need . . .' said Timothy.

'Is a friend indeed,' said Walter.

Then, very slowly, Timothy rested his hand on top of Walter's . . . and Walter let him leave it there.

That night, when the villagers of Ragley were sleeping and all was quiet, one light shone brightly from above Pratt's Hardware Emporium. Timothy had walked thoughtfully up the stairs, taking care as always to step evenly up the left-hand side of each carpet tread. When he came down he would reverse the process on the other side. Even wear of his stair carpet would thus be achieved and the equilibrium of Timothy's well-ordered life would be maintained.

Once in his bedroom he opened his sock drawer. There they were, neatly in line as always – black, blue and grey, familiar and comforting. He knew it would take an effort of will, but with the utmost concentration he pushed the blue socks nearer to the black ones and the grey ones a little more to the left. Then he placed his new pair of socks in the space that remained and stood back to admire the new configuration. It was a strange feeling, one he couldn't recall experiencing before, a sort of a cross between an optical migraine and a hot flush. Then a thought occurred to him. Perhaps this was what it felt like to fall in love.

Timothy looked one last time at his sock drawer before he turned out the light. He had socks for all seasons, but when would he wear the new ones?

And then he understood . . . friendship came at a price.

Chapter Six

Sewing for Boys

Our Activities afternoon was reintroduced to the weekly timetable with the support of parents and friends of school.
Extract from the Ragley School Logbook:
Tuesday, 22 November 1983

Terry Earnshaw loved being a boy. Life was one long sequence of adventures. Yesterday he was a pirate and today he was a secret agent. It was Tuesday, 22 November and the harsh frosts and smoking chimneys of Ragley village heralded the coming of winter. However, the freezing weather did not deter this intrepid son of Barnsley as a new day stretched out before him.

After saying goodbye to his mother and little sister, Dallas Sue-Ellen, he walked with his brother Heathcliffe to the bus stop in the High Street. The two boys had chosen their usual circuitous route alongside the muddy ditch at the back of the council estate. They had balanced on a fallen tree, tracked imaginary wild animals, made a grass trumpet and skimmed flat stones on the village pond before being shouted at by Sheila Bradshaw from her bedroom window above The Royal Oak.

Finally the brothers had parted and Heathcliffe boarded the bus to Easington Comprehensive School. Terry waved goodbye, then sought out a favourite vantage point by clambering up the lower branches of the weeping willow tree on the village green. From there he could look out for mysterious strangers and the occasional foreign spy. He was completely undeterred when Ted Postlethwaite, the village postman, told him to get down before he fell in the pond and became duck food.

Terry waved back to Ted in acknowledgement. He liked the village postman and thought it was a job he might do when he grew up; so he added it to his current list, which included professional footballer, butcher, shepherd, strawberry-picker, cowboy and Arctic explorer. Terry had also recently discovered, following a conversation with the knowledgeable and articulate Victoria Alice Dudley-Palmer, that boys *didn't* have babies and, in that moment, he knew that in the game of life he had shaken a six. Fortune had smiled on him and exciting times lay ahead.

Being a boy was, well . . . just *perfect*.

Meanwhile, at the other end of the High Street I had reached the front of the queue in the General Stores & Newsagent. 'Good morning, Miss Golightly.'

'Good morning, Mr Sheffield,' said Prudence, 'and here's your newspaper.' She moved on to the highest wooden step behind the counter to be on the same level as me. The diminutive sixty-five-year-old shopkeeper was a sprightly lady.

'Sad news I'm afraid, Mr Sheffield,' she said. 'Some

dreadful person has vandalized the *Blue Peter* garden. What's the world coming to?'

'Oh dear,' I said.

I glanced at the front page. It looked as if someone was trying to *rule* the world. A fifty-two-year-old Australian by the name of Rupert Murdoch, owner of the *Sun* and *News of the World* newspapers, had just bought one of America's largest newspapers for a small fortune. I shook my head in disbelief and then remembered my manners. 'And a very good morning to you too, Jeremy,' I said.

Miss Golightly had lost the love of her life in 1940 when her fiancé Jeremy, a young fighter pilot, had been killed in the Battle of Britain. Since then she had named her teddy bear after him and he had become her lifelong friend. Today he was wearing a hand-knitted scarf and a bobble hat, a thick Aran sweater, cord trousers and brown leather boots.

'It's a cold day, Mr Sheffield,' said Prudence, 'so Jeremy wrapped up warm.'

I nodded in agreement and folded my newspaper. 'Very sensible.'

'And how is Mrs Sheffield?'

'Fine, thank you.'

'And what about young John William?'

'He's on solids now,' I said proudly, '... well, more *mushy* than solid, so to speak.' A thought occurred to me. 'Oh, yes, I've just remembered. I need a jar of Pond's Cream from the pharmacy.' I glanced at my watch. 'I'll slip out at lunchtime to get it.'

'No need, Mr Sheffield, I'll ask Mrs Eckersley to call and drop it into school for you. She's my new part-time assistant – a lovely young lady. Her little girl, Lucy, has just started in Mrs Pringle's class.'

I thanked Miss Golightly and the bell above the door rang merrily as I walked out into the cold. Outside the shop Terry Earnshaw and Harold Bustard were peering into the brightly lit shop window. They each had a penny and were discussing the possibility of pooling their meagre resources to select from aniseed balls, gob-stoppers, sherbet dips, coconut lumps, treacle toffee and liquorice laces.

When I arrived at school a sharp hoar frost had coated the hedgerows like icing sugar and the air was clear and cold. Ruby was sprinkling salt on the frozen steps in front of the entrance door. 'Cold morning, Ruby,' I said as I hurried past.

'Nay, there's cold an' there's *cold*, Mr Sheffield, an' this is nowt.' Ruby was a tough lady.

'How's Ronnie?' I asked as an afterthought. 'I've not seen him in a while.'

Ruby leaned on her yard broom and shook her head. ''E were like death warmed up this morning. Ah rubbed a bit o' goose grease on 'is chest las' night but it did no good. 'E's goin' to t'chemist t'get summat t'shift it.'

I nodded, shivered and went into school.

'Men!' muttered Ruby under her breath as I walked to-wards the welcome warmth of the office.

After hanging up my duffel coat and old college scarf, I went into the staff-room. All the teaching staff plus Vera had arranged to meet briefly before school to confirm arrangements for our Activities afternoon. The aim was to use the particular skills of the teachers to the benefit of all the children and bring into school a few willing and supportive parents and friends. It had worked well in the past so we had decided to try it again.

'So I'm setting up my classroom with a selection of experiments in the physical sciences,' said Jo with enthusiasm. 'I've got pulley systems, glass prisms, magnets and mirrors, so I'm well prepared.'

'Thanks, Jo,' said Anne, 'sounds good.' Anne was particularly grateful. She had a superb knowledge-base in the *natural* sciences, and this was reflected in her year-round nature table; however, she was aware that the science curriculum for the children in her care needed to be wider.

'And I presume I've got the hall, Jack,' said Sally. 'I've got some simple props for the drama activities and I could do with projecting the words for the singing on the OHP.' Our overhead projector looked as though it should be in a museum, but it was a regular teaching aid for Sally, who spent many evenings writing out words, chords and musical notes on sheets of acetate.

'It would help if I could do my sewing in your classroom, Jack,' said Anne, looking at the long list of volunteers. 'There's more room – and you could use my carpeted book corner for your stories and creative writing.'

So that was it. We were prepared for a break from our usual timetable, enabling mixed age groups to have the chance to experience science, creative writing, stories, sewing, drama and music, with a different range of activities in future weeks. Personally, although I didn't mention this to the others, I found it difficult. Working with the youngest children in the school was *very* hard work, with each child demanding individual attention *all the time.*

Vera's official title was 'part-time clerical assistant' and, in consequence, she didn't work at Ragley School on Tuesday and Thursday mornings. However, no one would dream of referring to Vera as a 'clerical assistant'; she preferred the term 'secretary'. So it was that after our meeting she went down the High Street to her twice-weekly cross-stitch class in the village hall and then drove into York to Currys showroom, where she purchased an Electrolux 350E vacuum cleaner for £84.95. This was something she would never have been able to afford prior to her marriage to Rupert. The young salesman tried to impress her with a fluent pitch about the super-boost button that provided a thousand watts of energy and the advanced slide control, but Vera gave him short shrift. All she needed to know was that it would clean the vicarage stair carpet without Joseph's cleaner, Miss Figgins, getting a hernia. Joseph's current cumbersome model really needed to be relocated to a domestic-appliance museum.

At morning break Terry Earnshaw and Victoria Alice Dudley-Palmer were discussing the future.

'One day I'll marry a modern man,' said Victoria Alice, 'and I'll have two children and we'll live in Surrey.'

Terry pondered the enormity of this statement for a while. 'Vicky . . . 'ow d'you mean, *modern*?'

'Well, he'll be *sensitive* and he'll help me with washing up and decorating and he'll be able to sew his own buttons on.'

'What about football?' asked a concerned Terry.

'Oh yes, you could play football and rugby and cricket and tennis and . . . well, other games, like chess and croquet.'

Terry had never heard of croquet but didn't like to mention it. 'So if I do sewing this afternoon ah can be a modern man when ah grow up?'

'Yes, Terry,' said Victoria Alice, 'that would be a start – and it would be wonderful and I would be so proud of you.'

Terry thought for a moment. Perhaps sewing wasn't so bad after all.

Meanwhile, Mrs Kitty Eckersley had called in to the school office. Mother of eight-year-old Lucy, she was a tall, slim thirty-three-year-old with cropped blonde hair, high cheekbones and blue-grey eyes.

'It's one pound and nineteen pence for the Pond's Cream, Mr Sheffield,' she said.

'Thanks very much,' I said. 'I really appreciate you taking the time.'

'No trouble, Mr Sheffield,' she said with a smile. 'Anything to help. My Lucy has been really happy here and she's settled well thanks to Mrs Pringle.'

'That's good to hear,' I said.

'In fact,' she added, 'I've been talking to Mrs Pringle and Mrs Grainger about the Activities afternoon and I've volunteered to help with the sewing group. I'm free on Tuesday afternoons.'

'That's very kind,' I said. 'I'm grateful for your support.'

Predictably, it was Vera, the fount of all knowledge regarding the villagers, who knew all about Kitty Eckersley's background. At lunchtime Vera returned to school after a busy morning and we shared a pot of Earl Grey tea.

According to Vera, Kitty had been born in Wakefield in West Yorkshire and she had a fine reputation as a local dressmaker. She lived on the Morton Road with her husband, David, the art teacher at Easington Comprehensive, and her father-in-law, Winston, a local eccentric and restorer of street organs. In 1968 she had gained her City and Guilds Dressmaking Certificate, followed by the Advanced Certificate a year later. More recently, in 1981, she had passed her City and Guilds 730 Teaching Certificate and now taught adult education classes two nights a week at Easington Comprehensive School.

'That's wonderful news for the sewing group,' I said. 'A real professional in support.'

Sally was equally enthusiastic, as she had attended one of Kitty's dressmaking courses at Easington Comprehensive School while Colin looked after their three-year-old daughter, Grace. 'Yes, it's a perfect evening class for me,' said Sally. 'No examinations, so no pressure.'

When Kitty arrived I joined Anne and Vera in my classroom while they prepared the materials for the afternoon's sewing tasks. Kitty was happy to talk about her life. As a sixteen-year-old she had worked in a shirt factory in Wakefield; by her late twenties she was making silk blouses for the major stores in London, including Debenhams and Harrods.

'It was tough to start with,' said Kitty. 'There was a strict apprenticeship. I had to complete fourteen rows of machine stitching on a one-and-a-quarter-inch strip of material, the size of a shirt cuff, and they had to be perfect before they let me loose on real garments.'

She had learned very early that the north of England, and particularly Manchester, was the perfect place for cotton because in the damp climate it didn't snap, but eventually she had moved on to polyester threads that had the wonderful capacity to stretch. Her sewing machine was a Willcox & Gibbs from America with a treadle and a motor attached. It was a relic of the Second World War, when it had been used for making uniforms.

'I preferred using crimplene because it didn't fray in the wash,' Kitty added with conviction. She had also brought along many of the tools of her trade to show the children, including a tailor's ham and a wooden dowel covered in fabric to help with pressing the seams of a garment. Best of all, she had examples of simple patterns and materials for three easy-to-make tasks: a heart-shaped lavender bag, a reflective armband on a hoop of thick elastic, and a tissue-holder made from a six-inch-square piece of material folded in half.

'And I always wear these,' she added with a smile, slipping a pincushion attached to a thick elastic band on her left wrist and a metal thimble on the second finger of her right hand.

Meanwhile, on the High Street, Nora's Coffee Shop was filling up with the usual lunchtime trade and Elton John's 'I'm Still Standing' was belting out on the old juke-box when Ragley's favourite binmen walked in.

Big Dave Robinson and his faithful cousin Little Malcolm Robinson were popular village characters. Big Dave, at six feet four inches, and Little Malcolm, exactly one foot shorter, lived together on the council estate and toured the local villages each day in their refuse wagon. Big Dave went to sit at his favourite table next to the rack of old *Sun* newspapers while Little Malcolm hurried to the counter and looked up into the eyes of the woman he loved. 'Two teas, please, Dorothy.'

Dorothy Humpleby was filing her nails while skimming through her latest *Smash Hits* magazine. A peroxide-blonde would-be model, she was dressed in a tight, white, see-through blouse, red leather hotpants and her favourite Wonder Woman boots with four-inch heels. As Dorothy was five feet eleven inches tall in her stocking-feet, Little Malcolm found conversations difficult.

'What d'you think, Malcolm?' enquired Dorothy.

'What about, Dorothy?' asked a puzzled Little Malcolm.

'M'new image, o' course,' retorted Dorothy.

''Xactly what's that then, Dorothy?'

'It's m'new Max Factor extra-long, thick-lash mascara.'

'Oh, er, well . . . it's lovely,' said Little Malcolm.

Dorothy held up the tube and peered at the writing on the side. 'An' it's 'ypo allergenic.'

'Ah didn't know you 'ad any allergies, Dorothy,' said Little Malcolm. 'Ah'm reight sorry.'

'No, y'soft ha'porth,' said Dorothy, 'it lengthens an' thickens.' Little Malcolm began to blush. He was thinking of something else. Undeterred, Dorothy continued with enthusiasm. 'An' it stays all day wi'out smudging,' she explained. 'An' then there's m'new Endless Shine Nail Enamel, t'ultimate in shiny nails wi' no chippin' or peelin'.'

'That's lovely, Dorothy,' said Little Malcolm, glancing across at Big Dave, who was mouthing 'Hurry up!'

'Finally, m'*peas de insistence*,' said Dorothy, 'is m'soft ultra-lipstick wi' colour an' gloss t'last 'til closin' time.'

Big Dave gave Little Malcolm his 'big girl's blouse' look and Little Malcolm recoiled. 'So it's two teas, please, Dorothy,' he said hurriedly. He also had some news. He was clutching a copy of the *Easington Herald & Pioneer* and was too excited to remember to ask for two pork pies. He opened the paper and pointed to a dramatic advertisement. 'It says 'ere, Dorothy, "Tomorrow's World is 'ere f'you today" . . . an' ah think it is.'

'What y'talkin' about, Malcolm, an' does Dave want a pie?' asked Dorothy, reaching for a two-day-old pork pie.

Undeterred, Malcolm pressed on. 'If we go t'York we can rent one o' them new fancy video recorders.'

'An' d'*you* want a pie as well?' asked Dorothy.

'Er, yes please,' said Little Malcolm. 'An' it says we get six video films rent free.'

'Went fwee?' said Nora from behind the Breville sandwich toaster. She wasn't one to miss out on an interesting conversation.

Nora Pratt, the owner of the Coffee Shop, didn't miss much. She had long since come to terms with the fact that her inability to pronounce the letter 'R' had curtailed, in her view, a blossoming acting career.

Little Malcolm looked at the list. 'They've got *Chariots o' Fire*, *Fame*, *Superman II*, *T'Love Bug*, *Annie* an' m'favourite.'

'What's y'favouwite, Malcolm?' asked Nora as she scraped the black bits from a cremated cheese sandwich.

'*Rocky III*,' said Little Malcolm.

'Oooh, ah love that Wocky,' said Nora. ''E's pwoper sexy.'

'An' 'e's got big muscles like my Malcolm,' said Dorothy.

Little Malcolm loved it when Dorothy said *my* Malcolm.

He went a shade of puce. 'An' they chuck in a free blank cassette,' he added for good measure.

'OK, Malcolm,' said Dorothy, 'we'll go.'

'An' ah'll 'ave t'go,' said Nora, looking at the clock. 'As pwesident of Wagley Am-Dwams, ah'm 'elping wi' dwama at school an' ah'll 'ave t'wush,' and she grabbed her coat and scarf. 'An' don't fwet, Dowothy, 'cause Wuby's daughter, Shawon, said she'll come in to 'elp,' and she hurried out.

Petula Dudley-Palmer was equally excited. She had just purchased Delia Smith's *Complete Cookery Course* from her Book of the Month Club for a mere fifty pence. It was on special offer and, as Petula worshipped Delia as her ultimate kitchen goddess, it had been an opportunity too good to miss. She had decided to try out 'Spanish pork with olives' for Geoffrey's evening meal and had written two cloves of garlic and a green pepper on her shopping list.

However, by the time she had stepped out of her revolutionary power-shower, donned her dressing gown and unpacked her new state-of-the-art Design Centre electric hot-tray, ordered from her Littlewoods catalogue, she realized it was time to get dressed for the Activities event at school and an afternoon of creative writing. After all, as president of the Ragley Book Club, she needed to be seen *and heard*.

The sewing group was hard at work and Terry was really enjoying making a pair of reflective armbands. Victoria Alice and Maureen Hartley were in the same group and sewing neat stitches down the side of their tissue-holders.

Kitty Eckersley had given them wonderful support and they had enjoyed her stories.

'Well done, Terry,' said Kitty, 'that's excellent work – your mother will be thrilled.' She looked at Little Mo's sewing. 'And so will yours, Maureen.'

'No she won't, Miss,' said Little Mo quietly.

'Oh, why not?' asked Kitty innocently.

'She's in 'eaven,' said Little Mo simply and without looking up from her sewing.

Kitty bit her lip and glanced at the intense little dark-haired girl. She was reminded that honesty can break your heart.

That night in the Earnshaw household everyone was settling at the kitchen table for an evening meal.

'What did y'do at school t'day, boys?' asked Mrs Earnshaw.

'Nowt,' said the two boys in unison, eyeing up the single Spam fritter on their plate and wondering if there would be two each.

'Y'must 'ave done summat,' she persisted.

'Done summat,' echoed little Dallas Sue-Ellen.

Everyone ignored her.

'Ah did some woodwork,' said Heathcliffe and Mrs Earnshaw shovelled an additional fritter on to his plate.

'An' what about you, Terry?' asked Mrs Earnshaw.

Terry was wearing his reflective armbands proudly. 'Ah did some sewing.'

'Sewing!' exclaimed Mr Earnshaw. He put down his *Racing Post*. 'SEWING . . . f'BOYS!'

'Well ah think it's a good idea,' said Mrs Earnshaw and gave Terry a second fritter.

'What y'learning *sewing* for?' asked an incredulous Mr Earnshaw.

'Well, when ah grow up, Dad, ah'm gonna be a modern man,' said Terry earnestly.

'What's t'world comin' to?' muttered Mr Earnshaw.

'An' we've started d'mestic science – cookin' an' suchlike,' added Heathcliffe for good measure.

Mr Earnshaw gave his sons a look of disgust and buried his head back in his paper.

'Well, ah'm proud of y'both,' said Mrs Earnshaw and made sure the boys received a larger spoonful of mushy peas than Mr Earnshaw. 'Don't grow up like 'im,' she added, '. . . a bloody dinosaur.'

'Bloody din'saur,' repeated Dallas Sue-Ellen.

That night in bed Heathcliffe switched on his three-colour torch and began to read his *Roy of the Rovers Annual*.

'Heath',' said Terry from his single bed on the other side of the room.

'What?' asked Heathcliffe, not looking up.

'What's a *modern man*?'

'Dunno.'

'D'you think we'll both be modern men when we grow up?'

'Dunno,' said Heathcliffe again.

'Heath',' said Terry.

'Yeah?'

'What's d'mestic science?'

'Mekkin' cakes an' suchlike,' muttered Heathcliffe.

'Ah think ah'll mek cakes and do sewing when ah grow up,' said Terry.

'Ah'm not,' said Heathcliffe firmly.

''Ow come?' asked Terry.

'Ah'm gonna get married instead.'

While Terry was thinking this through Mr Earnshaw shouted from the next bedroom, 'Turn that light out – an' shurrup!'

A long silence followed.

Finally, Terry raised his head from the pillow and whispered, 'So . . . y'not gonna be a modern man then.'

'No,' said Heathcliffe, 'ah'm gonna be like Dad – a bloody dinosaur.'

Chapter Seven

Broken Blossoms

Mrs Pringle invited a visiting speaker into assembly as part of her Senses project. Miss Lillian De Vere spoke to the children about the work of the Royal National Institute of Blind People (RNIB). Class 1 began rehearsals for their Nativity play.

Extract from the Ragley School Logbook:
Friday, 9 December 1983

There are days that stay long in the memory. Friday, 9 December 1983 was such a day. It was the time I met Lillian De Vere and she was a very special lady.

The early morning had begun as usual, with Beth and me sitting at our old pine table in the kitchen. John was strapped into his baby seat while Beth spooned food into his mouth and I sipped black tea while scribbling a memo for the day ahead. At four and a half months old our son was growing fast and he smiled cheerily, showing off his first two teeth, as the mushy mixture dribbled down his chin.

It was snug and warm in the cottage, while outside on the far hillside the dense forests had lost their colour and skeletal leaves formed dank piles of leaf mould round the gnarled trunks. Beth was the constant in my life, and now, with the arrival of baby John, we had become a family. It had been a journey I would never forget.

'I think we made the right decision, Beth,' I said.

She looked up at me and smiled – but it was a tired smile. Looking after John was hard work and there was no respite.

'You mean staying at home?'

'Yes,' I said, 'and John's getting the best possible care.'

She refastened the elastic bobble that held back her hair. 'But I shall want to get back to my headship next September, Jack, and then we really do need to rethink our careers.' This was becoming a recurring theme.

For my part I simply wanted to be true to myself. 'I love being a village school teacher, Beth, and I'm not sure I want to be the head of a large school.'

'Just keep an open mind,' she said quietly.

I sighed. 'I'd miss the teaching, Beth – that's what I'm good at. I don't really see myself as a manager, like you or Vera.'

'I understand, Jack,' and she looked at me with the hint of concern in her green eyes. 'But there's a bigger picture to think of – and we have John now.'

I looked at the clock and could feel irritation building. 'Sorry, I have to go. I offered to help Sally get the hall ready for assembly.' Beth nodded knowingly and turned her attention back to our son and his growing appetite. I walked into the hallway and put on my duffel coat and scarf. 'I promise we'll talk about this tonight. It's the carol concert at the Hartford Home after school so I should be home around seven.'

'Try not to be later, Jack – you're babysitting tonight,' Beth called after me as she scraped the food from John's bib with a plastic spoon. 'It's Jo's girls' night in York.'

I had forgotten that Anne and Sally had planned a farewell party for Jo Hunter to include female staff and a few girlfriends. 'Where are you going?' I asked, looking back round the door.

'We've booked a room in the Dean Court. Very up-market – and private,' she added with a mischievous grin.

'Sounds a good evening,' I said.

Beth picked up John and we stood by the door as I kissed them both on the cheek. 'Have a good day,' she said.

'Don't worry, I won't be late,' and I opened the door and hurried out into a frozen world and the silence of snow.

Beth called after me, 'Oh, and by the way – Laura's coming.'

And suddenly my mind was elsewhere.

Three miles away on the Crescent in Ragley village, twelve-year-old Heathcliffe Earnshaw was delivering the morning papers. He paused in the lighted porch outside Barry Ollerenshaw's house, breathed on his frozen hands and from his bulky bag took out a copy of the *Beano*. It was rare for him to have twelve pence to purchase his second-favourite comic, so this was a great opportunity to catch up on the latest exploits of Dennis the Menace and Gnasher on the front page. He smiled as he read. Being a paper boy had its advantages, particularly if, like this son of Barnsley in South Yorkshire, you didn't feel the cold. He pushed a *Daily Mail* and the comic through the letter-box and strode on.

A fresh snowfall settled on Heathcliffe's hand-knitted balaclava as he paused under a street lamp and took out Frankie Kershaw's *Eagle* comic. This was his favourite comic of all time, but at twenty-two pence it was way out of his reach and, in any case, he was saving up to buy his mother a Christmas present. He had seen a pendant on a chain on Shady Stevo's market stall that Stevo had said was twenty-four-carat gold and a bargain at ninety-nine pence. Meanwhile, his brow furrowed as he read the front page. Dan Dare, Pilot of the Future, was clearly having problems in an alien space camp.

The church clock struck half past seven and Heathcliffe hurried back to the General Stores with his empty bag. On the way he waved a cheery greeting to the other early birds – namely the milkmen Ernie and Rodney Morgetroyd, and the postman, Ted Postlethwaite. Then it was time for a quick breakfast before boarding the school bus to Easington Comprehensive. Little did he know it then, but for Heathcliffe getting up at the crack of dawn to go to work was to be the norm for the next thirty years.

As I drove up the High Street, winter had gripped Ragley in its cold fist and a bitter sleet rattled against my windscreen. The villagers stooped like a group of matchstick millworkers from an L. S. Lowry painting as they bowed into the cutting wind and hurried towards the General Stores to buy a bag of logs for the fire or vegetables for a warming soup. Above their heads, the clouds were ripped like tattered rags as they raced across a steel-grey sky.

When I got out of my car and hurried across the playground Ruby was pegging down our rickety school bird table with makeshift guy ropes of orange baling twine to prevent it from blowing over. As she raised a heavy wooden mallet to drive in a tent peg, apparently oblivious to the sub-zero world around her, she smiled up at me. 'Posh lady jus' arrived, Mr Sheffield, wi' a little feller 'elpin' 'er.'

I glanced over my shoulder. On the driveway, parents and children emerged like wraiths from the darkness towards the lights of the entrance porch and the welcome warmth within. 'Thanks, Ruby,' I yelled, but my voice was lost in the wind.

Sally was hurrying through the entrance hall when I walked in. 'Just getting another table for assembly, Jack,' she said. 'The speaker, Miss De Vere, is here and she's got a huge box of artefacts for her talk.'

'I'll give you a hand,' I said and hung up my duffel coat and scarf in the office. The children in Sally's class were doing a project on 'The Senses' and this morning was to be an exciting addition to their practical work, with follow-up research, discussion and writing.

We carried the heavy pine table from the entrance area into the school hall, where a small, frail-looking, grey-haired lady was standing behind one of the dining tables and arranging a variety of interesting objects. She turned to an equally elderly man standing alongside, then picked up a ball and shook the bell inside.

'John,' she said confidently, 'let's put the Braille books on the extra table and I'll use this one for everything else.' She began to arrange her collection in neat order from left to right, including something that looked like a doorbell and a set of Braille salt and pepper shakers.

'Miss De Vere,' said Sally, 'this is the headteacher, Mr Sheffield.' We put the table down in front of them and Miss De Vere looked up and gave me a friendly smile, extending a delicate hand. We shook hands and I turned to the gentleman beside her, who appeared a little lost and was holding a stack of large manuscripts, each page punched in raised dots. He seemed to be looking over my shoulder. He was wearing a badge with the letters RNIB and I presumed he was blind or partially sighted.

'Jack,' continued Sally, 'this is John, Miss De Vere's colleague from the RNIB.'

I took his hand to shake it.

Vera suddenly appeared at the double doors that led back into the entrance hall. 'Telephone, Mr Sheffield,' she called. 'Miss Barrington-Huntley.'

'Please excuse me, I'll see you later – and thanks for coming, it will be a wonderful experience for the children.' I hurried off. Our chair of the Education Committee at County Hall didn't like to be kept waiting.

When I took my class into morning assembly Sally had arranged the children so that they were seated on three sides of the hall with a performance space in the middle. Miss De Vere was standing behind a table at the front with her colleague sitting beside her.

Sally gave a confident introduction. 'We have five senses, girls and boys. Who can tell me what they are?' Hands shot up everywhere and she pointed to six-year-old Rufus Snodgrass.

'Hearing, Miss, when y'list'ning t'things,' said Rufus confidently.

'Well done, Rufus,' said Sally. 'And another one?'

Eight-year-old Dawn Phillips raised her hand hesitantly. Dawn was a quiet girl and the daughter of the chairman of the PTA. 'Touch, Miss,' and she wiggled her fingers in the air as if to demonstrate.

'Excellent, Dawn,' said Sally and the tall fair-haired girl flushed with pride. 'That's two. Who can give me another one?' She pointed to eight-year-old Ryan Halfpenny, who was about to internally combust with the effort of not shouting out his answer.

'Smell, Miss,' said Ryan, 'like flowers an' chocolate an' that stuff they put on roads.'

'And what do we call that?' followed up Sally, looking at Terry Earnshaw, our building materials expert.

'Bitumen,' said Terry confidently. 'An' ah know another, Miss.'

'Go on.'

'Tasting things, like sweets – an' Mrs Mapplebeck's cabbage,' said Terry with feeling.

Sally wisely didn't pursue the cabbage theme and moved on. 'And one more – a very important sense and the one we shall be talking about this morning.'

Ten-year-old Victoria Alice Dudley-Palmer was waiting patiently, her hand raised in the air.

'Victoria Alice?' said Sally.

'Sight, Miss,' said Victoria Alice, 'and I know what RNIB stands for on the poster.'

'And what's that?' asked Sally.

'The Royal National Institute of Blind People,' said

Victoria Alice clearly and I saw Miss De Vere smile and nod in appreciation.

'That's right, well done,' said Sally. 'So please give a warm welcome to our speaker this morning – Miss De Vere.'

After the applause the confident Miss De Vere spoke clearly. 'Good morning, boys and girls,' she said, 'it's exciting to be here in your lovely school. My name is Lillian De Vere. I am seventy years old . . . and I am blind.'

There was silence.

'There are more than one million people in the country who have suffered from sight loss,' she said. The cadence of her words flowed like a gentle stream, soft and clear in harmonic resolution. 'I am one of those people, boys and girls . . . I am blind.' You could have heard a pin drop. I suddenly realized I had made a wrong assumption. When this elegant lady was arranging the artefacts in front of her with absolute confidence I assumed she could see. I was wrong. 'This is why my friend John is with me,' explained Miss De Vere. 'He can see just like you and he helps me to get around. So I'm a very lucky lady and I have had a wonderful life.'

The assembly was superb. Miss De Vere spoke eloquently to the children and demonstrated a clever device that alerted you to bring your washing in off the line if it started raining. There were games that fascinated the children, including dominoes and a large Braille dice. Then John blindfolded lots of willing volunteers and rolled a ball towards them with a ringing bell inside. Miss De Vere finished with the story of *The Selfish Giant* from a Braille book and we all watched in amazement as her fingers interpreted the sequences of raised dots that she explained had been invented by Louis Braille almost two hundred years ago. The children were full of questions and Miss De Vere was thrilled with the response.

At the end she said, 'I shall be hearing some of you after school today as I live at the Hartford Home and I know Mrs Pringle is bringing her choir to sing for us.'

At morning break she took her leave and John guided her to the car park, although it seemed she could have managed it herself. The children lined the path and waved goodbye and I wondered if she knew . . . I guessed she did. Back in class the children wrote about their experiences of the morning as I reflected on my life and how lucky I was.

At lunchtime, when I walked into the staff-room, Joseph Evans had arrived and was in animated conversation with Anne. The previous day he had attended an ecclesiastical conference in York. 'It was a wonderful event,' he said enthusiastically.

'What was the conference?' I asked.

Joseph rummaged in his pocket and pulled out the programme for the day. Above a photograph of Canon Henry Fodder was the bold title *'The Prayer and Fasting Annual Conference'*.

'Yes,' said Joseph with a shy smile, 'it was very lively.'

'So what did you do?' asked Anne.

Joseph made that familiar steeple of fingers as if he were about to pray. 'Well, we prayed a lot and discussed the importance of fasting – and of course we always get a lovely lunch.'

Anne gave me that familiar wide-eyed smile and hurried off to her classroom.

Following Joseph's lesson with Jo's class about the birth of Jesus he returned to the staff-room with a collection of children's writing. Everybody was busy with preparing end-of-term reports and the beginning of the run-up to Christmas, but we all found time to share some of the children's responses.

Seven-year-old Stacey Bryant had written, 'Jesus was born in Bethlehem which is a long way from Ragley.' Jemima Poole was almost correct in her understanding of the gifts to baby Jesus: 'I'm glad one of the kings gave Jesus some Franky Scent because I like perfume.' Meanwhile, Ted Coggins had his own opinion: 'It's a shame the kings didn't give Jesus a tin of biscuits or a Wagon Wheel. I get a Wagon Wheel at Christmas if I'm good and eat all my horrible sprouts.'

During afternoon school the rehearsal for our forthcoming Christmas Carol Service was going well. After school Sally had arranged a trial run at the local Hartford Home for Retired Gentlefolk, which was an annual treat for the residents. Parents had completed a reply slip saying they would bring the children in her choir and makeshift orchestra to the venue at five o'clock and collect them an hour later.

In the school hall Sally propped her *Carol, Gaily Carol* Christmas songbook on a music stand and selected number 9, 'Baby Jesus, Sleeping Softly'. As I tiptoed across the floor she began to strum gently on her guitar while the children sang:

Baby Jesus, sleeping softly
On the warm and fragrant hay,
Children all the wide world over
Think of you on Christmas Day.

The choir was accompanied by an enthusiastic orchestra that included treble and tenor recorders, Indian bells, castanets, a tambourine and triangles. Seven-year-old Rosie Sparrow, who possessed a perfect sense of rhythm, had been given the responsibility of playing chime bar F on the first beat of each of the four bars. It sounded wonderful and I marvelled at how Sally, year after year, managed to take a disparate group of children from all walks of life and transform them into a coherent and unified whole. This was followed by Anne guiding her children, with the patience of a saint, through a first rehearsal of their Nativity play. For the parents this was a highlight of their year and expectations were always high.

Towards the end of the day, when I walked into the school office, Vera was taking yet another obtuse telephone call from an anxious parent.

'Did you say a *leopard*, Mrs Crapper?' said Vera. 'No, I can assure you that Patience does *not* require a leopard costume for the Christmas play.'

There was a prolonged silence during which Vera adopted her Mother Teresa pose. 'Yes, I agree there isn't a leopard in the Christmas story.'

More mumblings from Mrs Crapper followed.

'No, it's actually a *shepherd* costume, Mrs Crapper.'

A happy resolution had been achieved.

'Yes, I'm sure you are relieved,' agreed Vera calmly.

Vera replaced the receiver and looked up at me. 'Don't ask, Mr Sheffield.'

Finally school came to a close. It was the time of the fading of the day and a cold December mist swirled over the High Street and the smoking chimneys. In the distance, over the purple bulk of the Hambleton hills, the setting sun glittered like beaten bronze.

I decided to call in to Prudence Golightly's General Stores. After the concert I had a quiet night ahead of me, at least I hoped so, and it was an opportunity to write a few Christmas cards. With winter coming on Vera had decided to buy a bottle of Sanatogen tonic wine and was standing at the counter ahead of me. She also purchased a large tin of Whiskas for thirty-three pence and a bottle of Robinsons Orange Barley Water for fifty-nine pence.

'Good luck this evening, Mr Sheffield,' she said. 'I'm sorry I can't be with you. Rupert and I have to go to Pickering.'

I bought a pack of twenty-five Christmas cards for ninety-nine pence and walked up the High Street for a welcome hot drink in Nora's Coffee Shop. As I walked in Dorothy Humpleby was filing her nails behind the counter and singing along to Billy Joel's 'Uptown Girl'. I ordered a coffee, sat by the window, watched the world go by and listened to Dorothy and Nora chatting in their usual inimitable way.

Breaking off from frying eight thick rashers of bacon for two of her special Belly Buster Bacon Butties, Nora picked up her latest copy of *Woman's Weekly* from under the counter, flicked through the pages and hurried over to Dorothy.

'Look at this, Dowothy,' she said. 'It's wight up y'stweet.'

Dorothy stopped filing her nails and looked up. 'What's that then, Nora?'

Nora held up her *Woman's Weekly*. 'It sez 'ere y'can find the *weal you*.'

'The real me?' repeated Dorothy, looking puzzled.

'Yes,' said Nora, 'by summat called gwaphology.'

'Graphology . . . what's that when it's at 'ome?'

'It's *psychological*,' said Nora mysteriously.

Dorothy's interest was now aroused. 'Psych'logical?' she said, her eyes wide in astonishment.

'Yes, it sez 'ere it's psychology o' 'andwiting,' said Nora.

''Andwriting?'

''Yes, 'andwiting – an' y'wight off t'one o' them post office boxes in somewhere called Tunbwidge Wells.'

'Tunbridge Wells?'

'It's a posh place down south. Y'send 'em a sample.'

'A *sample*?' asked Dorothy, suddenly becoming wary.

'Yes,' said Nora, 'o' your 'andwiting.'

'An' what 'appens then?'

Nora peered again at the advertisement. 'Y'weceive a confidential wepo't about y'stwengths an' weaknesses.'

'Oooh, ah'd like that, Nora,' said Dorothy, 'an' my Malcolm would be reight impressed wi' me goin' all *psych'logical*.'

I finished my coffee and thought that maybe Nora didn't have such a daft idea after all. We all have strengths and weaknesses . . . perhaps it was time to recognize mine.

*

The Hartford Home for Retired Gentlefolk was an imposing red-brick Victorian building hidden from the village cricket field by a high yew hedge. Set in two acres of land, it was an elegant and gracious place to live out one's twilight years. When I arrived it was a hive of activity, with residents, parents and children all heading for the main hall.

One of the senior carers, Janet Ollerenshaw, a tall, athletic young woman wearing blue jeans, trainers and a Cambridge-blue polo shirt with a Hartford oak tree logo, welcomed me. 'Good to see you again, Mr Sheffield, we're all looking forward to the concert. I've heard my little brother Barry is playing a triangle,' she said with a wry smile. 'He's never shut up about it. You'd think it was Last Night of the Proms.'

It was a memorable concert, warmly appreciated by the supportive audience, and there wasn't a dry eye in the house when little Rosie Sparrow sang her solo of 'Away in a Manger'. Afterwards the staff wheeled out tea, orange juice and mince pies and the children served the residents and engaged them in conversation, mainly revolving around what they hoped to get for Christmas.

I renewed acquaintance with a lovely lady, Violet Tinkle, who regaled me with wartime memories, including spending three old pence for her *Woman's Own*, keeping fit for the war effort by taking Iron Jelloids while listening to Joe Loss and his band playing 'We'll Meet Again' and 'We're Gonna Hang Out the Washing on the Siegfried Line'.

Meanwhile, Ragley's oldest inhabitant, ninety-seven-year-old Ada Cade, surprised and impressed Harold Bustard and Molly Paxton by telling them that her

twenty-first birthday present from her father had been a
drastic one. She had had all her teeth removed. 'He told
me,' explained Ada, 'that it would save a lot o' pain an'
suff'ring at t'dentist in t'years t'come,' and both children
thought this was a wonderful idea.

It was when everyone had left and I was saying a final
goodbye that Janet Ollerenshaw approached me with
Lillian De Vere on her arm. 'Lillian wondered if you
would like to see her photographs of movie stars, Mr
Sheffield. She's very proud of them.'

'Of course,' I said.

'It won't take long, Mr Sheffield,' said Lillian, 'but I
thought you might be interested.'

I followed them to Lillian's ground-floor room. It was
spacious and comfortable. On one wall were six large,
framed, black-and-white photographs of the Hollywood
greats. They stretched in a neat line across the wall
between the window and the grandfather clock in the
corner.

'They're my favourite film stars, Mr Sheffield,' she said.
'Lillian Gish, Clara Bow, Vivien Leigh, Rita Hayworth,
Judy Garland and the only man – my heart-throb, Marlon
Brando.' Her long slender fingers stroked the wooden
frame of the first photograph in the line. It showed a
frail and wistful-looking actress wearing a lace dressing
gown. Underneath it read *'Broken Blossoms 1919'*.

'This was my mother's favourite film, Mr Sheffield.'
She turned to face me. 'In fact, I was named after Lillian
Gish, the star of the film – and she's still alive and living
in America.'

'She's a very beautiful lady, Miss De Vere,' I said.

'It was the first silent movie I ever saw and I can

remember it perfectly,' she said wistfully, 'and then my eyes started to deteriorate.'

Janet Ollerenshaw turned to face me. 'I'm afraid Lillian had the disease *Retinitis pigmentosa*, Mr Sheffield.'

'It began when I was young,' explained Lillian. 'At first I had difficulty seeing at night and then my field of vision in each eye got less and less. If you look at the world through a rolled-up newspaper you will get an idea of what it's like. Then the tube gets narrower as you get older and the vision in each eye gets less and less. I'm told there's no cure.'

'I'm so sorry,' I said.

'Don't be,' she said simply. 'I made sure I challenged myself to lead a very full and active life, and at least I could see once and I have a good memory, even if I say it myself.'

'You're a remarkable lady, Miss De Vere,' I said and looked back at the photographs, 'and perhaps one day I'll watch *Broken Blossoms*.'

'You won't regret it, and you must come back and tell me what you think.'

'I shall,' I promised, and took her hand and squeezed it gently. Janet nodded in my direction. It was time to leave.

Back at Bilbo Cottage, as I walked in Beth was putting the finishing touches to her make-up in front of the hall mirror.

'Your meal is on the table, Jack,' she said as she screwed the top on her lipstick, 'and I've fed and changed John and put him in his cot.'

'Thanks,' I said, 'and you look wonderful.'

She smiled, gave me a brief hug and opened the front

door. 'Sorry, Jack . . . like ships that pass . . .' She hurried out to her Volkswagen Beetle and as she set off for her evening in York a barn owl flew above our heads like a grey ghost of the night.

It was after midnight when she came home and slipped into bed beside me, putting her freezing-cold feet on the back of my calves.

'Had a good night?' I whispered.

'Yes thanks – sorry I'm late.'

'John's fine,' I said.

'Good,' she said and snuggled closer. 'How did the concert go?'

'Really well,' I said. 'There was a blind lady there – a Miss De Vere . . . she got me to thinking how lucky we are.'

'Yes, we are,' she said softly.

'Remember our conversation this morning?'

Beth yawned. 'Yes,' she said simply.

'I *will* think about another job if you think it's for the best.'

There was silence followed by deep breathing and she fell asleep.

I took a little longer.

Chapter Eight

A Surprise for Santa

A presentation of a framed photograph was made in school assembly today by Mr Evans, chair of the school governors, to Mrs Jo Hunter as a token of thanks for her service at Ragley. Mrs Hunter takes up a new appointment in January at Priory Gate Junior School in York when Mr Tom Dalton will take over as full-time teacher in charge of Class 2. The school choir will perform at the Christmas Crib Service at St Mary's Church on Christmas Eve. School closed today with 93 children on roll and will reopen for the spring term on Wednesday, 4 January 1984.

Extract from the Ragley School Logbook:
Tuesday, 20 December 1983

Santa's feet were cold – they always were.

Gabriel Book adjusted his white beard, checked his Mickey Mouse wristwatch and stamped his feet on the freezing floor of his grotto. He made a mental note to bring in an electric heater for the rest of the week. Now in his sixties, he was beginning to feel his age but, as a member of the local Rotary Club, he felt it was his duty to do his bit. It was Monday evening, 19 December, and in the local market town of Easington the Christmas Fair was in full swing.

Immediately outside Santa's little wooden hut the Handbell Society was out in force. All six members, each with a pair of Norfolk-crafted handbells, were entertaining the queue with their rendition of 'Frosty the Snowman'. However, their efforts were not appreciated by all. The two teenage daughters of the president of the Rotary Club had been persuaded by their father to work in Santa's grotto and dress up in outfits that sported the bright badges 'Good Fairy' and 'Busy Elf'. They were not impressed . . . but two ten pound notes had exchanged hands.

'If they play that bloody song again, I'll stick them handbells where the sun don't shine,' said the grammatically bereft eighteen-year-old Good Fairy.

'Too right,' said the minimalist-use-of-language sixteen-year-old Busy Elf.

Gabriel was not impressed with their contribution. Good Fairy was moody and Busy Elf was bone idle, but he battled on bravely. It was almost six o' clock, only an hour left, and mothers and children were waiting patiently outside as snow began to fall again.

The church clock was striking six when Ruby locked her caretaker's store. 'Ah've 'ung up all m'presents on t'tree, Mr Sheffield,' she said. Each year Ruby bought a small gift for every child in the school, usually a packet of sweets from the Rowntree's factory, and wrapped each one in North Yorkshire County Council tissue paper. It was a generous gesture from this kind lady for whom every penny counted.

'Thanks, Ruby,' I said.

She fastened up her threadbare coat. 'Ah'm off to t'Christmas market in Easington now, Mr Sheffield, wi' our Duggie an' 'Azel. Y'can get some real bargains.'

'Yes, I'm going there as well,' I said, 'to get a present for Beth.'

Anne Grainger emerged from the office. 'Well, I'm going tomorrow night,' she said with a grin. 'It's the only way I'll receive a Christmas present that won't finish up on John's workbench.'

Tomorrow was the last day of term and Anne and I had stayed behind to make sure everything was ready for our final assembly, including a farewell to Jo Hunter who had taught at Ragley for over six years. Vera had arranged for a large-scale photograph of Jo with the school netball team, on the memorable day they had won the York Small Schools Netball Tournament, to be professionally framed by an upmarket framer in Gillygate in York. Anne had wrapped this carefully and hidden it in the school office along with a host of other gifts, including an engraved Acme Thunderer whistle and a huge card signed by all the children and staff.

I locked up the school and eased my Morris Minor Traveller out of the car park. On the village green a giant Christmas tree was festooned with bright-coloured lights and the pantile roof of The Royal Oak was covered in wavy snow patterns. As I drove up the Easington Road, beyond the frozen hedgerows the boughs of elm and sycamore hung heavy under their winter burden and the winter sky promised more snow.

*

Meanwhile, in Santa's grotto, Good Fairy rubbed some of the spray-on snow from the tiny window and peered outside. 'Only a few customers left,' she said to her sister with a sigh of relief, 'and then Frankie Spraggon is taking me to The Pig and Ferret in his Capri.'

'Can I come?' pleaded Busy Elf.

'No you bloody can't,' said Good Fairy, pointing her wand in annoyance. 'Dad would have a fit.'

'Only if you told him,' groaned Busy Elf. She shook her head in annoyance so that the little bell tinkled on her green pointed felt hat.

'Come on, girls,' said Gabriel, 'I thought you were friends.'

Good Fairy shrugged her shoulders and looked condescendingly at Gabriel. 'No, Santa, we're not friends – we're *family*.'

Gabriel stared down at his black boots. He knew the pain of family squabbles. Since his wife had died he saw little of his daughter, Abigail, except when she was stuck for a babysitter. Her partner, a Liverpool bookmaker, had long since flown the nest. Abigail had always considered Gabriel too strict as a parent and, as the years went by, he realized she was probably right. In consequence, they barely spoke these days.

Now the greatest joy of his life was when his granddaughter, five-year-old Zoe, sat with him on his sofa and he read stories to her. The little girl loved Little Red Riding Hood and Goldilocks and was almost word perfect as he pointed to the text. He recalled she had first called him 'Ga-ga' when she was only two years old and the name had stuck. Now it had progressed to 'Ga-ga

144

Book' – it seemed an appropriate name for a reader of stories. Gabriel wondered what Abigail and Zoe might be doing this holiday and reflected that Christmas could be a lonely time.

Good Fairy opened the wooden door. 'Next please for Santa,' she said with forced politeness.

In walked Connie Crapper with five-year-old Patience. 'Hello and a ho-ho-ho,' said Gabriel cheerily.

Connie plonked Patience roughly on Santa's knee.

'And what's your name?' asked Gabriel.

'Patience . . . what's yours?'

'I'm Santa,' said Gabriel, slightly taken aback, 'and have you been a good girl this year?'

Patience looked at her mother, who nodded fiercely. 'Yes, Santa,' said Patience with a glassy-eyed *it was never my fault* stare.

'And have you got any brothers or sisters?' asked Gabriel, trying another tack.

'No, Santa – ah'm a lonely child.'

Connie pointed at her wristwatch and glared at Gabriel. 'Tell Santa what y'want f'Christmas,' she said brusquely.

'Well, ah'd like a Snuzzle please.'

'A snuzzle?'

'She means a My Little Pony,' said Connie curtly. 'It's one o' them new soft toys.'

Gabriel was unaware of the advertisements for the new range of pastel-coloured horses with big soulful eyes, flowing polyester manes and tails and names such as Cotton Candy, Snuzzle and Blossom.

'Well, I'll look in my toy cupboard,' said Gabriel, 'and I'll see if one's there.'

Patience thought for a moment. 'Well, Santa,' she

145

said helpfully, 'ah'll come back tomorrow wi' m'mam's catalogue – they're all in there.' Then she jumped off his knee and hurried out after collecting a free sherbet dab from a bored Busy Elf and a mystery gift wrapped in tissue paper from Good Fairy, who made sure Connie and Patience were outside again before they opened it.

When I arrived in Easington the cobbled market square was full of stalls and surrounded by brightly lit shops. I parked next to the gable end of the toy shop and under a huge advertisement for a major new film coming in 1984, *Never Say Never Again* featuring Sean Connery as James Bond. As I fastened the toggles on my duffel coat, from a loudspeaker system next to the war memorial the Christmas number one, 'Only You' by the Flying Pickets, blasted out and the crowd hummed along.

I paused to look in the toy-shop window and realized with a hint of sadness that the world was changing. It felt as though I were witnessing the demise of the British toy industry. Famous names, Meccano, Dinky and Corgi, were all disappearing and being replaced by flashing video screens and the sound of laser fire. When I was a boy a Hornby Dublo train set was regarded as the perfect Christmas gift. Now the popular present seemed to be a *Star Wars* set at £23.

A small girl was staring at the labels on the boxes of games. 'Mam,' she said, 'was ah made in 'Ong Kong?'

I made my way to the electric showroom, where I spotted the perfect gift for Beth. It was a Sharp's micro-wave oven with a built-in turntable. Then I saw the price was £249.94 and I realized that my salary didn't stretch that far. I went in and settled for a Moulinex Multi Chef

146

for £45. 'It blends, chops and grates,' said the young lady assistant and, although I had little idea what she was talking about, it sounded very impressive. I put the large box in my car; then it occurred to me I would need a roll of Christmas wrapping paper to cover it so I wandered over to join the crowd next to Shady Stevo's stall.

He was a heavily built and swarthy man; it was rumoured the long, jet-black pony-tail that hung down his back was actually attached to his flat cap as one was never seen without the other. 'C'mon, ladies,' he was shouting, 'top-o'-the-range London fashion 'andbags, two poun' each or three for a fiver.' I saw Winifred Brown buy three while Connie Crapper bought a Remington Popcorn Maker for £14.95 and a 1983 *Adam and the Ants Annual* for £1.

Mrs Tricklebank was looking through the box of half-price Christmas cards, thinking ahead to Christmas 1985.

'Ah've got some lovely *classical* cards this year,' said Stevo, "ere's a set o' twenty f'fifty pence.' He held up a packet of cards featuring Giotto's painting *Madonna and Child*.

'I'll take 'em,' said Mrs Tricklebank and handed the pack to eight-year-old Sonia. Her little sister, five-year-old Julie, peered at the picture with curiosity.

'Who's that, Sonia?' she asked, pointing.

'That's Mary,' said Sonia, 'and she's holding baby Jesus.'

'So where's Jesus's dad then?' asked the little girl.

Sonia thought for a moment. 'Well . . . he'll be the one taking the picture.'

Lee Dodsworth's mother was in front of me and gave me a smile. She bought a Frogger electronic game (batteries not included) at £15 and an MB Pac-Man game for a fiver, then it was my turn. I bought a roll of wrapping paper for twenty pence, a box of four Memorex C90 Tapes for £2.50 and a three-pound jar of Quality Street for £3. As Ruby had said, it was definitely the place for a bargain.

Back at Bilbo Cottage I found myself untangling the string of Christmas tree lights once again. No matter how carefully I packed them away in January, eleven months later they had somehow contrived to resemble the Gordian Knot of ancient legend and, just like Alexander in 333 BC, I was struggling.

'Who's next for Santa?' asked Good Fairy. There were two mothers outside and two children. Brenda Ricketts came in with Billy, who had just celebrated his fifth birthday.

'Ho-ho-ho,' said Gabriel as Billy sat on his knee.

'What did y'say that for?' asked Billy, who had always been a direct little boy.

''E knows 'is onions, does my Billy,' said Brenda Ricketts proudly.

And he smells of them thought Gabriel.

'Tell Santa what y'want, Billy,' urged Brenda.

'Yes, Billy – what would you like for Christmas?' asked Gabriel.

Billy was looking curiously at Santa's beard and began to tug at it. 'Leave 'is beard alone,' shouted Brenda, 'an' say what y'want.'

Billy took a deep breath and looked up at Santa. 'Ah wanna rat.'

'A rat – a white rat?'

'No,' said Billy, 'a *Roland* Rat.'

'A Roland Rat?'

"'E's on breakfas' telly, Santa,' explained Brenda, 'wi' 'is friend Kevin.'

'Kevin?' Gabriel was struggling to comprehend. 'Is Kevin a rat as well?'

'Yes, Santa,' said Billy.

'I see,' said Gabriel. He was lost for words.

Billy was a good-hearted little boy and was always willing to help a friend in difficulty. 'Well if y'struggling, Santa,' he said, 'all you 'ave t'do is go t'Nugent's Toy Shop in York an' they've one in t'front window.'

Gabriel smiled. 'Well, before that I'll look in my toy cupboard to see if the little elves have made one.'

Billy looked at Busy Elf, who was yawning while flicking through the pages of her *Smash Hits* magazine. Meanwhile, Good Fairy was wrapping more mystery gifts in tissue and sticking lengthy strands of Sellotape round them.

'Santa mus' spend a lot on Sellotape,' observed Billy.

'Yes, luv,' said Brenda. 'Come on, time t'go. It's nearly seven o' clock and Santa 'as t'close now an' fly back to t'North Pole,' and she grabbed Billy's hand and they hurried out.

Across the market square Geoffrey Dudley-Palmer was in Dixons and thinking hard about purchasing a Polaroid Sun Camera 600 for Petula.

'It's a highly sophisticated system of electronics,' said the eager assistant with an attempt at a Rod Stewart spiky hairstyle that looked like an explosion in a Shredded Wheat factory.

'Really?' said Geoffrey, clearly impressed. He loved new technology.

Shredded Wheat Boy was now in full flow. 'The amount of light is measured by sensors so you get perfectly lit pictures.'

'Sounds good,' said Geoffrey.

The earnest young man moved in for the kill. 'It's pre-focused, so it only takes a split second to point and press.' He thrust the camera into Geoffrey's hands and recited his *pièce de résistance*. 'And only ninety seconds from pressing the button to peeling off the processed print.'

'But will my wife be able to work it?' asked Geoffrey in desperation.

Shredded Wheat Boy realized this wasn't the moment to declare his firm belief that advanced electronic hardware was clearly beyond the wit of a mere woman. He resorted to his man-to-man knowing wink and a patronizing smile perfected over his short apprenticeship. 'A trained chimpanzee could operate this.'

Geoffrey kept his thoughts to himself about his deep-seated and politically incorrect views of potential contests between his wife and educated primates. 'I'll take it,' he said.

'There's one more customer,' said Good Fairy, looking at her watch, 'but we should be shutting now.'

'We can't turn them away,' said Gabriel firmly.

Reluctantly, Good Fairy opened the door and a slim woman in her early thirties walked in with her fair-haired daughter. The mother stopped suddenly, surprised to see familiar eyes peering out from under Santa's fur-lined hood. Recognition was immediate – but it was too late: the eager little girl stepped forward and stared up at Father Christmas in his bright red suit.

'Hello, Santa,' she said . . . and Gabriel smiled down at his granddaughter.

'Hello, Zoe,' said Gabriel.

The little girl looked puzzled. 'Santa – how d'you know my name?'

Abigail gave him a sharp look, but Gabriel recovered quickly. 'Santa knows the names of all good little girls and boys,' he replied.

The little girl looked relieved.

'Go on, Zoe,' said Abigail quickly. 'Tell Santa what you would like for Christmas and then we'll be off.'

Gabriel ignored the rebuff even though it hurt. He knew his daughter hadn't forgiven him.

'Well, Santa,' said Zoe, 'please can I have a doll that wees and some books with Christmas stories – and some slippers.'

Abigail was surprised. 'Slippers?'

'Yes, Mummy,' said Zoe, 'for Ga-ga Book, because his feet are always cold when he reads stories to me.'

Abigail looked at her father and a flicker of a smile crossed her lips. She remembered when she was a child and Gabriel had read stories to her. He had cold feet even then. Meanwhile, Gabriel couldn't speak. He just stared in awe at the child he loved so much. Zoe put her hand in her pocket and took out a carrot. 'And this is for Rudolph,' she said.

'Thank you, Zoe,' said Gabriel, 'and a happy Christmas.'

Mother and daughter walked out into the darkness.

In the Earnshaw household all was not well. Mrs Earnshaw had clearly lost something, while Terry knew the day of judgement was approaching fast. He had opened the little cardboard flaps on the back of his sister's Co-op Advent calendar and eaten Dallas Sue-Ellen's chocolates from 20 December onwards.

'Baby Jesus 'as gone missing,' said a concerned Mrs Earnshaw. She held up the shoebox of Nativity figures.

'What's that, Mam?' asked Terry.

'Well, Mary and Joseph are 'ere but there's no baby Jesus.'

The Earnshaw family were taking part in what Joseph Evans described as the annual Posada: namely, the journey of Joseph, Mary and the donkey to Bethlehem. Over the period of advent the little clay figures were passed from one family to another. The idea was to re-enact their search for lodgings and it meant that Joseph, Mary and the donkey stayed in a different place each night, finally arriving back in church for the Crib Service on Christmas Eve.

'Baby Jesus?' repeated Terry, looking puzzled. 'But 'e's not been born yet, Mam. 'E dunt turn up 'til Christmas Day.'

The penny dropped and Mrs Earnshaw nodded in acknowledgement. 'Well . . . ah never thought o' that.'

Terry arranged the figures on the mantelpiece so that they were safe from Dallas Sue-Ellen's sticky fingers and then went up to bed.

'An' shut that door, Terry,' shouted Mrs Earnshaw. 'Y'weren't brought up in a barn!'

'But Jesus was,' retorted Terry, quick as a flash, 'an' 'e didn't get told off.'

Heathcliffe looked up from his *Roy of the Rovers* comic. ''E's right, Mam.'

Mrs Earnshaw smiled and pondered for a moment. *Well at least they're learning something at school* she thought.

Tuesday-morning assembly was a happy but tearful affair. After Joseph had retold the story of the birth of Jesus we said a prayer and then Jo Hunter gave a moving speech of thanks. Sergeant Dan Hunter was sitting next to me and, at the end, he shook my hand. 'Thanks, Jack,' he said quietly. 'We'll never forget Ragley School.'

However, during morning break it was clearly the Nativity story that had caught the imagination of the youngest children. 'Well, when ah grow up,' said Patience Crapper, 'if ah 'ave a baby an' it's a boy, ah'll sell it 'cause ah 'ate boys.'

Jemima Poole was more forgiving. 'Ah bet Mary would've liked a nice tin o' biscuits,' she said. 'My mam allus likes a biscuit when she's fed up wi' my big brother.'

Charlie Cartwright was unimpressed with the kings' gifts. 'If ah'd been Jesus ah would 'ave rather 'ad a Lego set or mebbe a light sabre.'

Meanwhile, that evening little Billy Ricketts went home and told his mother that Jesus had been born in a stabilizer. Fortunately Joseph was untroubled by the children's active imaginations; he was too busy preparing for the annual Crib Service on Christmas Eve.

Beth's parents, John and Diane Henderson, had travelled up from Hampshire on Friday evening to spend Christmas with us, while my mother and her sister May had decided to enjoy Christmas and Hogmanay north of the border with the Scottish clan. So it was that on Christmas Eve morning Beth was in the lounge looking at a knitting pattern and Diane was holding up the almost completed sweater that she was knitting for Laura. They were discussing something called reverse stocking stitch, but as I didn't even know what *forward* stocking stitch was it didn't seem the right moment to interrupt.

I walked into the kitchen where John, a lean, athletic six-footer with steel-grey hair, was playing in the hallway with baby John. 'So he slept through the night, Jack?' said John. 'That must be a relief.'

We had moved John's cot into our room so that he and Diane could use our tiny second bedroom. 'Yes, things are settling down now, thankfully,' I said. 'We're both getting some sleep at last.'

He lifted up his grandson, who immediately reached for his reflection in the hall mirror. 'He's an observant little lad, isn't he?' said John with a smile.

'He's trying to roll over on his tummy now,' I added with pride.

'Takes me back,' he said. 'Doesn't seem that long since Beth and Laura were this age.' He stared thoughtfully out of the leaded window at the winter scene beyond. 'Shame she couldn't be with us for Christmas,' he said, 'but she chose to go back to London.'

'So I heard,' I said.

At 2.30 we all piled into John's Land Rover and drove to St Mary's. The church bells were ringing as we walked up the pathway of Yorkshire stone while the snow settled in gentle curves against the weathered gravestones.

When we walked in through the great Norman doorway the sound of children's voices filled this beautiful church. Vera was lighting tall candles within the sanctuary of the altar so that a tapestry of flickering shadows illuminated the stained glass in the east window. Sally Pringle was preparing to accompany the children's Nativity on her guitar while Anne, helped by Sue Phillips plus a few willing parents, dressed the children in their costumes. It was a special time and we squeezed into one of the front pews so that John had a good view of the Nativity scene. The Posada was now complete, with the tiny figure of baby Jesus finally joining the tableau in the straw-covered stable.

Soon, the Valium-sedated Elsie Crapper played the introduction to 'Once in Royal David's City' and the choir mistress, Mary McIntyre, a lyric soprano who had a diploma from the Royal College of Music in London, sang the first verse as a solo as she led the choir down the central aisle. It was music blessed by angels.

As always, the children stole the show and, once more, the timeless tale was acted out by a cast wearing tea-towel headdresses and curtain-cloaks.

It was five o' clock when we got back to Bilbo Cottage. John lit a roaring log fire, I warmed some mulled wine, while Beth and Diane prepared a huge pan of leek and potato soup and a side plate of fresh bread.

Soon we were circling the programmes in the *Radio Times* that we wanted to watch or record over Christmas. I selected the Boxing Day film, *Bridge on the River Kwai* with Alec Guinness; Beth and Diane picked a Prokofiev ballet from La Scala, Milan, featuring Rudolph Nureyev and Margot Fonteyn; while John selected the *Only Fools and Horses* Christmas Special 'Thicker Than Water'.

Also, a host of new presents from John and Diane had

155

appeared under the tree, including, as we were later to discover, a Black & Decker Chuck Drill for me, a new dress for Beth and a carpet play-zoo for John.

Visitors to Santa's grotto had dwindled to a trickle as snow fell once more over the vast plain of York. Good Fairy and Busy Elf had not reappeared as Santa's helpers after the first night. Instead their mother, a friendly if over-apologetic lady, kept Gabriel company over the next few days, supplying him with endless cups of tea, an extra electric heater and a non-stop monologue concerning the problems of having teenage daughters.

It was nearly closing time when there was a tap on the door. The Rotary president's wife had left long ago to complete her Christmas shopping. Gabriel looked out and there was Abigail and a very excited Zoe. She was carrying a decorated shoebox. 'Santa, please could you give this to my Ga-ga Book on Christmas morning?'

Gabriel knelt on one knee before her. 'Of course, my dear.'

'There's something else,' said Abigail quietly.

Zoe played with Santa's beard while she considered what to say next.

'And please will you tell Ga-ga Book that he can come to our house for Christmas dinner?'

Only the gentle patter of snowflakes on the window disturbed the long silence. 'I will . . . I will,' said Gabriel. He looked up at his daughter. 'And thank you.'

He rubbed a tear from his eye and Zoe looked at his wrist. 'My Ga-ga Book has a Mickey Mouse watch,' she said.

'I know,' said Gabriel, '. . . I know.'

Abigail picked up Zoe and rearranged the warm scarf round the little girl's neck. 'Your mummy gave it to him when she was a little girl,' she said quietly.

As they walked out into the snow Gabriel called after them. 'Shall I tell him to bring anything?'

'No,' said Abigail simply, 'just himself.'

Gabriel picked up the box and looked at the label. It read: 'To Ga-ga Book, love Zoe XX'. He lifted the lid, peeped inside and smiled. The slippers were a hideous tartan but they were fur-lined. He had spent the last week promising surprises, but the best one had been saved until last.

'Warm heart, cold feet,' he chuckled as he locked up Santa's grotto for another year.

Chapter Nine

The Length of Our Days

Mrs Grainger and Mrs Pringle with children from the reception class and the school choir and orchestra will be supporting the Ragley annual village pantomime, The Wizard of Oz, *in the village hall on 31 December.*

Extract from the Ragley School Logbook:
Tuesday, 20 December 1983

'That was wonderful, darling,' said Felicity Miles-Humphreys through gritted teeth. Nora Pratt had just sung 'Over the Wainbow' without the use of the letter 'R' and Felicity was beginning to regret her choice of *The Wizard of Oz* for this year's annual village pantomime.

It was Saturday, 31 December and reluctant daylight had followed a dawn of wolf-grey clouds. At nine o' clock I had said goodbye to Beth and John and driven on the frozen back road from Kirkby Steepleton to Ragley village. The countryside was held fast in the grip of winter but slowly the first sharp light flickered across the frosty fields. Finally the sun broke through the mist and long, grey-blue shadows filtered through the bare trees. As I pulled up on the High Street the hedgerows were rimed with white frost and a diamond light lit up the bright berries on holly bushes laced with dark ivy. However, when I walked into the village hall armed with a can of lurid emerald-green emulsion paint and a two-inch bristle brush, the natural wonders of the world did not appear to be in abundance.

'Now . . . Munchkins, centre stage please,' shrieked the self-appointed producer and artistic director of the Ragley Amateur Dramatic Society. Felicity Miles-Humphreys adjusted a bright red headband that held back a mop of astonishingly frizzy hair dyed as black as her flowing kaftan. Felicity, a large lady – or *big-boned* as she often described her corpulent frame – was aware that the need for Valium had increased with each meeting of Ragley's motley crew of budding thespians.

The dress rehearsal was not going well. In fact, the word 'dress' was tenuous in the extreme, as few of the cast had brought their costumes. Also, Felicity's husband, Peter the stuttering bank clerk, was making his hesitant acting debut as the Tin Man, who, according to the script, didn't have a heart. Likewise, Felicity didn't have the heart to tell Peter that he was hopeless. Meanwhile, Rupert, her artistic son with delusions of theatrical greatness, had been cast as the Scarecrow and he kept forgetting his lines. However, as the Scarecrow was going to the Emerald City to get a brain, Felicity hoped the audience would assume this was in keeping with his character. As if that wasn't enough, Deirdre Coe as the Lion, incongruously, was simply too bossy and she strode the stage intimidating the rest of the hapless performers.

On top of all that, the Munchkins had munched all the Garibaldi biscuits and Jimmy Poole's Yorkshire terrier as Toto the Dog was chewing up the Yellow Brick Road. 'Let's take five,' announced Felicity in true Hollywood tradition.

Anne Grainger, as a reluctant but faithful committee member, and Sally Pringle as an ad hoc musical director, both recognized the signs of an imminent nervous breakdown and hurried off to the kitchen at the back of the village hall to make Felicity a cup of tea. It was a long-standing tradition to have a family pantomime in the village hall on New Year's Eve that included most of the children in the reception class, plus members of the school choir and orchestra, so the presence of Anne and Sally was appreciated by all. Sadly, it was destined to be a performance that would never be forgotten.

While Felicity found a few moments' respite in a cubicle in the ladies' toilet, she vividly recalled an earlier production of *The Wizard of Oz* that had been her inspiration. In 1977 she had gone to the Theatre Royal in York when Julie Dawn Cole, famous for playing Veruca Salt in the 1971 film *Willy Wonka & the Chocolate Factory*, had been perfect in the part of Dorothy, while Marsha Fitzalan had proved to be a particularly convincing Wicked Witch. She also recalled a particularly handsome chocolate tree played by a young man called Pierce Brosnan, who had gone on to star in an American TV programme called *Remington Steele*.

When she finally emerged and walked into the kitchen area, Anne Grainger gave her an encouraging hug and a cup of very sweet tea. 'Don't worry, Felicity,' she said.

'You see, Anne,' said Felicity, 'I've always been a *tactile* person – it's part of the creative instinct, you know – and I literally *feel* the pain when the performance doesn't meet my high expectations.'

'I'm sure this will be the best production we've ever had.' Strictly speaking, this was a bit of a back-handed compliment, seeing that all the previous pantomimes had been dreadful.

I had volunteered to help Anne's husband, John, put the finishing touches to the scenery and as I walked through the hall I saw Timothy Pratt arranging the chairs with military precision. I had long since avoided asking if he wanted any help, as Timothy firmly believed he was the only man in Yorkshire with sufficient spatial aware-ness to complete this boring task. So I merely smiled in acknowledgement as he checked the chalk guide lines for each row to ensure every chair was in its correct align-ment to the stage.

When I arrived backstage, John was painting a corrugated-card rainbow that, I noticed, sported only six colours instead of the recommended seven. While my history was a little hazy relating to Richard III being defeated by Henry Tudor at the battle of Bosworth in 1485, I could comfortably recall the popular mnemonic phrase: *Richard Of York Gave Battle In Vain.* However, this rainbow's indigo and violet had merged into one indistinguishable band.

'Felicity doesn't look pleased,' I observed as I stirred my tin of paint.

John, a big, bearded man in a thick Aran sweater, gave me a shy grin. 'Wait till she sees this bloody rainbow,' he said. 'She'll have a fit.'

I dragged out a sheet of plywood and, while I daubed

161

bright green turrets on a gaudy whitewashed castle, it crossed my mind that, fortunately, the expectation level of the audience was always very low. After all, back in 1977 we had been treated to *Snow White and the Six Dwarfs*, so a six-colour rainbow was pretty much par for the course.

Meanwhile, Nora Pratt, trussed up like a chicken in her hand-stitched Alpine leather corset, sought out Felicity in the kitchen. 'Wupert keeps fo'gettin' 'is lines, Felicity,' said Nora. 'It's weally upsetting.'

'Don't worry, Nora, it's just nerves,' said Felicity. 'All born performers get the collywobbles.'

Nora shook her attempt at a Bonnie Tyler hairstyle in despair. 'An' t'Tin Man knows *all* 'is lines but keeps wepeating 'em.'

'Yes, but it's his *debut* on the big stage, darling. We *professionals* have to make allowances.'

'Mebbe so,' said Nora, mollified, but only slightly. 'An' t'Lion 'as *too much* couwage if y'ask me,' she added for good measure. 'That Deidwe was weally wough when she dwagged m'down that Yellow Bwick Woad in t'wehea'sal.'

'I know, darling,' said Felicity with a sigh, sipping her tea nervously, 'but I'm sure this will be your greatest triumph.'

Nora gave what she hoped was a modest and understated nod of approval. *My gweatest twiumph* she thought as she wandered to the ladies' to loosen the unbreakable orange baling twine on her Alpine corset. After all, it was difficult to enjoy a secret KitKat when you could barely breathe.

*

When I returned to Bilbo Cottage, Diane Henderson was playing with baby John, who was now five months old and had begun to bang his rattle with gusto. He smiled as I hung up my old duffel coat and scarf in the hallway and stretched out his arms towards me in welcome. I picked him up and cuddled him, marvelling once again at the softness of his skin. Then I passed him back to Diane so I could wash the green paint from my hands.

'How did it go, Jack?' she asked. She looked relaxed and the old tensions between us seemed to have been forgotten.

I smiled. 'Well, the producer is having a nervous breakdown, the Tin Man has an unfortunate stutter, the Scarecrow can't remember his lines and the Lion is an objectionable bully. That apart . . . my Emerald City is a perfect shade of green and definitely worth the fifty pence admission.'

'So, just like the other pantomimes,' said Beth, who was chopping onions in preparation for a beef casserole.

'It will be good for the two of you to get out together,' said Diane. She lifted John and, much to his delight, put him in a baby bouncer I had fitted to the frame of the kitchen door. This had proved a blessing for Beth when she needed to prepare food in the kitchen.

It was shortly before seven o' clock that Beth and I left Bilbo Cottage and, for me, it felt like old times, just the two of us going out together.

With her perfect complexion and honey-blonde hair, and dressed in a casual, smart two-piece suit and her *Cagney & Lacey* coat with padded shoulders and a long belt tied casually at the waist, I wondered how she could ever have agreed to marry an awkward, bespectacled Yorkshireman like me. I glanced in the hall mirror and, to no avail, tried to flatten the palm-tree tuft of brown hair that refused to lie down on the crown of my head.

Beth drove her Volkswagen Beetle to enable me to have a drink after the performance and she parked by the village green outside The Royal Oak. We paid our fifty pence admission at the door to Elsie Crapper, who, as the official prompter for the pantomime, knew every word by heart, and we found two seats behind Dr Davenport and his wife, Joyce.

Backstage, all was not well.

'Now Rupert,' said Felicity, stroking his shoulder-length hair affectionately, 'you really must concentrate on your lines and bring that wonderful quality of pathos when you ask Nora, er, I mean *Dorothy*, for a brain.'

'But Mother, I'm working with a bunch of amateurs,' he said in disgust, as he applied his Leichner 5 and 9 make-up before knotting bundles of straw to his knees.

'I know, darling – but we must make allowances.' She put her arm round his slim waist and stared thoughtfully into the full-length mirror. Her son was well cast – in fact, he was the perfect physical specimen for the part of Scarecrow. A gangling, six-foot-four-inch, spotty, skinny and awkward young man, he had studied art and drama at college. Rupert certainly considered himself a cut above the others in terms of artistic talent. However, while his acting career had not blossomed, his ungainly height had secured him a day job as a shelf-stacker in the new supermarket in York. He now specialized in stacking

164

packets of Weetabix on the highest shelves in the cereals aisle. So, in a way, he *was* a cut above the others.

It was time for final preparations and Anne and a posse of mothers were trying to dress a lively band of Munchkins.

'Oh dear, your shoes are on the wrong feet,' said Anne to five-year-old Patience Crapper.

The little girl looked puzzled and refrained for a moment from chewing her Curly Wurly bar. 'But these are the only feet I've got,' she said, quick as a flash.

Anne sighed. *Where are the children's mothers when you need them?* she thought.

The auditorium was filling up fast, with the football team on the back row and villagers seeking out the best vantage points. Old Tommy Piercy had brought a cushion to sit on for a little extra comfort, while several of the senior citizens turned down their hearing aids in preparation for the ordeal of hearing Nora Pratt singing 'Yellow Bwick Woad'.

Ruby had arrived early and settled into her usual seat on the front row along with her daughters Racquel, Sharon, Natasha and Hazel, while 'Deadly' Duggie had joined his friends at the back. Meanwhile, a disgruntled Ronnie was taking time to settle in his seat.

'Stop shufflin', Ronnie,' said Ruby. 'Y'look as though you've got Saint Vitus' Dance.'

Ronnie rubbed his chest. 'Ah'm not feelin' m'self, luv,' he said.

'Shurrup,' said Ruby, 'show's startin'.'

To be precise, it wasn't due to start for another two minutes, but Scargill the Yorkshire terrier was tugging back the curtain with his sharp teeth so John Grainger, as official stagehand, took the unilateral decision to pull the cords that opened the curtains and a surprised Nora Pratt, resplendent in her Alpine corset and holding the straining Scargill on a taut leash, launched into her first song.

On the third row Betty Buttle muttered into Margery Ackroyd's ear, 'Look at 'er – dressed up like a dog's dinner.'

'Done up like t'Queen o' Sheba,' whispered Margery.

'Mutton dressed as lamb,' added Betty for good measure and they both relaxed, bathed in the innate superiority of the experienced theatre critic.

The performance literally stuttered on.

'But I haven't got a h-h-h- . . .' said the hesitant Peter.

'Hope,' shouted Deke Ramsbottom from the back row amid much unkind laughter from the inebriated footballers.

'Heart,' prompted Elsie Crapper from the side of the stage.

Peter frowned at Elsie. 'Why c-can't you be more p-p-p . . .'

'Patient?' suggested Elsie helpfully.

'Polite,' corrected Peter's son, Nigel, on the front row.

Peter nodded to his younger son in appreciation of his filial empathy and pressed on. 'B-but I haven't g-got a HEART,' he said, going red in the face, and the audience broke into spontaneous applause. It might not be Shakespeare, they thought, but at least they appreciated a soul in torment.

'Poor sod's tryin' 'is best,' said Big Dave on the back row.

'Y'reight there, Dave,' agreed Little Malcolm, holding Dorothy's hand as if he never wanted to let her go.

Apart from Deirdre Coe, who, as the lion, was booed every time she came on stage, the performance stumbled towards a conclusion accompanied by sympathetic applause.

Finally it was over. The audience breathed a sigh of relief and no one this year was going to ask for their fifty pence to be refunded, as had been the case ten years ago following *Goldilocks and the Two Bears*. Owing to the Tin Man saying each of his lines at least twice, the show had overrun by fifteen minutes. However, at last Nora took her fifth and final bow, accepted her bunch of flowers with feigned surprise and the curtain closed. We had survived another Ragley pantomime.

Parents hurried backstage to collect the Munchkins and the audience drifted out into the darkness.

On the front row all was not well. Ronnie was still in his seat and Ruby, clearly concerned, was standing over him.

'What's t'matter, luv?' she whispered. 'Y'look as though y've seen a ghost.'

Ronnie was short of breath and a pallor had spread across his usually florid complexion. 'Ah'm strugglin' t'breathe, Ruby. M'chest feels tight,' he gasped.

'Oh, Ronnie, Ronnie,' said Ruby as she looked on helplessly. Racquel seemed to sum up the seriousness of the situation before anyone else. She grabbed her sister's arm. 'Sharon, quick – find Doctor Davenport.' Then she turned to Natasha and gave her a meaningful look. 'Tek 'Azel t'fetch a glass o' water . . . an' find our Duggie.'

The sisters rushed off while Ronnie clutched the centre of his chest. He was sweating, his complexion had gone grey and there was now a bluish tinge to his lips. Duggie ran up and looked in horror as his father collapsed to his knees.

'Ruby . . . Ruby,' said Ronnie and he fell to the floor. The crushing pain in his chest was too much to bear. He tried to speak. 'Look after . . . look after . . .' he gasped.

Duggie leaned forward to hear the fading words. Ronnie's speech was slurred and was now barely a whisper. 'Look after what, Dad?' he asked.

Ronnie gripped his son's hand and whispered in his ear. 'Look after . . . look after . . . m'pigeons.'

Then there was silence as Ronnie stared vacantly at the ceiling.

'Ronnie, Ronnie,' cried Ruby, kneeling down and holding his hand. She turned tearful eyes to Duggie. 'What did 'e say, luv?'

Duggie looked back at the still figure of his father and then put his arms round his mother. ''E said, "Look after . . . y'mam."'

Dr Davenport did everything he could while Vera and Joseph tried their best to comfort Ruby and her daughters, but it was impossible to revive Ronnie. It was clear he had suffered a massive and fatal heart attack. The calm doctor moved into professional mode and took control of the immediate proceedings. The area around Ronnie was cordoned off and the few shocked villagers who had remained behind huddled near the entrance door, not knowing what to do next.

Timothy Pratt dimmed the lights to give Ruby and her family a little privacy, Anne and Sally made tea for everyone, and Big Dave and Little Malcolm went up the High

Street to The Royal Oak to break the dreadful news to the rest of the football team.

Ronald Gladstone Smith, aged fifty-two, husband of Ruby and father of six, died on the last night of 1983 in the village he loved, with his wife beside him and five of his children in close attendance. A bright moon shone down from the vast, jet-black firmament on this tiny corner of Yorkshire while a cameo of triumph and tragedy was played out.

At midnight the sounds of celebration echoed from behind the closed curtains of Ragley village, but in a dark corner of the village hall Dr Davenport was in conversation with the local funeral director. Duggie had been to collect his boss, Mr Flagstaff, from his home in Easington. They stood there, a sombre group, discussing arrangements.

Racquel had taken a lead and sent the distraught Hazel home with Sharon and Natasha, then she had asked Duggie to go across the road to Diane's Hair Salon and use her telephone to try to make contact with Andy at his army barracks.

This left Ruby in tears, sitting with Racquel and Vera. 'Why my Ronnie, Mrs F?' she sobbed.

'Only our Lord can tell us the reason, Ruby,' replied Vera quietly, 'and perhaps we'll understand in time . . . and in our prayers.'

Ruby's shoulders were shaking in grief. 'And why now?' she asked.

'It was his time,' said Vera simply.

'I don't understand,' said Ruby.

'My dear Ruby,' whispered Vera, 'none of us knows the length of our days.'

*

As midnight chimed to welcome the dawn of 1984, there were no balloons and no champagne. At number 7, School View in the little village of Ragley-on-the-Forest, Vera hugged her dear friend while Ruby's tears flowed and her daughters clung to her in a tableau of grief.

Finally, in the early hours, Beth and I drove home through a silent monochrome countryside of moonbeam shadows.

Lost in thought and suddenly overcome by the enormity of pent-up emotion, Beth began to weep. I pulled in at the side of the road beneath the sanctuary of sycamores and put my arms around her. We sat there, two souls in the darkness. Only a slight breeze whispered through the branches above our heads. There we sat under an eternal sky and reflected on a day of despair. I waited until her tears subsided then slowly drove home.

Chapter Ten

Bobble Hats and Breadcrumbs

The headteacher and Mrs Forbes-Kitchener represented the school at today's funeral of Mr Ronald Smith, late husband of our caretaker. Miss Flint provided supply cover in Class 4.

Extract from the Ragley School Logbook:
Tuesday, 10 January 1984

I've heard it said that it is always darkest before the dawn.

So it was on that winter morning when the world was still and the sky was a veil of sadness. It was the time of the long nights and a bitter, malevolent wind rattled the wooden casements of our bedroom windows. The driveway of Bilbo Cottage was coated with a blue film of crystal on this freezing morning. As I stared through the leaded panes I thought of what lay ahead – a different day, a time of farewell, a gathering of souls . . . a funeral.

It was Tuesday, 10 January and at Ragley School the new term had begun a week ago with a new teacher and fresh challenges. However, on this harsh winter morning a difficult time lay ahead. Eventually, fingertip softly, a grudging light began to spread across the distant fields and a land of grey-white snow and bare trees emerged from the void. From the second bedroom the muffled sounds of Beth feeding baby John provided sharp contrast. I smiled grimly at the paradox as new life struggled to greet a day of endings.

When I arrived at school Vera was sitting quietly in the corner of the staff-room. She had boiled a small pan of milk on our single-ring stove and prepared our usual mugs of steaming hot coffee.

Sally went immediately to sit beside her. She had spent eighteen pence that morning on a copy of the *Daily Mail*. 'I thought you might like this, Vera,' she said softly. She had removed the centre-page pull-out and passed it to her. Vera's eyes lit up in surprise.

'Oh, thank you so much, Sally,' and she settled back to enjoy the first colour photos of the new year. 'What wonderful pictures,' she murmured almost to herself. Young William appeared to be having a happy time toddling round Kensington Gardens. However, Vera frowned when she saw that the young prince had stuck out his tongue towards the press photographers. Nevertheless, her displeasure was fleeting when she recalled that the press had often made Diana's life distinctly uncomfortable. 'Such a handsome little boy,' she said, and for a few fleeting moments her thoughts were in another, happier place.

New Year's Eve had been a difficult time. The village hall had emptied quickly thanks to the quiet and orderly professionalism of Sergeant Dan Hunter and the major. A calm but subdued Dr Davenport certified Ronnie's death before he was moved to Easington hospital and, following a brief coroner's inquest, the event was registered. Finally, Joseph had moved into his pastoral mode in comforting the family and Vera had worked closely with Ruby's two eldest children, Andy and Racquel, to prepare a eulogy to be read at the funeral.

Sergeant Andy Smith had been given immediate compassionate leave and returned from duty in Ireland. Meanwhile, the funeral director, Septimus Flagstaff, had made it clear that he wanted Duggie to provide Ronnie with the best oak coffin with inlaid mahogany. It was now in their private chapel of rest, where the body could be viewed.

There was a subdued atmosphere in school on this dark morning and even the normally ebullient children moved quietly, as if sensing the mood of their teachers.

My classroom door opened. It was Vera, dressed in a black two-piece Marks & Spencer suit, black leather fur-lined boots and a small black pillbox hat. 'Time to go, Mr Sheffield,' she said.

I was in conversation with our supply teacher, Miss Flint, who had come in this morning to take charge of Class 4 while I represented the school at the funeral. 'Thanks, Vera, I'll be right there.'

Miss Flint walked with me to the classroom door and whispered, 'Take your time, Mr Sheffield, all will be well here.'

I nodded in appreciation and accompanied Vera to the office, where she helped me into one of the major's superb Crombie overcoats as I didn't own a black coat. It complemented my grey three-piece suit, white shirt, black tie and shiny black shoes. Fortunately we were a similar height, although he was broader in the shoulders. Even so, it was fit for purpose and had the added benefit of keeping me warm on this bitter winter's day.

We drove up Morton Road and parked on the vicarage forecourt. It seemed as if the whole village was on the move and a steady file of mourners walked carefully up the frozen path to the entrance of St Mary's Church. Joseph was standing there waiting for the arrival of the hearse. He had done this many times before and I realized what a reassuring presence he was on mornings such as this.

We crunched across the frozen gravel and paused to speak to him. Vera looked at her brother. 'Is there anything you need, Joseph?' she asked.

'It's all in God's hands,' he said.

Vera squeezed his arm. No words were needed, so we took our seats at the end of a pew near the central aisle. Elsie Crapper was playing soft organ music and Vera was pleased that our nervous organist had obviously taken her Valium.

The hearse drew up outside the church and the coffin was removed from the back with calm precision. Septimus directed his team of bearers to place it on the sturdy old wooden trestles under the lych gate. With silent decorum, he arranged the six men in pairs on either side of the coffin according to their height. Young Tommy Piercy and Little Malcolm were in front, two of the experienced official bearers employed by Septimus came next, with Big Dave Robinson and the equally tall Deke Ramsbottom bringing up the rear. Slowly and without effort, they raised the coffin to shoulder height and stood there, still as stone. A swirl of bitter sleet blew in the faces of the bearers but none of them flinched.

Joseph turned to Septimus, who gave him the briefest nod. Then Joseph glanced down at his well-thumbed *Shorter Prayer Book*, but it remained closed in his bony hand – he knew the words by heart. So it was, in a clear voice that could be heard by the congregation inside, he turned to face the church door and walked in front of the procession while the heavy crunch of matching footsteps on the rutted ice followed him. '"I am the resurrection and the life, saith the Lord,"' recited Joseph, '"he that believeth in me, though he were dead, yet shall he live: and whosoever liveth and believeth in me shall never die."'

Inside the church, Vera quietly echoed the familiar words of the gospel of St John, chapter 11, verses 25 and 26.

Behind the coffin and the bearers came Andy Smith, ramrod-straight in his sergeant's uniform, and Racquel, her tears hidden by the brim of her grey-black hat. They were on either side of Ruby, gripping her elbows through her winter coat. Next came Duggie, smart in his official funeral attire and pushing Ruby's mother, seventy-year-old Agnes, in a wheelchair. Sharon and Natasha followed behind, heads bowed, holding the hands of little Hazel, who stared ahead at the coffin as if in a dream.

As the procession entered the church, Joseph, in his cassock, surplice and a black scarf, removed his thick black cloak and passed it to the sidesman, Tobias Speight, who held it to his chest and bowed as the coffin passed him by.

'"Blessed are they that mourn: for they shall be comforted,"' said Joseph, reciting from the gospel of St Matthew, and his words filled the stillness of the church.

The family followed the coffin towards the altar, where it was placed on another set of trestles next to the pulpit. Behind them Tobias closed the ancient door and a soft blanket of silence descended on the congregation. The churchwarden, Wilfred Noggs, directed the family to the front pews and we all sat down with a rustling of heavy coats and scarves and the swish of paper as we turned to the first page of the funeral service.

We sang 'There Is a Green Hill Far Away' and then it was my turn. I stood at the lectern with the giant Bible resting on the outstretched wings of a brass eagle.

'Psalm Twenty-three,' I said, '"The Lord is my shepherd".' I was used to speaking in front of large groups of people, but this was different. I could almost feel Ronnie's presence in the coffin alongside me.

After returning to my pew, Vera put her hand on mine for a brief moment. No words were needed. Our second hymn was Ruby's favourite, 'All Things Bright and Beautiful', and tears were rolling down her cheeks as the choir mistress, Mary McIntyre, and one of our parents, Bonnie Shawcross, sang a beautiful duet for the first verse.

Andy Smith read the familiar extract from St John's gospel, chapter 14, verses 1–6, and ending with verse 27: '"Let not your heart be troubled,"' he said and then raised his eyes from the Bible and looked at his mother for the final words, '"neither let it be afraid."'

The Eulogy was carefully handled by Joseph, who encouraged everyone to remember Ronnie as a loving husband, a proud father, a popular member of the village community and manager of the Ragley Rovers Football Team.

This was followed by prayers and we all expected Joseph to lead the congregation in the Lord's Prayer; however, he explained that, before this, Ruby's four daughters had all written a short prayer of their own. It was something no one would ever forget. I have attended many funerals in my life but, when I look back, one of the most poignant moments was undoubtedly when little Hazel Smith took a folded piece of paper from her pocket and, holding tightly to Racquel's hand, read, 'I will miss my daddy and I hope he will be happy in heaven . . . Amen.'

The final hymn was one of Ronnie's favourites. He had sung 'Abide With Me' at Wembley Stadium in 1972 when Leeds United beat Arsenal in the FA Cup final. It was on that day he had purchased the bobble hat that had become his favourite among his motley collection. The rest of his bobble hats were in various states of moth-eaten repair in the hallway, but this one always had pride of place on the brass hook on the back of the bedroom door. Today it rested on his coffin, on top of a wreath with the word 'DAD' picked out in tiny white flowers.

Following the Blessing, the family and congregation filed out to 'We'll Meet Again' played on the organ. I stood up with Vera and we walked out in the bitter wind beneath an iron-grey sky of torn and tattered clouds. Albert Jenkins, school governor and self-appointed bell-ringer since the death of Archibald Pike, had climbed the bell tower and fitted a leather muffle over one side of the clapper of one of the bells. And so a sonorous muffled note rang out, fifty-two times to celebrate each year of Ronnie's relatively short life.

The burial followed and the finality of this affected us all. Joseph recited '"Lord, now lettest thou thy servant . . ."', until a sharp gust of wind snatched away the rest of his words.

Once again he had donned his long black barathea wool cloak and he led the procession to the graveside. It had been hard work for the gravedigger, even one with the mighty strength of the local handyman, Whistling John Paxton. Joseph had asked him to follow tradition and dig the grave to double depth so that in time, if required, a wife could share the same grave as her husband. However, frozen earth and tree roots had slowed him down.

John Paxton stood to one side in a collarless shirt and a donkey jacket, unmoved by the fierce wind and biting cold. He knew the job. The pile of earth, now solid frozen clods, would go back in but they would have to wait three months for the ground to settle before adding the headstone. This had been selected by Andy and Racquel according to the strict rules that determined a headstone must be oblong and not, as they had hoped, in the shape of a racing pigeon.

Meanwhile Septimus, with experienced precision, supervised the careful placing of putlocks over the grave. It was on these that the coffin was placed. The pallbearers knew their job and fed the thick webbing through the handles then underneath the coffin before lowering it into the grave.

A group of villagers waited at a respectful distance.

'What's in the box, Mummy?' asked the articulate three-year-old Bonnie Tricklebank.

'Older people die and go to heaven,' said Mrs Tricklebank in a quiet voice.

There was a pause. 'When will you be going, Mummy?'

'Not for a long time, luv,' she said with a wry smile.

'What about Daddy – he looks poorly.'

Mr Tricklebank picked up his daughter and held her close. 'We 'ave t'be quiet now, luv,' he said and kissed her cold cheeks.

As Ruby and the family gathered round the graveside snow began to fall again. Joseph recited, 'Man that is born of a woman hath but a short time to live, and is full of misery. He cometh up and is cut down, like a flower; he fleeth as it were a shadow, and never continueth in one stay.'

Finally, it was over and, as Ruby turned from the graveside and walked along the snow-covered path to the lych gate, she dropped a black leather glove from her trembling fingers. A short, stocky man with a ruddy face and a gentle smile stepped forward and picked it up. He raised his flat cap and handed it back to Ruby. 'An old Celtic tradition from m'mother's side,' he said quietly. 'If y'drop a glove another must pick it up.'

Ruby looked curiously at the man as if his face stirred a memory. Racquel said, 'Thanks,' and ushered her mother towards the waiting black Bentley provided by the major.

Ruby's mother, Agnes, paused. ''Ello, George Dainty,' she said. 'Y'back then.'

The man nodded and walked quietly away, deep in thought.

Back in Ragley village hall, Nora Pratt from the Coffee Shop and Sheila Bradshaw from The Royal Oak had worked hard to prepare for the wake. Trestle tables covered in snow-white linen were stacked with neat rows of crockery and steam was rising from a Baby Burco boiler and a coffee machine. The ladies of the Cross-Stitch Club had prepared a mountain of sandwiches, sausage rolls, slices of pork pie, home-made jam tarts and seed cake.

Soon a steady file of villagers queued to pay their respects to Ruby and her family. Through the crowd a frail, elderly lady came over and kissed Ruby on the cheek. 'My dear Ruby,' she said softly.

'Aunty Gladys,' said Ruby in surprise. ''Ow did you get 'ere?'

'Your Racquel arranged for me to get a lift from Skegness. I wanted to be here.' Ruby's aunt was known as Seaside Gladys and had found fame telling people's fortunes. She held Ruby's dumpy, work-red hands and looked into her eyes. 'Don't fret, Ruby,' she said. 'Happiness is waiting for you – but not where you expect to find it.'

Ruby held her intense gaze for a moment. There was often a hidden meaning to the words of her favourite aunt.

'Ronnie did love me,' she said simply.

'Yes, he did, my dear . . . in his own way.'

That evening Ruby closed the old frayed kitchen curtains and looked round her at the clutter. Ronnie's pigeon plate was there on the worktop, but today it was empty of breadcrumbs. When she walked through the untidy lounge, on the mantelpiece was a fading photo of the teenage Ruby on the day she was Ragley's May Queen. This young woman was slim and pretty with long wavy chestnut hair that hung down her back almost to her waist. A circlet of pretty flowers rested on her head.

Finally she went upstairs. In her bedroom Ruby sat on the edge of her bed and tried to remember the good times she had shared with Ronnie. Sadly, there weren't many. The happiest days in her life all revolved around her children. Ruby loved them all with a fierce resolve. She thought back to the day her first child, Andy, was born and how proud she had been. Her mother had knitted him a pair of blue bootees and these had been passed on to Duggie.

Ruby recalled the years of scrimping and saving and toil. Then she looked at the empty hook on the back of the bedroom door. The familiar bobble hat had gone and she knew her life had changed. She sighed and looked at the clock on the bedside cupboard. It was midnight and Ruby put on her nightgown and crept into Hazel's tiny bedroom. She lifted the covers, climbed in next to her and they lay there like a pair of spoons.

Ruby kissed her daughter gently and whispered, 'Goodnight, God bless.'

Chapter Eleven

George Orwell's New World

County Hall requested responses to their recent paper 'Equal Opportunities within the Curriculum'.

Extract from the Ragley School Logbook:

Friday, 27 January 1984

'Sooty's got problems,' muttered Sally as she glanced through the *Daily Mail* that Tom Dalton had left on the staff-room coffee table.

'Sooty?' asked Vera in surprise as she stirred the pan of hot milk.

It was Friday-morning break, 27 January, and outside the staff-room window the silence of snow covered the frozen earth. Under its smooth white blanket the world was still as stone. Tom was on playground duty and, like the rosy-cheeked children around him, didn't appear to feel the cold.

Anne and I were sitting near the gas fire, trying to keep warm while studying the Yorkshire Purchasing Organization catalogue and the price of bristle brushes.

'He's Harry Corbett's glove puppet,' said Anne with authority. 'I saw him on stage in Morecambe in 1950.'

'Actually,' said Sally, 'it's his son, Matthew Corbett, who's taken over and he's the one who writes the scripts.'

'So what is the problem?' asked a bemused Vera as she served up the piping-hot mugs of coffee.

'Well, apparently,' said Sally, 'Sooty keeps bossing his girlfriend, Soo, and telling her to work in the kitchen – so, he's clearly sexist.'

'I agree,' said Anne firmly.

'And so do I,' added Vera for good measure.

I reflected that Beth seemed to spend a lot of her time in *our* kitchen and decided to keep quiet.

It was 1984 and political correctness had arrived in Ragley village.

I was the last to leave the staff-room when the bell went. Vera glanced down at her notepad. 'By the way, Mr Sheffield,' she said, 'a company called New Age Systems telephoned to ask if their representative could call in this morning. So, I'll deal with it shall I?' It was rhetorical and I recognized it as such. 'Thanks, Vera,' I said, 'I'd be lost without you.' She smiled and began to fill our Gestetner duplicating machine with ink.

Thirty minutes later nine-year-old Charlotte Ackroyd, without looking up from her School Mathematics Project workcard on percentages, announced, 'Mr Sheffield, Ford Capri Mark II wi' twin 'eadlights comin' up t'drive.' I smiled. Charlotte knew her cars.

'Thanks, Charlotte,' I said and recalled it must be the New Age visitor.

A skinny young man with a goatee beard, John Lennon circular spectacles and wearing a purple corduroy suit walked into the office. He carried a smart black briefcase and placed it on Vera's desk. Vera, suitably horrified, picked it up, placed it on the floor and, in doing so, noticed his shoes had never been introduced to polish.

'Good morning, Mrs Four-Kitchens,' he said, peering myopically at the scrawled notes in his Roland Rat notebook. 'I'm Lionel Crudd from New Age Systems.' He passed his business card to Vera.

'Good morning, Mr Crudd . . . my name is *Forbes-Kitchener* and not what you said,' she said coldly.

Undeterred, the young entrepreneur pressed on. His confidence was high. He had experienced the full day's training and had passed with flying colours. 'Well, Mrs, er, t'day's your lucky day. I'd like t'introduce you to t'new world o' modern eighties communication.'

'Really?' said Vera, thinking that this was a man only a mother could love.

He held up an A3-size glossy photograph showing a sleek plastic box with a telephone handset cradled on one side plus a keyboard and a small pop-up monitor. 'This is it,' he said proudly.

'What is?' asked Vera.

Mr Crudd paused to check that the image was the right way up. *Clearly slow on the uptake* he thought. 'You are looking, Mrs Fork-Itchener, at an ergonomically designed desk communication terminal,' he said.

'You mean it's a *telephone*,' said Vera.

'Well, in a manner o' speakin',' said Mr Crudd, 'but what you in fac' are lookin' at is an *executive* telephone.' It was time to pull the rabbit out of the hat . . . *a hypothetical one of course* he thought. 'It's multifunctional,' he explained with pride. 'You can put two 'undred and fifty-five names in the dialling directory.'

'But I've got that number and more in my file index,' said Vera, 'and I know most of them off by heart.'

'Yes, but it sends TELEX messages,' said Mr Crudd triumphantly.

'Who to?' asked Vera.

He was thrown for a moment but recovered quickly. 'Well, er, anyone y'know who's got a telex.'

'But we don't know anyone with a telex.'

He was getting desperate. 'Well . . . it displays a monthly planner wi' all your appointments f'every day.'

'You mean like this,' said Vera, holding up her immaculately neat and precise desk diary.

'An' it has a *direct* link with other information networks,' he added.

'Information networks?'

'Yes, like Prestel.'

'In Lancashire?'

'Er, no.'

Vera had heard enough. This strange little man was talking a different language. 'Well, thank you, Mr Crudd . . . but not today.'

Lionel Crudd recognized defeat when it stared him in the face and, after a hesitant farewell, he packed his shiny briefcase and sloped off to his rusty Capri in the car park, reassured that three of his four headlights were working on this dark, gloomy winter's day.

It was lunchtime and we had gathered in the staff-room.

'Look at this,' said Sally. She picked up the *Daily Mail* from the coffee table. The headline read, 'Big Brother Is Watching You!'

Tom looked up from his computer magazine. '"It was a bright cold day in April, and the clocks were striking thirteen",' he recited. 'We did *1984* for my A-level English.'

Sally scanned the article that included extracts from George Orwell's vision of a totalitarian future in *1984* and the infamous Ministry of Truth. It described a world, rather like Russia, that was short of shoelaces and razor-blades and reminiscent of post-war London.

'Well, today's proles live in crowded tower blocks,' said Sally pointedly. She smiled at Tom. 'And Tom's computer will probably replace Orwell's telescreen in a world where there is no privacy.'

'Oh dear, I do hope not,' said Vera in dismay.

I was looking through the *Times Educational Supplement* and was attracted to the headline 'Curb the Cane'. 'There's a proposal here to end corporal punishment in schools,' I said.

'It never did me any harm,' said Tom casually. 'Kept me on the straight and narrow.'

'Well, I'm totally against it,' said Sally.

'Thankfully, I've never had to use it,' added Anne.

I thought *and neither have I*, and it struck me that we were fortunate teaching in this quiet corner of North Yorkshire where the vast majority of children were well behaved, understood right from wrong and loved coming to school. Bullying was almost non-existent and we all worked hard to provide an effective curriculum. It seemed we were a long way from the growing problems within inner-city schools and the difficulties faced on a daily basis by other members of our profession.

Also, it looked as though our *entente cordiale* with France had gone out of the window. Under the headline 'Lamb

Ambush', President Mitterand had apologized profusely following the arrest of two British lorry drivers. They had been kidnapped by Normandy farmers who were demonstrating against cheap food imports and the new Labour leader, Neil Kinnock, had told them it was 'outrageous'.

Meanwhile, across the frozen High Street in the village pharmacy, Deke Ramsbottom didn't look happy. 'Ah'm still strugglin' wi' t'same ol' problem, Eugene.'

'Well y'better 'ave some more o' these,' said Eugene sympathetically. He selected a packet of Germoloids suppositories. 'These 'ave got an improved formula so they should do t'trick,' he added.

'Ah'm not sure,' said Deke. 'Ah've already 'ad some o' these. Your Peggy gave me a box of 'em.'

Eugene looked thoughtfully at the packet. 'What's wrong wi' these then?' he asked.

'They taste rotten, Eugene,' said Deke, shaking his head.

'Ah,' said Eugene as the penny dropped. He glanced in the direction of Peggy, who had finished stacking the new stock of Johnson's Baby Cream. 'Deke, let's 'ave a quiet word o'er 'ere.' He tugged at Deke's sleeve and they were soon in deep and animated conversation in the far corner of the shop.

'Y'what?' muttered Deke. 'Y'jokin'.'

'No, ah'm not, Deke,' whispered Eugene. 'That's where y'put 'em.'

'Bloody 'ell!' grumbled Deke. 'What's t'world comin' to when y'told t'stick bullets up yer arse?'

'It's 1984, Deke,' said Eugene quietly, 't'world's changing.'

*

187

At the end of school Betsy Icklethwaite cleaned the black-board extra quickly. 'Ah'm in a rush, Mr Sheffield,' she said with a grin. 'Ah've got some shoppin' t'do on t'way 'ome an' then me an' Molly an' 'Azel want t'see *Grange 'ill*.'

'*Grange Hill*,' I said, 'is it good?'

'Brilliant, Mr Sheffield,' said Betsy as she replaced the board rubber on the shelf, 'but ah'm really worried about Zammo McGuire. 'E's in a spot o' bother.' She rushed off to her coat peg and the classroom was quiet again. I collected a pile of English books for marking and then set off for the entrance hall. We had all decided to check arrangements with Vera for the afternoon tea party at the vicarage to celebrate Joseph's birthday.

'What about Sunday afternoon?' asked Sally. 'I've got a recipe for muesli biscuits that I'd like to try out.'

'Shall we come early?' asked Anne. 'We can help pre-pare.'

'Well, Shirley and Doreen from the kitchen said they would come at three o' clock and set the tables,' said Vera, 'and Rupert's cook, Doris, has done most of the baking – but do come. Many hands will make light work.'

'And are you sure you don't mind us bringing John?' I asked.

'That's fine,' said Vera. 'In fact I'm hoping Sally will bring young Grace.'

'Colin will be pleased,' said Sally with a grin.

'What about me?' asked Tom. 'Shall I bring anything?'

'Just yourself,' said Vera with a smile, 'and it will be good to have moral support for Ruby too. I do hope she will feel able to come.'

*

On Saturday it was a quiet dawn and a grey light filtered over the sleeping land. The world was waking from the dark abyss of a seemingly endless night and the scurrying of small woodland creatures marked the beginning of another winter's day.

Once again Beth and I were up early to feed John, now six months old and with a big appetite. He was the centre of our world.

'I've been thinking, Jack,' said Beth after changing his nappy.

'Oh yes, what about?' I asked as she carried John downstairs.

'A bigger headship,' she said crisply.

I groaned inwardly. 'Really?' I said to give me thinking time.

Beth sat John on the kitchen floor. He could sit up unaided now for a few minutes and he smiled up at us.

'Yes, Jack,' and there was light and anticipation in her green eyes as she put cereal bowls on the table, 'but not for you – for *me.*'

'Oh, I see,' I said. This wasn't what I had expected.

She gave me a level stare. 'When I've finished my Masters degree I should have a good chance of a bigger challenge, maybe down in Hampshire where my mother could provide child care – and where you could be a village headteacher again, if that's what you want.'

I had guessed that one day Beth would want to return to her native county, but not yet . . . not yet. 'Is that what *you* want?' I asked.

I guessed she sensed my reticence. 'Yes, one day,' she said and we sat eating our cornflakes in silence. It was at times like this that I saw the strength in her. I had come to know Beth as a woman, a wife and a lover, but, increasingly, there were times of reflection. We had shared a pathway but it seemed her ambition was driving us towards different destinations. Love could be a tough companion.

Now our relationship was like a slow river, steady and reassuring, murmuring its gentle song over the everlasting pebbles . . . but what is love if not a friend in dark places, a companion in a forest of whispering trees, a haven in a journey of shadows? 'Then I'll support you,' I said and kissed her cheek.

On the kitchen radio Paul McCartney's number-one record 'Pipes of Peace' was playing for the umpteenth time and Beth hummed along.

'And by the way, Laura rang,' she said. 'She's moved into her new flat in York. I said I'd take John and meet up for lunch.'

I smiled, but kept my thoughts to myself.

Three miles away on the Crescent, Anne Grainger was in her bedroom, dressed only in her bra and pants, scrutinizing her figure in front of the full-length mirror. She sighed deeply. The problem was clear to see. She was no longer the shape she once had been. In consequence, following the excesses of Christmas, she had decided to take drastic action. Attracted by an advertisement in her *Woman's Own*, she had hurriedly written off to Needletrade International in Croydon, enclosing her measurements and a postal order for £9.95.

So it was that while John was in the garage making a deathtrap of a gate-leg occasional table, Ragley's deputy headteacher unwrapped her belated Christmas present to herself. She smiled as she held up her new and fashionable B-Slim Girdle with specially reinforced tummy-control panels. 'Oh dear,' she murmured to herself, 'the times they are a-changing . . . . Goodbye forties, hello fifties.'

After Beth left for York, Bilbo Cottage was quiet, so I decided to drive into Ragley and catch up with some paperwork in school. The back road from Kirkby Steepleton had been cleared by Deke Ramsbottom in his snowplough and I negotiated the three-mile journey carefully. When I arrived in the car park curve-stitching patterns of frost decorated the window panes in their wooden casements and the Gothic bell tower resembled a Christmas cake.

In the peace of the school office the heavy silence was a cloak of comfort and my thoughts wandered freely. I wrote a lengthy response to County Hall's discussion paper concerning equal opportunities. This was an issue that was clearly gathering nationwide momentum and the workplace was changing fast.

At one o' clock I decided to enjoy some hot food in The Royal Oak, so I locked up the school and headed across the village green. The spiky grass crunched beneath my feet and my breath hung in the air as a misty vapour. The frozen pond, bordered by brittle hoar frost, was covered with a thin sheet of ice, its surface cracked like shattered marble, while above it the bare branches of the weeping willow, like skeletal fingers, shivered in the winter wind.

The Ragley Rovers football match had been cancelled and the team and supporters were propping up the bar when I walked in.

'What's it t'be, Mr Sheffield?' asked Don the barman.

'A pint of Chestnut and one of your giant Yorkshire puddings, please,' I said.

Clint Ramsbottom sidled up. 'Ah'll 'ave a Budweiser, please, Don,' he said a little sheepishly.

Don reached down under the counter. 'Just got 'em in, Clint,' he said. 'They're new. Not tried one m'self.'

Shane glanced across to the bar. 'What's that y'buying, Nancy?' Clint winced as he always did when his psychopathic brother called him Nancy.

Don held up the bottle. ''E wants a Budweiser.'

'A what?' shouted Shane.

'Sounds foreign t'me,' said Old Tommy Piercy. 'What's wrong wi' proper English beer?'

'All m'mates i' York are drinkin' 'em,' said Clint defensively.

Don removed the metal cap from the top of the bottle. 'Here y'are then,' he said with a sigh. 'What abart a glass – 'andle or no 'andle?'

Clint shook his head. 'Y'drink it straight from t'bottle.'

Sheila leaned over the bar and for a fleeting moment the football team were distracted by her prodigious bosom. 'A cat could 'ave weed on that bottle,' she said.

'Or a dog,' added Big Dave Robinson for good measure.

'Y'reight there, Dave,' said Little Malcolm. 'Ah've seen Jimmy Poole's little terrier weeing on t'enamel buckets outside Tidy Tim's.'

'There y'are,' said Sheila.

'Ah'll 'ave a glass then,' said a demoralized Clint.

'Ah fought f'this country,' mumbled Old Tommy through a haze of Old Holborn tobacco, 'an' what thanks do y'get – German beer!'

'An' a pint o' Tetley's f'Mr Piercy,' added Clint hurriedly.

Mollified, Old Tommy nodded sagely. 'Ah well, y'only young once, ah s'ppose,' and he winked at Deke Ramsbottom, who raised his glass in appreciation of Old Tommy's generous conclusion to what could have been an embarrassing situation. Deke reflected that he hadn't raised his children to drink foreign beer. 'What's t'world comin' to, Mr Sheffield?' he grumbled.

'It's certainly changing, Deke,' I said.

'An' did y'know that Lord Mayor o' London is a *woman*,' said Don in disgust.

'They can't do that,' said Big Dave, clearly affronted by the suggestion.

'Y'reight there, Dave,' agreed Little Malcolm, 's'not nat'ral.'

'Sez on t'news she's called Lady Mary Donaldson,' said Don.

'Never 'eard of 'er,' said Big Dave.

'Well ah think it's a good idea,' said Sheila.

I said nothing and wandered off to a corner table where Sheila served me with a steaming plate of beef and onions in a huge crispy home-made Yorkshire pudding swimming in gravy – a feast on a freezing winter's day. The conversation at the bar ebbed and flowed and I recalled the equal opportunities paper I had left on Vera's desk. The Ragley football team had some conceptual catching up to do.

That evening Beth and I settled down in front of a roaring log fire with a bottle of red wine and watched television. The dashing John Nettles as Bergerac was followed by Terry Wogan interviewing David Attenborough, Randy Crawford and Matthew Kelly. Even though *Match of the Day* included the opportunity to win £100 worth of Premium Bonds, we switched over to BBC2 to watch a programme about two very unusual men. A man called John Duffy had chosen to be at home with his family to enable his wife to go out to work, while Vic Green, a redundant steel-worker, had to stay at home owing to force of circumstance. A sociologist, Jacqueline Burgoyne, examined the new developments that were challenging traditional roles in family life.

'That could be us one day,' said Beth with a grin. She snuggled up on the sofa and rested her head on my shoulder. Her hair was soft against my cheek and I pondered what the future would hold for us.

As we climbed the stairs to bed Beth said, 'Laura's been invited to Joseph's party tomorrow,' and that gave me something else to think about.

After checking John was sleeping soundly I stared out of the diamond panes of his bedroom window, lost in my own thoughts. A bitterly cold night had descended on the plain of York. The world was silent, all sound muted, and snowflakes drifted like winter confetti over the white landscape. Before me, as far as the eye could see, a spectral world of blue ice was covered in a shroud of newly fallen snow. The countryside was still in the fastness of winter and frozen moonbeams lit up the distant hills in sharp relief . . . and for a moment I thought of Laura.

Somehow our destiny had always seemed braided together . . . like silk and cord.

On Saturday afternoon when we arrived at the vicarage it was a hive of activity and Joseph was clearly thrilled that so many people had turned up. I met up with Vera in the kitchen while Beth showed off John's sitting-on-the-carpet skills to an enthusiastic group. Vera and I were both surreptitiously pouring our glasses of Joseph's home-made peapod wine down the sink. 'Sorry about this,' I said.

'It's probably got a future as a potent oven cleaner,' said Vera and we rinsed our empty glasses and walked into the hallway. We could see Ruby sitting in the lounge and she gave us a listless wave.

'Jack, I worry about Ruby,' said Vera.

I noticed that Vera had called me Jack. We were clearly off-duty and she was in a reflective mood.

'She's been very quiet at work,' I said. 'I wish we could cheer her up.'

'All the ladies at the Cross-Stitch Club have rallied round,' said Vera.

'And I heard about the Ronnie Smith Trophy,' I added.

'Yes,' said Vera, glancing across at Rupert, who was deep in conversation with Joseph about the state of the church roof. 'Rupert wanted something that would ensure Ronald's name lived on, so he purchased a lovely football trophy and had it engraved.'

'That was a good idea,' I said. 'I think Mr Ramsbottom is going to present it each season to Ragley's Player of the Year.'

The murmur of gentle conversation and the respectful clink of fine china and crystal glasses drifted over us in our private space.

'I pray for her every day,' said Vera, 'and she has the blessing of a loving family around her.'

'Time is a great healer,' I added.

'Let's hope so, Jack,' said Vera. 'It's difficult for Ruby to live in hope when she abides in sorrow.'

Vera hurried off to do her hostess duties while I wandered into the large, beautifully furnished lounge. I noticed Laura standing on the other side of the room talking to Jo Hunter. As usual she looked as if she had stepped from the cover of *Vogue* magazine – casually dressed in skin-tight Burberry jeans, a steel-grey denim jacket and matching waistcoat, and calf-length leather boots. Her long brown hair hung loose over her shoulders.

She caught my eye and came over. 'Hello, Jack,' she said simply and kissed me on the cheek. Her perfume was familiar. Then she straightened the creased collar of my herringbone jacket and stepped back as if considering the improvement.

'You look stunning as usual, Laura,' I said.

'Nothing much,' she said. 'Just our range of casual gear at Liberty.'

'So you've moved into York again.'

She smiled. 'Just until the summer. A lovely apartment – you must come and see it. Near the museum gardens again . . . just like old times.' Her green eyes never wavered.

'Perhaps,' I said.

She sighed. 'Well, Jack, I need a drink.'

I whispered in her ear. 'I wouldn't recommend the peapod vintage.'

She squeezed my hand. 'Don't worry, Jack,' she murmured, 'I learned a long time ago what to avoid,' and she walked away to the drinks table and began talking to Beth.

Tom Dalton was suddenly standing next to me. His eyes never left Laura as she poured herself a glass of Vera's mulled wine. 'Who's that beautiful woman with Beth?' asked Tom.

I put my hand on his sleeve. 'Tom, that's Laura and she's Beth's younger sister.' Tom simply stared, clearly captivated by Laura's confidence and slim figure. '. . . But only by a couple of years,' I added hastily.

'Jack, I'd love to meet her,' implored Tom.

'Perhaps later,' I said. 'Let's have a word with the major.' I ushered him towards the grand fireplace where the major was standing sentry in front of a roaring log fire.

The party went well and the food was magnificent. Shirley Mapplebeck had brought a savoury hot-cheese dip served with carrot sticks and cauliflower sprigs, while Doris, the major's cook, had prepared a crisp, creamy crab millefeuille. They were busy swapping recipes.

Meanwhile Jo Hunter was catching up with Tom on the news of her class. 'So, how's it going?' she asked.

'Fine,' said Tom. 'I'm getting to know them and they're definitely a bright bunch. In fact, keeping up with them with the new technology is a challenge. Some of them have got computers at home now and use them most days.'

'That's what I'm finding,' said Jo.

They discussed the special needs of the children and then Tom suddenly changed the subject. 'I'm told that's Laura, Beth's sister.'

'Yes, she's got a good job in London at Liberty, the fashion house, but she's doing some work at their branch in York at present. She's renting a flat there for a few months.'

'And she's not wearing a ring,' said Tom.

Jo looked up at him, slightly puzzled. 'Yes, she's single at the moment I think.'

Tom stood quietly, his jawline firm with the expectation of the moment and his piercing blue eyes sharp with anticipation.

We all toasted Joseph's health, then Vera walked in with a wonderful birthday cake for him. It was while we were eating a slice and drinking fine ground coffee that Beth finally introduced Tom to her sister.

'Laura,' said Beth, 'this is Tom – Tom Dalton, the new teacher at Ragley.'

'Hello, Tom,' said Laura with no great enthusiasm. She looked preoccupied.

I watched the meeting from a distance. Laura appeared indifferent, polite but not interested. Her thoughts were clearly elsewhere.

On Monday lunchtime we were back in the staff-room. 'They've sorted out the Sooty problem,' said Sally as she glanced through Tom's *Daily Mail*.

'Really?' asked Anne. 'How have they done that?'

'Apparently they've changed the scripts so that Soo is no longer submissive,' said Sally, 'and she's been taken out of the kitchen.'

'I should think so,' said Vera.

'So what's she doing now?' I asked.

Sally scanned the text under the photograph of the pair of furry glove puppets. 'Well, Soo's now reading motorcycle manuals and driving an excavator.'

Tom opened his mouth to say something and I shot him a warning glance. He settled back.

It was a new world and George Orwell didn't get a look-in.

Chapter Twelve

Raining in My Heart

Members of the Parent Teacher Association prepared the hall for tomorrow evening's 'PTA 50s Disco'.
Extract from the Ragley School Logbook:
Friday, 3 February 1984

As I drove up Ragley High Street, out of the darkness of a bitter winter morning light streamed from Nora's Coffee Shop. She was admiring a large poster in the window. It read:

RAGLEY SCHOOL PTA 50s EVENING
in the School Hall
7.30 p.m.
on Saturday 4th February 1984
Frothy Coffee & Cakes (Supplied by Nora's Coffee Shop)
50s Bring & Buy Stall
Clint Ramsbottom's Disco Experience
Tribute to Buddy Holly (featuring Troy Phoenix & the Whalers)
Tickets 50p from the school & local shops

The Ragley Parent Teacher Association, led by the indefatigable chair of the committee, Staff Nurse Sue Phillips, had decided to arrange a fundraising evening with a fifties theme. The date selected was the Saturday following the twenty-fifth anniversary of the day when, on 3 February 1959, Buddy Holly had died in the small plane he had chartered to take him to the next stop on his tour. Excitement in the village had been building for the past two weeks. Dusty suitcases were being pulled down from attics and searched for fifties memorabilia, and Clint Ramsbottom had visited Shady Stevo's market stall to add to his record collection. It seemed that everyone in the village had a story to tell about life in the 1950s – not least in Nora's Coffee Shop.

'Well, ah've got m'short pink skirt wi' a net petticoat an' m'bobby socks, so ah'm ready f'tomorrow night,' said Dorothy.

'That sounds all wight, Dowothy,' said Nora, 'an' ah've got that lovely cotton pwint dwess wi' a flowal design from that *Hey Pwesto* catalogue.'

'Twenty-five years – who'd 'ave thought it?' said Dorothy. 'Ah were only a baby.'

'It were wight sad, Dowothy,' said Nora, 'when 'e died in that plane cwash . . . weally upsettin'.'

Dorothy looked at the tired collection of buns and pastries. 'An' what are we taking?' she asked.

Nora was never one to miss an opportunity. 'Well, we can get shut o' them wock cakes fowwa staht.'

'We'll need t'get set up in t'school in good time,' said Dorothy.

Nora nodded. 'Mr Sheffield said he'd come wound t'collect all t'coffee an' cakes.'

'There'll be music,' said Dorothy.

'Ah love wock an' woll,' said Nora.

'An' me an' Malcolm'll be dancin'.'

Nora looked at the poster again. 'Clint Wamsbottom's Disco Expewience,' she said, 'an' that Twoy Phoenix – 'e sounds jus' like Buddy 'Olly so long as y'don't look at 'im.'

'Well, ah love that "Heartbeat" on t'juke-box,' said Dorothy. 'What's your favourite, Nora?'

Nora thought back to her teenage days. '"Waining in My 'aht",' she said without hesitation. However, Nora remembered that song for different reasons and she smiled at the memory.

When I arrived at school Ruby was knocking icicles from the eaves of the school entrance with a yard broom.

'We don't want 'em fallin' on t'kiddies' 'eads, Mr Sheffield,' she said.

'Thank you, Ruby,' I said, 'that's really thoughtful.' I looked at this sturdy Yorkshirewoman and sensed she was working extra hard to dull the pain of heartache. In my class, her daughter Hazel seemed to have recovered quickly with the resilience of youth. All the staff had kept an eye on the little girl, but she appeared to be her old enthusiastic self. It seemed that in Ruby's case it would take longer.

'An' t'boiler's goin' at full blast,' she said. Her eyes were red from recent tears.

'Ruby,' I said quietly, 'come inside for a cup of tea.'

She paused and reknotted her headscarf. 'Thank you, Mr Sheffield, ah will.'

When the bell rang for the start of morning school, she was still in the office, sharing her thoughts with Vera.

Morning assembly turned out to be a lively event and featured Sally's orchestra, comprising a few children from each class playing Indian bells, chime bars, a huge wooden xylophone, castanets, triangles, tambourines, recorders, drums and cymbals. Sally propped her *Okki-Tokki-Unga* songbook on her music stand and opened it to number 25, 'Do Your Ears Hang Low?', and began to strum the chords on her guitar while the children sang:

> *Do your ears hang low?*
> *Do they wobble to and fro?*
> *Can you tie them in a knot?*
> *Can you tie them in a bow?*
> *Can you toss them over your shoulder*
> *Like a regimental soldier?*
> *Do your ears hang low?*

This was accompanied by large, exaggerated actions featuring the little ones in Anne's class. The makeshift orchestra proved to be very noisy and enthusiastic, with little Billy Ricketts beating a drum as if his life depended on it.

Joseph was making his usual Friday-morning appearance and after assembly he spent half an hour in Class 3. This week's Bible studies theme concerned the Creation. All seemed to be going well until eight-year-old Ryan Halfpenny asked a question.

'Did Adam an' Eve 'ave any clothes, Mr Evans?'

'Well, er, no – they wouldn't have had any clothes,' said Joseph hesitantly, wondering where this conversation might lead.

'Ah don't s'ppose they would 'ave minded,' said Ryan with an innocent smile.

Joseph was puzzled. 'And why is that?' he asked.

''Cause mirrors 'adn't been invented,' said Ryan with a finality that brooked no argument.

At the end of the lesson Joseph collected in the children's 'Faiths of the World' topic folders. During morning break he was reading Barry Ollerenshaw's work. Under a wonderful picture of a mosque Barry had written, 'A mosque is a bit like a church but it's a bit different because the roof is doomed.' Joseph chuckled to himself, but with true Christian spirit he corrected the spelling.

At morning break when I walked into the office Vera handed me the telephone. 'It's Mrs Sheffield,' she said and set off for the staff-room.

'Good timing, Beth,' I said, 'exactly half past ten.'

'Yes, it's handy knowing your timetable,' she replied.

'So what are you and John doing?' I asked.

'We're meeting Laura for lunch, but before that I'm calling in to the bank to discuss that high-interest cheque account they're advertising. The drawback is they want a minimum balance of two thousand pounds in the account.'

'Way beyond a teacher's salary,' I said.

'Still worth a try, Jack,' said the financially aware Beth.

It occurred to me that my wife would have made a good accountant. Balance sheets left me cold. 'Fine, good luck,' I said.

'Oh yes, and Laura will be coming to the dance. Bye.'

I replaced the receiver and remembered Laura and the brief time we had spent together. Now our relationship was one of fleeting friendship and the distance of unfulfilment. For her perhaps it had ended as quickly as it had begun, like icicles in spring sunshine. Those days had long since passed . . . it was over.

When I walked into the staff-room Sally was reading out an article from Tom's *Daily Mail* and shaking her head in dismay. Billy Jean King, one of the most successful women in world tennis, had lost over £1 million in advertising deals after revealing her relationship with her personal secretary – a woman!

'We're living in the Dark Ages,' grumbled Sally and everyone nodded, but significantly Joseph and Vera said nothing.

Across the High Street Ruby's mother had a hair appointment at Diane's Hair Salon and Natasha Smith was pushing her grandmother's wheelchair. Every shopowner had cleared the snow from the pavement in front of their shop and Deke Ramsbottom had used a few barrowloads of council grit to make it safe for foot traffic.

Coming out of the General Stores was a portly, cheerful man with a bag of shopping. 'Who's that, Grandma?' asked Natasha.

'George Dainty,' said Agnes.

''E were at m'dad's fun'ral,' said Natasha.

'That's reight, luv – 'e used t'know y'mam a long time back.'

Natasha, curiosity aroused, pressed on. 'When was that?'

'Well . . . ah recall 'e tried t'court y'mam that day she were May Queen. 'E were seventeen an' y'mam were sixteen.'

Natasha parked the wheelchair and helped Agnes out of it and into the welcome warmth of the shop. 'An' what 'appened, Grandma?'

'Some things are best left unsaid,' said Agnes mysteriously and disappeared into the salon for her weekly morning of tea, pampering and comfort.

In my class after break the children were busy with their mathematics lesson. Charlotte Ackroyd came up with a novel answer to the question 'How do you change centimetres to metres?' Charlotte had written 'Just take out the *centi*' and, not for the first time, it occurred to me that a child's version of the so-called right answer was often better than mine.

Meanwhile, up the Morton Road, Petula Dudley-Palmer stared out of her state-of-the-art conservatory and felt that familiar sense of loneliness. As usual, Geoffrey had left early for work after complaining he couldn't find matching cufflinks and she had driven Elisabeth Amelia into York to the prestigious Time School for Girls and dropped off Victoria Alice outside the school gate in Ragley. By mid-afternoon the day had begun to drag and she picked up the *Radio Times*.

It was at this time each day that she wondered about her life. On occasions, she recalled a time when a sausage roll was not served on a small china plate accompanied by a regulation paper napkin. Crusts had never been removed from a loaf and cucumber sandwiches weren't necessarily triangular. She knew there must have been a time when she had stood at a crossroads in her life and taken the wrong turning. As she sipped her coffee, the conclusion was always the same – it was the day she had met Geoffrey.

Petula remembered a long-ago time in Manchester when she had collected empty pop bottles from the local tip and returned them to the corner shop at three old pence on each bottle. Then she would go with her friends to the Saturday-morning cinema and play in the local park on the way home. She wondered what had happened to them all and why she was always unhappy. In the *Radio Times* the Star Movie, *A Woman Rebels*, on BBC1 at 2.20 p.m. caught her eye. Katharine Hepburn was playing the part of a crusader for women's rights in Victorian England. It was the perfect accompaniment to a mug of coffee and a thickly sliced cheese sandwich . . . with crusts intact.

During afternoon school we worked on our Weather project, during which the busy, intense and extremely bright Lee Dodsworth put up his hand and pointed to his reference book. 'Mr Sheffield, it says here that the Antarctic holds about ninety per cent of the world's ice – so what happens if it melts?'

The follow-up discussion was fascinating as we considered the implications of sea levels rising, the possible flooding of London and how we could prevent it. During my training I had been told never to underestimate children and at the end of the school day I wished we could have sent a recording to the world's leaders.

Later, as darkness descended on Ragley village, members of the PTA plus a few mothers came in to prepare the school hall for tomorrow's dance. When I walked in with a box of pins and a pin-pusher, Margery Ackroyd was in conversation with Connie Crapper and Freda Fazackerly. "'E's got that *look*,' said Margery knowingly. Connie and Freda nodded in acknowledgement. 'An' lovely shoulders – y'know, real *manly*.'

'Ah never 'ad teachers like 'im when ah were at school,' said Connie wistfully.

'An' 'e's single by all accounts,' added Margery.

'Well, ah wouldn't kick 'im out o' bed,' said Freda.

They all laughed and I followed their gaze. Tom Dalton, jacket off and sleeves rolled up, was carrying a stage block effortlessly to the far corner of the hall. I coughed politely and, like naughty schoolgirls, they hurried away to decorate the entrance hall and continue their appraisal of Ragley's new teacher. Meanwhile I found myself having to decide where to pin up posters of Elvis Presley, Duane Eddy, the Everly Brothers and a very youthful Shirley Bassey.

In Diane's Hair Salon other more important decisions were being discussed. Amelia Duff, the postmistress, was under the dryer. 'What do you think, Diane?' she asked. 'I'm thinking of joining Kays catalogue.'

Diane went to the far corner of the salon and sat on the bay-window bench seat. "'Ow come?'

Amelia sighed and looked a little anxious. 'Well, Ted was in the Post Office this morning and he gave me a Freepost coupon from his *TV Times*. It said that with your first order you would get a Sunbeam electric blanket – a double-bed size.'

Diane lit up a John Player King Size cigarette and blew the smoke above her head. 'Sounds a bargain t'me,' she said.

'I haven't got a double bed, Diane.'

Diane smiled. 'Maybe it's time y'got one, Amelia.'

'Do you think so?'

Diane took a last puff, nipped the glowing end of her cigarette and placed it carefully in the ash tray on the coffee table next to the pile of *Woman's Weekly* magazines. 'Good men don't grow on trees an' you'd 'ave t'be blind not t'see 'e's smitten.'

There was a long silence while Diane removed the rollers from Amelia's hair. Finally, Amelia spoke. 'We've only cuddled up to now, Diane.'

Diane let this statement hang in the air for a while. She had learned long ago that psychology was a key part of being a successful hairdresser. Finally she spoke. 'They sell lovely double beds at the Cavendish store in York – an' they deliver free an' put it up f'you in y'bedroom. That Rosie in t'mobile library told me.'

Amelia was silent while she weighed up the gravitas of this decision.

'He's taking me to the dance tomorrow,' she said.

Diane removed the final roller. 'Well . . . tell 'im 'e could 'elp y'choose.'

Amelia stared at her reflection in the mirror and smiled. Perhaps the time had come.

That evening, over a piping-hot casserole, Beth told me about her visit to the bank. I listened politely, but in the end I knew I could trust her decisions. She was mapping out a future and even talking about pensions. There were times when the taut strands of our relationship became unravelled and I didn't know why.

That evening we settled down in the lounge to watch

the *Nine o'Clock News* with John Humphrys. At the end, weatherman Ian McCaskill told us what we already knew – that tomorrow would be like Siberia. We switched over to ITV and our favourite advertisement came on. It was an advert for Yellow Pages and featured an elderly gentleman trying to locate a copy of *Fly Fishing* by J. R. Hartley. The poor man was trawling around various bookshops to no avail until his daughter gave him the Yellow Pages to browse through and locate a shop that had the book in stock – and viewers discovered that he was the author!

Beth switched back to BBC1 and stretched out with a glass of wine to enjoy *Remington Steele*. She went very quiet. I guessed she was tired – or maybe she was interested in Pierce Brosnan – so I took the opportunity to creep upstairs to check on John. It was at moments like this I recalled the whispered times of quiet memories. For me love was a living promise, a journey shared. I watched him breathe and knew the elation of fatherhood. I felt blessed.

On Saturday morning the tattered rags of cirrus clouds fluttered across a blue-grey sky. Beth and John drove into York and I decided to open up school so Clint Ramsbottom could set up his Disco Experience. However, a hot drink seemed a good idea, so I called in to Nora's Coffee Shop.

Two seventeen-year-olds, Claire Bradshaw and Anita Cuthbertson, were sitting at the table next to the juke-box singing along to Cindi Lauper's 'Girls Just Want to Have Fun'. Claire and Anita had been in my class when I first arrived in Ragley. "Ello, Sir,' they shouted in unison. Claire had her Chegger's Jogger headphone radio hanging round her neck. Anita had spent sixteen pence on a *Jackie* magazine and they were drooling over a picture of Wham! on the front cover after reading articles on Tears for Fears and Boy George.

I had just sat down with my coffee and a bacon sandwich at a table by the window when Little Malcolm walked in to spend a couple of minutes with the woman of his dreams while Big Dave called into the chemist.

'Malcolm,' said Dorothy in a loud voice, 'does my stomach look flatter when ah'm lying on m'back?'

Little Malcolm looked round, hoping no one could overhear this conversation and also wondering where it was heading. 'Yer allus look slim an' beautiful t'me, Dorothy.' Malcolm might be a vertically challenged refuse collector but he had learned a lot about female psychology during his time with Dorothy and he nodded in a self-congratulatory way.

'Well ah'm not sure it does, Malcolm,' said Dorothy.

'Y'reight there, Dorothy,' agreed Little Malcolm hurriedly. Dorothy frowned at him and Little Malcolm fleetingly considered that maybe his intuitive empathy for female psychology wasn't quite what he had imagined it was.

'What d'you mean, ah'm right?' demanded Dorothy.

'Well, ah think y'beautiful,' said Little Malcolm, resorting to a previously successful strategy.

Dorothy frowned again at Little Malcolm, only partially forgiving. Meanwhile, Nora, eager to get involved, left the task of arranging a plateful of two-day-old meringues and picked up Dorothy's magazine. '"Have a body like Victowia Pwincipal for only twenty-five pence,"' she read. '"Get into shape. Feel and look gweat."'

'You 'ave t'send a postal order t'Newton Abbot in Devon,' said Dorothy. 'What d'you think, Nora?'

'That Victowia Pwincipal is weally beautiful,' said Nora, 'an' it says it's a wevolutionawy new pwogwamme so it mus' be good.'

Dorothy turned the article round so Little Malcolm got a perfect view of the television star's shapely curves. 'An' it sez 'ere,' said Dorothy, 'that it's *isometric.*'

Malcolm shook his head. 'Me an' Dave don't use metric,' he said, 'jus' feet an' inches – an' furlongs an' miles, o' course, when w'go t'York races.'

Dorothy gave Malcolm her *well he's only a man* look and turned away to slice a crusty loaf.

Further down the High Street in Prudence Golightly's General Stores a topical conversation was taking place. 'Prudence,' said Freda Fazackerly in her usual no-nonsense manner, 'will y'be taking the 'alfpence off t'price of a loaf or roundin' it up?'

The Times had announced, 'Britain's least loved currency, the halfpence has now left the nation's purses after thirteen years of unpopularity,' and added that the Conservative MP Anthony Beaumont-Dark considered that most people didn't even pick them up when they dropped them! However, this wasn't the case in Ragley village, particularly for pensioners or anyone on a small budget, when even a halfpence counted.

'Well, it depends on the price I have to buy it,' said Prudence after consideration, 'but I'll always do my best to keep prices down whenever I can.'

'Ah bet they'll put price of a second-class stamp up,' said Margery Ackroyd. 'It's twelve and a half pence now.

Pound to a penny it'll be thirteen pence in no time.'

There were grumblings further down the queue. 'Ah pay thirty-seven and a half pence f'me dog licence,' said Betty Buttle. 'Ah bet that'll go up as well.'

Amelia Duff made no complaint. When the shop had emptied, for the first time in her life she purchased a Valentine's card. Then she took it home, propped it on the mantelpiece behind her Women's Institute Potato Champion trophy and realized she had a week to consider how to post it to a postman.

The dance was a great success. Beth and I left careful instructions for Natasha Smith, our babysitter, but she was clearly very capable after helping to bring up her little sister Hazel. I had finally decided upon an unadventurous checked shirt and jeans, while Beth looked stunning in a Doris Day outfit.

Little Malcolm looked the part in his drainpipe trousers, brocade waistcoat, bootlace tie and brothelcreeper shoes and spent most of the evening with his face pressed between Dorothy's breasts, swaying to Pat Boone records. Dave didn't like dressing up, so he wore one of his old suits and, as his fiancée Nellie was visiting her mother in Barnsley, he sat with Deke Ramsbottom, who had also arrived in his normal everyday clothes. Even so, as he looked like a cross between Roy Rogers and an extra from *Wagon Train*, he blended in well.

Clint Ramsbottom's Disco Experience comprised three coloured light bulbs and a scratchy record deck, but as he was working for nothing we couldn't complain. He played lots of Buddy Holly classics, including 'That'll Be the Day', 'Oh, Boy!' and 'True Love Ways', and everybody danced. Laura had come in a slinky Brigitte Bardot outfit and had immediately attracted the attention of Tom Dalton, dressed as a teenage rocker. They danced together briefly and, for the first time, Laura seemed to take an interest.

Later in the evening, Troy Phoenix sang a few songs minus his two Whalers, who had to work overtime at the bakery in York. When, much to everyone's relief, he finally took a break, he tried hard to impress Claire Bradshaw and Anita Cuthbertson. The five-foot-two-inch fishmonger, known locally as Norman Barraclough, told them, 'Ah were so good lookin' ah 'ad t'tek ugly tablets.' However, they remained unimpressed, not least because after driving his little white fish van all day he stank of Whitby cod.

'They're giving a free rock bun with every frothy coffee,' said Claire, in the hope of a free drink. Unfortunately, as Troy was only receiving the price of a fish supper for his efforts, it fell on deaf ears.

I tried to have a word with everyone who had supported the event and met up with Old Tommy Piercy. He nodded towards Vera and Ruby, who were together on the other side of the hall. 'Don't you fret about Ruby, young Mr Sheffield,' he said. 'That's t'way o' things. Bairns are born, old uns die an' life goes on. Ruby'll be fine. It's time f'grievin', but one day sun'll rise an' she'll smile again, you mark my words.'

Meanwhile, the bring-and-buy stall was creating considerable interest. Not for sale but on display was Prudence Golightly's ration book and her 1953 Coronation scrap album. However, considerable bartering was going on between the stall-holder, Sue Phillips, and her customers.

John Grainger, for a reason beyond Anne's com-prehension, had bought an October 1957 edition of the new *Practical Money Maker Magazine*, originally priced at one shilling and threepence, for twenty-five pence. On the cover, much to Anne's amusement, was a picture of an ecstatic father painting wooden toys, a not-quite-so-thrilled mother cutting up pieces of leather for a handbag, and a strange but perfectly coiffured little boy who must have spent every waking hour weaving baskets.

'There'll be some good ideas in here,' said John, but basket-weaving was not Anne's idea of renewing the spark in their marriage. She bought an old Horlicks poster but guessed the banner headline '*Guards Against Night Starvation*' would be lost on John.

There was a brisk trade for the many artefacts, which included an empty tin of Lyons Green Label Tea, a *Rupert Bear Annual*, a collection of *Eagle, Tiger, Bunty* and *Girl* comics, a Philip Harben cookery set, a Magic Robot that always pointed to the right answers, a box of Dinky toys and an *Emergency – Ward 10* nurse's uniform. The lonely bachelor, Maurice Tupham, bought the Archie Andrews ventriloquist doll, presumably for company, while Timothy Pratt purchased a Dan Dare spaceship kit, apparently a working model and powered by a Jetex motor, for his dear friend Walter Crapper.

After the last dance, a smooch to 'Raining in My Heart', Beth went to help Anne, Sally and Vera to clear up. Laura was in conversation with Tom in the middle of the dance floor and then looked up and caught my eye. After a hurried farewell that left Tom looking a little crestfallen, she collected her long leather fur-lined coat and came over to me. 'I'm going now, Jack,' she said. She searched in her pocket and took out her car keys. 'I'm parked on the High Street – will you walk me to my car?'

'Of course,' I said.

As we stepped out in the freezing darkness a monochrome world of grey ice stretched out before us and we walked in silence down the cobbled drive. Above us, over the vast plain of York, the clouds were a silver shroud in the moonlight. Laura was deep in thought and when we reached her car she stood there as still as her moon-shadow. Then, true to her quixotic character, she took my hand and looked up at the sky where the stars, like far-off fireflies, held steadfast in the firmament. 'Do you ever wonder, Jack?'

'Wonder?'

She turned to face me. 'About how everything has worked out. You and me and Beth . . . a cosy solution.'

'What do you mean?'

She squeezed my hand. 'Jack, be the man you want to be – life is slipping away.'

'Laura . . . I don't understand.'

We stood there under the deep purple sky, two souls in a world of confusion. She stretched up and kissed me gently on the cheek. 'You never did, Jack . . . you never did.'

'I always thought of us as friends.'

'Did you?'

'Yes, of course, what else would we be?'

'What else would you like it to be, Jack?' Her eyes shone in the moonlight.

'Laura – I'm happily married . . . and I love Beth.'

'I thought you loved me once.'

'Did you?'

'Yes, and I loved you.'

There was silence. The full moon, like an oculus in the dark heavens, lit up the bare trees above us and cast sharp, ghostly shadows at our feet with an eerie light.

'Your turn will come, Laura,' I said. 'The right man is out there waiting for you and you'll know it when you meet him.'

'Maybe I already have, Jack.'

I watched the lights of her car slowly fade as she drove down the High Street and back to York.

When I walked back up the drive I saw Nora Pratt standing alone, deep in thought. She appeared upset. 'What's the matter, Nora?' I asked quietly.

'Ah'm fine, Mr Sheffield,' she said, 'don't mind me. It were jus' that "Waining in My 'aht" bwought back memowies of my Fwank.'

'Frank?'

''E were my boyfwiend an' ah loved 'im.'

'And what happened, Nora?'

''E thought 'e loved someone else.'

I watched her walk away under a vast sky studded with sentinel stars and I reflected that life was complicated.

There were loose ends . . . and unfulfilled promises.

Chapter Thirteen

Dorothy's Dirty Weekend

County Hall sent invitations for two members of staff to attend the weekend conference in the summer term at High Sutton Hall entitled 'A Vision of the Curriculum'.

Extract from the Ragley School Logbook:
Friday, 2 March 1984

It was early Friday morning, 2 March, and in Nora's Coffee Shop Queen's 'Radio Ga Ga' was blasting out from the red and chrome juke-box.

'Ah love that "Wadio Ga Ga",' said Nora, ''specially that Fweddie Me'cuwy,' but Dorothy didn't reply. Usually she would sing along and file her nails in time to the beat, but this morning was different. Her *Smash Hits* magazine lay unopened on the counter. It featured photos of Culture Club, Duran Duran, Michael Jackson, David Bowie, Billy Joel and The Police – but Dorothy's mind was elsewhere. She had a *book*.

It was rare for Dorothy to be seen with a book and Nora looked up from scraping the residue of a cheese sandwich from the Breville toaster and peered myopically at the cover. Then she gave a gasp. The title read *The Dirty Weekend Book* and Nora hurried to the stool next to Dorothy to share in its delights. Soon they were reading the tips for young lovers.

'Lots o' ideas 'ere,' said Dorothy as she began to read chapter one. 'Ah wanted t'pick one an' s'prise my Malcolm wi' it.'

'Sounds weally womantic, Dowothy,' said Nora. 'Wonder who wote it?'

Unknown to them, five women had collaborated to write a sexy hotel guide for a perfect dirty weekend. One of the authors, Charlotte Du Cann, niece of the Tory MP Edward Du Cann, said, 'It's not a smutty book and all the boyfriends we took knew they were taking part in the research.' It was also reported that Mrs Pamela Nell, who ran the Highbullen Hotel in Chittlehamholt in Devon, after appearing in the guide, said, 'Thirty years ago we would never have accepted an unmarried couple – but nowadays, who cares!'

'Dunno, Nora,' said Dorothy, 'but ah thought a weekend away from Big Dave would do 'im good. Ah wanted it t'be diff'rent an' exciting an' it'd be a bit o' *private* time, if y'get m'meanin.'

'Oooh, ah do,' said Nora, 'an' y'never know – 'e might pwopose.'

Three miles away, as I drove on the back road from Kirkby Steepleton to Ragley village, the heavy mist that had hung over the countryside slowly cleared and the distant Hambleton hills came into view.

The season was changing. The last of the snow had

gone and early spring sunshine promised warmer times ahead. Snowdrops, aconites and crocuses brightened the new grass in the fields with a splash of colour and the sticky buds on the horse chestnut trees were cracking open. Soon new shoots of lime and ash would burst into life. Rooks cawed loudly in the elm-tops and the first primroses brightened Ragley village green. In the General Stores, Margery Ackroyd was telling a disbelieving Prudence Golightly that she had heard the first cuckoo. The days of winter were over. The dark days were behind us.

When I drove up the High Street the local refuse wagon was parked outside Nora's Coffee Shop and Big Dave and Little Malcolm were hurrying in for a mug of tea and a hot buttered teacake before work. They waved a cheery greeting as my familiar Morris Minor Traveller trundled past.

Tom Dalton was in the school office with Anne and they were checking a list on a clipboard. Our new member of staff had settled in well. He was clearly a very good teacher and had begun to take on extra responsibility. Since Jo Hunter had left Tom had become our unofficial staff entertainment officer.

'I've checked with the Odeon Cinema, Jack,' he said 'and we've got a block booking.' A night out for staff and partners had been organized and we were going to see *Educating Rita*, starring Michael Caine and Julie Walters.

'Thanks, Tom. Let me know if I can help with transport,' I offered.

'All sorted, Jack,' he said with a smile.

*

Meanwhile, across the High Street in Nora's Coffee Shop, Big Dave went to sit at his usual table while Little Malcolm approached the counter and looked up at the woman of his dreams.

Dorothy hid *The Dirty Weekend Book* under the counter. "Ello, Malcolm,' she said.

"Ow are you, Dorothy?' he asked.

'Well, Malcolm, 'ah've been thinking about this weekend,' she said, recalling one of the tips in the book, 'when Dave goes t'stay wi' Nellie in York.'

'We can 'ave the 'ouse to ourselves,' said Malcolm hopefully.

'Ah know, Malcolm – an' ah'm gonna 'ave one o' them posh baths wi' bubbles an' foam an' all that,' said Dorothy.

Little Malcolm's eyes widened and he almost forgot to order two toasted teacakes with their teas. 'It sounds reight wonderful, Dorothy.'

'Ah've got m'Tahiti Foam Bath,' she said, reaching down behind the counter and selecting a bottle from her overflowing *Fame* shoulder bag. She read the label and nodded in satisfaction. 'It sez it's got monoï in it.'

'Money?'

'No, Malcolm, *monoï* . . . it's why women in Tahiti 'ave smooth skin.'

'So 'xactly, er, what is it?' asked Little Malcolm.

'Dunno, Malcolm, but it'll mek me like them women in t'South Seas.'

'But ah like you jus' t'way you are, Dorothy,' he said.

In Dorothy's eyes Little Malcolm had just pressed the right button and she looked at him as if he were the perfect man – namely, Shakin' Stevens with a Donny Osmond smile.

'Oy, lover-boy!' shouted Big Dave. 'Gerra move on. Y'like love's young dream. Where's m'tea?'

The spell was broken and Dorothy poured the tea.

The squeaky castors of our music centre could be heard as Anne wheeled it across the floor. From the box of her and Sally's carefully selected collection of LPs, Anne chose 'Spring' from Antonio Vivaldi's *Four Seasons*, slid it carefully out of its cardboard sleeve and then placed it on the circular rubber mat on the revolving turntable. She adjusted the dial to 33 revolutions per minute, then lowered the plastic arm until the stylus settled into the black grooves at the beginning of the track and the opening bars drifted through the still air of our crowded school hall.

At the end of Joseph's assembly, on the theme of asking for forgiveness for wrongdoings, a thoughtful Harold Bustard approached him. Harold had been envious of the Raleigh BMX Burner that Ben Roberts had got for Christmas.

"Scuse me, Mr Evans,' he said politely.

'What is it, Harold?' asked Joseph, pleased to be asked a question by this curious little boy with hair like a shoe-brush and ears like the FA Cup.

'Well, ah'd like t'ask God for a bike,' confided Harold.

'Ah well – I don't think He would want you to do that,' said Joseph with a reassuring smile.

'Well, 'ow about ah steal one an' ask f'forgiveness?'

It was at times like this that Joseph considered his communication skills with young children were not what they used to be.

*

At morning break in the staff-room Vera frowned as she looked at the front page of her *Daily Telegraph*. There was plenty of news. England soccer fans had run riot in France and Mick Jagger was about to become a father for the third time as Jerry Hall was rushed into a New York hospital.

However, it was another article that caught her eye. 'Oh dear,' she said almost to herself. Half of Britain's 187,000 miners had downed tools and the venerable Margaret was facing a problem.

'What is it, Vera?' asked Sally.

'Problems with the miners,' said Vera, shaking her head.

'The miners' leader, Arthur Scargill, was on television last night, Vera,' said Sally, 'and he sounded really determined.'

'Never fear,' said Vera confidently. 'Margaret will soon sort out that dreadful man.' She looked again at the photograph. 'And no one with a hairstyle like that can ever be trusted.'

Sally smiled and shook her head. Sometimes it simply wasn't worth the bother.

Back in Nora's Coffee Shop, Dorothy was flicking through an old copy of *Smash Hits* magazine. She had read the articles on Queen, Tracey Ullman and Kajagoogoo and was now staring at the front-cover photograph of Madonna.

'What y'stawin' at, Dowothy?' asked Nora.

'Madonna's 'air, Nora,' said Dorothy, her gaze still fixed on the sexy American rock star. 'Ah'm 'avin' me 'air done when Ruby's daughter covers for me an' that's 'ow ah want mine t'look.'

'Well . . . ah can't say ah'm impwessed,' said Nora with unwitting correctness.

Dorothy was not to be deterred. 'Ah like it 'cause it's sort of wild but nat'ral.'

'Mebbe so, Dowothy,' said Nora, 'but it could 'ave been waining when she 'ad 'er photo taken.'

At lunchtime we gathered in the staff-room. Tom had just bought the March edition of *Your Computer* magazine and was completely engrossed.

'Looks interesting,' I said, but without conviction.

'It is, Jack,' he said. 'A great article here about graphics extensions for BBC, Dragon and Spectrum.'

A new vocabulary had emerged and we were being left behind. 'Oh, that's good,' I said and both Sally and Anne nodded in agreement. It occurred to me that Tom appeared to have won over the hearts and minds of the female staff.

Sally gave a secret smile and settled back to read her *Daily Mirror*. She was delighted that Tony Benn was back in parliament as the new Labour MP for Chesterfield, while the Chancellor, Nigel Lawson, was attracting unpopularity with his intention to tax beer, cigarettes and even fish and chips. She ignored the provocative photograph of the seventeen-year-old model Samantha Fox in a string vest and studied the article about Rula Lenska moving in with her heart-throb, Dennis Waterman.

Ten miles away in York, Beth had responded to an earlier telephone call from Tom by dialling her sister's number in the Liberty fashion department.

'Yes, I'd love to come,' said Laura. 'I'm free tonight and

I'll try to get away in time – and did you say it was Tom who's organizing it?'

A sister-to-sister confidence was exchanged.

'Yes,' said Laura, 'I suppose he is.'

A short distance away Ruby's daughter Racquel was also in York, at the Currys sale. She wanted to cheer up her mother, who had been down for so long. While the electric Rowenta iron at £15.99 was a definite temptation, the offer of £500 in credit was almost too good to resist.

Soon she was in discussion with the shop assistant, completely unaware that, for the long years that lay ahead, this was the day she began a life of debt.

Meanwhile, on the school playground two eight-year-olds, Mary Scrimshaw and Sonia Tricklebank, were deep in conversation.

'This morning t'vicar said that God listens to our prayers,' said Mary thoughtfully.

'Y'right, 'e did,' agreed Sonia.

'We could say a prayer,' said Mary.

'OK,' said Sonia and she clasped her hands and closed her eyes.

'Thank you God for t'pancakes we 'ad f'lunch,' said Mary.

'But we 'ad liver an' onions,' said Sonia.

'Ah know,' said Mary. 'Ah'm jus' checkin' 'e's listening.'

Suddenly they saw a dead bird on the school field. 'What 'appened t'the bird?' asked Sonia.

'Mr Evans says when y'die y'go to 'eaven,' said Mary.

There was a long silence while Sonia stared dubiously

at the sky and then back to the little bird. 'So did God throw 'im back down then?'

Dorothy Humpleby was outlining her lips with a soft pencil, making sure it was a tone darker than her lipstick. After all, perfect coordination was a sign of the new eighties woman. After spending her lunchbreak in Diane's Hair Salon, she had returned to the counter looking as though she had been dragged through a hedge backwards. Little Malcolm was about to order two pork pies for himself, while Big Dave sat at a nearby table and read the sports page of the *Sun*.

"Ave y'noticed summat diff'rent, Malcolm?' asked Dorothy.

Little Malcolm was perplexed. He had noticed that Dorothy's hair looked like a rook's nest after a thunderstorm but, that apart, she looked just the same.

'It's yer 'air, Dorothy.' Fortunately he didn't elaborate.

'Oooh, Malcolm,' said Dorothy, 'ah 'oped you'd like it. It's m'Madonna look.'

A perplexed Malcolm put two pork pies in the pockets of his donkey jacket and picked up two mugs of sweet tea.

'Why's 'er 'air like that?' asked Big Dave when Little Malcolm sat down.

'She wants it to look like that little bloke what plays f'Argentina,' explained Little Malcolm.

Big Dave's knowledge of football was unsurpassed in Ragley village. 'Y'mean Maradona?'

'That's 'im, Dave,' said Little Malcolm.

*

226

Dorothy wasn't the only one seeking to impress. 'Don't worry, Vicky,' said Terry Earnshaw with the confidence of youth. 'Ah know 'ow t'be posh like you. Ah asked our 'Eathcliffe.'

'And what did he say?' asked Victoria Alice, unaware until now that she was posh.

'Well,' said Terry in a conspiratorial whisper, ''e sez if y'put *axshully* at t'start of a sentence, then you've cracked it.'

'Actually?' repeated Victoria Alice, looking perplexed.

'Yeah – axshully,' repeated Terry.

'I see,' said Victoria Alice . . . but she didn't.

The afternoon ended with story time in each class. Anne was reading *The Tale of Squirrel Nutkin*, Tom had his children enthralled with *Charlie and the Chocolate Factory*, Sally was acting out an Alan Garner folktale and I was reading *Prince Caspian* by C. S. Lewis. You could have heard a pin drop.

When the bell rang for the end of school Michelle Cathcart and Louise Hartley came up to me. 'Thanks for t'lovely story, Mr Sheffield,' said Michelle.

'Ah love C. S. Lewis,' said Louise. 'Ah'm going t'read all 'is books one day.'

'So am I – 'cause we're friends,' said Michelle.

'And ah'm going t'Michelle's house, Mr Sheffield, t'watch television and have m'tea,' said Louise.

'It's *Grange Hill* tonight at five past five,' said Michelle.

'And it's t'end-of-term dance,' said Louise.

'Then after tea at twenty to seven it's *Doctor Who*,' said Michelle.

'It's t'last part of *Planet o' Fire*, Mr Sheffield,' added Louise, 'so it'll be good.'

'But t'best bit is that we do t'cooking and make t'tea,' said Michelle. They ran off excitedly . . . completely unaware that they were destined to be friends for life.

I was in Anne's classroom when I noticed Mary Cartwright, mother of Charlie, and Connie Crapper, mother of Patience, walking up the drive and heading for Tom's classroom.

'Jack, a quiet word,' said Anne mysteriously. 'We need to keep an eye on that.'

'What is it, Anne?' I asked, puzzled.

'It's about Tom . . . I'm beginning to have a concern,' she said quietly. 'He's clearly a very conscientious teacher who is always willing to discuss a pupil's progress. However, he is also a *very good-looking man* and some of our younger mothers have begun to call in frequently, supposedly to discuss their child. It would appear that for some of them any excuse will do. I'm sure he's completely unaware,' she gave me a firm and meaningful look, 'so a word from you might be appropriate.'

'Thanks, Anne. I'll pick my moment.'

As darkness fell the children were back in their homes and in the Earnshaw household an interesting conversation had begun in the kitchen.

'T'vicar was tellin' us abart Jesus an' 'is disciples wi' Easter comin' up,' said Terry to his brother.

''E told us abart 'em when ah were in Mr Sheffield's class,' said Heathcliffe.

''E said t'worst disciple was that Judas Asparagus or summat.'

'Now that's a vegetable ah really 'ate,' said Mrs Earnshaw. 'We 'ad some at yer Aunty Mavis's an' ah were on t'toilet f'two days.'

'Y'mother's reight,' shouted Mr Earnshaw from the lounge.

Terry leaned round the kitchen door and looked at his father sitting in his armchair reading his *Racing Post*. 'Anyway, Dad, 'e were let down badly, were Jesus,' said Terry.

'Was 'e?' muttered Mr Earnshaw without raising his eyes from checking the runners and riders.

''Cause o' that Judas Asparagus an' that Pon-shus,' said Terry.

'It were *Pontius* . . . 'e were a pilot,' said Mr Earnshaw from behind his paper. He gave the contented nod of a father who imparts wisdom with the innate confidence of all misguided men who believe they know it all.

'Tek no notice of y'dad,' said Mrs Earnshaw, ''e knows nowt.'

'Knows nowt,' repeated Dallas Sue-Ellen.

Mrs Earnshaw was making pancakes and Heathcliffe and Terry were crowding round the old gas cooker, their noses almost in the frying pan, while Dallas Sue-Ellen stared vacantly at *Rainbow* on ITV.

'So what did y'learn at school t'day?' asked Mrs Earnshaw.

Terry scratched his head and fragments of dried mud and grass fell into the pancake mix. However, Mrs Earnshaw had been brought up to believe that a little muck hurt no one so, undeterred, she continued to stir.

'Well, Mam,' said Terry, 'we was doin' about Jesus an' t'Easter story wi' t'vicar.'

'We did that las' year,' said Heathcliffe. 'In fac', we did Jesus ev'ry year at Easter an' Christmas.'

'So what did t'vicar say?' asked Mrs Earnshaw.

'It were 'is las' supper, Mam – jus' 'im an' 'is d'ciples – an' they didn't 'ave pancakes.'

'Well, they wunt 'ave been invented then,' said Heathcliffe knowingly. Since moving on to secondary school he regarded himself as the fount of all knowledge in the Earnshaw household.

'Mam?' pleaded Terry.

'What?' said Mrs Earnshaw, shoving the rusty spatula under the first pancake.

'Can ah 'ave t'first pancake, Mam?' asked Terry.

'*Please* can ah 'ave t'first pancake, Mam, *please*?' said Heathcliffe, remembering that if you said *please* to Miss Golightly in the shop you usually benefitted.

Mrs Earnshaw tapped them both on their heads with the spatula. 'Do y'know, boys,' she said, 'if Jesus were 'ere, 'e would say "Let my brother 'ave t'first pancake."'

Terry frowned as he tried to work this out.

As usual Heathcliffe was quicker off the mark. 'OK, Mam,' he said. Then he turned to his brother. 'Terry – you can be Jesus.'

Meanwhile, in the Post Office, Amelia Duff was reading the *Daily Mirror*. She had opened it to the *Dear Marje* agony-aunt column featuring the acerbic wit of Marjorie Proops.

Underneath the letter that began, 'I am a 34-year-old and I'm in love with my daughter's boyfriend' was another of particular interest. It simply read, 'I am a mature 59-year-old lady who wishes to have a relationship with a man for the first time' and Amelia thought *that could be me.*

She looked at the clock. Ted the postman was coming round for his tea. Ted liked Amelia's experimental cooking and tonight she had prepared oriental bacon rolls with spinach. She wondered if she might push the boat out and welcome him with a refreshing cocktail of one part chilled white wine with one part soda water. *You never know where it might lead.*

Back at Bilbo Cottage there was barely time for me to wheel John up and down the hallway in his baby walker that he loved so much. At almost eight months he was now a strong little boy and could push himself up from a sitting position.

However, Natasha Smith soon arrived to babysit and Beth and I changed quickly for our night out in York. As always, Beth looked lovely. She had volunteered to drive and we squeezed into her Volkswagen Beetle. Her confident, speedy driving was a feature as she negotiated the busy Friday-evening traffic through the city centre and we parked on the approach to Micklegate Bar, one of the four great stone gateways to the city. As we walked along this wonderful medieval street I recalled its gruesome history. In the fifteenth century the head of the Duke of York was put on a spike and displayed on top of the highest turret so that, in the words of William Shakespeare, 'York may over look the town of York'.

We hurried across to Blossom Street and the Odeon Cinema, where a smiling Tom was waiting outside. He was casually dressed in an old St Peter's School rugby shirt, blue jeans and a waxed Barbour jacket. 'Everyone is here, Jack,' he said and gave me two tickets. 'You're sitting on the end of the row with Anne, John, Vera and the major, and I'm in front of you with Sally and Colin, plus Dan and Jo. I've put Dan in the aisle seat as he's so tall,' he added with a grin.

'Thanks, Tom,' I said.

He had a single ticket left in his hand. 'And this is for Laura in case she turns up.'

We hurried in and I whispered to Beth, 'I didn't know Laura was coming.'

Beth appeared unconcerned as we looked for our seats. 'Tom rang me and asked for her number. She'll enjoy the night out.'

When we sat down Sally passed round a large bag of sherbet lemons and there was animated conversation as we all exchanged greetings. Everyone was in excellent spirits and it was good to relax together. Suddenly Tom arrived with Laura. Dan and I were in the aisle seats and we stood up.

'Hello, everybody,' said Laura. 'Thanks for the invitation.' She slipped off her charcoal-grey maxi-length leather coat. 'Sorry – a bit of a rush,' she said by way of apology. Laura wore a blue denim shirt with a red knotted neckscarf, and a brown suede waistcoat with skin-tight Burberry jeans and calf-length black leather boots. She looked stunning, and her high cheekbones were flushed after her brisk walk from Liberty in the sharp northerly wind. Her green eyes looked at me steadily. 'Hello, Jack, hi, Beth,' she said and kissed us both on the cheek. I could smell her perfume, Opium by Yves Saint Laurent, and it brought back certain memories. She took the spare seat between Tom and Jo in the row in front and waved a brief greeting as the lights dimmed and we settled back for *Educating Rita*.

I knew the story well, having read Willy Russell's stage play. Michael Caine was superb as Frank Bryant, the self-loathing drunken professor of literature, and Julie Walters was perfectly cast as Rita, the 'ah-wanna-learn' hairdresser, a working-class woman who wants to find some meaning to her life. As the film reached its climax in the airport, with Frank about to board his plane, there was that iconic moment as Rita paused at the end of the corridor. She turned and looked back and we were left wondering if their unfulfilled relationship would ever be rekindled. I noticed Tom whisper something to Laura and she turned to look at me. The credits rolled, the lights came on, the spell was broken and midst a hubbub of conversation we made our way out into the street.

'Would you like to come back to my place for coffee?' offered Laura.

Everybody except Tom seemed to want to get home for one reason or another. 'I live close by so I'm free,' said Tom eagerly.

I looked at Beth. 'Well, we don't have to get straight home, do we?'

Beth looked at her watch. 'We can't be late for the babysitter, Jack.' She gave her sister a hug. 'So see you next week, maybe for lunch,' she said.

'Fine,' said Laura. She glanced at me. 'Goodnight, Jack,' she said and looked at Tom, then they walked off together.

*

At midnight Little Malcolm had long since given up trying to repair the boiler. Dorothy's hopes of a luxurious bathtime had been dashed and the first chapter of her *Dirty Weekend Book* had not been fully realized. As they snuggled up next to each other for warmth Dorothy wondered if chapter two might prove to be a little more exciting.

Meanwhile, as the bells of York Minster chimed the late hour, outside Laura's apartment on a quiet road near the museum gardens, parked close to her brand-new Nissan Micra, was a rusty royal-blue Renault 4. The engine was cold and would remain so for a long time.

Chapter Fourteen

The Miner's Daughter

A new temporary admission, Debbie Harrison, age eight, commenced full-time education in Class 3. Mrs Pringle and the headteacher accepted an invitation to view the new Jorvik Viking Centre in York on Saturday morning, 31 March. The school choir and orchestra are to perform at the Mothering Sunday Service at 11.00 a.m. in St Mary's Church on Sunday, 1 April.

Extract from the Ragley School Logbook:
Friday, 30 March 1984

It was Vera who saw her first and beckoned me to the office window. 'This must be the new girl, Mr Sheffield,' she said.

Debbie Harrison arrived at Ragley on the last school day in March. She was a sturdy, fair-haired eight-year-old and she was clinging nervously to her mother's hand. They were accompanied by Mrs Doreen Critchley, our dinner lady, and she looked in a determined mood as they arrived at the school gates.

It had been a long, cold winter but now the season had changed and the promise of light, colour and warmth stretched out before us. The little girl was staring up in wonderment at the horse chestnut trees that bordered the school wall. The sticky buds were coming alive and, around their gnarled trunks on the grassy mounds, the first daffodils were raising their bright yellow trumpets to a powder-blue sky. Her mother, a slim woman in a warm coat and a knotted headscarf, crouched down beside her and pointed back towards the dancing heads of primroses on the village green. The bond between mother and daughter was clear. Doreen pointed towards the entrance door and they walked up the cobbled school drive towards it. Vera turned from the window, looking thoughtful.

'What is it, Vera?' I asked.

Vera glanced down at her spiral-bound notepad. 'It's the new temporary admission, Mr Sheffield,' she said, '. . . the miner's daughter.'

As they say in Yorkshire, Doreen Critchley was never backwards in coming forwards. With a confident rat-a-tat on the office door she walked in.

'G'morning, Mr Sheffield,' she said. 'This is m'sister, Meg 'Arrison from Barnsley. She's staying with us 'til t'Easter 'olidays.'

The likeness between the two sisters was obvious, but whereas Doreen had the physique of a night-club bouncer, Meg Harrison was slim and gaunt. 'Ah spoke t'Mrs F a while back about young Debbie coming 'ere for a couple o' weeks,' added Doreen.

'Yes, it's all in order,' I said.

'That's correct,' confirmed Vera, holding up the file. 'All the paperwork has been completed.'

'So welcome to Ragley, Mrs Harrison,' I said and we shook hands. 'I'm Jack Sheffield, the headteacher, and this is our secretary, Mrs Forbes-Kitchener.'

Vera glanced at Doreen. 'As it's a bit of a mouthful, I answer to Mrs F,' she said with a smile.

Meg Harrison nodded shyly in response. 'An' this is my Debbie,' she said.

I looked at the little girl. Her clothes were old and faded but spotlessly clean and her hair was perfect in two neat plaits. It was evident that Mrs Harrison took pride in her daughter's appearance. 'And I'm sure you will be happy here, Debbie.'

'Say thank you t'Mr Sheffield,' prompted Mrs Harrison.

'Thank you, Mr Sheffield,' said Debbie politely.

Earlier in the week I had contacted the headteacher of Debbie Harrison's school in the South Yorkshire authority. It had been an interesting conversation. Then I had discussed Debbie's temporary admission with our Education Welfare Officer, Roy Davidson, and he had confirmed the arrangement.

'Ah'm really grateful, Mr Sheffield,' said Mrs Harrison as she removed her headscarf. 'Y'look to 'ave a lovely school.'

'Thank you,' I said, genuinely touched by the compliment. 'One thing is certain,' I looked at the towering presence of Doreen and smiled, 'we have the best school dinners in North Yorkshire.'

Doreen nodded. 'It's a fact is that,' she said – and she meant it. 'Well, ah best get on, Mr Sheffield,' she went on, glancing at her sister. 'Y'know where I am, Meg,' and she walked out into the entrance hall.

'Well, Mrs Harrison,' I said, 'there are a few things we need to discuss.'

She looked down at her daughter. 'It's awkward, Mr Sheffield.'

'I understand, so we'll get Debbie settled first.'

Vera responded as I knew she would. 'I'll ask Mrs Pringle to call in, Mr Sheffield,' she said and hurried out.

Moments later Sally tapped on the door and walked in with eight-year-old Mary Scrimshaw. She introduced herself to Mrs Harrison and then crouched down.

'Hello, Debbie, I'm Mrs Pringle and I'm going to be your teacher,' she said, 'and this is Mary. She's the same age as you and you'll be sitting on her table.'

The two girls, both the same height, looked at each other and smiled. Sally had chosen well. 'Would y'like to see where t'put your coat?' asked Mary. 'We've got t'names above our coat pegs and we can make a label f'yours.'

'Yes, please,' said Debbie.

'Call in to class before you go, Mrs Harrison,' said Sally as she was leaving, 'so you can see that Debbie is fine.' The ice was broken and Debbie held hands with Mary as they followed Sally back to class.

'Mrs Harrison,' I said, 'we'll do everything we can to make sure your daughter is happy here for the short time she is with us. The headteacher of Debbie's school in Cortonwood explained the situation to me and we understand why you're here. I know these are difficult times for you and we'll do our best.'

'Ah'm extremely grateful, Mr Sheffield,' she said and clearly meant it.

'I have to get back to my class now,' I said, glancing up

at the clock, 'so I'll leave you with Mrs Forbes-Kitchener to sort out arrangements for school dinners and any queries you may have.' I set off back to class as the bell rang to begin another school day.

Mrs Harrison looked at Vera. 'Ah'm sorry for the extra work we've caused you, Mrs F, but my 'usband *insisted* we come t'live wi' Doreen for a bit 'til things 'ave settled down, an' it's probably for t'best.'

'Do sit down, Mrs Harrison, and don't worry,' Vera said quietly. 'Debbie will be well looked after in Ragley School.'

Meg Harrison looked at Vera nervously. 'Debbie doesn't know yet,' she said.

'Doesn't know?' asked Vera.

She sighed as if she was carrying the weight of the world on her shoulders. 'Yes, Mrs F – she doesn't know 'er dad was one o' t'thirty-seven pickets arrested last Monday.'

Vera recognized a troubled soul when she saw one. 'Would you like a cup of tea?' she said.

Little did we know it, but at that moment Sergeant Dan Hunter was in a packed minibus driving south on the A1 to provide police reinforcements against the miners.

He was reflecting how fast everything had escalated. At the beginning of March the Coal Board chiefs had announced, 'Cortonwood Colliery must close in five weeks' and, in doing so, had lit the blue touchpaper for strike action throughout the British coalfields. A few days later the Yorkshire branch of the National Union of Miners announced strike action for its fifty-eight thousand members following the last shift on Friday, 9 March.

The following day the chairman, Ian MacGregor, issued his infamous closure programme, demanding a cut of twenty thousand jobs in the coming year. Durham, Kent and South Wales miners met and called their miners out, while Yorkshire miners from Armthorpe departed to pits in Nottinghamshire and, in doing so, defied a High Court injunction banning flying pickets.

The first martyr of the strike was David Gareth Jones, a twenty-four-year-old miner at Ackton Hall pit in Yorkshire, when he was killed on the picket line at Ollerton. Five thousand miners from all over the country attended an emotional funeral at South Kirkby on 23 March. Later, busloads of police were drafted in and at an illegal road block thirty-seven men were arrested. John Harrison was one of them.

Margaret Thatcher had spoken in Birmingham about 'rolling back the frontiers of socialism' and Dan Hunter knew the situation would get worse before a resolution was achieved. As they rumbled along he glanced up at a flapping bedsheet draped over a roadbridge. Large letters had been painted on it and the message for the police was clear. It read 'Thatcher's Thugs'.

Dan settled back in his seat and worried about the day's work that lay ahead. As the miles sped by he thought of his upbringing in the village of Pity Me in County Durham, where his brother Tom still lived. The name of the village had caused amusement in the past. Now, sadly, it appeared ironic – Tom was a miner.

In the school office Mrs Harrison was sipping tea and feeling more relaxed. 'I appreciate this, Mrs F,' she said.

Vera glanced down at the notes from the Education

Welfare Officer attached to Debbie's admission form. 'So he was arrested,' she said quietly.

'John's strong as an ox,' said Meg Harrison with obvious pride, 'but 'e's never raised a finger t'me or Debbie, or anyone f'that matter. 'E's a good man but t'best of us can get desperate.'

'I understand,' said Vera.

''E jus' stood there chanting,' said Mrs Harrison. Her voice was breaking. 'Ah'm afraid 'e 'ates Margaret Thatcher.'

There was an intake of breath from Vera. '"Hate" is a strong word,' she said pointedly.

'Ah know – but that's 'ow 'e feels,' said Meg Harrison. 'As for m'self, ah jus' think there mus' be a better way.'

'I'm sure there is,' said Vera. 'Perhaps the miners don't understand what Mrs Thatcher is trying to do.'

Mrs Harrison shook her head. 'My John is a fourth-generation miner in our village an' 'e's a proud man. 'E believes she's destroying our community.'

'I suppose Mrs Thatcher is thinking what's best for the *whole* country,' said Vera.

'Mebbe so, but me an' John jus' want our Debbie to 'ave a good life an' do well at school. That's what's important to us – but we need t'earn a living first.' Mrs Harrison clasped her fingers together as if in prayer. 'We're prepared t'work 'ard, but my John knows nowt else but working in t'pit. That's all 'e's' done since 'e were a lad.'

'We'll all do our best to help, Mrs Harrison,' said Vera, 'and have no fear, your daughter will be fine at Ragley School.' She glanced at the clock. 'Morning assembly is about to start. Let's go in and sit at the back and then you'll be able to see that Debbie is settled.'

Vera took Mrs Harrison into the school hall, where Sally's choir were singing a song from her new large spiral-bound singing book entitled *Game Songs*. Much to Meg Harrison's delight, her daughter Debbie was sharing a printed copy of the words with Mary Scrimshaw and they were singing in loud confident voices:

> *Take a little bit of yellow*
> *And a little bit of blue,*
> *Put it in a bowl and mix it up do,*
> *We've got a colour we've never had before,*
> *What have we got? We've got green.*

Vera and Mrs Harrison stayed for a few minutes, then crept out. Debbie gave a little wave that meant *I'm all right* and Meg Harrison looked relieved.

'Call back before the end of school, Mrs Harrison,' said Vera, 'and I'll take you to Debbie's classroom to collect her.'

'You've been very kind, Mrs F,' she said and hurried off, leaving Vera deep in thought.

After assembly Joseph was in my class, telling the Easter story. He had explained in some detail the idea of Lent, the period from Ash Wednesday to Good Friday. However, it was the notion of doing without something you liked that provoked immediate discussion.

'Ah 'ave t'do wi'out choc'late, Mr Evans, an' ah love choc'late,' said Ben Roberts plaintively.

'I do understand, Benjamin,' said Joseph, 'but it is an important sacrifice.'

'But ah 'ad t'do wi'out crisps las' year an' ah love crisps

242

an' all,' added Ben for good measure. Ben didn't know what *pathos* meant, but it underpinned every utterance.

'Er, well, that's good as well,' said Joseph, slightly concerned that Ben was rapidly becoming the class martyr.

However, Ben wasn't finished. 'An' nex' year ah'll prob'ly 'ave t'do wi'out summat else that ah like.'

'Yes, that's very likely,' said Joseph. 'We have to do without something *every* year.'

'For t'rest of our lives?' asked Ben in astonishment.

'Well, er, yes,' mumbled Joseph.

'Dunt seem fair t'me, Mr Evans,' said Ben.

'Why not?' asked Joseph.

'Well, Jesus only 'ad t'go wi'out *once* – an' we've gorrit every bloomin' year.'

It wasn't so much the misplaced logic that concerned Joseph, rather the enthusiastic applause that greeted Ben's conclusion.

It was during an impromptu staff meeting at lunchtime that it was decided that Sally and I would take up the invitation from the Jorvik Centre in York to send two teachers from each local school on Saturday morning to visit this wonderful new tourist attraction.

'I'll meet you here in the school car park, Jack,' said Sally, 'and we can travel in together.' She was really enthusiastic and had already arranged to take parties of children when it opened officially next month.

The staff-room emptied, leaving just Anne and me listing the books we needed to supplement our Ginn Reading 360 reading scheme. 'Jack, I think I know why Tom didn't volunteer for tomorrow's visit,' she said.

I was puzzled. 'Why's that?' I asked.

'He's meeting Laura in York for coffee. I heard him telling Sally.' She gave me a long lingering and knowing look, and I prayed this wasn't going to become a problem.

At afternoon break Tom was on duty and I wandered out to the playground. He gave me that familiar relaxed smile. 'Season's changing, Jack,' he commented, glancing up at the branches of the horse chestnut trees above our heads.

I sighed. It was hard to know how to begin. 'Tom . . . you don't seem to be short of ladies to help you in the classroom.'

'There's a lot of support in the village,' he said, 'and, as the vicar mentioned in interview, we need to utilize the skills of the community.'

'That's right, we do,' I agreed, 'but we also need to be aware of the possible problems of becoming . . . well, *over familiar.*'

Light was dawning in his keen blue eyes. 'I would never do anything unprofessional, Jack,' he said hurriedly.

'I know that, Tom,' I said quietly. 'It's just friendly concern on my part. We always have to be careful in our dealings with parents. We need to listen but keep a professional distance – if you take my meaning.'

He stared into his mug of tea. 'Yes, Jack, I understand.'

There was an awkward silence as the children skipped and played around us. 'Anyway, thanks for listening, Tom, and do talk to me if you have any problems. I'm here to help whenever I can.' I looked at my watch. 'Time for the bell,' I said and walked back towards school.

'Jack,' he called after me, '. . . this has nothing to do with Laura, I suppose?'

'No, it hasn't,' I said without breaking my stride.

*

At the end of school Vera took Meg Harrison to Sally's classroom and Debbie hurried out clutching a card for Mothering Sunday.

'Ah've 'ad a smashing day, Mam,' she said, 'and ah made a card f'you f'Sunday but y'can't see it yet.'

Meg Harrison gave her daughter a big hug and then smiled at Vera. 'Thanks, Mrs F. Ev'ryone's been so kind.'

'Come and see me on Monday if you want to talk,' said Vera.

'We might see you before then at church,' said Meg. 'Ah've been talking to our Doreen.'

'That would be wonderful,' said Vera. 'There's a family service at St Mary's at eleven o' clock and lots of the children will be there.'

'We 'ave a small gospel 'all in our village an' ah 'elp t'run it,' she said proudly. 'Our Debbie knows 'er Bible, Mrs F.'

As she left she held open the door for Ruby and then mother and daughter set off for home. Ruby smiled and paused with her mop and galvanized bucket. It was reassuring to note that as time passed she seemed to be getting back to her old self. 'She's a nice lady, Mrs F . . . Doreen says she meks a lovely egg custard.' Ruby said this with the reverence accorded to an Oscar-winner and trundled off to clean the girls' toilets.

On Saturday morning Vera was sitting in her kitchen reading her *Daily Telegraph* and sipping a cup of Earl Grey tea. Morton Manor was silent as Rupert and his daughter, thirty-one-year-old Virginia Anastasia, had gone to look at a new pony for her riding school.

245

The miners' strike dominated the front pages. It appeared to be gathering momentum. Vera read on and shook her head in dismay. The Association of Chief Police Officers had gathered on the thirteenth floor of Scotland Yard to prepare plans to prevent pickets talking to Nottinghamshire miners and setting up road blocks. Also, thousands more police had been drafted in from other county forces to prevent miners entering non-striking areas. The seeds of a long-running battle had been sown – and she thought of Meg Harrison and her daughter.

Sally and I arrived in York and followed a group of teachers into the remarkable £2.6 million centre under the Coppergate shopping precinct.

A distinguished gentleman greeted us. 'Welcome to the Jorvik Viking Centre,' he said, 'described by the Chairman of the English Tourist Board, Michael Montague, as "The most exciting tourism project yet seen in the country", and this morning you will see why.' I was encouraged by his obvious enthusiasm. 'We plan to open to the public on Saturday, April fourteenth, but we wanted local teachers to have the opportunity to see it for themselves prior to planning visits for their schools.'

We had arrived at a line of small vehicles that resembled four-seater dodgem cars from the seaside. 'Visitors will travel through the centre in these electronically guided cars, which have internal speakers with a commentary by Magnus Magnusson plus voice tracks in a language similar to Old Norse. However, for this visit you are welcome to browse on foot at your leisure.'

There was a mixed response as most of us would have

enjoyed the ride, but we knew this gave us a unique opportunity to explore the centre more fully. We followed him through the growing darkness of a 'time tunnel' to a remarkable world we could barely imagine.

'So this is it,' he said. 'We have travelled back over one thousand years to the year 948 to the middle of a Viking township we have called Jorvik. The street we have created is actual size and you will see a jeweller at work, a wood-turner and children beside a weaving loom. There are herrings, skins and hides being unloaded from a boat, plus a host of artefacts including cooking pots, antler combs, ice-skates made from cattle bones and a magnificent Anglo-Saxon helmet.' He gestured with a wave of his arm. 'So please feel free to explore.'

Sally, as always, was a veritable mine of information. There were literally hundreds of relics, including boots, padlocks and stone lamps that, according to Sally, had once been filled with floating wicks. I was puzzled by the double-ended spoons, but Sally told me they were used for measuring rare and expensive herbs.

Finally, when we emerged back into the bright light of the twentieth century, I realized I had experienced a rare glimpse of our history and our changing times. It was yet another jewel in the crown of York's tourism industry.

Outside a party of Americans were looking on with interest.

'Hi,' said one of them, a tall man with perfectly even teeth usually only encountered in a toothpaste advertise-ent. The badge on his zip-up bomber jacket read 'Hootie Spurlock II' from a place with an interesting name – Boring, Oregon, USA. His wife, Mabeline, was holding his hand and clearly used the same ultra-white toothpaste.

'Is this lil' place open yet, mah friend?' he asked.

'I'm afraid not,' I said. 'It opens to the public in two weeks.'

'Oh dear,' said Mabeline, 'we'll be in Paris, France, by then.'

'So are you doing a tour?' asked Sally politely.

'We sure are,' said Hootie. 'We were in London, England, yesterday and we saw the Tower.'

Mabeline shook her head sadly. 'Shame they built it right in the flight path of Heathrow Airport.'

'That's surely true,' said Hootie and with a friendly wave they hurried off to catch their coach to Edinburgh, Scotland, leaving Sally and I shaking our heads.

'Wonder what it's like to live in a place called Boring?' mused Sally with a grin.

Back in Ragley village Emily Cade had pushed her mother's wheelchair into Prudence Golightly's General Stores. Ada, the oldest lady in the village, smiled up at Prudence.

'You seem to be doing well, Mrs Cade,' said Prudence in a loud voice.

'Well, ah must be seventy by now,' shouted Ada in response.

'No, Mother,' said Emily, 'you're ninety-seven.'

'Ninety-seven – ninety-seven!' exclaimed Ada. 'If ah'd known that ah wouldn't 'ave come out!'

After buying a jar of Heinz sandwich spread, Emily hurried out with her mother as Meg and Debbie Harrison walked in. Meanwhile, at the door, Mary Cartwright, mother of six-year-old Charlie, was muttering to Freda Fazackerly.

'That vicar wants lockin' up,' she said. 'It were that lesson 'e did about gettin' baptized.'

'Why, what happened?' asked Freda.

'Well, our Charlie took 'im lit'rally and tried t'baptize our cat in t'kitchen sink. Poor little sod nearly drowned.'

At the counter, Meg Harrison was served promptly by Prudence, who picked up each item from the counter and rang the amount into her old-fashioned till. 'That's Heinz Baked Beans at twenty and a half pence, a tin of Princes corned beef at sixty-nine pence, a tub of Stork margarine at seventeen and a half pence and a loaf of bread at thirty-two pence.' She smiled at Meg. 'That's one pound thirty-nine, please.' Then, while Mrs Harrison looked in her purse, Prudence rummaged under the counter and produced a pack of six Penguin biscuits, priced at thirty pence. She added it to the collection of shopping. 'And a small gift for you and the little girl,' she said with a gentle smile.

There was an intake of breath from this tough lady from South Yorkshire. 'No offence intended, Miss Golightly,' said Meg, 'but ah'm reluctant t'accept . . . wi' it being *charity*, so t'speak.'

'But we always give something to new children in the village,' explained Prudence.

'Ah don't know,' said Meg, not wishing to offend this kind lady.

'Please accept it in the spirit it is given,' said Prudence.

There was a long silence broken eventually by Meg. 'Thank you,' she said and looked down at Debbie. 'Looks like you've got a treat f'after tea, Debbie. So thank the kind lady.'

'Thank you,' said Debbie, who was staring up in wonderment at Jeremy the bear on his shelf, dressed in his gardening outfit, complete with tiny gloves and a small pair of pruning shears.

'And one more thing,' said Meg, 'ah'm planning t'make a cake an' 'ere's t'list of ingredients. Ah wondered if ah could call back later t'collect 'em?'

'Of course,' said Prudence and smiled when she looked at the list. 'It looks interesting.'

'It's f'summat special,' said Meg.

It was Sunday morning and when I looked out of the bedroom window of Bilbo Cottage a pale sun was rising in the eastern sky and silver-grey clouds, back-lit with golden light, heralded a new dawn. A thin mist was rising and, spread out before me, a sinuous pattern of flickering sunshine brought the distant countryside to life. It was a time of regeneration, with nest-building in the hedgerows and new shoots of wheat and barley in Twenty-acre Field.

John was eight and a half months old and had developed new ways of travelling. Beth and I laughed as he rolled over in an attempt to get to another place on the carpet and then pulled himself up the side of the sofa and shuffled along the length of it. Clearly pleased with himself, he clapped his hands and said, 'Dadda, dadda.' My heart almost burst with pride.

When Beth and I parked on Morton Road outside St Mary's Church it was clear the Mothering Sunday Service was one of the most popular in the church calendar. Parents and children were hurrying through the lych gate in large numbers. Sally was already there with Anne, organizing our school choir and recorder group.

Beth grinned as she parked John's pushchair alongside the glass-fronted church noticeboard. Elsie Crapper had been at work again. Her latest additions read:

*Please come along and sing with the choir
– they need all the help they can get.
The choir require a few new choir robes owing to new members and the deterioration of the older ones.*

Underneath, the second notice read:

*BRING AND BUY SALE
Saturday 7th April at 2.30 p.m.
Ladies . . . get rid of all the unwanted items that clutter up the house . . . bring your husbands.*

Before the service began, Joseph caused a little humour when he read out the wedding banns for two young people in the village, Carl Briers and Louise Longbottom. He declared the date of their wedding followed by the announcement, 'Their marriage will, of course, finally bring to an end their friendship that began at school,' and Vera on the front pew went red with embarrassment.

It was a happy occasion, with a lovely performance by Sally's choir that included Debbie Harrison sharing a song sheet with her new best friend, Mary Scrimshaw. The service was shorter than usual with so many young children in the congregation and Joseph moved briskly to a final prayer. When it was over everyone filed out and shook hands with Joseph as the usual parting greeting. In the church Vera was collecting the hymn books and stacking them away neatly when she heard footsteps behind her. It was Meg Harrison with Debbie beside her. 'Hello again, Mrs F,' she said.

Vera had thought long and hard since their previous conversation, particularly about the views regarding her favourite politician. However, first and foremost Vera thought of herself as a Christian and she reached out without hesitation to shake hands with this lady of South Yorkshire. 'Good to see you,' she said and looked down at Debbie. 'Where your treasure is, there shall be your heart also,' she added with a knowing smile.

'St Matthew, chapter six,' said Meg simply.

'Verse twenty-one,' added Vera for good measure.

Meg Harrison had a cake tin under her arm. 'Ah've brought you a gift, Mrs F,' she said, 't'share out in t'staff-room.' She placed the tin on the front pew and removed the lid. 'Jus' a light fruit cake,' she went on, 'an' ah've covered it wi' a layer of marzipan an' there's another layer of marzipan baked into t'middle.' It was also decorated with balls of marzipan. 'As y'can see, there's eleven of 'em, Mrs F.'

Vera gave a knowing smile. 'Representing the eleven disciples,' she said.

'It's a tradition in our family,' explained Meg, 't'mek a simnel cake on Mothering Sunday.'

'This is a lovely gesture and I'm very grateful. The teachers will be thrilled.'

'Well, you've all been very kind,' said Meg.

Vera studied the face of this lady. 'And you've been very brave,' she said softly.

They were both quiet as they looked at each other.

'Mebbe there's different ways t'be brave, Mrs F,' said Meg with gravitas.

So it was, in the quiet of this lovely church, the heavy silence was a cloak of comfort as two women, separated by pride and politics, embraced for the first and last time.

Chapter Fifteen

A Cow Called Clarissa

School closed today for the two-week Easter holidays and will reopen on Monday, 30 April. The new village policeman visited school.

Extract from the Ragley School Logbook:
Friday, 13 April 1984

'Mr Sheffield,' said Ruby, 'there's a cow in t'cycle shed.'

The unexpected, by its very nature, takes you by surprise. However, some surprises are bigger than others. So it was that on Friday, 13 April at 7.00 a.m. I found myself answering a telephone call at Bilbo Cottage from Ruby the caretaker.

'I'll be there as soon as I can, Ruby,' I said. 'In the meantime, close the school gate so the children don't go near it and ring the police. If it gets on to the road there might be an accident.' I rang off and rushed into the bathroom. My morning routine usually took thirty minutes – shave, shower, dress. Today I did it in fifteen. By half past seven I had parked outside school and arrived at the gate where

Ruby was waiting for me, holding her yard broom like a trident.

'Ah rang Mrs 'Unter in York, Mr Sheffield, an' she said she'd tell 'er 'usband an' 'e would send someone out. An' ah rang Deke Ramsbottom 'cause 'e knows all t'local farmers.'

'Well done, Ruby, that's excellent,' I said and she beamed with pride. So, like a latter-day Sherlock Holmes and Dr Watson, we closed the school gate, crept up the drive and stopped outside the large Victorian cycle shed.

'Go on, Mr Sheffield,' said Ruby, leaning defiantly on her broom, ''ave a look for y'self.'

A black-and-white Friesian cow with a short rope dangling from its neck was scratching itself against one of the ancient wooden pillars. It gave me a lugubrious look with its big soulful eyes and chewed in a relaxed, contented fashion. I enjoy looking at a herd of cows grazing peacefully in a far-off field. However, standing face to face with a cow that weighs around half a ton in a confined space did not immediately bring to mind the aesthetic delights of the English countryside.

'Ruby, I'll stay here to make sure it doesn't get on the playground and you go and wait outside the school gate.' My caretaker's safety was obviously my first concern . . . my own came a close second.

Ruby ran down the drive at a surprising speed.

Presumably startled by this twenty-stone figure in a bright orange overall, the cow decided to bolt for freedom. It barged me out of the way, trod on my foot, lumbered through the back entrance of the shed, charged down the leafy path that bordered School View and disappeared out of sight as it headed for the football field and the wooded area beyond.

'Shit!' I shouted as I hopped on one foot – and I wasn't referring to the cow claps that decorated the concrete floor. My foot hurt like hell.

Meanwhile, Julian Montgomery Pike parked his little grey police van by the village green outside The Royal Oak, picked up his helmet from the passenger seat and stepped out.

He took a deep breath. This was it – his first day going solo. PC Pike was twenty-two years old and had just completed his two-year probationary period. Early that morning Sergeant Dan Hunter at the station in York had given him the directions to Ragley-on-the-Forest. 'Start at the school,' Dan had said, 'introduce yourself, be polite, don't do anything daft, make sure this runaway cow is returned to its owner safely and do everything *by the book*. Remember – it's a lovely, quiet village.'

Julian stretched up to his full height of five feet eight and a half inches, although with two pairs of thick insoles in his big black boots and a tall helmet he actually felt like a six-footer. He checked his uniform, made sure his shiny new Hiatt handcuffs were secure in their pouch on his leather belt, wondered if he should have put his truncheon in his truncheon pocket rather than his rolled-up copy of *Karate Illustrated* monthly magazine and looked across the village green at the school.

It was at that moment he spotted a tall, gangling man in strange, old-fashioned black-framed spectacles outside one of the school outbuildings, hopping on one leg and appearing to utter obscenities. There was also a very large lady carrying a yard broom and running towards the school gate as if her bum was on fire.

PC Pike moved smoothly into action. *Always remain calm in a crisis* he thought and marched swiftly across the village green.

'G'morning, madam,' he said. 'Having trouble?'

'Ah'm guardin' t'gate,' said Ruby. She was taking her sentry duty seriously.

'We had a call about an escaped cow,' said PC Pike.

'That were me,' said Ruby. 'Ah'm t'school caretaker,' she pointed at me, 'an' that's t'eadteacher.' I was still doing my impression of Zebedee from the *Magic Roundabout*. 'Y'better talk to 'im,' and she opened the gate.

When I saw a young policeman walking up the drive I curtailed my impromptu morris dancing. 'Hello – you're a welcome sight,' I said. 'I'm Jack Sheffield, the headteacher.'

'I'm the new village bobby,' he said, 'PC Pike,' and we shook hands.

I gestured towards the cycle shed. 'We discovered a cow on our school premises this morning, but it's just bolted for freedom towards the fields at the back of school.'

He took out his notebook and opened it to the first page. 'Can you give me a description?'

'A description?'

'Yes, sir,' said PC Pike, licking the end of his sharp new HB pencil. He had seen policemen do this on *Bergerac*.

'Well, it was a cow.'

He wrote 'cow' and paused.

'A Friesian,' I added for clarification.

'A what, sir?'

'A Friesian – it was black and white. Oh, yes, and it had a rope round its neck.'

'Ah, that's good,' he said and continued scribbling.

Then he smiled when he realized that an unexpected opportunity to shine had fallen in his lap. 'Just leave it t'me, sir, I'll apprehend the animal and I'll call back later,' and he set off at a brisk trot towards the football pitch.

'Fine, thanks,' I called after him, feeling very relieved. Then I limped down to the school gate to retrieve my car. 'You can open the gate now, Ruby,' I said and looked at my wristwatch. It was 7.45 a.m. and the last day of the spring term had begun.

By the time the rest of the staff arrived everything was back to normal. The cow story caused amusement in the staff-room, particularly the part when it stepped on my foot. I wondered when PC Pike would reappear, but there was no sign of him. However, there were children to teach and soon we were busy again.

In my class we were using descriptions of animals to encourage the development of vocabulary. The Buttle twins, Rowena and Katrina, had both chosen to write about a dog. When I marked their books I called them to my desk for a quiet word.

'Rowena, did you copy?' I asked.

'No, Mr Sheffield,' said Rowena.

'What about you, Katrina?'

'No, Mr Sheffield,' echoed Katrina.

'Well, why is your description identical to your sister's?' I asked.

'It's t'same dog, Mr Sheffield,' said Katrina, quick as a flash.

I smiled. There was something special about twins.

Fortunately their mathematics work was more convincing. They were working with Betsy Icklethwaite on a problem-solving task that involved converting fractions to decimals and it was clear they understood the concept, particularly Betsy, who tried to get a percentage in every sentence.

'Three minutes to morning break, boys and girls,' I said.

'Only five per cent of an hour,' said Betsy with a grin.

When the bell rang for morning playtime, Charlotte Ackroyd made another announcement. 'Little copper comin' up t'drive, Mr Sheffield.' She was writing up her experiment after making copper sulphate crystals and once again her eyes never flickered from her work. I looked up from my desk and peered out of the window. I could see a small grey police van parked outside the school gate and a diminutive, slightly dishevelled policeman staring around him.

Vera had spent twenty-five pence that morning on her *Woman's Weekly* magazine and, when I walked into the office, she was admiring the attractive photograph of Lady Di on the front cover. 'The white hat with the blue band is perfect for her,' she said. She proceeded to flick through the pages and I was treated to a parade of hats as worn by Queen Elizabeth the Queen Mother, Princess Margaret and the Duchess of Kent.

'They're all wonderful, Vera,' I said without conviction.

'It's all down to good taste, Mr Sheffield,' she added. Then there was a knock on the door and PC Pike came in and gave us a shy smile.

'Hello again, PC Pike,' I said. 'This is Mrs Forbes-Kitchener, our school secretary.'

'Pleased to meet you, Mrs Forbes-Kitchener,' he said

politely. 'I'm the new village policeman, Julian Pike.'

'I'm delighted to meet you, Julian,' said Vera, 'and I'm sure you've spoken to Sergeant Hunter, who gave considerable support to the school.'

'Yes, of course, and I hope to do the same,' he said.

Vera studied him for a moment. 'I recall your mother, Emily Montgomery, as she was then,' she said. This should have surprised me, but Vera's local knowledge was unsurpassed. 'A lovely lady. She helped with the school library van . . . very keen on Enid Blyton, I recall.'

'Particularly the Famous Five, I'm afraid,' said PC Pike and his cheeks flushed, 'which is why I'm called *Julian*. She thought it was distinguished – "a leader of men", she used to say.'

'Yes, that's definitely Emily,' said Vera.

'So . . . is there any news of the cow?' I asked, keen to bring everyone back to the here and now.

'I'm afraid not,' he said and looked down sadly at his grass-stained boots. 'She's proving elusive, so I'm going to ask around in the village. I presume we don't know who the owner might be?'

'No idea,' I said.

'Well I've been told to work *by the book*,' he said.

'Oh dear, Julian,' said Vera, 'you mustn't be a *pedant*.'

Julian was confused. He didn't know whether to be pleased or hurt, as the word was unfamiliar. So he gave what he thought was a knowing nod of acknowledgement. It was the mannerism he had perfected after watching ninety-one episodes of *Skippy the Bush Kangaroo*. As the super-intelligent Skippy explained that, three miles away, two boys had fallen down a disused mine shaft that was slowly filling with water at the rate of six inches per hour, the head ranger of Waratah National Park used to give that familiar, all-knowing nod. To Julian that really was the sign of a leader of men.

'Well, I'll get on and report back later,' he said.

During playtime all the children were out enjoying the sunshine, with the exception of three. Sally had given permission for Debbie Harrison, Mary Scrimshaw and Barry Ollerenshaw to remain in class to complete a special task.

Next to the sink, the three children were busy making an Easter Tree, as it was Debbie's last day at Ragley. Sally had provided a block of oasis and cuttings from her garden so that Debbie could take home a present for her mother. The girls were arranging branches of pussy willow, forsythia and blackthorn while Barry Olleren-shaw looked on. He was impressed. 'Y'could 'ang little choc'late eggs from them twigs.'

'That's a good idea, Barry,' said Debbie.

Barry liked Debbie – she wasn't frightened of worms. 'So . . . what did y'think o' Mr Evans' story 'bout Jesus?' he asked.

'Bit scary,' said Debbie.

'A miracle,' said Mary.

Barry nodded knowingly. 'Well, when t'vicar said it were a *miracle* that Jesus rose from t'dead ah thought it were good – but ah were more impressed as to 'ow 'e got that big 'eavy stone away from t'cave entrance.'

The pecking order of miracles was a lot to think about, so the two girls simply carried on arranging the branches.

*

PC Pike was standing outside Prudence Golightly's General Stores, wondering where to go next. Prudence was an advocate of free local advertising but Julian was too busy thinking to be distracted by the three postcards on the noticeboard.

They read:

Antique desk – suitable for lady with thick legs and large drawers.

Let us oil your sewing machine and adjust tension in your house.

Dog for sale – eats anything – likes children.

He walked in and introduced himself to Prudence, who suggested he visit the butcher's shop next door. In the hope this did not forebode the demise of the missing cow, he went in.

Old Tommy Piercy's grandson, Young Tommy, was displaying pigs' trotters on metal trays in the shop window. One of Old Tommy's specialities, they had been cleaned, brined and ready-cooked. Old Tommy, a long-standing member of the Guild of Butchers, was also particularly proud to be a member of the Sausage Appreciation Society and he was in the back room of the shop wrapping up £2 worth for Betty Buttle.

Betty was in animated conversation with Margery Ackroyd, telling her about her wonderful new John Moore's catalogue. 'It's reight good, Margery,' she said. 'Ah jus' filled in t'Freepost coupon in m'magazine an' ah got a free automatic coffee maker wi' m'first order.'

'But nobody drinks coffee in your 'ouse,' said Margery. 'They all drink tea.'

Undeterred, Betty just grinned. 'Ah know, but it might come in if America declares war wi' Russia like it says in t'paper. Then t'Yanks'll be 'ere again an' accordin' to m'mother they all gave 'er coffee an' chocolate an' cigarettes.'

And that's not all thought Margery, but said nothing.

PC Pike popped his head round the door. 'Excuse me, but has anyone seen a runaway cow this morning?'

George Dainty was at the back of the queue. 'Funny y'should mention that, officer,' he said, 'there was a cow walkin' through my back garden, large as life, but when ah went out it 'ad gone.'

'When was that, sir?' asked PC Pike.

George looked at his expensive duty-free wristwatch. 'Only ten minutes back, ah reckon,' he said.

He took out his notebook. 'And what's your address, sir?'

'Big bungalow, number thirty-six,' said George, 'on t'right up t'Morton Road.'

'Thank you, sir,' said Julian and rushed off to his little grey van.

'Coppers are getting smaller,' said Betty.

'And younger,' added Margery with a sigh.

Old Tommy reappeared. 'Did someone mention a missing cow? Billy Icklethwaite were lookin' for 'is Clarissa this morning, so Deke Ramsbottom said. Ah'd best ring 'im.'

*

PC Pike was driving like Nigel Mansell along the Morton Road. He had once done ninety-six miles an hour at 5.00 a.m. on a summer's morning in a Hillman Minx on an empty downhill stretch of the M1 between Leeds and Sheffield – so he had known excitement. In fact, he recalled he had almost wet himself.

However, Julian was also a sensitive soul. He had cried when the Waltons shouted goodnight to each other at the end of each episode and there had been times he wished he had been christened John-Boy rather than Julian. So, with caution in mind, he slowed up, parked outside a spacious modern bungalow and walked stealthily into the back garden of number 36.

Back on Ragley High Street, after George had bought his lamb chops, he met Ruby and raised his flat cap. 'Ruby, luv, ah'm sorry about your Ronnie . . . 'ow y'keeping?'

"Ello, George. Ah 'eard y'were back . . . Ah'm fine, thanks, all things considerin',' she said with a tired smile. 'You 'ave t'keep goin' for t'children's sake, don't you?'

George had retired from his fish-and-chip shop in Alicante in Spain and, after making his fortune, had returned to the little Yorkshire village he had known as a boy and he had bought a smart bungalow on Morton Road. 'Life's tough, Ruby, but you're tougher,' he said.

'Ah miss 'im ev'ry day – in spite of all 'is faults,' sighed Ruby.

'That were allus t'problem wi' love, Ruby,' said George. 'Y'don't pick who y'love – it chooses you.'

'Mebbe so, George . . . an' ah'm sorry ah didn't recognize you at t'funeral. Ah've gorra memory like a sieve some days,' she said, pushing her chestnut curls from her face.

'Never you mind, Ruby,' he said with a gentle smile and he squeezed her hand. 'Good memories are worth waiting for,' and he walked off up the High Street.

Ruby looked after him and wondered what he meant.

At number 38, Morton Road, in the privacy of the new Scandinavian log cabin built in their back garden, Petula Dudley-Palmer stripped naked, donned a pair of sunglasses and prepared to relax in her private cocoon of warmth.

She had purchased a revolutionary Classic Regency-style Solarspeed Sunbed using Geoffrey's new American Express credit card. It had been hand-built to her specifications and came with a two-year guarantee. An all-year, all-over tan was clearly the answer to the depression she had begun to feel. Now she would look like a million dollars and be the envy of all the mothers in the village. She would be brown and they would be green.

With that comforting thought she opened the slatted wooden doors to the morning sunshine and the view of the very private and professionally landscaped garden. However, clumping over the Japanese bridge next to the lily pond and the *Acer palmatum* was a large black-and-white cow. With a scream she turned and ran back into the house.

Julian had never seen a full-frontal naked woman before. His girlfriend, Monica, a prim waitress in Betty's Tea Rooms in York, had always insisted that a *top-half-only* pre-nuptial relationship was sufficient and he had gone along with it. *All good things come to he who waits*, she had told him. Now he was pleased that the dense avenue of perfectly manicured variegated conifers hid him from view. However, he did feel a little voyeuristic as he stared through a small gap in the hedge at the retreating bare backsides of both Petula and a cow he would come to know as Clarissa.

Betsy Icklethwaite was completing the last in a series of workcards about percentages. 'Ah'm good at fractions an' percentages now, Mr Sheffield,' she said, 'an' it's just as well.'

'Why's that, Betsy?'

'Well, when ah read that letter an' ah found out what they were goin' t'do t'our Clarissa.'

'Clarissa?'

'Yes, Mr Sheffield, Clarissa, our cow – ah 'elped 'er escape this morning.'

And the little girl told me the whole story.

After a few telephone calls Billy Icklethwaite arrived in the school office looking embarrassed. 'Ah'm sorry for all t'fuss, Mr Sheffield.'

'Don't worry, Billy,' I said. The poor farmer was clearly distraught.

'Ah 'eard y'met my Clarissa this morning, Mr Sheffield,' he continued. 'Ah milked 'er at t'crack o' dawn like ah usually do an' then ah went t'look at a pig in Thirkby. When ah got back Clarissa 'ad gone. Then Deke an' Old Tommy were ringing round saying one 'ad turned up at school an' it were on t'loose in t'village. So ah' 'pologize for t'inconvenience.'

'We'll need to have a word with Betsy so she doesn't do it again,' I said cautiously.

'O' course, Mr Sheffield. Mrs F explained and ah've

brought t'letter that she found on t'table.' He passed it over. It was printed on very official headed notepaper and stated that Mr Icklethwaite must reduce his herd by 50 per cent to keep in line with regulations issued by the EEC. 'Reduce my 'erd by 'alf it says . . . but ah've only got *one* cow.'

I heard the church clock in the distance striking one. 'Well, Mr Icklethwaite, the new village bobby is out searching for her now so I'm sure Clarissa will soon turn up.'

Beyond the terraced cottages on the High Street, clumps of daffodils studded the grassy banks and in the fields anxious ewes were keeping a close vigil on their new-born lambs. Sadly, PC Pike was too tired to appreciate the beauty of the North Yorkshire countryside. He had run miles through the lanes, forests and byways of this little village. 'I'm knackered,' he mumbled to himself . . . and his feet were killing him. The church clock struck one as he leaned against the village hall noticeboard. Sadly, he was too tired to appreciate the latest notices. They might have raised his spirits.

The first read: *The Low Self Esteem Support Group will meet in the church hall . . . please use the back door.*

The second was equally poignant. It read: *The sixth form drama group from Easington School are presenting Hamlet by William Shakespeare. You are all invited to attend this tragedy.*

Across the road he spotted the village pharmacy. Inside, Nine-Fingers Freddie, the pianist who played Russ Conway hits in The Royal Oak, was at the front of the queue. 'Jus' m'prescription, Eugene,' said Freddie.

'Here y'are,' said Eugene. 'One tablet twice a day wi' meals. Y'lookin' a bit down, Freddie,' he added.

Freddie picked up his tablets. He sounded distraught. 'Well – that tonic ah bought las' week for m'wife's nerves didn't work.' He walked to the door.

'What makes y'think that?' asked Eugene.

'Well,' said the disconsolate Freddie, 'she's jus' packed 'er case an' left me,' and the bell above the door rang madly as he left.

Everything went quiet.

Norman Critchley, husband of our formidable kitchen assistant, was next in line and behind him was Ernie Brown, husband of Winifred, the village battleaxe.

Finally Norman spoke up. 'Ah'll 'ave a bottle o' that tonic, Eugene.'

'An' so will I,' echoed Ernie and they wandered off with hope in their hearts.

It was PC Pike's turn. 'Excuse me, but have you got anything for blisters?' he asked.

'Tek y'boots off an' let's 'ave a look,' said Eugene.

Julian removed his boots and gingerly peeled off his socks.

'Bloody 'ell,' said Eugene. 'They're t'worst ah've seen.' Eugene believed in telling people how it was. After applying a variety of cushioned plasters, Julian settled up and departed. 'Live long and prosper,' said Eugene, his version of Mr Spock's Vulcan salute. Julian was puzzled – he didn't watch *Star Trek*. 'An' by the way,' shouted Eugene as he reached the door, 'was it you looking for Billy Icklethwaite's cow? 'Cause she found 'er way 'ome, so Deke Ramsbottom said.'

PC Pike took out his notebook. He was on to his third page. 'And where's that, sir?'

'Cokes Bottom Farm,' said Eugene, 'far end of Morton Road, on t'right beyond t'posh bungalows.'

At Cokes Bottom Farm the local press were already there. News travels fast in a small village. Clarissa looked none the worse for her tour of the village and Betsy Icklethwaite's decision to release her was being treated sympathetically.

'So you're the new bobby,' said the keen young reporter. 'It appears you somehow managed to guide Clarissa home again.'

'I was just doing my job,' said Julian modestly. 'We're trained to do things by the book,' he thought of Sergeant Hunter, 'and you can quote me if you like.'

At afternoon break the telephone rang in the office and Vera smiled. She passed the receiver to me. 'Mrs Sheffield,' she said and then walked through the little passageway to the staff-room to enjoy a cup of tea.

'Hello, Jack,' said Beth, 'how's it going? I've not heard from you since you rushed off this morning.'

'It's a long story,' I said. 'We got all the end-of-term reports out on time and, oh yes, there was a runaway cow on school premises – but it's sorted now and we got a call saying it was back in its own field.'

As a headteacher's wife, Beth was completely unfazed by the occasional incongruous message. 'I'm ringing about Laura – and Tom,' she said in a whisper.

'Oh . . . I see.'

'I've just spoken to her and she's going back to London for Easter.'

'So how is Tom involved?'

'Laura has invited him down there. She said it was just to show him the sights.'

'It could be quite innocent,' I said.

There was a silence as we each tried to read the other's thoughts.

'I think Tom likes Laura,' said Beth.

'He's far too young for her,' I replied, perhaps a little too sharply. 'He needs to be more sensible.'

'So does my sister,' said Beth. There was the sound of John crying in the background. 'Must go,' she said and rang off.

As the school day neared its end the four classes were enjoying their traditional end-of-day story time. Anne was reading the story of Chicken Licken to her class and they sat there open-mouthed as the drama unfolded. 'Chicken Licken shouted to the farmer, "The sky is falling! The sky is falling!" – so, girls and boys, what do you think the farmer said?'

There was silence as the group of small children pondered the problem. Suddenly, Billy Ricketts put up his hand.

'Yes, Billy?' asked Anne.

'Well, Miss, ah reckon t'farmer might o' said, "Bloomin' 'eck, we gorra talkin' chicken,"' and Anne was reminded why she chose to teach the youngest children in Ragley School.

Meanwhile I was reading our class story, *The Silver Sword* by Ian Serraillier, a tear-jerking tale of a family trying to be reunited.

'A bit like Clarissa, Mr Sheffield,' said Harold Bustard, 'y'know – trying t'get 'ome again.' The story had swept around the school like a jungle telegraph.

'I suppose it is, Harold,' I said and Betsy Icklethwaite gave me a shy look.

It was a happy group of children that ran down the drive with thoughts of holidays and Easter eggs, while a slightly less exuberant group of teachers tidied their classrooms and did a stock check.

The following week, the new edition of the *Easington Herald & Pioneer* was delivered to Bilbo Cottage and I cut out the front-page article for the staff-room noticeboard.

Over a photograph of Clarissa the cow, flanked by a smiling PC Pike on one side and a perplexed Mr Icklethwaite on the other, was the banner headline '*New Bobby Rescues Runaway Cow – The Full Story of Clarissa, the Friesian Fugitive*'. It reported that the Ministry of Agriculture had sent a letter of apology to Mr Icklethwaite stating, 'Obviously there has been a mistake and Clarissa will remain as she is.' The article also added the view of his wife: '"Percentages can cause a lot of problems," said Mrs Icklethwaite, 45, of Cokes Bottom Farm. "When I was at school we did fractions."'

It occurred to me that you can't please all the people all the time . . . only 50 per cent of them!

Chapter Sixteen

Terry Earnshaw's Bob-a-Job

Mrs Grainger and Mrs Pringle have agreed to display an exhibition of children's art work in the refreshment marquee at the May Day Fair on the village green on Monday, 7 May. School closed today for the Bank Holiday and will reopen on Tuesday, 8 May.

Extract from the Ragley School Logbook:
Friday, 4 May 1984

'You were supposed to look for fauna and flora,' said Raymond the Scout leader.

Terry Earnshaw and a few of the youngest members of the Ragley Scout Troop had spent the last hour climbing trees, playing Red Indians and generally having a good time. 'Ah've gorra Aunty Flora,' said Terry helpfully. 'She lives at t'seaside in Skegness.'

Raymond shook his head and sighed. There were over 600,000 Scouts in the country and he had finished up with Terry Earnshaw. Sometimes it was tough to communicate with the youngest members of the Ragley Scout Troop, particularly this son of Barnsley in South Yorkshire. He was one of a kind – *or maybe not*, Raymond thought. His big brother, Heathcliffe, turned up occasionally and he was definitely *unconventional*.

'Well,' said Raymond, 'it's time to go, but don't forget to take your receipt books and collecting tins for Bob-a-Job and remember – Major Forbes-Kitchener will present the Scout of the Year trophy at the May Day Fair to whoever does the most *helpful* job.'

It was that time of the year when Boy Scouts gave a helping hand to their community by cleaning cars, gardening, window-cleaning, shopping and helping the elderly cross the road even though they may not wish to . . . and all for a bob, or five pence in decimal currency. Terry looked at the other boys, whose sleeves were barely long enough to accommodate all the badges they had won, and thought *I've no chance.*

It was Friday, 4 May and an eventful Bank Holiday was in store.

Following an evening of gentle rain, Saturday dawned bright and clear. When I opened the bedroom window the heavy scent of wallflowers was in the air to herald a day of promise and, once again, the swallows had returned to the safe haven of their nesting sites in the eaves of Bilbo Cottage. The hedgerows were teeming with new life and the world seemed blessed in this tiny corner of God's Own Country.

After a lazy breakfast I left Beth working on her dissertation for university while John rolled around on his play-mat. The drive into Ragley was a joy and, bordering the High Street outside the village hall, the almond trees were in blossom. On the village green, overhanging the pond, new leaves on the weeping willow caressed the lush grass and, outside school, the first flower stalks on the horse chestnut trees gave hope of the summer days to come. I left my Morris Minor Traveller in the school car park and walked back out of the gate, where bright yellow forsythia lifted the spirits.

I had agreed to meet Tom Dalton on the village green at ten o' clock, prior to setting up the marquees under the supervision of Major Forbes-Kitchener. Tom had said he was available to help out today but had commitments on May Day and I did wonder what they might be. I glanced at my watch. There was time to spare, so I decided to call in to Nora's Coffee Shop for a hot drink.

Meanwhile, in the Earnshaw household, Heathcliffe and Terry were straining at the leash.

'Can we go now, Mam?' pleaded Heathcliffe.

'Look 'ere,' said Mrs Earnshaw, 'ah don't want you boys getting into trouble.'

The two brothers looked the picture of innocence. 'No, Mam,' they replied in perfect unison and with the stoic expression of absolute sincerity.

'It's Bob-a-Job, so we're gonna be *'elpful* t'people,' said Terry.

'An' t'best Scout gets a trophy, Mam, so ah'm 'elping our Terry,' explained Heathcliffe.

'Well, remember,' warned Mrs Earnshaw as she wiped the jam from Dallas Sue-Ellen's face, 'be'ave y'selves.'

The boys gave a glassy-eyed look of innocence. 'So can we go, Mam?' asked Terry.

'Where y'goin' t'first?' asked Mrs Earnshaw.

'Miss Golightly's, Mam,' said Heathcliffe.

'OK, but no going into Mr Tup'am's rhubarb patch.' The colour left the boys' cheeks. *How does she know?* was the question that flickered through their minds. 'Else you'll get what-for,' she added for good measure.

There was a moment's hesitation as both boys considered the exact nature of what-for, but for the Earnshaw boys life was for living, not thinking about, so they ran off to begin a day of helping the needy, the unwary and the completely mystified.

It was crowded when I walked into the coffee shop and last month's number one, Lionel Ritchie's 'Hello', was on the juke-box. Dorothy was behind the counter reading her *Smash Hits* magazine and studying a photograph of Michael Jackson celebrating with his girlfriend Brooke Shields after winning eight Grammy awards, including Album of the Year for *Thriller*.

Dorothy looked up. 'What's it t'be, Mr Sheffield?'

'Just a coffee, please, Dorothy.'

'Fwothy coffee comin' up,' said Nora, who had just spent twenty-five pence on a *Woman's Weekly*. 'Ah'm weading about Bwitain's most popula man, Mr Sheffield,' she said.

'Oh yes,' I answered vaguely.

'Y'mean David Essex?' asked Dorothy.

Nora frowned.

'Shakin' Stevens?' Dorothy tried again hopefully.

'No, ah'm talking about that weally nice Iwishman, Tewwy Wogan.'

'Oh, 'im?' mumbled Dorothy without enthusiasm and returned to studying Michael Jackson's handsome profile.

'Yes, Nora, I've heard him on the radio,' I said as I paid for my mug of bubbling foam.

"E 'as some weally lovely ca'digans,' she called after me as I sought a spare seat.

Seventeen-year-old Claire Bradshaw and Anita Cuthbertson were drinking bottles of 7Up through plastic straws. They looked up. "Ullo, Sir,' said Anita, "ere's a spare seat.'

'Thanks,' I said with a wry smile. It seemed only yesterday that I was helping them with long division.

"Ow's y'little boy?' asked Claire when I had sat down.

'Fine, thanks,' I said. 'Growing up fast.'

They had clearly moved on from *Jackie* magazine. On the table in front of them was an old December issue of *Cosmopolitan*, selected from the pile on the shelf near the door. It was open at the page entitled 'Should You Discuss Ex-Boyfriends?' and I guessed in the case of these two inseparable friends the answer was a definite yes.

'So how are you?' I asked.

'Fine thanks, sir,' said Anita, 'an' we've got some news.'

'Really?'

Claire turned to a new page and pointed to a photograph. 'Mr Sheffield, we're gonna be like 'er.'

The headline read 'Madonna – the Hottest Wildest Woman in Rock'.

'Madonna?'

'Yes, Mr Sheffield,' said Anita, 'she sells seventy-five thousand records a day.'

'Does she?'

'We're in Clint Ramsbottom's rock band,' said Claire.

'An' we're gonna be famous,' added Anita.

'So who's in this band?'

'Well, there's Clint Ramsbottom o' course – 'e's on lead guitar – an' 'is brother Shane 'as got a drum,' said Claire.

'Then there's Kenny Kershaw on bass guitar an' Wayne Ramsbottom – 'e's got a drum as well,' added Anita, eyes bright with excitement.

'You've got *two* drummers?'

'Yes, Mr Sheffield,' said Claire, ''cause they've *both* got a drum and they want t'be in t'group.'

'An' me an' Claire are t'singers,' said Anita proudly.

'And what's the name of your group?' I asked.

'The Throb,' they said in unison.

'The Throb . . . er, that's really catchy,' I said uncertainly.

'Well we all like The Clash an' Claire's got that record *London Calling,*' said Anita.

'Clash?'

'Yes, Sir,' said Claire, 'our music's a bit like them wi' a bit o' Status Quo thrown in.'

'An' Claire sings like Tina Turner,' said Anita. 'An' ah sing a bit like that Izora Armstead.' They could see they were losing me. 'Y'mus' know T'Weather Girls, Mr Sheffield,' said Claire.

I seemed to remember Wincey Willis on *TV-am* telling me it was going to be sunny this weekend, but I couldn't work out what this had to do with their proposed pop group.

'They sang "It's Raining Men",' prompted Anita.

'Oh, did they?'

I smiled uncertainly, supped the last of my coffee and beat a hasty retreat.

In the General Stores, Heathcliffe and Terry had pooled their pocket money and were staring intently at the jars of cinder toffee, Pontefract cakes and liquorice pipes. Sustenance was important before they began helping people. They were working out the cost:weight ratio, which, had they known it, would have promoted them to the next level of difficulty in the School Mathematics Project.

After deciding on two identical bags of liquorice torpedoes they asked the question: 'Bob-a-Job, Miss Golightly?'

Prudence Golightly was a kindly soul. 'Yes please, boys. You can clean the shop window,' and she gave them a bucket of water and two chamois leathers.

Unfortunately, the configuration of the counter combined with the vast collection of items on display prevented Prudence from having a clear view of the intrepid window cleaners.

Minutes later Heathcliffe said, 'We've finished, Miss Golightly.'

'It were 'arder on my side,' said Terry, red in the face.

Puzzled, Miss Golightly followed them outside and stared at the window in dismay. 'Where's all the writing gone?'

As a favour to Miss Golightly, George Postlethwaite, the one-armed fisherman who could do perfect mirror-writing, had painted the bargains of the day on the inside of the shop window in large white letters.

'Ah cleaned it off, Miss Golightly,' said Terry.

'But I only wanted you to do the *outside*,' pleaded Miss Golightly.

'But y'gave us *two* cloths,' insisted Heathcliffe.

Miss Golightly gave a wry smile. 'Yes I did, I suppose . . . oh well, here's your shilling.'

'Axshully, Miss Golightly – it's five pence *each*,' said Heathcliffe with considered politeness. 'An' don't worry, we'll find Mr Postlethwaite an' mek it right,' and they put the money in the collecting tin, recorded their first transaction in their receipt book and ran off.

Outside the Post Office a large van pulled up and two men began to unload a huge bed. Ben Roberts watched intrigued – it was the biggest bed he had ever seen.

He took one last look at the card to his grandma in Market Weighton. It read: 'Dear Grandma, thank you for the 50p stuck to my Easter egg box and I'm sorry I didn't write to you sooner. I promise I'll write a lot quicker if you send anything for my birthday on May 21st. Love, Benjamin. X'. He posted the letter and waved to Mrs Poole and her Yorkshire terrier, Scargill, and wished that one day he might own a dog.

Mrs Poole was tying Scargill's lead to the drainpipe outside Diane's hairdresser's when the Earnshaw boys approached. 'Bob-a-Job, Mrs Poole?' asked Terry.

Mrs Poole looked relieved. 'Yes, luv,' she said and put a coin in the tin. 'Look after Scargill while ah'm 'aving me 'air done an' ah'll see y'back 'ere in a couple of 'ours.'

'OK, Mrs Poole,' said Terry, taking the lead.

'Axshully, there'll be *two* of us looking after y'dog, Mrs Poole,' said Heathcliffe, shaking the tin. Mrs Poole took the hint, removed another coin from her purse and hurried through the shop door.

Slightly hampered by the lively Yorkshire terrier straining on his leash, the intrepid duo sought out their next customer.

"Ow about Mr Pratt?' suggested Terry, staring at Pratt's Hardware Emporium. Outside the shop was a trestle table on which Tidy Tim had displayed a collection of clay pots. They tied Scargill's lead to one of the table legs and walked in. 'Bob-a-Job, Mr Pratt?'

Before Timothy could reply there was a crash outside.

Scargill had pulled his lead clear, attacked one of the life-like hedgehog boot-scrapers and then run off as a multitude of clay pots rolled off the table and smashed on the concrete forecourt. The boys followed Timothy out of the door.

'Oh 'eck,' said Timothy, 'what a mess!' He looked up and down the street but no culprit was in sight. 'Oh well, boys, here's a job. 'Ow about y'sweep up this mess and ah'll pay when you've done it.'

'Good as done, Mr Pratt,' said the holier-than-thou Heathcliffe and he gave Terry a knowing look that indicated 'admit nothing'.

When Veronica Poole walked into Diane's Hair Salon Betty Buttle was sitting under the dryer reading a copy of the *Sun*. However, Betty wasn't interested in the photograph of Boy George and George Michael leaving for America, although she did notice that Wham!'s macho George Michael was showing off his hairy chest whereas Boy George was wearing a skirt. It was the picture of Joan Collins that caught her eye. 'Well, would y'believe it!' said Betty.

'What's that?' asked Veronica.

'It sez 'ere a twenty-nine-year-old housewife won on that *Mastermind* programme. Her specialist subject was

Dynasty an' she got twenty-six correct answers. Ah could 'ave won that.'

'But there's *general* knowledge as well, Betty,' said Veronica guardedly.

'Ah well, mebbe so,' said Betty.

'So what's it t'be t'day, Veronica?' asked Diane.

Veronica thought for a moment and looked down once again at the photograph in Betty's newspaper. 'Ah'll 'ave a Joan Collins, please, Diane – y'never know, that dishy young teacher might fancy an older woman.'

Diane picked up a bottle of shampoo and smiled. She knew when to keep her thoughts to herself.

'Ah see Amelia is 'aving a posh double bed delivered to t'Post Office,' said Veronica, changing the subject.

'It'll be f'Ted Postlethwaite,' said Diane.

Veronica looked into the mirror at Ragley's favourite hairdresser. 'Diane – what are *you* looking for in a man?'

Diane thought for a moment and sighed. 'Well . . . a *pulse* would be a start.'

'Ah wonder where 'e's gone,' said Heathcliffe, peering up and down the High Street for the four-legged fugitive.

'Let's ask Clint,' said Terry.

Clint Ramsbottom was sitting on the bench outside the village hall, smoking a cigarette. The young farmhand was becoming politically aware and was particularly pleased with his stylish Campaign for Nuclear Disarmament earstud. Sadly, it was unfortunate that he had selected one of the reject stock sold by Bent Bernie in Thirkby market. Instead of the letters CND it read COD. So it was that

Clint Ramsbottom, trendsetter of Ragley village, now resembled a punk fisherman with attitude. He looked deep in thought.

"Ello, Clint,' said Heathcliffe.

'Sorry, lads, ah've no change,' said Clint, eyeing up the collecting tin.

'We've lost Scargill,' said Heathcliffe. "Ave y'seen 'im?'

'Yeah, 'e ran round t'back o' t'pub. Old Tommy were shoutin' at 'im f'pinchin' one of 'is sausages.'

'Oh 'eck,' said Heathcliffe, 'we'd best go find 'im.'

Terry had another thought. 'Clint, if y'goin' in t'pub can y'tell old Mr Postlethwaite that Miss Golightly wants t'see 'im 'bout painting 'er window again.'

'OK,' said Clint, '. . . an' guess what, lads.'

'What?' said the boys.

'Ah've gorra rock band,' said Clint proudly.

'Who's in it?' asked Terry.

'Me an' Kenny on guitars, m'brothers on t'drums an' Claire an' Anita singing . . . 'cept they can't sing.'

"Ow about y'play louder so no one can 'ear 'em?' suggested Terry.

Clint nodded appreciatively. 'Good idea, Terry,' he said, 'but w'need somewhere t'practise.'

Heathcliffe grabbed the opportunity. 'If w'find somewhere will y'give us a bob?' he said.

'It's a deal,' agreed Clint with a grin.

Tom and I were hot and tired after erecting the marquee and The Royal Oak beckoned for some well-earned refreshment. Don the barman was up a ladder, peering hesitantly under the roof tiles as we walked in. A few members of the football team were propping up the bar and Sheila was pulling pints for Deke Ramsbottom and his son Shane.

I looked at the menu on the blackboard. Sheila made sure her meals, whenever possible, featured local produce and the influence of a recent visit from Pete the Poacher could be seen by the introduction of squirrel soup.

"Ello, Mr Sheffield, Mr Dalton . . . Whitby fish, fresh in t'day,' said Sheila.

Norman Barraclough, the local fish merchant, had made the round trip to the east coast in his little white van and a whole smoked herring, still with its backbone, was an appetizing delicacy.

Tom smiled and nodded. 'For two then please, Sheila,' I said.

'Full o' protein, Mr Dalton,' said Sheila, devouring my handsome colleague with her eyes. 'We got t'keep 'is strength up, 'aven't we, Mr Sheffield?'

'You get a table, Tom,' I said, 'and I'll bring the drinks over.'

He nodded, gave Sheila a flashing smile and walked over to the bay-window table.

"E's a looker, y'new teacher, Mr Sheffield,' said Sheila. "As 'e got a girlfriend?'

'I've never asked,' I said.

The television above the tap-room bar was switched on and Sheila glanced up at it disconsolately as she pulled a frothing pint of Chestnut. "Ave y'noticed, Mr Sheffield, they allus start wi' a *Good afternoon* and then tell y'why it isn't.'

'You sound a bit fed up, Sheila.'

'Ah'm worried about them bees in t'roof, Mr Sheffield . . . big day on Monday an' we can't find s'lution.'

*

Don Bradshaw was standing at the foot of his ladder looking concerned.

'Bob-a-Job, Mr Bradshaw?' asked Heathcliffe.

Don sighed deeply. 'Ah'd give you a lot more than a bob t'get shut o' them bees. They'll be in t'attic next.'

Terry looked up the ladder. 'Ah'll go up an' poke 'em wi' a stick, Mr Bradshaw,' he offered.

Don smiled. 'No thanks, young Terry,' he said, 'it's too dangerous, but thanks for offerin'.'

'You've got an attic, Mr Bradshaw?' queried Heathcliffe. 'It's jus' that Clint wants a room for 'is new rock band t'practise.'

Don grinned. 'Ah don't think so.'

'But your Claire's t'lead singer,' said Terry quickly.

Don thought for a moment. 'So that's what she's been up to.' He put his hand in his pocket and pulled out a few coins. 'Just stack t'ladder round back for me, lads – an 'ere's summat for y'collectin' tin.'

'Thanks, Mr Bradshaw,' they said and carried the ladder to the back yard. To their surprise, there was Scargill the Yorkshire terrier, chewing away at one of Old Tommy Piercy's prize-winning sausages.

'Bloomin' 'eck,' said Heathcliffe, 'we'd better look after 'im now.'

'Let's tek 'im for a walk,' said Terry.

"Ow about to t'big Manor?' said Heathcliffe. 'Mrs Forbes-Kitchener'll give us a job.'

Don reappeared behind the bar, looking hot and bothered. 'Ah can't seem t'shift 'em,' he said. 'Ah've tried ev'rything. T'little buggers are under t'eaves. Ah'd 'ave t'tek some tiles off t'roof, ah reckon. Looks like a big job.'

Sheila looked concerned. 'We can't 'ave a swarm o' bees stingin' all t'customers, Don, an' we'll be packed in both bars on May Day.'

'Ah'll do m'best, luv,' said Don forlornly.

Clint Ramsbottom appeared and, after a conversation with George Postlethwaite, he sauntered up to the bar. 'Mr Postlethwaite's going t'Miss Golightly's t'paint signs,' he said.

''E could write wi' both 'ands,' said Deke.

'Y'mean afore 'e 'ad 'is arm blown off in t'war?' asked Don, looking for clarification.

'O' course, y'great lump,' said Sheila.

'So 'e could write left-'anded an' right-'anded?' said Don.

'That's reight, Don,' said Deke, ''e were ambiguous.'

Stevie Supersub Coleclough, the only member of the football team with any academic qualifications, said, 'Ah think y'mean ambidex—' but stopped quickly when he saw the psychopathic glare from Shane Ramsbottom.

'Them Earnshaw boys said y'lookin' for a place for y'band t'practise,' said Don, 'so y'can use our attic.'

'Our attic?' said Sheila.

'Yes, luv,' said Don. 'Our Claire's t'lead singer.'

'Oooh, that's wonderful,' said Sheila. She pulled a pint for Clint and he wandered off to talk to his brother.

''E's allus been sensitive, 'as our Clint, ever since 'e were a little lad,' said Deke with a sigh.

Sheila continued to pull mightily on the hand pump and glanced across at Clint, who was fingering his new pendulous earring. 'Well, that's a good thing,' she said.

'Ah've gorra thing f'sensitive men. Y'don't get many in 'ere.'

Deke leaned over the bar. 'But it can be embarrassing, Sheila,' he said. 'Ah've 'ad m'moments wi' 'im.'

'Ow d'you mean?' asked Sheila.

'Well,' said Deke, 'when they were kids ah recall tekkin' 'im an' Shane to t'pictures t'see *Bambi* an' when Bambi's mother got shot our Clint burst into tears.'

'Ah'm not s'prised,' said Sheila as she placed a foaming pint of Tetley's bitter on top of a York City tea towel on the bar. 'Ah were upset m'self. So . . . what about your Shane?'

Deke took a pensive sip. 'Well 'e's never been into sensitivity.'

'Why, 'ow did 'e tek it?' asked Sheila.

''E asked if 'e could 'ave a shotgun f'Christmas.'

Sheila looked at Shane and the giant fist that held his pint tankard with the letters H-A-R-D tattooed on his knuckles. 'Y'can pick y'friends but not y'family,' she said.

When Deke walked back to the football team, Don put his arm round Sheila's shoulders. 'It's a cryin' shame f'Deke,' he said. 'All y'want in life is *normal* . . . and y'finish up wi' a psychopath an' a poofter.'

At the magnificent Morton Manor, Vera was deep in thought. She was standing in the comfortably furnished Victorian conservatory and the furniture was looking decidedly worn. However, she had just discovered the perfect solution in her *Radio Times*. There was an opportunity to purchase matching stretch covers for the ageing sofas and the beauty of it was that they came with matched frilled valances. Also the title of the range was simply perfect. The 'Diana Linen Look' appeared to have the seal of royal approval – even though the address was a company in Preston. *Still, you can't have everything* she mused.

It was then she saw two scruffy boys with a lively dog on the gravelled driveway. They waved at her and pointed to their collecting tin. She smiled in recognition – the Earnshaw boys – and she picked up her purse and went out to meet them.

'Bob-a-Job, Mrs Forbes-Kitchener?' they recited politely.

Vera looked around. There was a small attractive flower bed outside the kitchen door. *Safe enough* she thought. 'Yes, boys, fetch the wheelbarrow from the shed over there and get a trowel and weed this flower bed, please. Come round to the conservatory when you've finished and I'll pay you.'

Minutes later it was clear that the boys were not avid watchers of *Gardeners' World*. "Ow d'you tell which is weeds, 'Eath?' asked Terry.

Heathcliffe replied emphatically. 'Pull 'em all out, Terry, an' if they come up again, them's weeds.'

When Vera returned it took a great effort to remember the Christian values that underpinned her life. Her flower bed now resembled Cleethorpes beach at low tide. It was with a heavy heart that she placed two five-pence pieces in their mud-covered collecting tin.

On Sunday evening in the tap room of The Royal Oak the usual crowd were supping contentedly and watching the new television series of *Surprise Surprise* with Cilla Black and Christopher Biggins.

'Lovely singer,' said Sheila.

'But she s'pports Liverpool,' said Don with a frown.

'Ah know, but she can sing love songs wi' feelin' – jus' like that French woman from way back.'

'Edith Pee-off,' said Old Tommy through a haze of Old Holborn tobacco. What Old Tommy didn't know about old songs wasn't worth knowing.

Suddenly the ceiling began to shake. 'Bloody 'ell!' exclaimed Don. 'What's that?'

'Sounds like thunder,' said Old Tommy, adjusting his hearing aid.

'It's them kids upstairs,' said Sheila benignly. 'Let 'em 'ave their bit o' fun.'

The more Wayne Ramsbottom beat his drum the more his big brother Shane tried to outdo him. The noise was like a physical blow. Claire and Anita had sung themselves hoarse but they couldn't compete with the wall of sound coming from the other end of the attic. On the rooftop above them the tiles trembled. The members of The Throb were living up to their name.

The May Day celebrations were always a special time in the Ragley calendar and large crowds gathered on the village green. Marquees with garlands of bright bunting fluttered in the gentle breeze, and the sun shone down on the morris dancers in their white linen shirts and cord trousers with coloured ribbons tied round their knees. Old Tommy Piercy's hog roast was as popular and appetizing as ever and Sally's maypole dancers stole the show. The beer tent was a popular meeting place for the men of the village and the ladies of the Women's Institute served cream teas in the large marquee, where Anne and Sally had organized a wonderful display of children's art work. We were disappointed that Tom had missed the big day, but knew it must be something important that kept him away.

Beth, with John on her knee, was sitting on the semi-circle of straw bales watching Captain Fantastic's Punch and Judy Show when Don Bradshaw tugged my sleeve.

'It's a miracle, Mr Sheffield,' he said in a hoarse whisper. 'They've gone, ev'ry las' blinkin' one.'

'Gone?'

'Them bees,' he said, full of excitement. 'Sheila reckons it must 'ave been t'noise of our Claire's rock band – it would 'ave woken t'dead. So it's thanks t'them Earnshaw boys for suggesting it. Ah've told t'Scout master an' 'e were pleased.'

'That's good news,' I said.

Even so, what was to follow came as a surprise. As the entertainment was dying down, the major picked up the microphone.

'Ladies and gentlemen, boys and girls, for helping where help was needed most, the winner of the Scout of the Year for 1984 is – Terence Earnshaw.'

The major shook hands with Terry and handed him the trophy. Terry held it aloft as if he had just won the World Cup and the Earnshaw family led the applause. The major passed the microphone to Terry and the bristle-haired boy surveyed the crowd. There was George Postlethwaite, who had had to repeat his morning's sign-painting task, Vera Forbes-Kitchener, whose garden had been stripped of flowers, and Old Tommy Piercy, who had lost his plate of prize sausages.

'Thank you very much, Sir,' said Terry. 'Me an' m'brother . . . we jus' want to 'elp.'

Chapter Seventeen

Extra-Curricular Activities

Mr Dalton left at lunchtime to deliver a lecture on 'The Impact of New Technology in the Primary School'. Miss Flint provided supply cover. After school the headteacher and Mr Dalton attended the North Yorkshire Schools 'The New Curriculum' briefing at High Sutton Hall.

Extract from the Ragley School Logbook:
Friday, 8 June 1984

'Blast!' exclaimed Beth. 'There's a stain on the tablecloth.'

I stared at the mark on the snowy-white cloth. 'It's only tiny,' I said.

Beth was unconvinced. 'And I haven't time to wash it before Mother comes.'

It was Friday morning, 8 June, and I was about to leave for school. 'No one will notice,' I added, though I didn't believe it myself.

The tiny portable television set was murmuring away on the kitchen worktop. On *Good Morning Britain* Nick Owen was informing the nation that the miners' strike was gathering momentum. While forty-four pits were working normally, one hundred and nineteen were idle. The strike was in its thirteenth week and Arthur Scargill was seeking support from dockers, lorry drivers and seamen. When Margaret Thatcher announced, 'I do not see any role for government intervention,' I turned the sound down.

'You know what my mother's like,' said Beth, 'and this is the tablecloth she bought us as a first anniversary gift, so we need to use it.'

Diane Henderson was driving up from Hampshire to spend the weekend with us and we always had a tidy-up before she came. 'We can cover it with a placemat,' I said.

'I suppose so,' said Beth, slightly mollified. She turned to pick up John and put on his new shoes as he giggled with pleasure. He was walking now after a sudden growth spurt and spent a lot of time exploring his new upright world by playing with the coasters on the coffee table. 'Anyway, good luck at the conference and I'll see you tomorrow.'

I bent down to kiss them both and picked up my overnight bag from the hallway. 'Love you,' I said and hurried out. A long day was in store with an overnight training course at High Sutton Hall immediately after school.

It was to prove eventful.

At 7.30 a.m. in Ruby's house Mike Read was playing Wham!'s number-one record 'Wake Me Up Before You Go-Go' on his Radio 1 show. The volume on the old Bush radio was on full, Sharon, Natasha and Hazel were singing along and the walls were shaking. While this appeared to be a normal start to a day at 7 School View, something was different. After over five months of mourning, Ruby was humming contentedly. She no longer viewed life through a veil of tears. Her world was changing and the first flicker of hope warmed the scattered ashes of her life. The healing process had begun.

Meanwhile, in her kitchen on the Crescent, Anne Grainger was listening to Radio 2 and Ray Moore's breakfast show. Kenny Rogers and Dolly Parton were singing 'Islands in the Stream' but Anne was definitely *not* singing along. She was in the middle of an enough-is-enough moment. Her husband John had just spent the exorbitant sum of ninety-five pence on his May issue of *Woodworker Magazine* and was pointing to a photograph of a wooden rocking chair on the front cover. 'I'm going to make this for you,' he said. 'I could knock it up in an afternoon.'

To John it was the chair of the twenty-first century – modern, minimalist and magnificent – whereas to Anne it appeared to be the most uncomfortable piece of furniture she had ever seen – a sort of a curved duck-board.

'John, have you ever thought there might be something *we* could do together during an afternoon?' she asked in desperation.

John's eyes lit up. 'You mean you want to help me make it?'

Anne looked up at the kitchen clock in despair. It was another fourteen hours before her television heart-throb David Soul appeared in *Starsky and Hutch*, along with her opportunity to relax with a glass of wine. 'I don't think so, John,' she said with feeling. 'I had other extra-curricular activities in mind.' John was engrossed and the remark passed him by.

*

At Morton Manor, Vera turned down the Debussy and Bizet concert on Radio 3 and walked into the lounge, where Rupert was watching Selina Scott reading the breakfast news. Vera had noticed that Rupert definitely preferred Selina Scott on BBC1 to the slightly more chatty Anne Diamond on ITV, and guessed she knew why.

However, Rupert was shaking his head in dismay. 'What's the country coming to?' he muttered. During the Round Britain Milk Race cyclists had had to scramble through gardens to get past Welsh farmers after they had blocked the road into Aberystwyth with tractors, in protest at cuts in the EEC milk production quotas. Also, the National Union of Railwaymen had voted for a 31 per cent pay rise with a minimum wage of £100 for a thirty-five-hour working week. Meanwhile, the threatened postal strike had been called off following a new pay offer. By the time the elegant Selina announced that there were now five million people smoking cannabis in Britain, Rupert was switching off in disgust.

'The country's in a mess, old thing,' he said and smiled at the woman he loved. He picked up his *Financial Times*, sat in his favourite armchair and reflected on the changes in his life since he had married Vera – not least when Timothy Pratt delivered three large bags of Fullers Earth Cat Litter to the tradesman's entrance of Morton Manor.

Vera was not entirely happy at being referred to as 'old thing'. However, she kissed his forehead and returned to the kitchen to share a slice of toast and home-made marmalade with Debussy and Bizet.

*

I parked on the High Street outside the General Stores and called in for my newspaper. At the counter Margery Ackroyd was clutching her *Daily Mirror* and almost bursting to share her latest bit of television gossip with Prudence Golightly.

'I knew they were in love,' announced Margery. *Emmerdale Farm*'s Jack Sugden and his television wife Pat had decided to marry in real life. Apparently thirty-nine-year-old Clive Hornby and forty-two-year-old Helen Weir broke the news over a bottle of bubbly. 'Y'can't *act* love,' said Margery knowingly. 'It was as plain as t'nose on y'face.'

My newspaper didn't mention this blossoming love affair. Instead it concentrated on the National Association of Headteachers, who had proposed a four-term year plus a change to the law compelling all schools to start each day with morning assembly, in order to cater for other religions. Our school population was changing, particularly in the big cities.

Morning assembly was a memorable occasion. Joseph gave a short talk entitled 'Love Thy Neighbour' and illustrated it with a few Bible stories. However, it was his asking the children for examples in our daily lives that made the staff sit up and listen. Katie Icklethwaite seemed old before her years when she announced knowingly, 'I think love is when y'kiss all the time and then y'get married and jus' talk to each other like my mum and dad.'

Little Becky Shawcross touched us all when she said, 'Love is when your mummy kisses you to sleep at night cos in my house there's no one else to do it.'

Billy Ricketts had a more down-to-earth view of this

complex concept. He said cheerily, 'Mr Evans, ah think love is when our dog licks m'face – even though it's clean.'

Meanwhile, Rosie Spittlehouse expressed a practical viewpoint: 'Love is when Mummy gives Daddy t'last sausage.'

It was left to Hazel Smith to sum up. 'Mr Evans,' she said quietly, 'ah wish ah could've told my dad ah loved 'im jus' one more time before 'e went to 'eaven.' On the other side of the hall Anne looked down, took her handkerchief from the sleeve of her cardigan and wiped a tear from her eye. I had always believed that teaching was the best job in the world but, on occasions, it could be heartbreaking.

Happily, we finished on a cheerful note when Anne sat at the piano and led an impromptu sing-song from the *Count Me In* songbook she had used this week to support her role-play shopping experiences. The children in Class 1 stood up and sang:

> *Six sticky buns in a baker's shop,*
> *Big and brown with a currant on top.*
> *A boy came along with a penny one day,*
> *He paid one penny and took a bun away.*

During the performance Billy Ricketts as a diminutive baker collected plastic pennies and the children took turns to be the shopper. It was a happy end to a poignant assembly.

During morning break Sally was on playground duty and Tom and Anne were busy discussing the afternoon talk.

'It's a feather in your cap, Tom,' said Anne, 'if Miss High-and-Mighty has invited you to speak.'

Tom flicked through his stapled sheaf of notes for his talk, entitled 'The Impact of New Technology in the Primary School'. 'I've got a slide show as well,' he said and pulled out a small yellow plastic box containing twenty-four 35mm slides. 'I've got a really good photograph of an Apple computer.'

'Apple?' said Anne.

'Yes, it's the first to use a pull-down menu.'

'Really,' said Anne, now completely mystified.

'And it uses a mouse.'

'A mouse!' exclaimed Anne, looking alarmed.

Tom smiled and showed her a photograph of something that resembled a small plastic soap dish with a wire sticking out like a mouse's tail. 'Like that,' he said with a grin.

At lunchtime Miss Flint arrived to teach Class 2 for the afternoon, following Tom's invitation to give a talk at High Sutton Hall to newly qualified teachers on the new technology. Soon she was sharing a pot of Earl Grey tea with Vera, her long-time friend, and discussing the recent photographs of Princess Diana, who, wearing a white coat over her maternity dress, had visited a sweet factory. Wisely, as she was expecting her second child in September, she had selected low-calorie fruit gums as she was watching her weight. 'Very wise,' said Miss Flint and both ladies nodded knowingly.

Vera refused to read the article about John McEnroe, who had told assembled VIPs to 'Shut your fat mouths' at the French Tennis Championships.

'Let's hope they ban him from Wimbledon for life,' she said with feeling.

Suddenly Tom popped his head round the staff-room door. 'I'm off now,' he said, 'and thanks, Miss Flint. I've left the programme of work for the afternoon on my desk and the children know what's expected.'

'Thank you, Tom,' said Miss Flint.

'Any plans for the weekend, Tom?' asked Sally.

Tom paused before replying. 'Well, I should be seeing Laura tomorrow afternoon when I get back from the course.' He looked hesitantly at me. 'She's coming round to help me buy some furniture for my flat in York.' He pulled out an advertisement from his pocket. 'A bit dear, but it looks good.' It read: 'Cavendish-Woodhouse All-in-One Living Room £499.95'.

Everything went quiet until the ever-positive Sally broke the ice. She stood up and walked out into the corridor with him. 'Let's have a look,' she said.

I said nothing, Vera frowned and Anne looked concerned.

The afternoon finished quietly, with me completing a few more of my termly reading tests. Louise Hartley had just read the final line of the Schonell Graded Word Reading Test, namely: rescind, metamorphosis, somnambulist, bibliography and idiosyncrasy. It was a spectacular achievement by this hardworking girl from a single-parent family and I knew her father would be proud.

I cleared my desk, updated the school logbook and set off in my Morris Minor Traveller as the weather was changing. The journey over the moors on the Ripon road was dramatic, as dark, heavy cumulus clouds built up over the Hambleton hills.

At last I drove through the giant wrought-iron gates and along the long, winding gravelled driveway and past the beautiful lake. High Sutton Hall was just as I remembered it, a fine Georgian mansion set in five hundred acres of magnificent Yorkshire countryside. Just beyond a walled garden covered in honeysuckle and variegated ivy was a sign that read 'Stable Block' and I pulled in to the old cobbled square that was now used as a car park.

It was good to be here again. This was a special place, a wonderful retreat for teachers to meet, share ideas and enjoy excellent hospitality. It was a reminder of the grandeur of bygone days. However, it was still an oasis in the wild North Yorkshire moors and, above my head, a lone kestrel, like a prince of the sky, hovered menacingly, searching out its prey.

By six o' clock all the local headteachers had arrived to swell the audience of recently appointed teachers who had been there during the day, and smiles of recognition were exchanged as we settled in our seats. There was an air of expectancy as Miss Barrington-Huntley thanked us for our attendance and emphasized the importance of today's meeting.

The main lecture featured North Yorkshire's charismatic Senior Primary Adviser, Richard Gomersall. It was a concise summary of the new demands that were coming our way in the primary curriculum. As he repeated the term 'value for money', it was clear to us all that a brave new world was on the horizon and it would be people like Tom Dalton and his peer group that would be leading it. There were supplementary presentations by other advisers, including an intriguing one concerning extra-curricular activities and the minefield of possible pitfalls. The closing remarks by Miss Barrington-Huntley merely confirmed the challenges that lay ahead.

Dinner was a relaxed affair, with no one from the same school sharing a table with a colleague. So it wasn't until shortly before nine o' clock that I met up with Tom in the spacious bar and could ask him about his afternoon talk to the rest of the group. We ordered two pints of John Smith's bitter and sat in one of the comfortable alcoves.

He looked a little anxious and kept glancing out of the bay window as he sipped his drink.

'So, how did it go?' I asked.

He looked hesitant. 'Well, I think it went well, Jack – but you can never tell.'

'Tom, you're way ahead of everyone here in the new technology, so it's good for your career and the reputation of Ragley School that you've been invited to speak.'

'Yes, I met Miss Barrington-Huntley,' he said with a sense of awe and wonder.

'And what did she say?'

'Simply "Well done" . . . and that I was fortunate to be at Ragley and to make the most of my time there.'

I understood the hidden message. Miss Barrington-Huntley had marked his card.

Then the unexpected happened.

To my surprise Laura walked into the bar and all heads turned. She was wearing a chic checked blouse and waistcoat, a pencil-thin, figure-hugging grey skirt, high-heeled black leather shoes and a fake moleskin long-line jacket – in marked contrast to the standard two-piece business suits worn by the female delegates.

'Hello, Tom. Good directions – I found it easily.' She turned to me, stretched up and ran her long slender fingers down the lapels of my jacket, then straightened my crumpled tie. The scent of Opium perfume filled my senses and her soft brown hair brushed against my face. Finally, she stood back to admire her work. 'That's better, Jack.'

'I didn't know you were coming here,' I said.

Laura smiled. 'Just an impulse thing, Jack.' She looked at her watch. 'Tom said he would be finished by nine and I was free.' She looked at Tom. 'There's a hotel in the village if you want to go out for that drink.'

'Yes, of course,' said Tom, 'that is if you don't mind, Jack.'

Laura looked at me with challenge in her green eyes. 'We don't need Jack's permission – and it's only a drink.'

I chatted with a group of headteachers I knew and exchanged stories over a few more drinks – more than I was used to. It was around ten thirty when I decided to go back to my room.

The evening was warm and sultry and, in the distance, lightning flashed and thunder boomed. I closed the curtains to shut out the night and, after undressing, I slipped on a pair of boxer shorts and lay on my bed. It was good to relax and I picked up the novel that Laura had bought me for Christmas, *The Thorn Birds* by Colleen McCullough; soon I was immersed in the life of the Australian outback, where the beautiful Meggie made Ralph de Bricassart the centre of her life. Suddenly there was a knock on the door. I picked up the paperback and padded barefoot across the carpet. I guessed it was Tom and opened the door wide. I was wrong.

'Hello, Jack,' said Laura. Her cheeks were flushed and her eyes were bright. Her hair was damp and hung in wild strands over her face. She smiled at my surprise and glanced down at my novel. 'Good story,' she said. 'I hoped you might read it one day.'

'Why are you here, Laura?'

She stepped forward, leaned against the door jamb and put her cool fingers on my bare shoulder. 'Jack, I don't want to drive home,' she swayed a little and I guessed, like me, she had enjoyed one drink too many, 'not in this weather . . . and I've had a few drinks.'

Outside, sheet lightning split the ebony sky, followed almost immediately by the boom of thunder, and the earth shook under giant footsteps. The storm was almost upon us.

'There are spare rooms here,' I said. 'Just have a word with reception and there should be no problem.'

'I'll do that,' she said and fixed me with that confident and rebellious level stare I knew so well, '. . . and I'll see you later.'

By mid-morning on Saturday the first of the summer storms had passed and the tension of oppressive heat had gone. I drove home through a refreshed land where only the distant cry of a pheasant disturbed the peace of the countryside. In the hedgerows, the cow parsley sparkled with cuckoo spit and the magenta bells of foxgloves nodded in the gentle breeze. The closed fists of sycamore leaves had unfurled in the summer sunshine, while at their feet the scent of wild garlic drifted from the shady woodland floor. The world appeared content once again.

When I arrived back at Bilbo Cottage John was asleep in his cot and Beth was setting the table in the dining room. Diane had obviously settled in quickly and was in the kitchen preparing a simple lunch of carrot and parsnip soup and home-made soda bread, all transported via a triumph of Tupperware from her kitchen in Hampshire.

'Hello, Jack,' she said. 'I hope you're hungry.'

'Smells wonderful,' I said and kissed her lightly on the cheek.

'How was the conference?' said Beth.

'Fine . . . Miss High-and-Mighty was asking after you.'

Beth collected our only matching soup spoons from the dinner service in the Welsh dresser, a welcome wedding gift, two years ago, from the Parent Teacher Association. 'He means Miss Barrington-Huntley, Mother,' said Beth, 'chair of the Education Committee.'

'She wanted to know how your Masters degree was progressing. I told her you only had your third year to complete, along with the dissertation.'

'Interesting question,' said Beth.

'She also asked if you were definitely returning to work in September.'

Beth looked up at me. 'I hope you said yes.'

'I did.'

Diane paused from serving up the soup. 'Pity you don't live closer,' she said quietly, with a glance at Beth, 'then I could be your childminder.'

I went up to see John, who was sleeping peacefully, although he had rolled in his sleep to the bottom of his cot with his head pressed against the wooden bars. I moved him gently to make him more comfortable, then went back downstairs to the dining room and tucked in to the wholesome food.

'Delicious soup, Diane,' I said, 'and I love the bread.'

'Home-made,' she said simply.

'Mother makes it every Sunday down at home, Jack,' said Beth a little wistfully.

We ate in silence for a while and my thoughts wandered.

'I'm hoping to see Laura later,' said Diane suddenly.

Beth stood up and began collecting the soup bowls. 'I rang her apartment in York last night but I couldn't make contact.'

'Probably seeing that young man I keep hearing about,' said Diane pointedly. 'What's his name, Jack?'

I stared down at the tablecloth and noticed the stain was there. I covered it with my placemat and wondered if it would remain for ever.

'Tom Dalton,' I replied quietly.

Chapter Eighteen

A Bolt from the Blue

Pupils' individual report books went out to parents for signing and return. The headteacher and staff visited York Minster after school to offer help following the fire during the early hours of the morning.

Extract from the Ragley School Logbook:
Monday, 9 July 1984

'Jack – the Minster's on fire!'

It was 6.00 a.m. on Monday, 9 July and Beth was giving John his early feed in the kitchen at Bilbo Cottage. I hurried downstairs in my dressing gown. The newsreader on the radio sounded urgent and I turned up the volume.

'In the early hours of this morning,' he said, 'a massive fire engulfed York Minster. The roof of the thirteenth-century south transept has been destroyed and there are fears for the magnificent Rose Window. Latest reports say that over one hundred firefighters are struggling to bring the blaze under control. The cause of the fire is unclear, but it may be the result of a lightning storm.'

I looked at Beth. 'This is terrible,' I said and glanced at the kitchen clock. 'I think I'll go down there before school and ask if they need volunteers this evening.'

Beth looked concerned. 'Well do be careful, Jack – and I'll ring Vera and Joseph. I'm sure they would want to know.'

As I approached York it looked like a war zone. A huge pall of smoke hovered over the city and there was the sound of sirens in the distance. I parked in Lord Mayor's Walk and walked under Monk Bar and on to the Minster. The police had cordoned off the immediate area and large crowds were gathering as the news spread. It was a dramatic sight. I had never seen so many firemen in one place. Above me the West Tower soared into an acrid smoke-filled sky and I stared in awe at this wonderful building, revered by man and, seemingly, built by gods.

I caught sight of the tall figure of Sergeant Dan Hunter and waved to him. He ducked under the protective cordon, his uniform soaked and covered in ash. 'Bad business, Jack,' he said shaking his head.

'You look exhausted.'

He gave me a tired smile. 'I got here at three o' clock, the roof collapsed shortly before four.' We both stared up at the south transept. 'It sounded like the end of the world, Jack, molten lead and debris everywhere. Those firefighters are brave guys.' A team of firemen on giant ladders were spraying the stonework around the famous Rose Window in order to cool it, while dark pools of water spread at our feet.

'I'm sure a lot of volunteers will turn up,' I said. 'I thought I would come down after school.'

Dan scanned the crowds. 'You'll need to go round to Chapter House Yard,' he said. 'We're keeping the public well back from here for safety reasons.'

'Fine,' I said, 'and good luck.' We shook hands and he hurried off.

I pressed through the growing crush of onlookers and found the yard, where a group of clergy were piling books and rugs. An old friend, Canon Henry Fodder, was there and clearly distressed. 'Hello, Jack,' he said with a sigh. His grey hair was plastered to his face. 'It's too dangerous to go back in now, but we have managed to retrieve a great deal.' He gestured towards a neat pile of crosses and candlesticks gathered in haste from the six altars and stacked on a tarpaulin.

'I'm sure everyone will rally round,' I said. 'This has always been a special place.' I looked up at the glory of this great building. 'My mother brought me here as a boy and told me it was one of the great cathedrals of the world.'

There was a hint of a smile on his unshaven face. 'Jack,' he said and put his hand on my shoulder, 'she was right – and with God's help we shall prevail.'

Back at Bilbo Cottage Beth had prepared a cooked breakfast for me. 'I guessed you might need this,' she said and gave me a hug. 'I'll keep it warm while you shower.' I certainly needed one. My clothes and hair stank of woodsmoke. 'So how was it?'

I shook my head. 'As bad as you can imagine.'

'On the news they said it was a group of unknown teenagers who raised the alarm,' said Beth, 'otherwise it would have been a lot worse.'

'Lucky they did,' I said. 'The quick response looks as though it saved the West Tower.'

'Laura lived only a stone's throw away,' said Beth. 'She left just in time.'

I had heard that Laura had returned to London. 'How is she?' I asked.

'Not sure,' said Beth. 'I'll probably ring her later.' She sounded perplexed. 'Come to think of it, she's been very quiet for weeks now – probably pressure of work back in London.' I went upstairs deep in thought. Life was a hall of mirrors: nothing was as it seemed.

It was later than usual when I drove into Ragley village.

'Gerra move on!'

Miss Lillian Figgins, our Road Crossing Patrol Officer, defended her zebra crossing with the zeal of a lioness protecting her cubs. She stared back at Stan Coe in his mud-splattered Land Rover and shook her head in dismay. 'Wait y'turn, Stanley Coe,' she shouted as she guided a group of children across the road.

It was a hot and humid morning and Stan Coe removed his greasy flat cap, wiped his balding head with a dirty handkerchief and shouted once again. 'Y'like a little 'Itler on that crossing. Some of us 'ave work t'do.' The local pig farmer was well known in the village as a boorish bully and he had few friends. He blasted his horn as he accelerated away and Lollipop Lil wished that one day he would get his come-uppance.

Before school, the staff-room was buzzing with the news.

'I heard the sirens in the early hours, Jack,' said Tom. 'Then it was as if a bomb had landed. I got dressed and went out with some of my neighbours to see the fire. The flames must have been a hundred feet high.'

'Joseph and Miss Figgins are getting a lift into York at lunchtime with Wilfred Noggs, the churchwarden, to see if they can help,' said Vera, 'and I shall go straight from school.'

'John is already down there with his woodworker's toolkit,' said Anne, 'and I've agreed to drive down there this evening with Sally and meet up with Tom.'

I glanced at the clock. 'Time's up, everybody – we've got children to teach.'

In morning assembly Sally managed to lift our spirits. She had purchased a new songbook, *Jukebox*, a selection of thirty-three pop songs, and was strumming along to number 26, 'There Is a Happy Land'. The children laughed as they sang:

> *Charlie Brown's got half a crown,*
> *He's going to buy a kite.*
> *Jimmy's ill with chicken pox*
> *And Tommy's learned to ride his bike.*

I paused as I listened to the enthusiastic chorus of 'There is a happy land where only children live' and reflected how true it was. Their world really was a precious place, a magical time of giants, princesses, dragons and tall towers – a home for dreams within the cocoon of childhood.

In contrast, shortly before lunchtime in Tom's class, Rufus Snodgrass put down his pencil and shook his head. 'Ah'm strugglin',' he said.

'Why is that?' asked Tom.

Little Rufus stared down at the empty page. 'Well, 'cause you've asked us t'write about my favourite pet.'

'That's right, I did,' said Tom.

'But ah can't think of anything,' pleaded Rufus.

'You've got a hamster, haven't you?' asked Tom.

'Yes, but ah still can't write,' said Rufus in despair.

'Why's that, Rufus?'

'Well, Mr Dalton, 'cause all ah can think of is m'mam shouting at m'big sister f'gettin' pregnant.'

Tom looked out of the window as the breeze whipped the branches of the horse chestnut trees at the front of school and considered that there were days when teaching was a complex profession.

Meanwhile, at the vicarage, a heated exchange was taking place on the gravelled drive. Joseph was looking in despair at the overgrown graveyard and surrounding lawns. 'But you promised you would arrange for the grass to be cut *every* week,' he implored, trying to keep his anger under control.

'Ah do it when ah've gorra man t'spare,' said Stan Coe dismissively, 'an 'ah've been busy lately.'

'But look at the state it's in,' said Joseph.

Sadly, no one else had volunteered to tend the spacious lawns around the church and graveyard. When the contract had come up for renewal, one of Stan's long-time drinking partners on the parish council had made sure he got the job and a new motor mower had been purchased. It was kept in an old shed hidden from view round the back of the vicarage.

'Beggars can't be choosers,' said Stan dismissively.

'Then we shall have to make other arrangements,' said

Joseph emphatically. 'I shall inform the parish council that you have not completed the work.'

'You'll be sorry if y'do,' threatened Stan. He weighed sixteen stones and loomed over the stick-thin vicar. 'An' ah'll be back for t'mower later,' he added as he walked back to his Land Rover and trailer.

'It belongs to the parish council,' shouted Joseph as Stan accelerated away in a spurt of gravel.

Lillian Figgins had heard the exchange after mopping the kitchen floor and came out to see what was happening. She gave the departing pig farmer a look that would have curdled milk. Then light dawned and she smiled. 'Joseph,' she said quietly, 'ah may 'ave a solution – can ah use y'telephone?'

Half an hour later Deke Ramsbottom reversed his trailer up the vicarage driveway, unloaded an unusual cargo and drove off with a cheerful wave.

'Mr Evans, this is Delilah,' said Lillian proudly.

'My goodness – what a magnificent creature!' exclaimed Joseph.

The huge sheep that trotted confidently towards the graveyard clearly thought all her birthdays had come at once. Spread out before her was enough lush grass to keep her happy for the foreseeable future.

'It's a Four-Horned Jacob ewe, Mr Evans.'

This was a distinctive sheep with a coat of black and white wool and a face that resembled a badger, black with a white band from forehead to muzzle. 'The major is looking after 'er for a friend,' said Lillian, 'and she'll make short work of all t'grass – an' 'e says she's better than a guard dog.'

*

Meanwhile, further up Morton Road there were different problems. In her state-of-the-art conservatory, Petula Dudley-Palmer was unpacking a large box. As chairwoman of the Ragley Book Club, Petula had extended her brief to include a mail-order initiative and champion reading in the community – however, the ordering system hadn't gone to plan. It hadn't helped that all the books had arrived in sealed brown envelopes with only a number code to identify the contents. Sadly, Petula had mixed them up, although, with the passing of time, many of her fellow members had forgotten which book they had ordered.

Even so, Sheila Bradshaw in The Royal Oak was looking forward to the follow-up to *The Joy of Sex*, appropriately entitled *More Joy of Sex*. Timothy Pratt had ordered *The Fretwork and Model Making Annual* for his best friend Walter, the model-aircraft enthusiast. Timothy firmly believed that one day Walter might branch out into dolls' houses, forts and ships; after all, Walter Crapper was the most exciting man he had ever met. Petula herself had ordered *Jane Fonda's Workout Book*, plus a special treat for her husband Geoffrey – namely, Mark McCormack's *What They Don't Teach You at Harvard Business School*. Diane Wigglesworth, the hairdresser, was anticipating a quiet night in with *Hollywood Wives*, the blockbuster novel by Jackie Collins, while the increasingly figure-conscious Sally Pringle had ordered *The Weight Watchers Food Plan Diet Cookbook*. Amelia Duff, the postmistress, had selected *Fishing with Friends* from the catalogue for her new love, Ted Postlethwaite, and Margery Ackroyd, having crept unwillingly into her forties, decided to continue her search for eternal youth with *The Mary Kay Guide to Beauty*. Finally, Betty Buttle, the *Muppets* fan, was simply looking forward to a good laugh with *Miss Piggy's Guide to Life*.

As Petula toured the village in her Oxford Blue 1975 Rolls-Royce Silver Shadow, she prayed that everything would work out.

At the end of school, the children clutched their report books in sealed envelopes to take home for signing by their parents and eventual return to their teachers. Vera and I weren't far behind. We walked out to my Morris Minor Traveller and drove into York. Traffic appeared to be gridlocked so we parked at St John's College and walked up Gillygate towards the Minster. Much had happened during the day and a chequerboard of tapes covered the fallen debris to enable the individual timbers to be recorded.

We set to work in Chapter House Yard under the supervision of Canon Henry Fodder, who had worked non-stop all day. We did exactly as we were told and there was a genuine warmth and camaraderie among the volunteers. For three hours we folded curtains and rugs, cleaned ornaments and packed them into boxes to be labelled and transferred to safe storage. It was back-breaking work on a sticky, humid evening, and storm clouds were gathering to the north as we finally took our leave. John Grainger took Anne and Sally home, Wilfred Noggs volunteered to drive Vera back to Morton Manor and Joseph and Miss Figgins walked back with me to my car.

We were tired and thirsty as we drove up Ragley High

Street and the lights of The Royal Oak shone brightly. I spoke up, 'How about a drink?'

'We've certainly earned one,' said Joseph.

Lillian had always been a *direct* woman. 'Well ah could murder a port an' lemon.'

As we pulled up by the village green the first rumble of thunder could be heard in the far distance. When we walked in Ruby's son, Andy Smith, who was on leave from his post in Ireland, was standing at the bar with the football team and a smattering of the regulars. The discussion seemed a little more serious than usual. 'Well we won in t'Falklands,' said Andy.

Old Tommy Piercy seemed unconvinced. 'Ah've seen too many wars, young Andrew,' he said, 'an' there's no *winners.*'

'But we stood up for what were reight,' said Andy. 'We fought for a better world. Don't you agree, Mr Piercy?'

'Nay, lad,' replied Old Tommy, puffing thoughtfully on his pipe, 'if ah agreed wi' you, we'd *both* be wrong.'

''Ow d'you mean?'

'Well, young Andrew ... war doesn't tell y'who's *reight*,' said Old Tommy, 'only who's *left*.'

There was silence as the football team weighed up the gravitas of Old Tommy's words. Even the old farmers playing fives and threes at the dominoes table paused momentarily and nodded their approval in his direction.

'Mebbe y'reight, Mr Piercy,' said Andy, holding up an empty tankard. ''Ow about another?'

The spell was broken, normal service was resumed and Don gave us a cheery welcome as he pulled a fresh pint of Tetley's bitter for Old Tommy. 'Evenin', Miss Figgins,

Mr Sheffield – an' welcome, vicar, good t'see you. What will it be?'

'A port and lemon, please, Don,' I said, 'a pint of Chestnut and a large glass of your finest red wine.'

Don grinned and, of course, as an infrequent visitor to our local public house, the irony was lost on Joseph. The Royal Oak was not renowned for anything other than good ale, hearty meals and companionship. Lillian and Joseph wandered off to one of the bay-window tables while I waited for the drinks.

Outside there was a flash of lightning when suddenly Stan Coe walked in. He stopped in the doorway when he caught sight of Joseph chatting amicably with Lillian. A smile crossed his face and he hurried out again. Ten seconds later there was a crash of thunder. 'Storm's two miles away,' said Old Tommy with authority.

'Light travels faster than sound,' said Stevie Supersub Coleclough knowingly.

'That's why some folk look bright until you 'ear 'em speak,' said Old Tommy, nodding at the door that Stan Coe had left swinging on its hinges, and everyone smiled in agreement.

I delivered drinks to Joseph and Lillian and returned for my pint. Sheila appeared behind the bar with a list on a clipboard. 'Will y'sponsor our Claire, Mr Sheffield? She an' Theresa an' all t'teenagers are gonna do a walk in t'summer 'olidays t'raise money for t'Minster fund. It's jus' been on t'news an' all t'villages are rallying round to 'elp.'

'Certainly, Sheila,' I said and I added my name.

''E writes wi' 'is left 'and, tha knaws,' said Old Tommy.

'So 'e's a southpaw,' said Don, doing a quick exhibition

of shadow boxing in front of the shelf of bottled shandy.

'Who'd o' thought,' said Sheila wistfully, 'a cack-'anded 'eadteacher.'

Old Tommy sucked deeply on his old briar pipe and peered at me through a haze of Old Holborn tobacco. 'Y'look worried,' he said.

'Just a lot going on, Mr Piercy,' I said.

Old Tommy was a perceptive man and he leaned over and whispered in my ear. 'Now listen in, young Mr Sheffield,' he said, 'tha' needs to give a problem two coats o' lookin' over. Allus remember – an ounce o' plannin' saves a pound o' trouble.'

'Thanks, Mr Piercy,' I said and picked up my pint of Chestnut.

'Think on, young Mr Sheffield, y'never know 'ow clever you are 'til y've failed.'

Stan Coe was not one to miss an opportunity. It had been a stroke of luck seeing the vicar. The vicarage would be empty and there was nothing to stop him collecting the grass mower. After all, as his father had told him, 'possession is nine-tenths of the law'. While he was unsure what this actually meant, he knew that if the mower was in *his* shed and not the vicar's he had more chance of keeping it. Time was of the essence, so he roared off up Morton Road.

Delilah had enjoyed her day – the grass was sweet and the graveyard was peaceful. As darkness fell she discovered the perfect resting place. Next to a tall gravestone was a rectangle of gravel that had retained the heat of the day. The overhanging branches of a mature beech tree also provided shelter from the oncoming storm. Life was good for this Jacob ewe and she settled down for the night.

In The Royal Oak, Lillian and Joseph were keen to get home. It had been a long day. We finished our drinks quickly and agreed I would drop Joseph off at the vicarage and then drive on to Lillian's pretty little cottage in the tiny hamlet of Cold Hampton before returning home to Kirkby Steepleton. We said our goodbyes and hurried out to my car. Wind was whipping the drooping branches of the weeping willow on the village green – the storm was coming.

Stan Coe parked his Land Rover and trailer outside the entrance to the vicarage and stepped out. All was quiet apart from the lonely hoot of an owl and the rustling of the high branches of the elm trees. Stan was often out at night, usually in The Pig and Ferret, playing dominoes with his equally boorish companions. One of them had mentioned to him that a cure for baldness was the rough edge of a cow's tongue at midnight. So it was that Stan would often roam the local countryside at night to seek out a willing Friesian to lick his follicularly challenged head. Strange customs such as these were common in some of the remote villages of North Yorkshire. However, tonight was different. The silent graveyard was not the place to find a solution to his baldness. He was on a different mission.

He walked confidently down the well-worn path to-wards a group of outbuildings at the back of the vicarage. Clouds scudded across the sky and moonlight flickered through the swaying branches, lighting up the lichen-covered gravestones. Suddenly he heard a mysterious scraping sound behind the gravestone he was passing and he stopped and stared into the darkness. Then there was a new sound, almost like the clip-clop of hooves on a cobbled road, and he hesitated, wondering whether to turn back.

Then it happened.

A shape appeared above the gravestone and it was a sight to freeze the blood. Lightning flashed and, in that moment of sharp white light, Stan saw a black-and-white visage from hell. It had two long sharp vertical horns on its forehead, plus a pair of curled horns, and it leered at him to reveal large tombstone teeth. The manic glare from the bulbous staring eyes was the stuff of nightmares. As thunder crashed down around him he ran for his life.

Outside the gate of the vicarage I slowed up.

'Goodness me!' exclaimed Joseph.

'It's Stan Coe,' I said, 'and it looks as if he's seen a ghost.'

'Or Delilah,' said Lillian with a chuckle, as a Jacob ewe peered inquisitively round the vicarage gate.

The sight of the village bully bolting out of the blue shadows and driving off was one that Lillian treasured for years to come. It was also noticeable that, from that day on, Stan tended to avoid Lollipop Lil's zebra crossing during the busy early mornings, particularly after she burst into a chorus of 'Delilah' as he drove past.

It proved to be a stormy night and the villagers of Ragley locked their doors, closed their curtains and settled down for the evening.

I sat on the sofa with Beth to watch the news. Sue

Lawley reported that the cause of the York Minster fire was most probably a 'bolt from the blue'.

Perhaps it was – however, it was the sight of Stan Coe that came to mind.

Meanwhile, the unexpected had arrived through the letter-boxes of the members of the Ragley Book Club. Walter Crapper was thrilled to receive *What They Don't Teach You at Harvard Business School*, Ted Postlethwaite was picking up a few tips in *Hollywood Wives*, while Betty Buttle was unimpressed with *The Fretwork and Model Making Annual*.

Best of all, Amelia Duff, the recently liberated village postmistress, was relaxing in her new double bed with *More Joy of Sex* and reflecting that, next Friday after work, Ted the postman would be getting more than a fish supper.

Chapter Nineteen

School's Out!

14 fourth-year juniors left today and will commence full-time education at Easington Comprehensive School in September. 95 children were registered on roll on the last day of the school year. School closed today for the summer holiday and will reopen on Monday, 3 September.

Extract from the Ragley School Logbook:
Friday, 20 July 1984

It was a perfect morning and the countryside was sleeping. I opened the window and peered out at the tiny village of Kirkby Steepleton and beyond. The breathless promise of a new day hung heavy on the distant land and the fields of barley shimmered under the heat haze. Gradually a rim of bright golden light spread across the eastern sky and a quiet dawn emerged from behind the Hambleton hills. Above me the branches of the elm trees murmured with a sibilant whisper like the fluttering of a thousand butterflies. The time of the breaking of our world had arrived, the end of an era, the final day. It was

Friday, 20 July and Ragley School was about to close for the summer holiday.

Beth was preparing John's breakfast – and he was tottering around the kitchen floor, seemingly unperturbed by the events around him. Meanwhile, as I ate a hasty bowl of Weetabix, Cyndi Lauper was singing 'Time After Time' on Radio 2.

As I was about to leave, Beth gave me a hug. 'Good luck,' she said. 'My turn in September.'

'We'll need to sort out what we're doing about a nanny,' I said.

Beth glanced down at a scribbled note on the telephone pad. 'Well, I might have some news by the end of today. The chair of governors at Hartingdale has invited me to their end-of-term assembly. She mentioned she had a few child-minding ideas.'

'That's good news.'

Beth's eyes were bright with excitement again, as if a new chapter in her life were about to begin. 'She's really positive and wants to help – and they seem keen to have me back.'

'You must be looking forward to it.'

'I am . . . and I'm not.' John was in her arms and he chuckled as she kissed his cheek. 'I've got used to being with John every day and it will be a wrench to leave him.'

'Well, enjoy your visit. All the children will love him.'

We kissed goodbye and, as I drove on the back road out of Kirkby Steepleton, I thought of Beth returning at last to her school in the lovely village of Hartingdale with its beautiful church, its pretty High Street and the old stocks in the middle of the village green . . . and I wondered what the future might hold for us.

*

When I reached Ragley High Street, the sun broke through and lit up the honeysuckle as it clambered over the trellis outside the village hall. The floribunda roses in Maurice Tupham's front garden were in full bloom and the hanging baskets outside Prudence Golightly's General Stores were vivid with fiery red pelargoniums and trailing magenta lobelia. On this summer morning it was a sight to gladden the heart.

'Last day, Mr Sheffield,' said Louise Hartley as she rang the bell to welcome the children of Ragley village.

Ruby had stayed late the previous evening to give the hall floor an extra polish and I saw her hanging up her overall. She was wearing her best dress. 'Thanks, Ruby,' I said, 'the hall looks a real treat.'

'Well, it's a special day, Mr Sheffield,' she said with a smile on her flushed face. 'An' ah'm lookin' forward to our 'Azel gettin' 'er prize.' She hurried off to collect Vera so that they could claim their usual two seats next to the piano.

Our end-of-year Leavers' Assembly was always a poignant occasion and the hall filled quickly with parents, grandparents and school governors. The Parent Teacher Association had purchased a book for each school leaver and these were presented by Major Forbes-Kitchener with great ceremony. As each name was called out, beginning with Sam Borthwick, the Buttle twins and Michelle Cathcart, their parents, sitting on the back row, found it difficult to hold back the tears. I watched them as, in turn, they walked to the front of the hall, confident now and a world away from the tiny children I had once known. I smiled as Louise Hartley, Betsy Icklethwaite and Molly Paxton went up to collect their prizes. Many of these pupils had been with me since the year of their fifth birthday; now they were eleven years old and ready to move on to secondary education.

Easington School had closed a day earlier than us for the holiday so a few ex-pupils had turned up to support their younger brothers and sisters. Twelve-year-old Heathcliffe Earnshaw was sitting with his mother and Dallas Sue-Ellen on the back row. It occurred to me that little Dallas would be five in November so another Earnshaw would be in the reception class next September – a sobering thought. Heathcliffe gave me a grin when Terry's name was called out. It was almost seven years since he had arrived at Ragley School from Barnsley with his brother, who could barely say a word. The memories were etched in my mind. Time seemed to have passed by so quickly. These children had known only me as their headteacher. A whole generation had come and gone – it really was the end of an era.

Last of all was Hazel Smith and Ruby's tears flowed as the applause rang out. Vera gripped the hand of her special friend as the cheerful eleven-year-old, the image of the young Ruby, strode confidently to the front amidst tumultuous applause and received a beautiful leather-bound copy of *The Lion, the Witch and the Wardrobe* along with a few reassuring words from the major. I looked round at the rest of the staff. Anne gave me that familiar quirky smile from the other side of the hall, Sally nodded with a *yes we feel the same* look and Tom appeared genuinely touched, as if he was beginning to understand the wonder of teaching in a village school. Shirley Mapplebeck, the school cook, in her bright summer frock, clutched her handkerchief on her lap, while Doreen Critchley rested a giant callused hand on Shirley's arm and squeezed it with gentle affection. It was a tiny gesture but huge in its significance and, in that moment, I knew why being a village headteacher was so important to me.

We were more than a school . . . we were a family.

Finally, after our last hymn, 'Lord of All Hopefulness', the school prayer was read beautifully by Michelle Cathcart, then Joseph led us in the Lord's Prayer. Anne put Vivaldi's *Four Seasons* on the turntable and we filed out. The school leavers stayed behind to show their new books to their parents, who huddled in groups, discussing not so much the happy memories of Ragley School but rather the price of the Easington School uniform.

The morning passed quickly and the excitement of the children was clear with the summer holiday stretching out before them.

At lunchtime Anne and I walked out on to the school yard and drank our tea in the sunshine. 'Another year, Jack,' she said softly. 'We've survived our fair share of ups and downs.'

'We certainly have,' I said, 'and Anne – thanks as always.'

Ruby arrived at the school gate. It was time to put away the dining tables and she waved as she walked up the drive. 'Ruby's definitely getting back to her old self,' said Anne. 'She seems to be coping better these days.'

I leaned against the school wall and reflected on recent months. 'Vera has been a good friend to her.'

We sipped our tea and luxuriated in the warmth of the

day. Finally, Anne broke the silence. 'And what do you think about Tom?' she asked.

'Well, he's clearly a good teacher,' I said a little defensively.

'I agree,' said Anne, 'but he's certainly got what you might call a way with the ladies.' She let the message hang in the air. Around us butterflies hovered above the buddleia bushes in the sunshine and we settled back, each with our own thoughts, to watch the children at play.

For them the cycle of school life carried on as it always did. They skipped and played and sat contentedly in little groups on the school field. These were the carefree days of endless summers and the forging of innocent friendships. Within the secret garden of childhood, small boys and girls ran around the school field, united by one apparently indisputable fact – they would live for ever.

At the end of the school day I stood on the steps of the entrance porch and said farewell to the children who were leaving to go to secondary school.

Michelle Cathcart gave me a home-made card with the message 'Thank you for being my teacher' above a beautiful drawing of the school bell tower. Her mother was standing nervously by the school gate, her familiar pink candyfloss hair bright in the sunshine. She blew a kiss, shouted 'Thank you' and waved goodbye, and I was touched by the gesture from this troubled lady.

In contrast, the blunt and gregarious Betty Buttle was suddenly by my side with her twin daughters, Katrina and Rowena. 'A proper sad day, Mr Sheffield,' she said. 'Thanks f'keepin' 'em safe.' The girls gave me a carefully wrapped copy of a fascinating book, *The Snickleways of York*, with their almost identical signatures on the title page, then hurried off down the drive to continue their inseparable lives.

'Goodbye, Sir,' said Lee Dodsworth politely and he gave me a tiny model of a Morris Minor Traveller, destined to be a paperweight on my desk for the next thirty years. He strode off confidently, not knowing that a remarkable destiny as a jet pilot awaited him.

Charlotte Ackroyd gave me an apple. I smiled in puzzlement. 'But you're not leaving,' I said. 'You're coming back next year.'

'Ah know, Mr Sheffield,' she said, 'but mebbe y'can keep me in mind t'be tuck-shop monitor next year.'

'We'll see, Charlotte,' I said and slipped the apple in my pocket. While I didn't encourage bribery, *initiative* was always appreciated.

Finally, Terry Earnshaw was standing on the step next to me. 'Thanks, Mr Sheffield,' he said. 'Ah'm looking forward to t'big school, but ah'll allus remember Ragley.'

'You'll enjoy being with your brother again,' I said.

He grinned. 'Ah will, sir. It's not t'same wi'out 'im,' and he ran off down the drive to begin the rest of his life and countless years of hard graft in all weathers.

One by one the teachers left.

Sally Pringle gave me a hug as she left to hurry home to share her precious summer break with her daughter, Grace, while Anne gave me my annual kiss on the cheek and a wry smile. I knew what she was thinking – six weeks with a DIY fanatic wasn't the stuff of dreams for the hardworking deputy headteacher of Ragley School.

Meanwhile, Vera tidied her desk as she always did. 'Rupert said if you and Beth and John have time to call in before you go down to Hampshire, you're more than welcome.'

'Thank you, Vera, we shall,' and she gave me that knowing look I recognized so well.

She paused in the doorway. 'And Jack, I'm making a summer fruit cornucopia – and that is *not* to be missed,' she added with a smile and walked out to the car park.

The last knock on my door was at 6.30 p.m. and Tom Dalton came in. 'Thanks for your support, Jack,' he said and shook my hand.

I put down my pen. 'What are your plans for the holiday?'

He looked at me curiously for a moment, presumably trying to decode any hidden message. 'I'm helping my father build a patio at his house in Bishopthorpe and then I'm having a couple of weeks' touring in France with some old college friends.'

'Sounds good, Tom.' I looked at him as he leaned against Vera's desk, hands in the pockets of his cord trousers and his old St Peter's School tie loose around the unbuttoned collar of his denim shirt, '. . . And I'm glad you've settled so well at Ragley. If there's any help you need next year, then let me know.'

'Thanks, Jack,' he said, 'I appreciate that and, yes, Ragley's a wonderful place to work.' He walked to the door and then hesitated. 'And I doubt I'll be seeing Laura – she says she's very busy at the moment.'

There was an awkward silence. 'Well . . . see you next term,' I said.

*

It was half an hour later when I made my final entry in the school logbook. I wrote, 'School closed today for the summer holiday and will reopen on Monday, 3 September.' Then I put the top on my fountain pen, blotted the words, closed the leather-bound tome and returned it to the drawer in my desk.

I stared around me at the walls of the office I knew so well and recalled the events of the past year, the triumphs and the tragedy. In the echoing emptiness of this Victorian school the faces of past pupils and teachers stared out from the neat rows of photographs, captured in a moment of their youth and living on in an image of earlier times. Finally, I locked up the school and drove away, leaving the academic year 1983/84 behind me.

Back at Bilbo Cottage Beth was full of news following her visit to Hartingdale.

'Guess what, Jack?' she said as she hurried from the kitchen. 'I've got the perfect childminder – a highly recommended lady with a son at secondary school. She called in to see me at Hartingdale and we got on well. It's all fixed for next term.'

It was a relief. 'Perfect,' I said as I hung my jacket on the hall stand.

Beth fingered the frayed cuffs and then peered out of the window at my precious car. 'Jack, the Morris Minor is getting like your jacket – too old for purpose – and we've got a long journey down to Hampshire next week.'

I looked at my herringbone jacket with its worn leather patches on the elbows. It was ten years old, familiar, comfortable – like an old friend. However, my Morris Minor Traveller was something much more special; the thought of changing it was sacrilege. 'Perhaps we ought to change yours, Beth,' I said. 'After all, the Beetle is looking decidedly rusty.'

'Good idea,' said the ever-practical Beth and I realized I had got off lightly.

On Saturday morning I had some shopping to do in Ragley and I called in to Nora's Coffee Shop for some welcome refreshment. Phil Collins was singing 'Take a Look at Me Now' on the juke-box and the teenagers Claire and Anita gave me a wave. Ever since watching *Flashdance* they had taken to wearing baggy sweatshirts that hung off one shoulder. The ensemble was completed with their ballet flats.

As Nora served me with a frothy coffee she nodded towards Dorothy, who was sitting with Little Malcolm, Big Dave and his fiancée, Nellie. 'Weally intewesting, Mr Sheffield,' said Nora, never one to miss out on a bit of gossip. 'Ah think Dowothy's gonna get mawwied at last.'

I settled down at a spare table within earshot of Ragley's favourite refuse collectors.

'A joint wedding?' said a surprised Big Dave.

'That's reight, Dave – you an' Nellie an' me an' Dorothy,' said Little Malcolm, who appeared quicker on the uptake on this occasion.

'On t'same day,' added Nellie for clarification.

'It'll be wonderful,' said Dorothy, flashing her new engagement ring.

'It were Nellie an' Dorothy's idea, Dave,' explained Little Malcolm.

'Ah weren't thinkin' o' rushin' things,' said Big Dave lamely.

Nellie gave Big Dave her *don't mess wi' me* look and he recoiled from the impact. 'Dave, d'you love me or not?' She pointed to Dorothy's garish engagement ring. ''Cause it's obvious Malcolm loves Dorothy.'

'O' course ah do,' said Big Dave.

Malcolm pulled a crumpled copy of the *Easington & District Advertiser* out of his pocket. 'Look at this, Dave,' he said. 'It looks perfec'. We could give Dorothy an' Nellie t'oneymoon of a lifetime.'

'An' it would be proper romantic,' said Dorothy.

''Ow much?' asked Big Dave. It was crucial to get the important items sorted first.

''Ave a look,' said Little Malcolm.

The advertisement read:

SUPER SAVER OCTOBER HOLIDAY TO BENIDORM £59.00
HOTEL TORRE DORADA
Full board at the Poncente beach
All bedrooms have a bath/wc
Swimming pool
Midlands Airport/Coventry

Big Dave frowned. 'Where's Coventry?'

'Dunno, Dave,' said Little Malcolm, 'it sez in t'Midlands – so it's down south somewhere, but there'll be buses.'

'Or trains mebbe – nowt but t'best f'my Nellie,' said Dave, '. . . s'long as it's not 'xpensive.'

'Well me an' Malcolm can save up,' said Dorothy and Malcolm nodded in rapturous agreement.

'It sez October,' said Big Dave.

'That's reight, Dave,' said Nellie, 'so . . . what's it t'be? Shall we get married in October?'

The binmen of Benidorm looked at each other and nodded.

Little Malcolm had finally got the woman of his dreams and Big Dave had got a cheap holiday with a woman who could recite football's offside rule.

'OK, you're on,' said Big Dave.

'Well, let's celebrate wi' a drink,' said Nellie, looking out of the window at The Royal Oak.

Big Dave rooted in his pocket for some small change. 'OK, Nellie luv, 'ow abart a mug o' tea?'

My next port of call was the butcher's shop. Beth's list included a large joint of ham, intended as our contribution towards the feast that awaited us at her parents' house in Hampshire.

It was soon clear that Old Tommy was very proud of his cured York ham. Maurice Tupham reared a few select Large White pigs in his back yard and fed them on brewer's spent grain, carefully matured over six months. Old Tommy knew this was the true secret of York ham. The meat, lean and rose-pink, was on display in the window. It had been smoked in the traditional way over wood shavings and herbs to produce a rich, salty ham with a dry texture and distinct flavour. It was Old Tommy's masterpiece and the trademark of the master butcher. 'Teks a lifetime t'learn 'ow t'get 'am as perfec' as this,' he said as he wrapped up a huge joint for me. Then he sighed deeply. 'Nostalgia . . . nostalgia,' he murmured. 'It ain't what it used t'be.'

'Thanks, Mr Piercy,' I said. 'Anyway, must rush.'

'There's more t'life, Mr Sheffield, than tryin' t'mek it go quicker,' he shouted after me.

*

Across the High Street, next to the village hall notice-board, Vera was in conversation with Joyce Davenport, who had just displayed details of their most recent charitable activity. It announced that the Ragley and Morton WI were supporting the June Whitfield Knit and Sew Charity Bazaar. However, their animated discussion did not concern the forthcoming task of knitting teapot and egg cosies but rather the fact that the treasurer had run off not only with the WI funds but also with the secretary's husband.

Entirely oblivious to this story of sexual dalliance, outside Timothy Pratt's Hardware Emporium Ruby had bumped into George Dainty. They appeared relaxed together and Ruby was smiling. It was good to see her at ease. She appeared to have found a new friend in this gentle, kindly man and they both waved as I clambered back into my car and drove home.

Tuesday, 24 July was a special day. It was John's first birthday and we packed the car very early and set off for a few days in Hampshire, to be followed by a visit to my mother, Margaret, and her sister, May, in Leeds. As we drove south out of Yorkshire we turned on the radio and joined in with the cult Alice Cooper hit of over ten years ago. There was a sense of freedom in our souls as we sang *'School's out for summer, School's out for ever'* as the miles swept by and Ragley School was left far behind.

It was early afternoon when we sampled the delights of Hampshire, a beautiful county of water meadows and dense forests. Soon we saw the sign for Little Chawton and drove into a classic English village. Outside The

Cricketer public house a few young men were quenching their thirst with the distinct amber local brew. On the village green families were enjoying their picnics while toddlers played hide-and-seek round the old cast-iron hand pump. We turned left at the church with its square Norman tower and arrived at a familiar row of thatched cottages faced with red brick and Hampshire flint.

Austen Cottage was a mellow brick-and-beam building and the tall, grey-haired John Henderson came out to meet us. 'Welcome home,' he said to Beth as he embraced his daughter.

'Lovely to be here, Dad,' said Beth.

Our son yelled to be free of the restraints of his car seat. 'You have a very active grandson,' said Beth as she unstrapped him. 'He'll be into all your cupboards.' She carried John into the kitchen, where Diane broke off from stirring a huge pan of watercress soup to greet her grandson with a tender kiss.

'Prepare yourself for a feast, Jack,' said John as he helped me with the luggage. 'Diane's been baking for the past week.'

Laura was in the entrance hall. She was casually dressed in jeans and a T-shirt and appeared preoccupied as she hugged everyone. Diane glanced at her occasionally as we gathered in the kitchen. John could walk confidently now and immediately began to climb the stairs. For the next half-hour it was a full-time job keeping track of his whereabouts as he explored the cottage.

After lunch, while he slept, I sat in the lounge with Beth and her father. Diane had slipped out to find Laura, who had gone to her room. Across the landing Laura's door was ajar. She was standing in front of the full-length mirror, staring thoughtfully at her reflection. A shaft of bright sunlight streamed across the room and lit up her still figure as if she were on a stage in the spotlight.

Laura looked thoughtfully at the slim woman staring back at her. Then she slowly spread her fingers across her stomach. She held them there and pressed gently, fingertip softly, as if searching for an answer to an elusive question.

'My God . . . what have you done?' she said to herself.

She stared at her reflection, her eyes suddenly moist with tears.

The door creaked and a voice said, 'Laura – what is it?' Diane stepped into the room and closed the door softly behind her.

'Not now, Mother,' said Laura distantly.

Diane stood by the door, staring at her younger daughter while Laura was as still as her reflection.

'I know you,' said Diane.

'Do you, Mother?'

'Laura – I've always known you.'

Diane walked slowly across the room. She stood beside Laura and looked into the mirror. 'So . . . are you?'

There was silence between them, two women in a tableau of confusion.

Finally, Laura murmured almost to herself. 'A child . . . a teacher's child.'

Diane stiffened. 'Yes . . . but which teacher?'

Laura raised her head and turned to face her mother while Diane looked into the green eyes of her daughter.

And in a heartbeat she understood.

ABOUT THE AUTHOR

Jack Sheffield was born in 1945 and grew up in the tough environment of Gipton Estate, in north-east Leeds. After a job as a 'pitch boy', repairing roofs, he became a Corona pop man before going to St John's College, York, and training to be a teacher. In the late seventies and eighties, he was a headteacher of two schools in North Yorkshire before becoming Senior Lecturer in Primary Education at Bretton Hall College of the University of Leeds. It was at this time that he began to record his many amusing stories of village life as portrayed in *Teacher, Teacher!*, *Mister Teacher*, *Dear Teacher*, *Village Teacher*, *Please Sir!* and *Educating Jack*.

School's Out! is his seventh novel in the *Teacher* series and continues the story of life in the fictional village of Ragley-on-the-Forest. He lives in York and Hampshire.

Visit his website at www.jacksheffield.com